Henry E. J. Stanley, Francisco Alvares

Narrative of the Portuguese embassy to Abyssinia

During the years 1520-1527

Henry E. J. Stanley, Francisco Alvares

Narrative of the Portuguese embassy to Abyssinia
During the years 1520-1527

ISBN/EAN: 9783337288273

Printed in Europe, USA, Canada, Australia, Japan

Cover: Foto ©Andreas Hilbeck / pixelio.de

More available books at **www.hansebooks.com**

NARRATIVE

OF THE

PORTUGUESE EMBASSY

TO

ABYSSINIA

DURING THE YEARS 1520–1527.

BY

FATHER FRANCISCO ALVAREZ.

TRANSLATED FROM THE PORTUGUESE,

AND EDITED,

With Notes and an Introduction,

BY

LORD STANLEY OF ALDERLEY.

LONDON:

PRINTED FOR THE HAKLUYT SOCIETY.

MDCCCLXXXI.

T. RICHARDS, PRINTER, 37, GREAT QUEEN STREET.

WORKS ISSUED BY

The Hakluyt Society.

NARRATIVE OF THE PORTUGUESE
EMBASSY TO ABYSSINIA.

COUNCIL

OF

THE HAKLUYT SOCIETY

THE present work on Abyssinia is the earliest extant; for though Pedro de Covilham, the explorer of King John II, who was despatched from Portugal in May 1487, reached Abyssinia more than thirty years before our author, he does not appear to have left any written memorial of his long residence in that country.

This work of Francisco Alvarez has been translated from the original edition printed in black letter by Luis Rodriguez, bookseller of the King, on the 22nd October 1540, the *British Museum Catalogue* supposes at Coimbra.

The narrative of Alvarez has been translated into several languages, but most of these translations are considerably abridged. The following are a list of the translations:—

"Viaggio fatta nella Ethiopia, Obedienza data à Papa Clemente Settimo in nome del Prete Gianni." Primo Volume delle navigazione. 1550. Fol.

"Viaggio nella Ethiopia, Ramusio." 1 vol. 1554.

"Description de l'Ethiopie." 1556. Fol.

"Historia de las cosas de Etiopia." Traduzida de Portugues en Castillano, por Thomas de Padilla. Anvers: Juan Steelsio, 1557. 8vo.

"Description de l'Ethiopie." Translated by J. Bellere, from the Italian version of Ramusio. Anvers: C. Plantin, 1558. 8vo.

"Historia de las cosas de Ethiopia." By Miguel de Suelves. Printed in black letter. Saragoza, 1561. Fol.

"Warhafftiger Bericht von den Landen .... des Königs in Ethiopien." Eisslebē, 1566. Fol.——Another edition. Eisslebē, 1576. Fol.

"Die Reiss zu dess Christlichen Königs in hohen Ethiopien." 1576. Fol.

"Historia de las cosas de Ethiopia," traduzida por M. de Selves. Toledo, 1588. 8vo.

"The Voyage of Sir Francis Alvarez." *Purchas, his Pilgrims,* Part II. 1625.

Francisco Alvarez relates in this volume how much he desired, on his return to Portugal, to be sent on a mission to Rome, to present the Prester John's letters to the Pope, and it appears from the Portuguese *Biographical Dictionary* of Innocencio da Silva, that he succeeded in going to Rome, and afterwards returned to Lisbon.

Figaniere, and José Carlos Pinto de Souza say, in their Portuguese *Bibliographies*, that Alvarez was a native of Coimbra.

The utility and good effect of this Portuguese mission to Abyssinia suffered very much by the dissensions and quarrels which arose between Don Rodrigo de Lima, the Ambassador, and Don Jorge d'Abreu, the Secretary of Embassy, quarrels which, as usual in such cases, caused disunion amongst the whole staff of the Embassy. Father Alvarez acted a most useful part as peace-maker on all occasions; but he is very reticent, and has avoided saying upon which side the blame for these quarrels should be laid. It appears from the narrative that the Ambassador was very selfish, and thought too much of his personal interests; his conduct appears all the more blameable, from the account of the very different conduct of Hector da Silveira, who brought away the mission from Africa; but Jorge d'Abreu was very quarrelsome, and carried his quarrels further than can be excused, even by the fact that he could not refer his complaints home to his Government. The conduct of the Ambassador must, however, have been even worse than appears from the narrative, or the Abyssinians would hardly have supported Jorge d'Abreu as much as they did.

The reader is invited to compare the description of the entrance to the mountain in which the Abyssinian Princes were confined at the time of our author's visit, at pp. 140-144, and the motives for this confinement, with this opening passage of *Rasselas*, describing the Happy Valley.

" The place which the wisdom or policy of antiquity had destined for the residence of the Abyssinian Princes was a spacious valley in the kingdom of Amhara, surrounded on every side by mountains, of which the summits overhang the middle part. The only passage by which it could be entered, was a cavern that passed under a rock, of which it has long been disputed whether it was the work of nature, or of human industry. The outlet of the cavern was concealed by a thick wood, and the mouth which opened into the valley was closed with gates of iron. . . . . . .

" This lake discharged its superfluities by a stream, which entered a dark cleft of the mountain on the northern side, and fell with dreadful noise from precipice to precipice, till it was heard no more."

These descriptions agree sufficiently to leave no doubt that Johnson borrowed the idea of Rasselas from actual descriptions of Abyssinia, and from the translation of Alvarez in Purchas's *Pilgrimes*, when he wrote that work in 1759; but the matter is proved beyond doubt, by the fact that Johnson's first literary work was a translation from the French of Lobo's *Voyage to Abyssinia*. It was published in 1735, by Bettesworth and Hicks, of Paternoster Row, and for this task Johnson received only five guineas, which he was in want of for the funeral expenses of his mother.

Therefore, whatever frivolous persons in society may have done on insufficient information, Mr. Justin McCarthy, in his *History of our Own Times*, should have avoided the inaccuracy of writing: " He (Lord Beaconsfield) wound up by proclaiming that ' the standard of St. George was hoisted upon the mountains of Rasselas'. All England smiled at the mountains of Rasselas. The idea that Johnson actually had in his mind the very Abyssinia of geography and of history, when he described his Happy Valley, was in itself trying to gravity."

Mr. McCarthy goes on to say that: "When the expedition to Abyssinia is mentioned in any company, a smile steals over some faces, and more than one voice is heard to murmur an allusion to the mountains of Rasselas".

It is unfortunate that Mr. Justin McCarthy should

not have fallen in with those Englishmen who sighed over the excuse for the expedition to Abyssinia, that "it would keep the Bombay army in wind", or who reprobated the conduct of Lord Napier of Magdala to King Theodore, after having accepted from him a present of cows. But accurate ideas of political morality are not to be expected from an advocate of the most extreme proposals of the Irish Land League.[1]

The reader will find many descriptions of Abyssinian Ritual, and interesting discussions between the Abyssinians and Father Alvarez, who always showed much tact in these arguments.

It appears from this book, that the population of Abyssinia was far larger at that time than at the present; and that the contact of Europeans with the Abyssinians has not been to the advantage of the latter.

An interesting part of the narrative of Alvarez is the description of the churches cut out of the rock; he is very enthusiastic over the beauty of these structures. The style of Alvarez is never very clear; and there was much difficulty in translating this portion of his book, owing to the number of architectural terms, some of which are almost obsolete. No modern traveller has described these churches. Mr. Markham was within a short distance of them, but was unable to visit them.

[1] See the *St. James's Gazette*. Criticism of Mr. Justin McCarthy's language, October 29th, published since the above was written.

M. Antoine d'Abbadie visited them, but he has not yet written any account of his long residence in Ethiopia, having been occupied with the publication of his very copious astronomical observations, and being now engaged in printing a dictionary of the Ethiopic language.

M. d'Abbadie is anxious that the work on Ethiopia of the Jesuit Almeida, a MS. of which is in the British Museum, should be translated and published, as he considers it to be the most exact account of that country. I am indebted to M. d'Abbadie for several explanations of Ethiopic words and names which have been given in the notes : many of these were too much disfigured to be recognisable.

On one occasion, the Portuguese performed before Prester John a representation of the Adoration of the Magi, or an Epiphany miracle play. This would probably be similar to one that was found in a thirteenth century Service Book of Strasbourg, and which was published by Mr. Walter Birch in the tenth volume of the *Transactions* of the Royal Society of Literature.

The Abyssinian envoy, Mattheus, who went to Portugal and returned to his country with the Portuguese Embassy, suffered much on his way to Portugal, and also on his return, by reason of the doubts cast upon the authenticity of his mission. What happened to him in India on his way to Portugal, is mentioned at length in Mr. Birch's translation of the *Commentaries of Albuquerque*, vol. iii, p. 250. The truth appears to be that he was sent by Queen Helena, the queen-mother.

In several cases, the dates given by Alvarez of the days of the week and the days of the month do not agree, but as these dates refer to the departure from some village, and not to any historical event, I have not thought it worth while to verify and correct these discrepancies.

Mr. Clements Markham has compiled a map of Abyssinia for this volume, extending from Massowah to Shoa.

Some years ago a rather savage criticism of the publications of the Hakluyt Society complained of the excessive length of their Introductions. This one is much shorter than it should have been, not in deference to the critic, but because the researches necessary for doing justice to the work of Alvarez have been interfered with and prevented by other less agreeable occupations; but the delivery of this volume could not be delayed any longer, and the members of the Society are entreated to excuse its brevity.

June 29th, 1881.

TITLES OF THE CHAPTERS.

[1] Sic.

c

*In this Part is related the Journey which was made from the country
of the Prester John to Portugal.*

ERRATA AND NOTES.

Page 36, line 22, *for* " Rodrigro", *read* " Rodrigo".

„ 84 note, "mancal". "Baton ferré des deux bouts".—Roquette's *Dict.*

., 151, line 18, *for* "sleeep", *read* "sleep".

„ 178, line 28, "a crucifix painted on it", or perhaps, "a painted crucifix on it".

„ 186, note. See Grove's *Dictionary of Music* for a note on the Monochord.

., 199, note. "Alaquca, laquca, pierre des Indes qui arrête le flux de sang."—Roquette's *Dict.*

„ 228, line 25, *for* "Bruncaliam", *read* "Brancaliam".

„ 241. Col. Meadows Taylor describes a similar miracle play represented at Aurungabad by the Portuguese monks.—*Story of my Life*, p. 39.

„ 295, line 2, *for* "pesons", *read* "persons".

„ 324, last line, *for* " littlo", *read* " little".

,. 325, "cap. cxvii", *read* "cxviii".

., 344, line 33, "Cosme, Damiano", or the church of Saints Cosmo and Damian, martyrs united in the Calendar under 27th September.

„ 408, note, "Tahu." This is the Tau-cross or T-shaped crutch emblem of St. Anthony, so called from the name of the letter in the Greek alphabet.

Perchance your Highness may judge me to be as ignorant as over bold, since with such weak knowledge, and little capacity, I have desired to offer to you my poor works: but the love which I bear to your service excuses my error, because I have done it with such strenuous daring, as in truth I would do other greater things, if the favour of your Highness should also oblige me as in this work of Prester John of the Indies. Because, besides that the Bishop of Lamego incited me to this, your Highness bade me print it, saying that you would receive much satisfaction from it, which was a great favour to me; I give for it great thanks to God, because with this commencement others came to me with hope of a good end, blessed ends I hope. And if, my Lord, you keep this in your remembrance, I well believe that with a royal mind you will so accept the little, as you will bestow much. For a poor man passing by one day where his King travelled, brought him a little water with both his hands, saying: drink my Lord, for the heat is great. He accepted it gaily from him, not looking to the small quality of that service, but only to the good will with which he offered it. Therefore, though in this same manner I offer to your Highness this small service of the book of Prester John, receive with content its usefulness; for in it are related many notable things; the truth of which is as much shown in the deeds as in the words. Because it is a very important thing for a Prince to recall to memory the examples of profitable lives that have passed away, for a

1

lesson to the living. And as, my Lord, always since I have been yours my desire has been directed to your service in order to derive some fruit by it, even though power may have been wanting to me, good will has not failed: with this I went to Paris to seek for printing types of official letters and other things fitting for printing, which are no less of the best quality than those of Italy, France, and Germany, where this art most flourishes, as your Highness may see by the work which I have established in this city, with no small satisfaction, because it seemed to me that your Highness took pleasure in it, as has been shewn by the favours which you have done to me, and which I hope you will do. Thus, with this confidence, I took this little opportunity of Prester John, which (as the poets say) is not the less to be praised on this account. May your Highness receive with a royal and benignant mind this small service, the first fruits of my small capacity, which may bring profit and recreation from the labours which your great and arduous affairs bring with them. And if your Highness should find in this book any words that do not please you, remember that the men there abroad are lords of the words, and that Princes are lords of deeds and of fortune.

The treatise commences with the entry into the country of Prester John.

CAP. 1.—*How Diogo Lopez de Sequeira succeeded to the government of India after Lopo Soarez, who was governor before him, and how he brought Mattheus to the port of Maçua.*

I say that I came with Duarte Galvan, may God keep him, and this is the truth, and he died in Camaran, an island of the Red sea, and his embassy ceased in the time when Lopo Soarez was Captain General and Governor of the Indies, as I have already written at length, and here I omit to write it as it is not necessary : I shall write that which is necessary. I say that Diogo Lopez de Sequeira succeeding to the government of India after Lopo Soarez, he set to work to do that which Lopo Soarez had not completed, that is to bring Matthens the ambassador, who went to Portugal as ambassador of Prester John, to the port of Maçua, which is near to Arquiquo, port and country of Prester John. And he fitted out his large and handsome fleet, and we set sail for the said Red sea, and arrived at the said island of Maçua on Monday of the Octave of Easter, the seventh day of April of the year fifteen hundred and twenty, which we found empty, because for about five or six days they had had news of us. The main land is about two crossbow shots, more or less, from the island, and to it the Moors of the island had carried off their goods for safety : this mainland belongs to Prester John. The fleet having come to anchor between the island

and the mainland, on the following Tuesday there came to
us from the town of Arquiquo a Christian and a Moor: the
Christian said that the town of Arquiquo belonged to
Christians, and to a lord who was called Barnagais, a
subject of Prester John, and that the Moors of this island
of Maçua and town of Arquiquo, whenever Turks or
Roumys who do them injury came to this port, all fled
to the mountains and carried off such of their property as
they could carry, and now they had not chosen to fly
because they had heard that we were Christians. Hearing
this the great captain gave thanks to God for the news, and
name of Christians which he had met with, and which
greatly favoured Mattheus, who came rather unfavourably:
and he ordered a rich garment to be given to the Christian,
and to the Moor he showed great favour, and told them that
they had done what they ought in not stirring from the
town of Arquiquo, since it belonged to Christians, and the
Prester, as they said, and that his coming was only for the
service and friendship of the Prester John and all his people,
and that they might go in peace and be in security.

CAP. II.—*How the Captain of Arquiquo came to visit the
Captain General, and also some Friars of Bisam.*

The following day, Wednesday of the Octave, the captain
of the said town of Arquiquo came to speak to the Captain
General, and he brought him a present of four cows: and
the Captain General received him with much show and honour,
and gave him rich stuffs, and learned from him more details
about the Christianity of the country, and how he was already summoned by the Barnagais, the lord of that country,
to go there. This captain came in this manner: he brought
a very good horse, and he wore a cloak over a rich Moorish
shirt, and with him there were thirty horsemen, and quite

two hundred men on foot. After the long and agreeable conversation which they held by interpreters, the Captain General speaking Arabic well, the captain of Arquiquo went away with his people much pleased, as it appeared from what they said. At a distance of seven or eight leagues from this town of Arquiquo, in a very high mountain, there is a very noble monastery of friars, which Mattheus talked of a great deal, and which is called Bisan.[1] The friars had news of us, and on Thursday after the Octave there came to us seven friars of the said monastery. The Captain General went out to receive them on the beach with all his people with much pleasure and rejoicing, and likewise the friars showed that they felt much pleasure. They said that for a long time they had been looking forward for Christians, because they had prophecies written in their books, which said that Christians were to come to this port, and that they would open a well in it, and that when this well was opened there would be no more Moors there. They talked of many other things in similar fitting conversations, the ambassador Mattheus being present at all; and the said friars did great honour to Mattheus, kissing his hand and shoulder, because such is their custom, and he also was much delighted with them. These friars said that they kept eight days after the feast of Easter, and that during that time they did not go on a journey or do any other service, but that as soon as they heard say that Christians were in the port, a thing they so much desired, they had begged leave of their superior to come and make this journey in the service of God; and also that news of our arrival had been taken to the Barnagais; but that he would not leave his house except after the eight days after Easter had passed. The conversation with these friars and their reception having been concluded, the Captain General returned to his galleon with his captains, and the friars with him. These friars

[1] Or " of the Vision", according to some.

were received on board with the cross and priests with sur-
plices, giving them the cross to kiss, which they did with
great reverence. They were treated with many conserves
which the Captain General ordered to be given them,
and much conversation passed with them of joy and pleasure over a matter so much desired on both parts. The
said friars departed and went to sleep at Arquiquo.

Cap. iii.—*How the Captain General ordered mass to be
said in the chief mosque of Maçua, and ordered it to
be named St. Mary of the Conception, and how he sent
to see the things of the Monastery of Bisam.*

On Friday after the Octave of Easter, the thirteenth day
of the said month of April, very early in the morning, the
said friars returned to the beach, and they sent for them
with honour; and the governor with his captains passed
over with the friars to the island of Maçua, and he ordered
mass to be said in the principal mosque, in honour of the
five wounds, as it was Friday. At the end of the mass the
Captain General said that the mosque should be named St.
Mary of the Conception: from that time forward we said mass
every day in the said mosque. At the end of that mass, on
betaking ourselves to the ships, some of the friars went with
Mattheus, others with the Captain General: to all cloths were
given for their clothes, that is to say, stuffs of coarse cotton,
for that is the stuff which they wear; they also gave them
pieces of silk for the monastery, and some pictures and bells
for the same monastery. These friars all carried crosses in
their hands, for such is their custom, and the laymen wore
small crosses of black wood at their necks. Our people in
general bought those crosses which the laymen wore, and
brought them with them, because they were novelties to
which we were not accustomed. Whilst these friars were

going about amongst us, the Captain General ordered a man named Fernau Diaz, who knew Arabic, to go and see the monastery; and for greater authority, and for the matter to be better known for it to be written to the King our sovereign, he sent besides the said Fernau Diaz, the licentiate Pero Gomez Teixeira, auditor of the Indies. These each for their own part said that it was a great and good thing, because we ought to give great thanks and praise to the Lord for that we had come from such distant lands and seas, through so many enemies of our faith, and that we here fell in with Christians with a monastery and houses of prayer where God was served. The said auditor brought from the monastery a parchment book written in their writing,[1] to send to the King our sovereign.

CAP. IV.—*How the Captain General and the Barnagais saw each other, and how it was arranged that Rodrigo de Lima should go with Mattheus to Prester John.*

On Tuesday, the seventeenth day of the said month of April, the Barnagais came to the town of Arquiquo, and sent a message to the Governor of his having come. As it seemed likely to the governor that he would come to speak to him on the beach, he ordered a tent to be pitched and stuffs to be arranged in the best manner possible, and ordered seats to be made for sitting on. When all was done, a message arrived that the Barnagais would not come there: then the same day Antonio de Saldanha went to this town of Arquiquo to speak to the Barnagais, and he brought a message and agreement that they should meet and see one another midway, and so we all got ready to go with the

---

[1] Gaspar Correa says it was a breviary on parchment, and describes a picture contained in it on paper which had come from Jerusalem or Rome.

governor: some by sea and some by land, as far as half way
where they were to see one another. There the Governor
ordered his tents to be pitched and seats to be made. The
Barnagais coming first would not come to the place where
the tents were spread and the seats made. The Captain
General having landed, and learned that the Barnagais would
not come to the tents, ordered them to go with the seats and
leave the tents; but still he would not stir with his people
to where the seats were placed. The Captain General again
sent Antonio de Saldanha and the ambassador Mattheus to
him : then they agreed that both should approach each other,
that is, the Captain General and the Barnagais. So they
did, and they saw each other and spoke in a very wide plain,
seated on the ground upon carpets. Among many other
things that they talked of, the principal one was that both
gave thanks to God for their meeting, the Barnagais saying
that they had it written in their books, that Christians from
distant lands were to come to that port to join with the
people of Prester John, and that they would make a well of
water, and that there would be no more Moors there: and since
God fulfilled this, that they should affirm and swear friendship. They then took a cross which was there for that purpose, and the Barnagais took it in his hand, and said that he
swore on that sign of the cross, and on that on which our
Lord Jesus Christ suffered, in the name of Prester John and
in his own, that he would always favour and help to favour
and assist the men and affairs of the king of Portugal and
his captains who came to this port, or to other lands where
they might be able to give them assistance and favour, and
also that he would take the ambassador Mattheus into his
safe keeping, and likewise other ambassadors and people, if
the Captain General should wish to send them through the
kingdoms and lordships of Prester John. The Captain
General swore in like manner to do the same for the affairs
of Prester John and the Barnagais, wherever he might meet

with them, and that the other captains and lords of the kingdom of Portugal would act likewise. The Captain General gave to the Barnagais arms, clothes, and rich stuffs: and the Barnagais gave the Captain General a horse and a mule, both of great price. So they took leave of each other very joyful and contented, the Captain General to the ships, and the Barnagais to Arquiquo.[1] The Barnagais brought with him quite two hundred horsemen, and more than two thousand men on foot. When our gentlemen and captains saw this novelty which God had so provided, and how a path was opened for aggrandising the holy Catholic faith, where they had small hopes of finding such ; because they all held Mattheus to be false and a liar, so that there were grounds for putting him on shore and leaving him alone ; many then clamoured and asked favour of the Governor, each man for himself to be allowed to go with Mattheus on an embassy to Prester John, and here they all affirmed by what they saw that Mattheus was a true ambassador. Since many asked for it, it was given to Don Rodrigo de Lima; then the Captain General settled who were to go with him. We were the following : First, Don Rodrigo de Lima, Jorge d'Abreu, Lopo da Gama, Joam Escolar, clerk of the embassy, Joam Gonzalvez, its interpreter and factor, Manoel de Mares, player of organs, Pero Lopez, mestre Joam, Gaspar Pereira, Estevan Palharte, both servants of Don Rodrigo ; Joam Fernandez, Lazaro d'Andrade, painter, Alonzo Mendez, and I, unworthy priest, Francisco Alvarez.[2] These went in company

---

[1] Gaspar Correa says that at this leave-taking the Portuguese sounded their trumpets and drums and the fleet saluted, and a ball from a camel gun made three rebounds amongst the men of the Barnegaes, without hitting anyone. The Governor sent to ask pardon of him, saying it was a mistake of the bombardier. The Barnegaes answered that no one was safe unless God pleased, and that the ball had done no one any harm.

[2] Gaspar Correa says of the Embassy that Don Rodrigo de Lima was a man of good presence, and a fit man for such a service ; that Jorge

with Don Rodrigo; the Captain General here said, in the presence of all: Don Rodrigo, I do not send the father Francisco Alvarez with you, but I send you with him, and do not do anything without his advice. There went with Matthous three Portuguese, one was named Magalhaes, another Alvarenga, another Diogo Fernandez.

Cap. v.—*Of the goods which the Captain sent to Prester John.*

They then prepared the present which was to be sent to the Prester: not such as the King our Sovereign had sent by Duarte Galvan, because that had been dispersed in Cochim by Lopo Soarez: and what we now brought was poor enough, and we took for excuse that the goods which we brought had been lost in the ship St. Antonio, which was lost near Dara in the mouth of the straits. These were the goods which we took to Prester John: first, a gold sword with a rich hilt, four pieces of tapestry, some rich cuirasses, a helmet and two swivel guns, four chambers, some balls, two barrels of powder, a map of the world, some organs. With these we set out from the ships to Arquiquo, where we went to present ourselves to the Barnagais. Thence we went to rest about two crossbow shots distance above the town, in a plain at the foot of a mountain. There they soon sent us a cow, and bread and wine of the country. We waited there because they had to

d'Abreu, the second person of the Embassy, was a very well dressed gentleman; that Francisco Alvarez was a very prudent man, and well informed in all matters of the altar and divine services; that Estevan Palharte was a good fencer; the three Portuguese who accompanied Matthous were Miguel Fernandez, Diogo Tatys, and João d'Alvarenga, all men skilful in manual arts, and who could sing at mass, for which the priest carried rich ornaments and all that was necessary, and irons for making wafers.

send to us, or give us from the country, riding horses and camels for the baggage. This day was Friday, and because in this country they keep Saturday and Sunday, Saturday for the old law and Sunday for the new, therefore we remained thus both the two days. In these days the ambassador Mattheus settled with Don Rodrigo and with all of us, that we should not go with the Barnagais because he was a great lord, and that we should do much better to go to the monastery of Bisam : and that from that place we should get a better equipment than from the Barnagais. Don Rodrigo, doing this at his wish, sent to tell the Barnagais that we were not going with him, and that we were going to Bisam. And the Barnagais, not grieving on this account, went away and left us. And because our equipment had to be made by his order, they gave us eight horses and no more, and thirty camels for the baggage. So we remained discontented, knowing the mistake we were making in leaving Barnagais to please Mattheus.

Cap. VI.—*Of the day that we departed and the fleet went out of the port, and where we went to keep the feast, and of a gentleman who came to us.*

We departed from this plain close to the town of Arquiquo, on Monday the thirtieth of April. On this day, as soon as we lost sight of the sea, and those of the sea lost sight of us, the fleet went out of the port, although the Captain General had said he would wait there until he saw our message, and knew in what country we had arrived. And we did not go more than half a league from where we departed from, and then rested at a dry channel, which had no water except in a few little pools. We held the midday rest here on account of the great drought of the land : for further on we should not have water, and the heat was very

great. We all carried our gourds, and leather ewers, and
waterskins of the country, with water. In this dry river
bed there were many trees of different species, amongst
which were jujube trees, and other trees without fruit.
Whilst we were thus resting at the river bed there came
to us a gentleman named Frey Mazqual, which in our
tongue means servant of the cross. He in his blackness
was a gentleman, and said he was a brother-in-law of the
Barnagais, a brother of his wife. Before he reached us he
dismounted, because such is their custom, and they esteem
it a courtesy. The ambassador Mattheus, hearing of his
arrival, said he was a robber, and that he came to rob us
and told us to take up arms : and he Mattheus took his
sword, and put a helmet on his head. Frey Mazqual,
seeing this tumult, sent to ask leave to come up to us.
Mattheus was still doubtful, and withal he came up to us
like a well born man, well educated, and courteous.* This
gentleman had a very good led horse and a mule on which
he came, and four men on foot.

CAP. VII.—*How Mattheus made us leave the road, and
travel through the mountain in a dry river bed.*

We departed from this resting place all together, with
many other people who had been resting there; and this
gentleman went with us on his mule, leading his horse :
and he approached the ambassador, Don Rodrigo, and
caused the interpreter we had with us to approach, and
they went for a good distance talking and conversing. He
was in his speech, conversation, questions, and answers, a
well informed and courteous man, and the ambassador
Mattheus could not bear him, saying that he was a robber.
And while we were going by a very good wide and flat
road, by which were travelling all the people who had

rested with us at the rest, and many others who were travelling behind, Mattheus, who was in front, left this road and entered some bushes and hills without any road, and made the camels go that way, and all of us with them, saying that he knew the country better than anyone else, and that we should follow him. When Frey Mazqual saw this he said that we were out of any road, and that he did not know why that man did this. We all began to cry out at him, because he was taking us through the rough ground to lose and break what we carried with us, leaving the high-roads, and that we were travelling where the wolves went. Mattheus, perceiving our outcry, and that we were all against him, took a turn, and we went round some mountains to the road, more than two leagues before reaching it. And before we reached it Mattheus had a fainting fit, during which we thought he was dead for more than an hour. When he came to himself we put him on a mule, and two men on each side to assist him. So we went, all accompanying and looking after him, and Frey Mazqual with us, until we arrived at the road, which was a long way off. When we reached it we found a very large cafila of camels and many people who were coming to Arquiquo, because they only travel in cafilas for fear of robbers. These were all amazed at the road we had travelled. We all slept at a hill where there was water and a certain place for cafilas to halt at, and Frey Mazqual also. We all slept, we and the two cafilas keeping good watch all night. From here we set out next morning, always travelling by dry river beds, and on either side very high mountain ridges, with large woods of various kinds of trees, most of them without fruit: for among them are some very large trees which give a fruit which they call tamarinds, like clusters of grapes, which are much prized by the Moors, for they make vinegar with them, and sell them in the markets like dried raisins. The dry channels and road by which we went showed very deep clefts, which are made by the thunder storms: they do not much impede travelling, as they told us, and as we afterwards saw similar ones. All that is necessary is to turn aside and wait for two hours the overflow of the storm, they then set out travelling again. However great these rivers may be with the waters of these storms, as soon as they issue forth from the mountains and reach the plains, they immediately spread out and are absorbed, and do not reach the sea: and we could not learn that any river of Ethiopia enters into the Red sea, all waste away when they come to the flat plains. In these mountains and ridges there are many animals of various kinds, such as lions, elephants, tigers, ounces, wolves, boars, stags, deer,[1] and all other kinds which can be named in the world, except two which I never saw nor heard tell that there are any of them here, bears and rabbits. There are birds of all kinds that can be named, both of those known to us and of those not known, great and small: two kinds of birds I did not see nor hear say that there are, these are magpies and cuckoos; the other herbs of these mountains and rivers are basil and odorous herbs.

CAP. VIII.—*How Matthews again took us out of the road, and made us go to the monastery of Bisam.*

When it was the hour for resting ourselves, Matthews was still determined on taking us out of the high road, and taking us to the monastery of Bisam, through mountain ridges and bushes,[2] and we took counsel with frey Mazqual, who told us that the road to the monastery was such that baggage could not go there on men's backs, and that the road we were leaving was the high road by which travelled

---

[1] Anta.   [2] "Matos idiabrados", not in Bluteau.

the caravans of Christians and Moors, where no one did them any harm, and that still less would they do harm to us who were travelling in the service of God and of Prester John. Nevertheless, we followed the will and fancy of Mattheus. At the halt,[1] where we slept, there were great altercations as to the said travelling, and as to whether we should turn back to the high road which we had left. Seeing this, Mattheus begged of me to entreat the ambassador Don Rodrigo and all the others to be pleased to go to the monastery of Bisam, because it was of great importance to him, and that he would not remain there more than six or seven days (he remained there for ever, for he died there); and that when those seven or eight days were passed, in which he would trade in what belonged to him, we should be welcome to go on our road. At my request all determined to do his wish, since it was important to him, saying that we would remain at a village at the foot of the monastery. We departed from this halt by much more precipitous ground and channels than those of the day before, and larger woods. We on foot and the mules unridden in front of us, we could not travel; the camels shrieked as though sin was laying hold of them. It seemed to all that Mattheus was bringing us here to kill us; and all turned upon me because I had done it. There was nothing for it but to call on God, for sins were going about in those woods: at midday the wild animals were innumerable and had little fear of people. Withal we went forward, and began to meet with country people who kept fields of Indian corn, and who come from a distance to sow these lands and rocky ridges which are among these mountains: there are also in these parts very beautiful flocks, such as cows and goats. The people that we found here are almost naked, so that all they had showed, and they were very black. These people were Christians, and the women

---

[1] Meijoada, not in Bluteau.

wore a little more covering, but it was very little. Going a little further in another forest which we could not pass on foot, and the camels unladen, there came to us six or seven friars of the monastery of Bisam, among whom were four or five very old men, and one more so than all the rest, to whom all showed great reverence, kissing his hand. We did the same, because Mattheus told us that he was a bishop; afterwards we learned that he was not a bishop, but his title was David, which means guardian, and besides, in the monastery there is another above him, whom they call Abba, which means father: and this father is like a *provincial*. From their age and from their being thin and dry like wood, they appear to be men of holy life. They go into the forests collecting their millet, both that grown by their own labour, and the produce of the dues paid to them by those who sow in these mountains and forests. The clothes which they wear are old yellow cotton stuffs, and they go barefooted. From this place we went forward until the camels had taken rest, and in the space of a quarter of a league we arrived at the foot of a tree with all our baggage, and Mattheus with his, and frey Mazqual with us, also the friars, particularly the old ones, were there with us: and the oldest, whom Mattheus called a Bishop, gave us a cow, which we at once killed for supper. We were here in doubt by what way we could get out, and as there was no help for it we all slept here together, ambassadors, friars and frey Mazqual, ready to start.

Cap. ix.— *How we said mass here, and Frey Mazqual separated from us, and we went to a monastery where our people fell sick.*

The following day was Holy Cross of May; we said mass at the foot of a tree in honour of the true cross, that it might please to direct us well, entreating our Portuguese to make this petition with much devotion to our Lord, that like as He had opened a way to Saint Helena to find it, so He would open a road for our salvation which we saw to be so closed up. Mass being ended we dined, and the ambassador Mattheus ordered his baggage to be loaded on the backs of negroes, and taken to a small monastery which was half a league from where we were, and they name the patron of it St. Michael, and they call the site of the monastery Dise. Joam Escolar, the clerk of the Embassy, and I, went with this baggage on foot, as it was not ground or a road fit for mules. We went to see what country it was there, and whether we should go to that monastery, or whether we should turn back. Here frey Mazqual departed from us. With the journey we made, the clerk and I, we were almost dead when we arrived at the monastery, both from the precipitous path and steep ascent, and the great heat. After having taken rest, and seen the said monastery, and seen that it had buildings in which to lodge our goods, and ourselves also, the clerk returned to the company, and I remained at the monastery. On the following day, fourth of May, all our people came with the goods we were bringing with us, and which had remained at the foot of this mountain, all being carried on the backs of negroes. And on the night on which our people remained and slept there, Satan did not cease from weaving his wiles, and caused strife to arise among our people, and this on account of the ambassador's carrying out that which he had to do, and ought to do for the service of God and the King, and for the safety of our lives and honour: and one said that there were men in the company who were not going to do all that seemed fit to him, upon this they came to using their spears. God be praised that no one was wounded. As soon as we were all at the monastery I made them good friends, blaming them for using such words, since he was our captain, and that which was for the service of God and

2

the King was an advantage to us all, and that we ought not
to do anything without mature deliberation. We lodged in
this monastery of St. Michael under the impression that we
should depart at the end of seven or eight days, as Mattheus
had said, and they gave us very good lodgings. Upon this
Mattheus came and told us that he had written to the court
of Prester John, and to Queen Helena, and to the patriarch,
and that the answer could not come in less than forty days,
and that we could not depart without this answer, because
from there mules had to be sent for us and for the baggage.
And he did not stop at this, but went on to say that the
winter was beginning, which would last three months, and
that we could not travel during that time, and that we
should buy provisions for the winter. Besides, he said that
we should wait for the Bishop of Bisam, who was coming
from the court, and that he would give us equipment. This
one that he called Bishop is not one, but is the Abba or
provincial of Bisam. In this matter of the winter, and the
coming of this provincial, the friars of this monastery con-
certed with Mattheus, and they did not lie, for nobody in
this country travels for three months, that is, from the
middle of June, July, August, to middle of September, and
the winter is general: also as to the coming of him they
called Bishop, he did not delay much. A few days after
our arrival the people fell sick, both the Portuguese and also
our slaves, few or none remained who were not affected, and
many in danger of death from much bloodletting and purging. Among the first mestre Joam fell sick, and we had
no other remedy. The Lord was pleased that purging and
bloodletting came to him of itself, and he regained his
health. After that the sickness attacked others with all its
force, among them the ambassador Mattheus fell sick, and
many remedies were used for him. And thinking that he
was already well, and as though delighted and pleased, he
ordered his baggage to be got ready and sent to a village of

Bisam named Jangargara, which is half way between this monastery and Bisam. In that village are friars of the said monastery, who keep their cows there, and there are many good houses in it. He had his baggage taken there, and went with it, and two days after his arrival he sent to call the mestre, for he had fallen ill again. He left all the sick people and went, and we did not wait long after him, the ambassador, Don Rodrigo, and I, but went to visit him, and we found him very suffering. Don Rodrigo returned, and I remained with him three days, and I confessed him and gave him the sacraments, and at the end of the three days he died, on the 23rd of May 1520; and he made his will in the Portuguese language by means of mestre Francisco Gonzalves, his spiritual father, and also in the Abyssinian language by a friar of the said monastery. As soon as he was dead there came thither at once the ambassador, and Jorge d'Abreu, and Joam Escolar the clerk, and a great number of the friars of Bisam. We took him with great honour to bury him at the said monastery, and did the office for the dead after our custom, and the friars after their custom. In the same night that Mattheus died, Pereira, servant of Don Rodrigo, died. When the burial of Mattheus was done, the ambassador, Don Rodrigo, and Jorge d'Abreu, and Joam Escolar, clerk, and certain friars of the monastery, returned to the village where Mattheus died, and where his goods remained. And it was intended to make an inventory of his goods, in order that they should be correctly sent to the person whom he named, by Francisco Mattheus, his servant, whom the King of Portugal, our Sovereign, had given him and had set free, because before he was a Moorish slave, and the goods were in his keeping. The said Francisco Mattheus took it into his head not to choose that the inventory should be made : and the friars for their part hoping to get a share of the goods. Seeing this, Don Rodrigo left them to their devices and came away in peace;

2 2

and Francisco Mattheus and the friars took these goods to the monastery of Bisam, and thence sent them to the court of the Prester for them to be given to the Queen Helena, to whom he, Mattheus, ordered them to be given.

Cap. x.—*How Don Rodrigo sent to ask the Barnagais for equipment for his departure.*

As we were thus without any remedy, and had been waiting for a month and no message came, and we did not know what to do, and Mattheus having died, we determined on sending to ask the Barnagais to send us some equipment for our departure, so that we might not remain here for our destruction. Knowing this the friars grieved much at it, and pressed Don Rodrigo not to send, and to wait for the arrival of the said provincial, as he would be at the monastery within ten days, and that if he did not come that they would provide the means for our departure. And because these people are unconfiding they would not trust in the ambassador, although he had promised it them ; and they took an oath from all of us on a crucifix that we would wait for the said ten days, and they also swore to fulfil that which they had promised. And in order that we might not be disappointed on one side or the other, or in case both should take effect, we might choose the best, Don Rodrigo arranged to send Joam Gonzalves, interpreter and factor, and Manoel de Mares and two other Portuguese to the Barnagais to ask him to remember the oath which he swore and promised to the Captain General of the King of Portugal, which was to favour and take into his keeping the affairs of the King, and to be pleased to give us an equipment for our travelling. When the ten days were ended the factor sent one of the Portuguese that went with him with a good message, and with him came a man from the Barnagais saying that he came to give us oxen for the baggage and mules for ourselves. On the part of the friars nothing came.

CAP. XI.—*Of the fashion and situation of the monasteries and their customs, first this of St. Michael.*

The manner of these monasteries as to their sites and customs : all are situated on the greatest and highest cliffs, or the deepest they can find. This one of St. Michael is situated on a very steep rock at the foot of another very high rock, where no one can ascend. The stone of which these rocks consist is of the grain of the walls of the port of Portugal.[1] They are very great rocks. The land around these rocks is all covered with very great forests, and besides wild olive trees and high grass between them, in which there is much basil. The trees which are not wild olive trees are not trees known to us ; all are without fruit. In the narrow valleys which belong to this monastery there are orange trees, lemon trees, citron trees, pear trees and fig trees of all kinds, both of Portugal and India ; peach trees, cabbages, coriander, cardamine, wormwood,[2] myrtle and other sweet-smelling and medicinal herbs, all ill profited by because they are not good working men : and the earth produces these like wild plants, and it would produce whatever was planted and sown in it. The monastery house looks quite like a church building, constructed like ours. It has around it a circuit like a cloister, covered above in the same manner as the body of the monastery. It has three entrances, as ours are, one principal one, and two side ones. The roof of the church and of its cloisters is of wild straw, which lasts a man's life : the body of the church is built with naves very well constructed, and their arches are

---

[1] Oporto.   [2] Alosna.

very well closed; all appears to be vaulted. The church has
a chancel and a transept, in the centre transept are curtains
from end to end; and there are other curtains before the
side doors, from wall to wall. They are curtains of silk :
the entrance through these curtains is in three places, they
are open in the middle, and they reach one to another, also
they can be entered close to the walls. In the said three
entrances there are little bells suspended to the curtains
themselves, and nobody can enter by any part without these
bells ringing. Here there is not more than one altar, which
is in the chancel : this has a stand on four props, and the
altar reaches to these four props. This stand is covered
over above as though with a vault, and there is an altar
stone which they call *tabuto*. Upon this altar stone there
is a basin of copper, very large and flat below, and with
low sides. This basin also reaches to the supports of the
stand, which are disposed in a square. Within this large
basin there is another smaller one. This stand has curtains
hanging down from it to the ground, that is, at the back
and sides, which screen the altar, except that in front it is
open. One can go all round the altar. The bells are of
stone, and in this manner: long thin stones, suspended by
cords passed through them, and they strike them with
sticks made for the purpose, and they make a sound as of
cracked bells heard at a distance. Also at festivals they
take the basins from the altar and strike them with sticks,
and they help to make a sound. They have also other iron
bells, not round, but with two sides, they have a clapper
which strikes first on one side and then on the other, and it
makes a noise as of helving a mattock. They also have
other small ill-made bells, which they carry in their hands
at processions, and they ring the whole of them at the
festivals. On other days the bells of stones and iron are
used. In all churches and monasteries they ring for matins
two hours before dawn. They say the prayers by heart and

without light, except in the lamps or chandeliers, for they have not got lamps. They burn butter in these chandeliers, for they have not got oil. They pray or chaunt very loud, without art of singing, and they do not recite (alternate) verses, but all sing straight on. Their prayers are psalms, and on feast days besides psalms they recite prose, according as the feast is so is the prose. They always stand in the churches; at matins they only say one single lesson : this is said by a priest or a friar, rather shouted than intoned, and he reads this lesson before the principal entrance. When this lesson is finished, on Saturdays, Sundays, and feast days, they make a procession with four or five crosses on their poles, and a cross not, so much raised as carried like a stick in the left hand, because they carry a thuriblo in the right hand, since as many as carry a cross carry a thurible, there are always as many thuribles as crosses. They wear some silk cloaks, not well made, because they are not wider than the width of a piece of damask, or other silk from top to bottom. Before the breast, a cross piece to the flanks on each side, of any other stuff and of any colour, even though it should not match the principal part, and of this principal part a good ell hangs behind dragging on the ground. They make this procession through the circuit, which is like a cloister. This being ended, on the said Saturdays, Sundays, and feasts, he who has to say mass enters with two others into the chancel; they bring out an effigy of Our Lady, which they have in ancient pictures in all churches and monasteries. He who has to say mass places himself in the centre of the transept with his face towards the principal entrance, and the image in his hands held before his breast : and those who stand by his sides hold lighted candles in their hands, and all the others commence a chaunt like prose, and all walk, shouting and leaping as if dancing[1] they hold hands and go round, before the

[1] *Como em chacota*, dancing and singing, *i.e.*, not reverentially.

image,[1] and at the sound of that chaunt or prose which they
sing, they also ring the little bells and sound the cymbals to the
same tune. Each time that they pass before the image they
make a great reverence to it. Certainly it has a good appearance and causes devotion, from being a thing done for the
praise of the Lord God. There also proceed crosses and thuribles in this feast as in the procession. When this is ended,
which lasts a good while, they put by the picture and go to
a small building which is on the North side, and of the
gospel according to our mass; and outside the covered
circuit, where they make the bread which they call *corbom*,
and we *hostia*. They carry cross, thurible, and bell, and
bring thence the bread of wheat flour, and without leaven,
made at that moment, very white and nice, of the size and
roundness of a patena, in this monastery in which are few
people. In other monasteries and churches, where there are
many people, they make large loaves, and many of them
according to the people, because all are communicants who
go to the church. According to the width of the bread
they make its thickness, from half a finger's breadth to an
inch, or larger. They bring this loaf in a small vase,
which is one of those of the altar, covered with a cloth, and
with the cross and thurible, sounding a bell. Behind the
church, that is, behind the chancel,[2] in that circuit which is
like a cloister, nobody must remain unless he were in holy
orders, and all the others must be before the principal
entrance in another large circuit, which all the churches have;
for near this, which is like a cloister, anybody who likes may
stand. Whilst bringing the bread, as many as are in the
church or in its circuit, when they hear the bell, bow their
heads until the bell is silent, which is when they place the
wafer on the altar with the small vase in which they brought

---

[1] *Como quem anda per mãos diante da imagem.* According to the
Spanish translation of Miguel de Salves. Saragossa, 1561.
[2] *Oussia.*

it. They place this vase in the other larger one, and cover the bread with a dark cloth, after the fashion of a *corporale*. They have a silver chalice in this monastery, and so in all honourable churches and monasteries there are silver chalices, some have them of gold: in poor churches, which they call churches of *Balgues*, that is, of rustics, there are copper chalices. The vases are very wide and ill made, and they have not got patenas. They put into the chalice wine of raisins, in large quantities, because as many as partake of the communion of the body also partake of the blood. He who has to say mass begins it with Hallelujah in a loud voice, rather shouted than sung; all respond and continue the chaunt. He of the mass is silent and continues his benedictions, which he does with his small cross, which he holds in his hand. Those who are outside sing as well as those who are inside the church and cloister, up to a certain distance. Here one of those who is at the altar, takes a book and goes to read the epistle at the principal door of the church. When it is ended, he who read it at once begins a chaunt as a response; those who are at the altar, or in the church, follow him. This ended, he who says the mass takes a book from the altar, and gives it to him who has to read the gospel, and he bows his head and begs a blessing. After he has received it he goes to the place where the epistle was read, and with him two others, one with a cross and thurible, the other with a bell. They read the gospel, and likewise the epistle, fast and loud, as much so as the tongue can speak and the voice be raised. Returning to the altar, on the way another chaunt commences, and those that accompany them join in it. On reaching the altar they give the book to kiss to him who says the mass, and they deposit the book in its place; because at the altar they say nothing from a book. Then he who says mass takes the thurible, or they give it into his hand, and he incenses the altar above it, and then takes

several turns round it, giving incense. When these circuits
and incensing are ended, he turns to the altar and gives
many blessings with the cross, and then uncovers the bread
which was covered up, and which is for the sacrament: they
take it with both hands, and let go the right hand and it
remains in the left hand : with the thumb of the right hand
he makes five marks like little hollows, that is to say, one
in the upper part, one in the middle, another at the lower
part, another on the left, and another on the right hand,
and then he consecrates in his language, and with our own
very words, and does not elevate it. He does as much with
the chalice, and says over it our own very words, in his
language : and again covers it, and takes the sacrament of
the bread in his hands and divides it in the middle, and of
the part which remains in his left hand, from the top of it
he takes a very small portion, and places the other pieces
one upon another. The priest takes this small portion for
himself, and also takes a portion of the sacrament of the
blood. After that he takes the vase with the sacrament
covered up and gives it to him who read the gospel, and
likewise takes the chalice with the sacrament and gives it
to him who read the epistle. He then administers the
communion to the priests who are near the altar, taking the
sacrament in very small portions from the vase which the
deacon holds in his right hand, and as often as he administers
it the sub-deacon takes of the blood with a spoon of gold,
or silver, or copper, according to the church, and gives a
very small quantity to the person who has received the
body. There is also on one side another priest with a ewer
of holy water, and the person who has received the communion puts out the palm of his hand and he pours some of
that holy water, and with it he washes his mouth and
swallows it. This being done all go to the altar with this
sacrament before the first curtain, and in this manner they
give the communion to those that are there, and thence to

those who are at the other curtain, and thence to the
secular people who are at the principal door, both men and
women, if it is a church to which women come. At the
giving of the communion, and likewise at all the offices of
the church, all are standing up. When they come to
receive the communion, all come with their hands raised
before their shoulders, and the palms forward. As soon as
each one receives the sacrament of the blood he takes the
said water as has been said, and so generally as many as are
communicants. Before mass they wash their hands with
the water which is in all the churches and monasteries.
The priest who said the mass, and those who stood with him
at the altar, when the communion is ended, return to the
altar, and wash the vase in which the sacrament was, with
the water which remains in the ewer, which they say is
blessed, this water they pour into the chalice, and the priest
who said mass takes it all. This done, one of these ministers
of the altar takes a cross and a bell, and beginning a low
chaunt goes to the principal entrance, where the epistle and
gospel were read, and the administering the communion
ended, and as many as are in the church, and outside of
it, bow their heads, and go away in peace. They say this is
the blessing, without this no one goes away. On Saturdays
and Sundays, and feast days, in all the churches and
monasteries, blessed bread is distributed. The method
which they have in this small monastery, which will not
have more than 20 or 25 friars, is that which is followed in
all the monasteries and churches, great and small. The
office of the mass, exclusive of the processions, is short;
and the mass on week days is quickly finished.

CAP. XII.—*Where and how the bread of the Sacrament is made, and of a Procession they made, and of the pomp with which the mass is said, and of entering into the church.*

The making of this sacramental bread is in this manner. The building in which it is made, in all churches and monasteries, is, as I said above, on the gospel side, outside of the church and its circuit, which is like a cloister, in the space contained by the other outer circuit, which is not covered in, which space serves for a churchyard. All the churches and monasteries have such a building, and it does not contain anything else except what is requisite for this purpose; that is to say, a mortar for pounding wheat, a machine for making very clean flour, and such as is required for such a purpose, for they do not prepare this sacrament from flour or wheat on which women have laid their hands. They have pots for preparing the paste, which they make thicker than ours. They have a furnace, as for distilling water, and upon it a plate of iron, and in some churches of copper, and in other poor churches of clay. This plate is round and of a good size; they place fire underneath it, and when it is hot clean it with a waxed cloth, pour on it a portion of paste, and spread it out with a wooden spoon of such size as they intend to make the bread, and they make it very round. When it is set they take it off and place it on end, then they make another in the same way. When this second one is set, they take the first and place it upon it, that is to say, the side of the first which was uppermost they put upon the top of the other, fresh with fresh, and so the bread remains one whole one, and they do nothing more than make it round and turn it from one side to the other, and move it about on the plate, that it may bake on both sides and on the circumference. In this manner they make one or as many as they wish. In this same house are the raisins from which the wine is made, and a machine for pressing. In this same house the blessed bread is made which is given away on Saturdays and Sundays and feast days; and on great feasts, such as Christmas, Easter, Our Lady of August, etc., they carry this bread of the sacrament with a pallium,[1] bell, and cross devoutly. Before they enter the church with it they go round the church by the circuit like a cloister; when it is not a feast they enter the church at once and without the pallium. On a Saturday before Ascension these friars made a procession, and from being in a new country it seemed to us very good, and they did it in this way. They took crosses, and the altar stone covered with a silk cloth, a friar carried it on his head, which was also covered with the said cloths; and they carried books and bells, and thuribles, and holy water; and all went chaunting to some millet fields : there they made their devotions and cries after the fashion of litanies, and with this procession they returned to the monastery. We asked why they did that, and they said that the animals ate their millet, and so they went to pour out holy water and pray God to drive them out. In this country he that says the mass has no other difference from the deacon and sub-deacon in his vestments than a long stole with an opening in the middle to allow the head to pass through; before and behind it reaches to the ground. The friars say mass with hair on their heads; the priests do not wear hair, and are shaven and so say mass. Also, both friars and priests say mass barefooted, nobody enters the church with his feet shod, and they allege for this what God said to Moses : "Take off thy shoes from off thy feet, for thou art on holy ground."

[1] Under a canopy.

CAP. XIII.—*How in all the churches and monasteries in the country of Prester John only one mass is said each day; and of the situation of the monastery of Bisam where we buried Mattheus; and of the fast of Lent.*

In the monastery of St. Michael, where we were staying, we said mass each day, not in the monastery, but in the circuit which is like a cloister. In this country they do not say more than one mass in each church or monastery. The friars came to our mass with great devotion, as it appeared; and they supplied a thurible and incense, because we had not brought any with us, and they do not think mass is properly said without incense; and they said that they approved of all, except that we had only one priest to say mass; because among them not less than three, five, or or seven stand at the altar to say mass. They also were surprised at our coming into the church with our shoes on, and still more at our spitting in it. In this manner we said mass every day up to Trinity Sunday, and when we intended to say mass on the following Monday they did not allow us to say it, at which we were much scandalised and aggrieved, and it seemed to us that they had some evil suspicion of us, not knowing why they so acted. Later we learned how they preserved some things of the Old Law together with the New; such as that of the fast of Lent, which they began on Monday after Sexagesima Sunday, that is, ten days before the beginning of our Lent; and so they make fifty days of Lent. They say they take these days in anticipation for the Saturdays when they do not keep the fast. When they fast they eat at night, and because all fast they say mass at night, because all have to take the communion. Likewise, as they take fifty days' fast in Lent, so they take as many days after Easter which are not fast days. Then, when there is no fast, they say mass in the morning. This secret we did not know, and we had no one to explain it to us : as soon as their liberty not to fast had ended, their mass could not be said, except at night, and so they did not consent to our saying it ; thus we felt aggrieved without cause. This time having ended and Trinity passed by, all priests and friars are obliged to fast every day except Saturdays and Sundays. They keep this fast up to Christmas Day, and as all fast they say mass at night. They allege for this the supper of Christ, when He consecrated His true Body, having been a fast time, and almost night. The general people, that is secular men and women, are obliged to fast from Trinity to Advent, Wednesdays and Fridays of each week, and from Christmas day to the Purification of Our Lady, which they call the feast of Simeon,[1] they have no fast. The first three days after the Purification, not being Saturday or Sunday, are great fast days for priests, friars, and laymen. They say that in these three days they do not eat more than once : it is called the penitence of Niniveh. At the end of these three days, up to the beginning of Lent, they again fast as from after Trinity. During Advent and the whole of Lent, priests, friars, lay friars, men and women, small and great, sound and sick, all fast. Thus from Easter to Trinity, and from Christmas to the Purification, they say mass in the morning, because there is no fast, and all the other time at night, because they are fasting. Where we buried Mattheus is a great and honourable monastery, which is named Bisam, and its patron, Jesus. From the monastery where we stayed to this is a league of very precipitous country. It is on a very high rock, and looking round all sides of it there appear like the depths of hell. The monastery house is very large in bulk, and larger in revenues, and this monastery is very well fitted. The fashion of this house is of three large and beautiful naves, with their arches and vaulted roofs. They appear to be of wood, and because all

[1] *Symeon.*

is painted, it is not certain whether it is stone or wood. It
has two sets of cloisters round the body of the church, both
covered in, and much painted with figures of apostles,
patriarchs, prophets, and many things of the Old Law, and
many angels, and St. George on horseback, who is in all the
churches. This monastery also possesses a great cloth, like
a piece of tapestry, on which is the crucifix and effigy of
Our Lady and the apostles, and other figures of patriarchs
and prophets, and each one has his Latin name written, so
that no man of the country made it. It has many small
and ancient pictures, not well made, and they are not upon
the altars, for it is not their custom : they keep them in a
sacristy, mixed up with many books, and they bring them
out on feast days. There is in this monastery a very large
kitchen and bakehouse, also a very large refectory, in which
they eat. They mostly eat three and three[1] in a large dish,
it is not deep, but flat like a tray, and their food is very
poor. The bread is of maize and barley, and other grain
which they call *taffo*,[2] a small black grain. They make this
bread round, and of the size and roundness of a citron,[3] and
they give three of these to each friar : to the novices they
give three loaves to two of them, it is a matter of amazement how they can maintain themselves. They also give
them a few vegetables, without salt or oil. Of this food
they send to a great many old pensioners, who do not come
to the refectory. Besides seeing these things when we
buried Matthens, I saw them many times, because I came
there to pass time with the friars, principally on feast days,
when we were near there. In this way I learned about them
and their property, and revenues and customs. In my
opinion there were generally always a hundred friars in this

---

[1] By threes.
[2] Mansfield Parkins calls it teff, the species of corn most esteemed in
this country.
[3] Zambra, not referred to in Selves' translation.

monastery, most of them old men of great age, and as dry as wood; very few young men. This monastery is entirely surrounded by a wall, and this wall is closed with two gates, which are always locked.

CAP. XIV.—*How the monastery of Bisan is the head of six monasteries, of the number of the brothers, and ornaments, of the "castar"[1] which they do to Philip, whom they call a Saint.*

This monastery is the head of six monasteries, which are around it in these mountains; the furthest off is at a distance of three leagues from it, and all are subject to it, and are governed and ruled by it. In each of them is a David, that is a guardian appointed by the Abbot or provincial of this monastery, who is also David under the Abba. I always heard say that there were in this monastery three thousand friars, and because I doubted it much I came here to keep the feast of our Lady of August, in order to see if they would come together. Certainly I rejoiced to see the riches of this monastery, and the procession which they made: in my judgment the friars did not exceed three hundred, and most of them were very old. There is a circuit to this monastery which surrounds the two which are like cloisters covered in, and this one which is not covered in was on that occasion all covered in with brocades and inferior brocades, and velvets of Mekkah, all long pieces, sewn one to another in order that they might shelter the whole circuit. They made a very beautiful procession through this canopied circuit; all wore cloaks of the same stuffs, brocades, and velvets of Mekkah, badly made as I mentioned above. They carried fifty small crosses of silver, of bad workmanship, and as many

---

[1] Should be *teskar*.

3

thuribles of copper. When mass was said, I saw a great gold chalice and gold spoon, with which they administered the communion. Of the three hundred friars who came to this monastery, very few were those that I knew as belonging to it: and I asked some of my friends how it was, that with so large a number of friars in the monastery as they said, they were not present at such a feast. They told me that even though there were more than they had said, that they were scattered about in these monasteries and churches, and markets, to seek for their living, because that could not be in the monastery whilst they were young men; and when they were old men, and could not walk, they came to die in the monastery. On that day I saw the habit put on seventeen young men. There is a tomb in this monastery which they say is of an Abba or provincial of this monastery who is named Philip, and they give him the merits of a Saint, saying that there was a King Prester John who commanded that Saturday should not be observed in his kingdoms and lordships, and this Abba Philip went to that King Prester with his friars, and undertook to show how God had commanded that Saturday should be kept, and that whoever did not keep it should die by stoning, and that he would maintain this before all the fathers of Ethiopia : and he made it good before the King. Therefore they say that he was a Saint for making Saturday to be kept, and they treat him as a Saint, and they hold a feast for him every year, in the month of July, which they call *Castar* Philip, which means funeral or memorial of Philip.[1] On this account the people of this monastery are the most Judaizing of all the kingdoms of Prester John. I came twice to this Castar of Philip, at which they did me much honour, and they kill many cows at this feast. In one year they killed thirty, and in another year twenty-eight, and in

[1] *Castar* should be *Teskar*; Mansfield Parkyns calls it a sort of funereal feast, where charities are bestowed on the poor and the priests.

each of the years that I came there they gave me two
quarters of the fattest cow that was killed. This flesh is
distributed amongst the people who come to the Castar, and
the friars have none because they do not eat meat. And
these cows are all brought as offerings by their breeders in
the district, who vow them to Philip. This monastery, and
the others that are subject to it, have this rule in addition,
that no females enter them, that is to say, neither women,
nor she-mules, nor cows, nor hens, nor anything else that is
female. And these cows which they kill are killed a long
way from the wall, and when I came there they came to the
distance of a cross-bow shot to take my mule, and they
took her away to their farm of Jamgargara, where Mattheus
died.

CAP. XV.—*Of the agriculture of this country, and how they
preserve themselves from the wild beasts, and of the
revenues of the monastery.*

The friars of this monastery, and of the other monasteries
subject to it, might do good works by planting trees and
vines, and making gardens and orchards for their exercise;
and they do nothing. The country is ready to produce
everything, as is seen from that which is uncultivated: they
do not plant or grow anything except millet and bee-hives.
When it is night, neither they nor anybody else go out from
their houses from fear of the wild beasts that are in the
country, and those who watch the millet have very high
resting places upon the trees, in which they sleep at night.
In the district of this monastery there are, in the valleys
between the mountains, very large herds of cows, kept by
Arab Moors, and there go with each herd forty or fifty
Moors, with their wives and children: and their headman is

3 ?

a Christian, because the cows that they keep belong to Christian gentlemen of the country of the Barnagais. These Moors have nothing else for their labour than the milk and butter which they get from the cows, and with this they maintain themselves and their wives and children. On some occasions it happened to us to sleep near these Arabs, they accosted us to ask if we wished to buy cows, and for the price allowed us to choose them. They say that these Moors, and headmen who go with them, are all robbers under the favour of the lords to whom the cows belong, and so only large caravans travel. The revenues of this monastery are very large; those which I saw and heard of are, chiefly, this mountain in which the monastery is situated, of an extent of ten leagues, in which they sow much millet, barley, rye, and all these pay dues to the monastery, and they are also paid on the herds. On the skirts of this mountain there are many large villages, and most of them belong to the monastery, and at a distance of one or two days' journey an infinite number of places belonging to the monastery, and are called *Gultus* of the monastery, which means *coutos* or *celeiros*,[1] according to our Portugal. Don Rodrigro the ambassador and I were going on the road to the Court, a good five days' journey from this monastery, and arriving at a town which is named *Caina* we kept Saturday and Sunday in a small village which might contain twenty people, and they told us they belonged to the monastery of Bisan. Besides that town there were a hundred villages all belonging to the monastery, and that in which we halted was one of them. We were also shown many of the others, and they told us that every three years they paid a horse to the monastery, and that each village did this, which makes thirty-three horses every year. And in order to be certain of this I went to ask it of the *Alicaxi* of the monastery, which means the auditor or major-domo,

---

[1] *Couto*, an asylum, an enclosure; *celeiro*, a granary.

because he receives, and does justice : he told me that it was true that they paid the said horses. I asked why the monastery wanted so many horses, since they did not ride on them. He told me that they were obliged to pay horses, but that they did not give him horses, but paid fifty cows for each horse, and that this due of horses was so because these were villages of the King which paid him this due, and as he had endowed the monastery with these villages, between the monastery and the villagers this due of horses had been transmuted into cows. And over and above these dues of cows they also pay dues on fruits. Besides, at fifteen days' journey from the monastery, in the kingdom of Tigre mahom, there is a very large town belonging to the monastery named Aadete, which may be a large dukedom. This pays every year sixty horses, and an infinite number of dues and customs. In this district there are always more than a thousand friars of the monastery, because there are many churches in it, and the monastery is much favoured there. Of these friars some are very good, honourable, and devout, and others are not such. Besides these dues of horses paid to this monastery and to others, there are many villages belonging to the King which pay dues of the said horses, because this is always his due, and there are villages neighbouring to Egypt in which are large and good horses, and others near Arabia in which they are very good, but not so much so as those of Egypt.

Cap. xvi.—*How the friars impeded our departure, and of what happened to us on the road.*

Returning therefore to our journey ; whilst we were still at the monastery of St. Michael there arrived the man sent by the Barnagais to take us away, and with him two of our Portuguese, on the fourth day of the month of June; and he brought a few oxen and men to carry our baggage. The said man who had thus come went off at once to the mountains to fetch more oxen and people, and he came back with them. Whilst our baggage was out in the road for our departure, and the men and oxen ready, the friars came and talked so much to the people without their understanding us that they disarranged our departure, so that we again took in our baggage, and the ambassador again sent another time to the Barnagais, and Joan Escolar the clerk went thither with the man of the Barnagais, and they remained there six days. They came with orders and equipment for our departure, that is to say, that they were to conduct us and our goods, and to give us as many oxen and mules as we had need of. Even then the friars were set on impeding us greatly, as though they wished us evil. We left this monastery of St. Michael on the 15th day of June, and because there was detention in loading the baggage, on account of the oxen only coming in a few at a time, and there not being mules enough for all of us, and some having to go on foot, and also because there were few people to carry the baggage which could not go on the oxen where the country was precipitous, the bombards and four barrels of powder remained behind. Not very far from the monastery, half a league at most, the ambassador came up, and those that had remained with him, and we found all the baggage unloaded. Not being able to understand the cause for their having done it, we made them load it again; and not having yet started it all, a rumour arose amongst the negroes who were carrying our baggage, and they said that there were robbers there who were waiting for us in the road. Nevertheless we did not on that account desist from making the baggage go on in front through the bushes, because the road was narrow. The ambassador and all those that were with him determined to die upon the King's goods. The negroes were much amazed at the courage of ten or twelve men, who did not fear passing such steep mountains, where it was said that there were multitudes of robbers. Thus we went away, divided, with the oxen and negroes, with their burdens in front of us, going forward on our course. We travelled through very wild mountains, over ascents and descents, and very bad stony road. Most of the woods of these mountains are very large wild olive trees, from which good olive trees could be made. Issuing from these mountain ranges we entered into dry channels, which in winter time are great rivers, that is to say, as long as the showers last. As soon as the shower is finished the river is dry. These channels have on each side of them very high mountains, as rugged as those we had left behind. In these river beds there are large clumps of unknown trees, amongst which, near the rivers, there are a few wild palm trees. We slept this night in a river bed with little water in it.

Cap. XVII.—*How we passed a great mountain in which there were many apes, on a Saturday, and on the following Sunday we said mass in a village called Zalote.*

On the following day we again crossed another very high and rugged mountain ridge, over which we could not make our way, either on the mules or on foot. In this mountain there are many animals of different species, and an infinite quantity of apes in herds: and they are not generally spread over the mountain, but only where there are clefts and holes in the rock; they are not found in quantities less than two or three hundred, and beyond that number. If there is any flat ground above these precipices, that is their promenade, and no stone remains that they do not turn, and they scrape the earth so that it looks as though it were tilled. They are very large, the size of sheep, and from the

middle upwards hairy like lions. We passed the mountain,
and went to sleep at the foot of a village called Zalote.
There will be about four or five leagues from this place to
the monastery from which we set out. We halted by a
running river of very good water, and when our baggage
had been unloaded we went to the said village to see a very
honourable gentleman, the headman of it—a very old man,
who was lodged here very honourably. He gave us a very
hospitable reception, giving us many fowls cooked in butter,
and much mead, and he sent us a very large fat cow to
the place of our halt. On the following day, which was
Sunday, we went to say our mass at the church of the
village, which is called St. Michael, a poor church, both the
fabric and the ornaments. There are in this church three
married priests and three others, deacons,[1] that is to say, of
the gospel, and all are necessary, for no less can say mass.
This honourable captain I met with later as a friar in the
monastery of Bisan, and he left his condition and revenues
to his sons, who were honourable persons; and I saw him
stand at the gate outside, and he did not enter within the
monastery, and there he received the communion with the
novices, and when the offices of the church were ended he
remained in honour with the provincial. On this Sunday
we set out again in the afternoon, because the country
people who conducted us wished it so. Here we began to
travel through flat country fallows and tillage, in the fashion
of Portugal, and the bushes which are between the tilled
lands are all wild olives, without other trees. We slept by
some running streams, between many good villages.

[1] *Zagonaes.* Ethiopian corruption of *diakonos.*

CAP. XVIII.—*How we arrived at the town of Barua, and how the Ambassador went in search of the Barnagais, and of the manner of his state.*

We reached the town of Barua,[1] which will be three leagues from the village of Zalote, on the 28th day of June. This town is the chief place of the country and kingdom of the Barnagais, in which are his principal palaces, which they call Beteneguz,[2] which means house of the king. On this day that we arrived here the Barnagais departed hence, before our arrival, to another town, the chief place of another district, which is named Barra, and the town is called Çeruel. It seemed to us that his departure was in order not to have to receive us, and some told us that he had gone away with pain in his eyes. We were very well lodged for this country, in good large houses of one story, terraced above. On the third day of our arrival, Don Rodrigo the ambassador determined on going to see the Barnagais; and we went with him, five of us on mules, and reached the place where he was staying at vespers. The distance to this place from that at which we were halting might be three and a half or four leagues, and we went to dismount before his palace, close to the door of a church, where we offered our prayers. Then we went our way to the palace, or Beteneguz, as they call it, thinking that we should at once speak to him; and they did not allow us to enter, saying that he was sleeping. And although we waited a good bit we had no means of speaking to him. We went to rest in a goat shed, in which we barely found room; and they gave us two ox-hides with the hair on to sleep upon, and for supper bread, and wine of the country in abundance, and a sheep. On the following day we waited a long time for them to call us, and a message came for us to come. Then in the outer gate we found three men like porters,

---

[1] *Dibarua*, hillock seen from afar. [2] *Bait en-negus*.

each one with his whip[1] in his hand, and they would not let
us enter, saying that we should give them some pepper, and
they kept us for a good while at the gate. Passing through
this gate we arrived at another, at which stood three other
porters who seemed more honourable persons; these made
us wait more than half an hour standing on a little straw,
and the heat was so great it killed us. Upon this the ambassador sent to say that he should bid us come in or he
would return to his abode. Then the message went by one
who seemed to be of higher position, and word came that
we should enter. The Barnagais was in this manner, in a
large house of one story (for in this country there are not
houses of several stories), sitting on a bedstead, as is their
custom, fitted with poor curtains; he had sore eyes, and his
wife was sitting at the head of the bedstead. Having made
our obeisance, the ambassador offered him a *master* to cure
him; and he said that he had no need of him, as though he
did not thank him for it. Upon this the ambassador asked
him as a favour, and required on the part of Prester John,
that he should order equipment to be given us for our journey, assuring him how much service he would be doing in
this way to the king of Portugal, which would be well
repaid to him by the King and by his Captain-major; and
he, the ambassador, would tell Prester John the honour and
favour which he received from him. The Barnagais asking
what it was that we required, the ambassador said he
wanted oxen and asses for baggage, and mules for the Portuguese. To this the Barnagais replied that he could not
give any mules, and that we might buy them ourselves;
that he would give orders for the rest, and would send a
son of his with us to the court of Prester John, and with
that he gave us our dismissal.

[1] *Azorague*, a kurbach, or whip of hide, *cracache*.

CAP. XIX.—*How they gave us to eat in the house of the Barna-gais, and how in this country the journeys are not reckoned by leagues.*

When we were out of the house where the Barnagais was, they made us sit down in the receiving room of another house on mats on the ground, and they brought here a large trencher of barley meal, but little kneaded, and a horn of mead. And, since we had not seen such food, we would not eat it; but when we were more accustomed to the country we ate it readily. Without eating of this, we arose and came to our resting-place and then set out. This might be at two hours before midday. Having gone on our road half a league or more there came to us a man running and telling us to wait; that the mother of the Barnagais was sending us food, and took it as a misfortune our coming away without eating and not accepting the food they gave us, which was that customary in the country. We waited, and the food came to us, that is to say, five large rolls of wheat bread and a horn of mead. Let not anyone be amazed who hears of a horn of wine, because for the great lords and Prester John cows' horns are their cups for wine, and there are horns holding five or six canadas.[1] Besides this, the mother of the Barnagais sent us some of the same kneaded flour, and now we ate some of it. This meal is of parched barley, made into flour, and they mix it up with very little water, and so eat it. After this banquet we made our way to the town of Barua, where our goods and companions had remained. In this country, and in all the kingdoms of Prester John, there are no leagues, and if you ask how far it is from this place to such a place, they say : If you depart in the morning at sunrise, you will arrive when the sun is in such a place ; and if you travel slowly you will arrive there when they shut up the cows, that is at

_____
[1] A Portuguese measure equal to about three pints.

night. And if it is distant they say, you will arrive in a
sambete, that is a week, and so they define it according to
the distances. When I said that from Barua to Barra there
were from three and a half up to four leagues, that was
according to our opinion, and it would not be more. We
afterwards travelled there many times, and we started from
one town and dined at the other, and did our business and
returned to the town we had started from by daylight.
The people of the country reckon this as a day's journey,
because they travel very slowly. Between these two towns
there is very remarkable country, tilled fields of wheat,
barley, millet, pulse, lentils, and all other sorts of vegetables
which the country possesses unknown to us. From the
road from one place to the other more than fifty towns are
to be seen : I say large towns and very good ones, all on
heights. In these plains and fields there are herds of wild
cattle, forty or fifty in a herd. It is a chase that is very
pleasant for the Portuguese, but the country people are able
to do them little hurt, although they receive from them
much injury to their crops.

CAP. XX.—*Of the town of Barua, and of the women and their
traffic, and of the marriages which are made outside of
• the churches.*

This town of Barua in which we were staying, and where
later we passed more time, may have three hundred hearths
and more, a great part of them belonging to women, because this is like a court in many respects. One is that
people of the Prester's court never go from here, and as
many as come are not without wives. The other is because
this is the residence and seat of the Barnagais, and there
are continually in his house three hundred mounted men
and upwards, and as many more who come every day for

business of petitions, and few are without wives. This causes many single women to live here, and when they are old they have another resource, for in this town every Tuesday there is a great market or fair at which three or four hundred persons are brought together; and all the old women and some young ones have measures to measure wheat and salt, and they go to the market to measure and gain their living; they give hospitality to those that sleep there that day, and also take care for them of what remains to be sold for the next market day. There is another reason why there are many women in this town, it is because the men who have plenty of food to eat keep two or three wives; and this is not forbidden to them by the King nor by their magistrates, only by the Church. Every man who has more than one wife does not enter the church, nor does he receive any sacrament: and they hold him to be excommunicated. For a year and a half a nephew of mine and I lodged in the house of a man named Ababitay, and he had three wives still alive and acquaintances of ours, friends in honourable friendship: they said that he had had seven wives and thirty children of them. Nobody forbade them, except the Church, as has been said, which did not give them the benefit of the sacraments; and before our departure, he put away from him, and from intercourse with him, two wives, and remained with one, that is to say, the one he had last, who was the youngest, and already they gave him the sacraments, and he entered the church like anybody else, and as though he had not had more than one wife. On this account there are many women in this town, because the men are well off and are like courtiers : and they take two or three, or more if it pleases them. In this country marriages are not fixed, because they separate for any cause. I saw people married, and was at a marriage which was not in a church, and it was done in this manner. On the open space before some houses they placed a bedstead, and seated upon it the bridegroom and the bride, and there came thither three priests, and they began a chaunt with Hallelujah, and then continued the chaunt, the three priests walking three times round the bedstead on which the couple were seated. Then they cut a lock of hair from the head of the bridegroom, and another from the head of the bride. They wetted these locks with mead, and placed the hair of the bridegroom on the head of the bride, and that of the bride on the head of the bridegroom, on the place from which they had cut them, and then sprinkled them with holy water: after that they kept their festivities and wedding feasts. At night they put them in a house, and for a month from that time no one saw the bride, except one man only whom they call the best man,[1] who remains all this month with the married couple, and when this month is ended the man or best friend goes away. If she is an honourable woman she does not go out of the house for five or six months, nor remove a black veil from her face: and if before that she becomes pregnant she removes the veil. When these months are ended, even though she is not pregnant, she removes the veil.

CAP. XXI.—*Of their marriages and benedictions, and of their contracts, and how they separate from their wives, and the wives from them, and it is not thought strange.*

I saw the Abima Marcos, whom they call Pope, giving blessings in the church, that is to say, before the principal door; the bride and bridegroom were also seated on a bedstead, and the Abima walked round them with incense and cross, and laid his hands on their heads, telling them to observe that which God had commanded in the gospel; and that they were no longer two

[1] *Padrinho.*

separate persons, but two in one flesh; and that so in like
manner should their hearts and wills be. There they remained
until mass had been said, and he gave them the communion,
and bestowed on them the blessing. And this I saw done
in the town of Dara, in the Kingdom of Xoa.[1] I saw
another performed in the town of Çequete, in the Kingdom
of the Barnagais. When they make these marriages they
enter into contracts, as for instance: If you leave me or I
you, that one that causes the separation shall pay such a
penalty. And they set the penalty according to the persons,
so much gold or silver, or so many mules, or cloths, or
cows, or goats, or so many measures of wood. And if
either of them separate, that one immediately seeks a cause
of separation for such and such reasons, so that few incur
the penalty, and so they separate when they please, both the
husbands and the wives. If there are any that observe the
marriage rule, they are the priests, who never can separate,
and cultivators, who have an affection for their wives
because they help them to bring up their sons, and to har-
row and weed their tillage, and at night when they come to
their house they find a welcome reception : thus in effect or
perforce they are married for the whole of their lives. As
I said that they imposed penalties at marriages, the first
Barnagais that we knew, whose name was Dori, separated
from his wife, and paid her the penalty of a hundred gold
ounces, which were a thousand cruzados, and he married
another woman. And the wife that he separated from
married a noble gentleman who was named Aaron, a brother
of the said Barnagais. Both the brothers had sons, known to
us, of this woman, and these were, or are, great lords, both
are brothers of the mother of Prester John, whom all of us
knew. All of us who were there knew Romana Orque,[2]
sister of the Prester John, who is a noble lady married to a
great lord, a noble young gentleman. In our time she

---

[1] Shoa.   [2] *Rumanā Wark*, the golden pomegranate.

separated from this husband and married a man more than
forty years of age, who is one of the great lords of the
court; the title of this one whom she married is Abuquer,
and his father Cabeata. This is the greatest lord there is in
the court. Thus I saw and knew many of these separations;
I have named these because they are of great personages.
And because I said that Aaron married the wife of his
brother, let not him that reads it be amazed, because it is
the usage of the country. They do not think it strange for
a brother to sleep with the wife of his brother. This Aaron
moreover had sons of her who had been the wife of his
brother, and he left her and married another to whom he is
now married.

CAP. XXII.—*Of the manner of baptism and circumcision, and
how they carry the dead to their burial.*

Circumcision is done by anybody without any ceremony,
only they say that so they find it written in the books, that
God commanded circumcision. And let not the reader of
this be amazed—they also circumcise the females as well as
the males, which was not in the Old Law. Baptism they do
in this manner: they baptize males at forty days, and
females at sixty days after their birth, and if they die before
they go without baptism. I, many times and in many places,
used to tell them that they committed a great error, and
went against what the Gospel says: Quod natum est ex
carne caro est; et quod natum est ex spiritu spiritus est.
They answered me many times that the faith of their mother
sufficed for them, and the communion which she received
whilst in a state of pregnancy.[1] They perform this baptism

[1] This opinion of the Abyssinians appears to have anticipated the
Sorbonne judgment of 1733, given in the 20th chapter of *Tristram
Shandy.*

in the church, with water which they keep in a vase, and which they bless, and they put oil on the forehead and on the breasts and shoulder-blades. They do not put ointment,[1] nor do they have it, nor the oil of extreme unction. This office of catechism which they celebrate seems to me to be much the same form as the Roman, and at the time of pouring the water on the child they do it in this way. One who is the godfather takes the child from the hands of the woman that has it and raises it, holding it under the arms, and holds it suspended; and the priest who baptizes, with one hand holds the vase and pours the water over the child, and with the other washes it all over, saying in his language the words which we say, that is : I baptize thee in the name of the Father, and of the Son, and of the Holy Spirit. They always perform this office on a Saturday or a Sunday, and it is done in the morning at mass, because every child that receives baptism receives the communion, and they give it in very small quantities, and cause it to be swallowed by means of water. With regard to this, also, I used to tell them that this communion was very dangerous, and in no wise necessary. As I said that they put oil on the forehead, you should know that every child comes to baptism shaved with a razor, and the scars or marks which they bear on the nose, between the eyes, and at the corners of the eyes, are not made by fire nor for anything of Christianity, but with cold iron for ornament, and because they say that it is good for the sight. There are here women who are very skilful at making these marks. They make them in this manner : they take a clove of garlic, large and moist, and place it on the corner of the eye ; with a sharp knife they cut round the garlic, and then with the fingers widen the cut, and put upon it a little paste of wax, and over the wax another paste of dough, and press it down for one night with a cloth, and there remains for ever a mark which appears like

[1] *Crisma.*

4

a burn, because their colour is dark. On the occasion of death, I never saw great personages borne away; but of small people, and of others rather better, an infinite number. Their burials are in this manner. They do not use candles after death, but much incense. They carry them away wrapped up[1] in a shroud, and some of the more honoured have over the shroud tanned ox-hides, and are placed on trestles. The priests come for them, and pray shortly, and then set out at once with them on the way to the church, with cross, thurible, and holy water, running so that a man cannot catch them up. They do not bring the dead man into the church, but place him close to the grave; they do not use our office for him, nor do they recite psalms, neither do they say anything from the Book of Job. I asked what it was that they prayed; they told me that they read the Gospel of St. John all complete. And so they give him to the grave with their incense and holy water, and they do not say mass for the defunct, nor of devotion for any living person, nor more than one mass a day in each church; and all are communicants, as many as go to it.

CAP. XXIII.—*Of the situation of the town of Barua, chief place of the kingdom of the Barnagais, and of his hunting.*

This town of Barua is very good, and it is situated on a very high rock above a river, upon which are situated the king's houses, which they call Beteneguz, which means houses of the king. They are well situated in the manner of a fortress. All the rest is a great plain and an infinite number of large villages at the extremities of the fields. There is much breeding of all sorts of flocks, cows,

---

[1] *Encorilhados* for *enrodilhados*.

goats, and sheep, and of much game of all sorts. In the
river there is much fish, and many wild ducks of different
kinds,[1] and on land much game of all kinds, such as wild
cattle; in the plains hares in great quantity, so that every
day we killed twenty or thirty of a morning, and that without dogs, but caught with nets. There are partridges of
three kinds, which do not differ from ours, except in size
and the colour of their legs. There are partridges like big
capons of the same colour and fashion as ours, except that
their beaks and feet are yellow. There are others the size
of hens; these have red beaks and feet like ours. There
are others the size of ours, not different in colour or in anything else, except that their beaks and feet are grey. To
the taste all are very good partridges, as they are good in
colour. They do not frighten them to the earth.[2] Wild hens
cover the ground, quails are in infinite numbers, and so of
all other birds that can be mentioned, such as parrots and
other birds not known to us, great and small, and of many
shapes and colours; birds of prey, such as royal eagles,
falcons, hawks, sparrow hawks, blue herons, and river
cranes, and all other sorts that can be mentioned. In the
mountains are many hogs, stags, antelopes, gazelles, deer.
It will be said, how is it that there is so much game on the
land and fish in the river, when the country is so populous?
I say that nobody hunts or fishes, nor have they engines
nor devices, nor the will to do it; on this account the game
is very easy to kill, because it is not pursued by the people.
There are many wild beasts—lions, ounces, tigers, wolves,
foxes, jackals, and other animals not known to us. I never
heard that these wild beasts did any harm, although the
people are in great fear of them; only in one place which
is called Camarua, and which is about half a league from

---

[1] *Adens* and *marrecas.*

[2] *No las assombram a terra*: perhaps this means with a paper kite.
This passage is omitted in Selve's translation..

this town of Barua, a man was lying asleep at night at the
door of his enclosure, and his little son was with him,
keeping his cows, and a lion came and killed this man without anyone perceiving it, and he ate his nose and opened
his heart, without touching the child. The people of the
country were greatly afraid, and said that he would remain with a taste for man's flesh,[1] and that no one would
escape from him. The Lord was pleased that he never did
any more harm. We used to go hunting at that time near
this place, and we never found any lion, but we found
ounces and tigers; we did them no harm, neither did they
do us any.

CAP. XXIV.—*Of the lordship of the Barnagais, and of the
lords and captains who are at his orders and commands,
and of the dues which they pay.*

The lordship of the Barnagais is in this manner: its title
is that of King, because nagais means King, and bar means
sea, so Barnagais means King of the Sea. When they give
him the rulership they give it him with a crown of gold on
his head, but it does not last longer than what the Prester
John pleases. For in our time, which was a stay of six
years, there were here four Barnagais, that is to say, when
we arrived Dori was Barnagais; he died, and at his death
the crown came to Bulla, his son, a youth of ten or twelve
years of age, by order of the Prester John. When they
crowned him he was at once summoned to court, and while
he was at the court Prester John took away his sovereignty
and gave it to a noble gentleman, who was named Arraz anubiata. This man held it two years, and they took from him this
lordship and made him the greatest lord of the court, which
is Betudete,[2] and the lordship of Barnagais was given to

---

[1] *Cevado*, literally, allured.
[2] The favourite or preferred, *Bitwuddad*, because he was liked.

another lord, who was named Adiby, who was now Barnagais. Beneath the Barnagais are some great lords whom
they call Xuums, which means captains; and these are, first,
Xuum Cire, a very great captaincy, he is now married to a
sister of Prester John. We never went to this country and
Xuumeta because it is distant and out of the way. There
is another Xuumeta named Ceruil. We knew this lordship,
and they say that its Xuum brings into the field fifteen
thousand spearmen with shields and archers. Also Xuum
Cama, and Buno Xuum, and Xuum bono. These Xumetas
had been one, and on account of its being large, and the
Prester having misgivings that they might set themselves
up against the Barnagais, he made it into two, and even
yet each of them is very large. They say that this lordship
which is now two was the dominion of Queen Candace,
without having been larger in her time. She was the first
Christian that there was in this country, and whom the
Lord called powerful. Also two other captaincies, one is
named Dafilla, the other Canfila; these two border on
Egypt, and their captains are like lords of the marches.
All these captains before mentioned are of kettledrums,
which nobody except great lords can carry: and all these
serve with the Barnagais in wars when he goes to them, and
wherever he may go. They have other great gentlemen
under their command who are called Arraz,[1] which means
heads. We knew one of these, who was named Arraz
Aderaan, he is head over fifteen thousand men at arms,
whom they name chavas. I saw this Arraz Aderaan twice
at the court, both times I saw him before the gate of the
Prester John going without a shirt, and from his waist
downwards a very good silk cloth, and on his shoulders the
skin of a lion, in his right hand a spear, and in his left hand
a shield. I asked how it was so great a lord went
about in that manner, they told me that the greatest honour

[1] Ar-ras.

he had, since he was Arraz of the Chaufas, that is, head or
captain of the men at arms, was to go about like a man at
arms.   In the fashion that he went, there followed behind
him twenty or thirty men with spears and bucklers, so that
he goes about the court like a provost with his men.
I knew another Arraz Tagale, and Arraz Jacob, lords
of large lands, and many other Xuums, lords of lands,
but without titles.   Thus the Barnagais is the lord of many
lords, and of many lands and people, and so he and all
these lords that have been mentioned are subject to the
Prester John, and he removes and appoints them as he
pleases : so they pay to him large dues.   As all these lords
and their lordships are on the side of Egypt and Arabia,
from whence come the good horses, and the brocades and
the silks, they pay in these same goods : that is to say,
horses, brocades, and other silks.   They come to the
Barnagais with all these dues, and the Barnagais to Prester
John, and pays for himself and for the others, in each year,
a hundred and fifty horses ; as to the brocades and silks, it
cannot be known   how   much   they   amount   to,   only
I heard say that they were many ; I also heard that they
pay a large sum of cotton cloths from India for the customs
which they levy in the port of Arquiquo.

Cap. xxv.—*Of their method of guarding their herds from
wild beasts, and how there are two winters in this country : and of two churches that are in the town of Barua.*

The settlement of this town of Barua and of those
adjoining it, is this.   There are ten, twelve, or fifteen houses,
and one walled and closed yard, served by a gate : in this
yard they shut up their domestic cows which they use for
their milk and butter, and also small flocks, and mules and
asses.   They keep the gate well fastened, and a great fire,

and men who sleep there to watch, from fear of the animals
that roam about the villages all night : and if they did not
keep this watch nothing alive would remain which they
would not devour.   The people who go to sow millet in the
mountains of Bisan belong to this country and the neighbouring towns.   The reason why they go and do it is this.
Here there are very numerous grain crops of every kind
and nature that can be mentioned, as I have already said ;
and because it is near to the sea, by which go all the
provisions for Arabia, Mekkah, Zebid, Jiddah, and Toro,[1]
and other parts ; and they carry the provisions to the sea to
sell them.   And because in this country the winters are
divided into seasons, and the seed crops do not grow
except with the rains, they go to sow these millet
fields at the mountain of Bisan, where it is winter in the
months of February, March, and April.   There is this same
winter in a mountain called Lama, in this kingdom of the
Barnagais, which is fully eight days' journey from the
mountain of Bisan.   In another country, which is named
Doba, and which is quite a month's journey from this lordship of Lama, there is winter in these same months.   As
for those millet fields, they require rains, and as these winters happen out of season, they go and sow them where it
rains, and so profit by both winters.   In this town of
Barua are two churches with many priests, one close to the
other, one is for men, the other for women.   The men's
church is called St. Michael, that of the women is named
after the apostles Peter and Paul.   They say that a great
lord, who was then Barnagais, built the men's church, and
gave it the privilege that no woman should enter it, except
only the wife of the Barnagais, with one damsel, whenever
she went to take the communion, and even she does not
now enter the church, but takes the communion at the
door in the inner circuit with the laity, and so the

----

[1] Mount Sinai.

other women do in the church of the apostles, who take it
in its place. I always saw the women of the Barnagais go
to the women's church to take the communion with the
other women, and I did not see them use the privilege
which they say they have, of taking the communion, with
one damsel, in the church of the men. The circuits of the
churchyards join to one another; they are of very high
walls. They make the sacramental bread for both churches
in one building, and they say the masses in both churches
at the same time, and the priests who serve in one church
serve also in the other; that is two thirds of the priests
in the men's church, and one third in the women's church,
and so they are distributed. These churches have not got
tithes, but they have got much land belonging to the priests,
and they put it out to profit and divide the revenues of the
lands among themselves: the Barnagais gives what is
necessary to the churches, such as ornaments, wax, butter,
incense in sufficient quantity, and he supplies them with
everything. There may be in these churches twenty priests
and always twenty-two friars. I never saw a church of
priests which had not got friars, nor a monastery of friars
which had got priests; because the friars are so numerous that they cover the world, both in the monasteries
as also in the churches, roads, and markets: they are in
every place.

CAP. XXVI.—*How the priests are, and how they are ordained,
and of the reverence which they pay to the churches and
their churchyards.*

The priests are married to one wife, and they observe the
law of matrimony better than the laity: they live in their
houses with their wives and children. If their wife should
die they do not marry again; neither can the wife, but she

may become a nun or remain a widow as she pleases. If a priest sleeps with another woman whilst his wife is alive he does not enter the church any more, nor does he enjoy its goods, and remains as a layman. And this I know from having seen a priest accused before the patriarch of having slept with a woman, and I saw that the priest confessed the offence, and the patriarch commanded him not to carry a cross in his hand, nor to enter a church, nor to enjoy the liberties of the church, and to become a layman. If any priests after becoming widowers marry, they remain laymen. As it happened to Abuquer, who married Romana Orque, sister of Prester John, who I have already said was a priest, chief chaplain of Prester John, and he was disordained[1] and made a layman. He no longer enters the church, and receives the communion at the door of the church as a layman, and among the women. The sons of the priests are for the most part priests, because in this country there are no schools, nor studies, nor masters to teach, and the clergy teach that little that they know to their sons : and so they make them priests without more legitimisation, neither does it seem to me that they require it, since they are legitimate sons. All are ordained by the Abima Markos, for in all the kingdoms of Ethiopia there is no other bishop or person who ordains. The orders are given in two stages, as I will relate further on. I with my own eyes saw them given many times. In all this country the churchyards are inclosed by very strong walls, that the wild beasts may not disinter the dead bodies. They show them great reverence, no man riding on a mule passes before a church, even though he is going in a great hurry, without dismounting, until he has passed the church and churchyard a good bit.

---

[1] *Foy desordenado e feito leigo* ; not a correct expression.

CAP. XXVII.—*How we departed from Barua, and of the bad equipment we had until we arrived at Barra.*

We were at Barua the first time, without their giving us equipment for our departure, for eleven days; we departed on the 28th day of June 1520, joyful and contented, because we were travelling on our way; and those that conducted us went with our baggage a distance of half a league, saying that their bounds went no further, and that another town had to take us further on. As I said, it was in June, in the force of the winter of this country, and they set us down, and our goods, in a plain, and very heavy rain. The ambassador and three of us went on the road to Barra to speak to the Barnagais, the factor and clerk and the other Portuguese remaining with our goods. As soon as we arrived we went to the palace of the Barnagais to tell him what his vassals were doing to us. They did not give us an opportunity to speak to him that day. On the following day we did not sleep in the morning, and went to speak to him: as soon as we spoke to him he told us he would at once send for the goods. He ordered it to be brought a distance of a league and a half, in which it passed through three districts, by reason of the great population which is in that country, and they came and placed the baggage in another plain, where they let it remain four days in the rain and storms. In these days the ambassador and those that were with him were not quiet: at one time we went to the baggage, which was a league and a half off from us, at other times at our resting place, at others in the house of the Barnagais, to require him to send for these goods which belonged to the King, and were going to Prester John, or to tell us that he did not choose, and we would have it set on fire, and go our way disembarrassed. His speech was always fair, but the fruits of it never came. When four days were completed he sent for the goods.

CAP. XXVIII.—*How the goods arrived at the town of Barra, and of the bad equipment of the Barnagais.*

On the 3rd day of July of the said year, '20, our baggage arrived at the town of Barra, where we were. We hoped to start at once, and went to speak to the Barnagais requiring him to despatch us. We met with good words from him. On the following day a gentleman from the court of Prester John arrived, and the Barnagais gave him such a reception that he forgot us. When this gentleman arrived the Barnagais went out of the town to receive him at a small hill near the houses; and there went out with him many people, and he was naked from the waist upwards. The gentleman placed himself on the highest spot above the rest, and his first words were : the King sends to salute you. At these words all went with their hand upon the ground, which is the courtesy and reverence of this country. After that, he spoke the message which he had brought, and when he had finished hearing it the Barnagais clothed himself with rich garments, and took the gentleman to his house. It is the usage of this country to hear the words which the Prester sends outside the house, and on foot, and he to whom they are sent has to be naked above the waist until they have been delivered, and if the message is one of satisfaction on the part of Prester John, as soon as it is given he at once dresses himself: if it expresses his dissatisfaction, he remains naked as when he heard it. This Barnagais is brother of the mother of Prester John. After this the ambassador, and we with him, came to speak to the Barnagais, and he sent us away saying that for the love of God we should leave him, that he was sick. When we came they did not allow us to enter, saying that he was sleeping. So much passed of this sort that the ambassador said that he ill remembered what he had sworn and promised to the Captain-major of the King of Portugal, that is to say, to assist us and order equipment to be given us for our journey, that he forgot all this, and also that he was not mindful of the friendship which they had established and sworn, since he did so little for the affairs of the King of Portugal. Neither on this account did he make any more haste, but always excused himself with his guest, and with being ill. On the 6th of July seven or eight horsemen arrived, very gaily caparisoned, these were Moors, and seemed to be honourable persons, they came from other countries, and brought many very beautiful horses, which they were bringing to pay as tribute which they owed to Prester John and the Barnagais. As the arrival of the Moors redounded to his profit, neither his guests nor his sickness impeded him. The great reception and honour which the Barnagais paid to these Moors gave us great trouble. The ambassador had told him that he wanted twelve mules, and asked him to order them to be lent : he said that he could not lend them, and that we should buy them. When we wished to buy these mules which the people of the country were selling to us, the servants of the Barnagais came and interrupted the purchase, telling the vendors not to sell them, and that if they sold them they would be punished, and the gold would be taken away from them, for in this country money is not current. This happened in such manner that the rumour of it spread throughout the country, and the people told us that even if they wished to sell to us they did not dare, from fear of the Barnagais, because he wished to sell his own mules, and therefore forbade their selling them. (He has another method with the people of his country.) In all the kingdoms of Prester John money is not current, but only gold by weight, and the principal weight is called *ouquia*,[1] and this, which is an ounce, makes in weight ten cruzados, and for change there is a half ouquia, and from twelve drachms to ten make

---

[1] A gold coin in some parts of Africa.

an ouquia. This Barnagais forbade the people in his country having any other weights except his own, and they had to ask the Barnagais or his factors for the weights whenever they had to sell or receive gold, so that he had knowledge of what was in the country, and he takes it when he pleases, according to what his country people say, who must know it well.

CAP. XXIX.—*Of the church of the town of Barra, and its ornaments, and of the fair there, and of the merchandise, and costumes of the friars, nuns, and priests.*

In this town of Barra there is a church of Our Lady, large, new, very well painted and well built, and handsomely ornamented with many brocades, crimson silks, and Mekkah velvets, and red camlets. The church in this town is served like that at Barua, only that the offices are more solemnized because the Barnagais resides here, and because here there are more clergy and an infinite number of friars. The church is managed by priests. I saw them make a procession round the church in the greater circuit, which is of the churchyard. In it there were many priests, friars, and men and women, because in this church the women receive the communion in the place where the laity do so. In that procession I saw the ornaments which I have mentioned: they must have taken quite thirty turns round the church chaunting like a litany, and sounding many drums and cymbals, as they sound them when they make a procession before the effigy of Our Lady on Sundays and feast days; and they sing and celebrate a feast; and likewise when they give the communion on feast days. They said that this procession was made in supplication to God for rain for their sowing. The bells are of stone, like those of other churches, and the bells badly made. In this town there is a great fair like that of Barua, and so likewise in all the

places which are chief towns of districts, every week. The
fairs consist of bartering one thing for another, as for instance, an ass for a cow, and that which is of least value
gives to the other two or three measures of bread. By
means of bread they buy stuffs, and with stuffs they buy
mules and cows, and whatever they want, for salt, incense,
pepper, myrrh, camphor, and other small articles.[1] They
buy fowls and capons, and whatever they need or want to
buy is all to be found at these fairs in exchange for others,
for there is no current money. The principal merchants
at these fairs are priests, friars, and nuns. The friars
are decent in their habits, which are full, and reaching to the ground. Some wear yellow habits of
coarse cotton stuff, others habits of tanned goat skins
like wide breeches,[2] also yellow. The nuns also wear the
same habits; the friars wear, besides, capes of the fashion
of Dominican friars, of the same yellow skins or stuffs, they
wear hats; and the nuns wear neither capes nor hats, but
only the habit, and are shaven with a razor; and they wear
a leather strap wound or fastened round the head. When
they are old women they wear fillets[3] round their heads
over their tonsures. These nuns are not cloistered, nor do
they live together in convents, but in villages, and in the
monasteries of the friars, on account of belonging to those
houses and order. The order is all one, and the nuns give
obedience where they receive their habits. With regard to
entering churches and monasteries, the nuns do not enter
except as other women do. There is a great multitude of
nuns, as well as of friars; they say that some of them are
very holy women, and others are not so. The priests show very
little difference from the laity in their dress, because all
wear a good cloth wrapped round, like smart men, and their
difference is that they carry a cross in their hand, and are
shaven, and the laity wear long hair. The priests also have

[1] *Bechngarias.*   [2] *Zafoens* or *Safoens.*   [3] *Tufas.*

this, that they do not cut their beard, and the laity shave below the chin and the throat. There are other priests, whom they call Debeteraas, which means canons; these belong to great churches, which are like their cathedrals or collegiate churches, and are not monasteries. These are very well dressed, and at once appear as what they are: these do not go to the fairs and markets.

CAP. XXX.—*Of the state of the Barnagais and manner of his house, and how he ordered a proclamation to be made to go against the Nobiis,[1] and the method of his justice.*

The service of this Barnagais is very poor in state, although he is a great lord and has the title of king. As many times as we spoke to him we always found him seated on a bedstead beneath a coverlid, and himself covered with hairy cotton cloths which they name *basutos*; they are good for the country, and there are some here of a high price. Behind the sides of the bedstead, walls, without anything except four swords hung each on a pole, and two great books, also suspended on poles. In front of the bedstead, mats on the floor, upon which sit those who come; the houses rarely swept, his wife always seated on a mat near the head of the bedstead, many people always before him, the great people seated on mats. In sight of his bedstead stand four horses, one always saddled, and the others covered, not caparisoned for war, but as horses are in the stables. In these houses of his are two inclosures, and each one has its gate, and in it porters with whips in their hands, and in the one nearest to him are smarter porters. Between these gates, the inner one and the outer one, is always his Alicaxi, which means his judge, hearing causes and administering justice. If the cause is important,

[1] Nubians.

he hears the parties until he has determined upon it, and then
he goes and relates the cause to the Barnagais, who gives the
sentence: if it is a small cause, or if the parties wish it, the
Alicaxi gives sentence, and the cause is concluded. Moreover,
in all judgments, whether the Barnagais or the Alicaxi
judges, there must be present an honourable man, whom
they call by the name of his office Malaganha, who is like a
tabellion or notary of Prester John, and if either of the
parties wishes to appeal, he requires from this man the
certifying of the cause for Prester John and his judges. All
the lords of the countries of any of the kingdoms of Prester
John have an Alicaxi and a Malaganha appointed by the
Prester; so also have the captains subject to the Barnagais
and to the other great lords. The gentlemen who are
about the house of the Barnagais, and other grandees who
come on business, have this manner of coming from their
abodes. Whilst at the place he is living at he mounts his
mule, seven, eight, or ten men on foot go before him as far
as the first gate, and there he dismounts. If he is a person
of greater importance, he takes seven, eight, or ten mules,
or else three or four, according as the person is. So he
dismounts at the first gate, and arrives at the second, after
that, if they are bidden at once to enter, they go in, if not,
they sit outside like beehives in the sun, without any other
pastime. All these honourable persons wear sheep skins at
their necks or on their shoulders, and he who wears the
skin of a lion, tiger, or ounce, is more honourable. When
they come before the lord they take off the skin, as we take
off our caps. Whilst we were in this town of Barra on a
market day, they made a solemn proclamation that the Barnagais intended to make war on the Nobiis, five or six days'
journey from the limits of his country, towards Egypt,
neighbouring to the countries of Canfilla and Dafolha,[1] which
are subject to the Barnagais, as I have before mentioned.

¹ Dafilla.

These Nobiis are neither Moors, nor Jews, nor Christians. It is said that they had been Christians, and had lost their faith, and are thus without any faith. They say that there is among these Nobiis much fine gold. They said that but a short time ago they had killed a son of the Barnagais, and that he wished to go and avenge his death. I heard say that in the frontier districts of these Nobiis there were four or five hundred horsemen, very great warriors, and that it is a country very well supplied with provisions, and it cannot be otherwise because it is on this and the further side of the Nile, which they say is a very fertile country. The proclamation said that he would set out in fifty days from that time : but up to this there had been no muster nor movement of arms. This would be because in the country there are not many, and few people possess them except the Chavas, who are the men at arms. These men have javelins, bows and arrows. These great lords have a few swords, hangers, and shirts of mail (not many of them). On the occasion of this little revolt, the Barnagais asked the ambassador for swords, and the ambassador gave him his own, which he wore on the road, and which was very good, and he still persistently begged another rich sword with ornaments which he carried with him, saying he wanted it for the war he was going to make, and the ambassador not being able to excuse himself, it suited him to buy another from his companions with gilt ends and a velvet scabbard, which he gave him instead of his own. And in the house where we kept our goods, and where our Portuguese slept, which was a house without doors, on the following night they stole from them two swords and a helmet. All this would be on account of the war.

CAP. XXXI.—*How we departed from Barra to Temei, and of the quality of the town.*

Here we bought mules for our own riding, and the Barnagais gave us three camels, and with great fatigue we set out from this place, amidst heavy rains and storms, which harassed us very much; for in this time the winter was in force; it begins the 15th of June, a little sooner or later, and ends the 15th of September; whatever it takes more in one month it gives up in the other. In all this time they do not travel, and yet we were hurrying on our journey, for we did not know the usage of the country, nor the danger we were running into. So we began our journey with a part of our goods, for the rest of them remained at the said town, and our factor with it. We went and halted at a town which is named Temeisom, belonging to the district of Maiçada, and which is about four leagues from the town of Barra, from which we had set out. We got over this distance in three days on account of the severe storms; everything that we carried with us getting spoiled. In this town of Temei, where we arrived, there dwelt a Xuum of this district of Maiçada, who was first cousin of the Barnagais, a very honourable man, who used to show us great honour, and who was also a brother of the mother of Prester John. They say that there are in his Xumeta or captaincy twenty towns and no more, for this is (as they say) the smallest district and Xumeta which there is in the kingdom of the Barnagais. This town is on a high eminence (without rocks), but all tilled land and plains with small hollows: and on three sides it has a view over fourteen or fifteen leagues, but on the other, at the distance of a league, there commence great declivities which descend to a great river, and in the neighbourhood of this river appear more than a hundred large villages. It seems to me that in the world there is not so populous a country, and so abundant in

crops, and breeding of infinite herds, game of all kinds and
of the wildest. There is nothing here but tigers, wolves,
foxes, jackals, and other game. Let not this amaze any
one who hears or reads this : that there should be game in
a plain country with so much population : because, as I
said before, they neither kill nor are able to kill anything
except some partridges, which they kill with arrows. Many
other kinds of game they do not kill because they do not
eat them, others because they do not know how, and have
no devices for that purpose. So they breed because they
do not kill them. All the game is almost tame, because it
is not pursued. Without dogs we killed and carried away
twenty hares with nets in an hour, and as many partridges
with springes, just like piping goats to a fold, or hens to the
roost : so we killed the game that we wanted.

CAP. XXXII.—*Of the multitude of locusts which are in the
country, and of the damage they do, and how we made a
procession, and the locusts died.*

In these parts and in all the dominions of Prester John
there is a very great plague of locusts which destroy the fresh
crops in a fearful manner. Their multitude, which covers the
earth and fills the air, is not to be believed; they darken
the light of the sun. I say again that it is not a thing to
be believed by any one who has not seen them. They are
not general in all the kingdoms every year, for if they were
so, the country would be a desert in consequence of the destruction they cause : but one year they are in one part, and
another year in another ; as if we said, speaking in Portugal
and Spain, one year they are in the parts of Galicia, another
in Entre Douro and Minho, in Traz os Montes, another year
in Beira, another in Estremadura, another in Andalucia,
another in Old Castile, and another in Aragon. Sometimes
they are in two or three parts of these confines. Wherever

they come the earth remains as though it had been set on
fire. These locusts are like large grasshoppers, they are
yellow in the wings; when they are on the way it is known
a day before, not because the people see them, but because
they see the sun yellow, and the earth yellow, that is, the
shadow which they cast. Then the people are dismayed,
saying we are lost because the Ambatas are coming, and
this is their name among them. I will relate what I saw on
three occasions. The first was in the town of Barua, we
had then been three years in this country, and many times
we had heard say, such a kingdom, such a country is destroyed by the Ambatas; while we were there, we saw this
sign : the sun became yellow, and the shadow on the earth
likewise, and the people were all dismayed. Next day, it
was a thing not to be believed, for they spread over a width
of eight leagues, according to what we learned later : and
when this plague was close by, most of the priests of the
town came to ask me to give them some remedy for it. I
answered them that I did not know of any remedy, except
to commend ourselves to God, and pray Him to drive the
plague out of the country. Upon this, I went to the
ambassador to tell him that it seemed to me well that we
should make a procession with the people of the country,
and that it might please the Lord to hear us. This seemed
good to the ambassador, and next day in the morning we
caused the people of the country to come together, and all
the priests, and we took our altar stone, and those of the
town theirs after their usage, and our cross and theirs, and
singing our litany we went out from the church, all the Portuguese and the greater part of the townspeople. I told them
not to go in silence, but to cry out like us, saying in their
language, Zio marenos,[1] which means in our language, Lord
Jesus Christ have mercy upon us. With this cry and litany
we went through a plain of fields of wheat for the space of

[1] *Igzio maranna Kristos, Amharic.*

a third of a league to a small eminence, and there made an admonition which I had brought already written out that night with a requisition and admonition of excommunication[1] on it, that within three hours they should begin to set out on their way, and go to the sea, or to the country of the Moors, or to mountains of no profit to the Christians: and should they not do so, it called upon and invoked the birds of the air and the animals of the earth, and the stones and tempests to disperse and break and devour their bodies. For this, I commanded to catch a quantity of the locusts, and thus made this admonition to those present, in their names, and those of the absent ones, and ordered them to be let go in peace. It pleased the Lord to hear the sinners. When we were returning to the town, because their road was to the sea from whence they came, there were so many coming after us, that it seemed as though they would break our ribs and heads driving against us, such were the thumps they inflicted on us. When we arrived at the town, we found all the men, women, and children who had remained in it, placed on the top of the terraces of the houses, giving thanks to God for the manner in which the locusts went flying before us, and others coming after us. Meanwhile a great storm arose from the sea, which met them, confronting them with violent rain and hail, which lasted quite three hours. The river and streams swelled very much, and when they had ended running off, it was a wonderful thing that they measured two ells deep of their dead bodies, on the brink of the water of the great river, and likewise at the little brooks, a great multitude dead on the edges. The next day in the morning there was not a single one alive in the whole country. The people of the towns all round whence the locusts had arrived, hearing of this, came to see what had happened; some said : These Portuguese are holy, and by the power of God they

---

[1] The Latin text of a similar excommunication of noxious animals was given in the *Pall Mall Gazette*, or *Times*, in 1879.

have cast out the Ambatas. Others, and chiefly the priests
and friars of the neighbourhood (not those of this town)
said: Rather they are sorcerers, and by sorcery have cast
out the Ambatas; and so they have no fear of the lions and
other animals, on account of the sorceries they work.
Sixteen days after this, there came to me a Xuum, that is,
captain of a town, named Coiberia,[1] with men and priests and
friars, to entreat us for the love of God to succour them, for
they were all ruined by the Ambatas. This town is fully
eight leagues and more from Barua towards the sea. They
reached us at the hour of vespers. That same hour we set
out, five Portuguese, and we travelled all night, and arrived
an hour after sunrise. Already the people of the town were
collected, and those of other towns around (in which also
there were locusts), to beg us for the love of God to go there.
This town is on a high hill, from which a great extent of
country and many villages were in view, all yellow with
locusts. The church is at the foot of the town; we went to
it, and with our procession went to the town and took a
turn round it, and in four directions and in four villages we
made an admonition, having caught some locusts and letting
them loose as we had done the other time. When the procession was ended, we went to eat, and having finished eating
and gone out of the house, in all the country not a single one
showed itself. The people of the country would not leave
us alone, and insisted that by all means we should go to their
villages, and they would give us whatever we wished for.
It did not avail me to say that they were gone, and that it
was not necessary. They persisted in importuning us to go
and give them the blessing, as they were afraid of their
returning. So the people went away in peace, and on the
following day we returned to our resting-place. Here they
began to affirm more strongly, that through devotion and
prayer the locusts went away.

---

[1] Kuibayra.

CAP. XXXIII.—*Of the damage which we saw in another country caused by the locusts in two places.*

Another time we saw the locusts in another country called Abrigima, whence the Prester ordered provisions to be given us, in the kingdom of Angote. This country is distant from Barua, from which place we were thirty days in travelling the journey. While we were in this country I went with the ambassador who came from Portugal, and five Genoese with us, towards a country named Aagao. We travelled five days through country entirely depopulated, and through maize canes as thick as canes for propping vines, it cannot be told how they were all cut and bitten, as if bitten by asses, all done by the locusts. The wheat, barley, and tafo, as though they had never been sown there, the trees without any leaves, and the tender twigs all eaten, there was no memory of grass of any sort, and if we had not been prepared with mules laden with barley and provisions for ourselves, we and the mules would have perished. This country was entirely covered with locusts without wings, and they said these were the seed of those which had been there and destroyed the country, and they said that as soon as they had wings they would at once go and seek their country. I am silent as to the multitude of these without wings, because it is not to be believed, and it is right that I should relate what more I saw in this country. I saw men, women, and children, seated horror-struck amongst these locusts. I asked them : Why do you remain there dying, why do you not kill these animals, and revenge yourselves for the damage which their parents did you, and at least the dead ones will do you no further harm. They answered that they had not the heart to resist the plague which God gave them for their sins. The people were going away from this country, and we found the roads full of men, women, and children, on foot, and some in their

arms, with their little bundles on their heads, removing to
a country where they might find provisions (it was a pitiful
sight to see them). When we were in this lordship of
Abrigima, in a town named Aquate, there came travelling
thither such a multitude of locusts as cannot be told, and
they began to arrive there one day about the hour of tierce,
and till night they did not cease, and as they arrived they
settled to rest. Next day, at the hour of prime, they began
to depart, and at midday there was not one there; and not
a leaf remained upon a tree. At that moment others began
to arrive, and they remained like the others till next day at
the same hour, and these did not leave any ·crop with a
husk, nor a green blade. In this way they did for five days,
one after the other; and the people said these were the
children going in search of their fathers. They showed the
way for the others who had not got wings. After these had
passed we learned the width of the passage of these locusts,
and saw the destruction they had caused. The breadth of
this exceeded three leagues, in which there did not remain
a husk or a tree, and the country did not looked burned,
but much snowed with the whiteness of the sticks and dry-
ness of the grass. God was pleased that the fruits had
already been gathered in. We did not know whence they
came, because they came from towards the sea of the
kingdom of Dandali, which is of hostile Moors; neither did
we learn where was the end of their journey.

CAP. XXXIV.—*How we arrived at Temei, and the ambassador
went in search of Tigrimahom, and sent to call us.*

Let us return to our journey : two days after our arrival at
this town of Temei, before our baggage arrived which had
remained in Barra, the ambassador, Don Rodrigo, set out with
six men riding, on his way to the Tigrimahom's residence. He

has the title of King of extensive countries, and has very great lords under his orders and rule. Don Rodrigo went to ask him to give us equipment for our journey, as soon as we should enter his lands. We remained in this town of Temei, Joam Escolar and I, and two other Portuguese : in this time the factor arrived with the baggage which had remained in Barra; and so we brought it all together in this town of Temei, where we had a very hospitable reception from the first Xuum of the district, who is a brother of the Barnagais. On the 28th July of the said year of 1520 there came a message to us from the ambassador, to go with the goods to where he was staying in the house of the Tigrimahom,[1] with the Portuguese who had accompanied him. We were still waiting two days for the people of the country to carry our goods, and then a Xuum arrived who gave us assistance (and this with heavy squalls, storms, and rains); we travelled the space of a league through plains, and then began to descend a very steep road and a very deep descent for the distance of another league, and we went to sleep within the circuit of a church from fear of the tigers, and much vexed by the storms. The following day we went through mountains, both rocky ridges and forests of trees without fruit, until we came to a very large river, which, as it was winter, we found very large for passing over: this is the river on which the town of Barua is situated, and it runs to the Nile, where[2] the kingdom of the Barnagais ends, and that of Tigrimahom begins. From where we slept to this river will be two leagues, a little more or less, and, notwithstanding the mountains and woods, all peopled.   .

[1] *Tigri mahom*, should be *Tigri mākuānām*.

[2] " Where", should be " here" ; this river, the Mareb, not the Nile, separates the country of the Barnagais from that of Tigré.

CAP. XXXV.—*How the Tigrimahom sent a captain in search of our goods, and of the buildings which are in the first town.*

On reaching the river, the men who came with us unloaded the baggage, and from the other side of the river we heard drums and a noise of people : we asked what it was, and they said that a captain of Tigrimahom had come for us. We passed over without our goods to the other side of the river with a good deal of difficulty, on account of the strong body of water : we found a fine body of people come to fetch us ; they might be five or six hundred men to carry our goods. There was at once uncertainty between the people of either side of the river. Those of the country of Tigrimahom said that they had not got to take the baggage except in their country ; and those of the Barnagais, that they had no obligation except to place it on the shore close to the water in their country ; and they engaged in great shouting and obstinacy upon this matter. As the water was running high, they concluded upon passing over the baggage together, in a brotherly way, so that it should not remain out of doors on one or the other bank, but that which was just should be done. As soon as the baggage had been got across, and taken up by the people of Tigrimahom, they travelled with the baggage as fast as we did with our mules. We still travelled on, this portion of the day, through mountains like those we had left behind. On this road we saw herds of wild swine ; some passed of fifty hogs ; partridges and other birds covered the ground and the trees. Here, also, it was said there was every kind of animals, and according to what the mountains are it could not be otherwise. This night we slept in the open air, surrounded by fires from fear of the animals. Here the people began to change, also the country and the trees, and the costume of the people. Principally here we began to enter amongst very high peaks, which appear to rise up to the sky, so high are they; the space at their feet is not extensive, and all are separate one from another, and they are in a line, and not very wide at the base. All those that can be ascended, even though there is danger in it, have chapels on them, most of them of Our Lady. On many of these peaks we saw chapels, and we could not determine by what way people could go to them. We went this day to sleep at a town between the peaks called Abafazem, in which town is a very good church of Our Lady, well built, with the middle nave raised on two sides or walls, with its windows very well constructed, and all the church vaulted.[1] We had not seen any of this fashion in this country : in Portugal, in Entre Douro, and Minho, there are monasteries of this fashion. Close to the said church is a very large and hand-some tower, both for its height and the good workmanship of the walls, and for its width, it is already getting damaged, and yet it has all the look of a regal building, all of well hewn stone : we have not seen such another building. This tower is surrounded by houses, which match well with it, with both good walls and terraces above, like residences of great lords. They said that these edifices belonged to Queen Candace, and because her house where she became a christian is very near here, this would be the truth. This town, church, and country, are situated between these peaks, in very pretty fields, all irrigated by conduits of water descending from the highest peaks, artificially made with stone. The sowings which they irrigate here are wheat, barley, beans, pulse, peas, garlic, onions, garden rue, much mustard; in the water conduits, many good water cresses. In this town there are many priests, and well dressed ; they seemed to be good men, and they told us that

---

[1] This and other passages show that some of the churches in Abyssinia, which are sometimes called Portuguese churches by travellers, are anterior to the Portuguese.

in the commencement of christianity in this country seven
churches had been built, and that this was one of them : and
there is much appearance of its being so, because christianity commenced very near here, that is, in the town of
Aquaxumo.

CAP. XXXV.[1]—*How we departed from Bafazem, and went to the
town called Houses of St. Michael.*

We departed from this town as we had come, and also
the people of the country who carried our baggage (this
carrying is called Elfa), and we went to sleep at another
town called St. Michael.　On arriving at this town they did
not give us lodging, saying that the town was privileged;
and on account of the rain we went to the circuit of the
church, and in the outer circuit, which serves as a churchyard, we put our mules, because there was plenty of grass
on account of the winter rains.　In this country it is not
the custom to give victuals more than once a day, and it is
the custom to do that at night, in all the kingdoms and
lordships of Prester John.　Having arrived thus, and not
having had quarters given us, so also they did not give us
anything to eat, according to their custom, and we were
hungry.　Our factor said to me: Father let us eat.　I replied,
What shall we eat ?　He said to me, I have brought two
fowls cooked, let us eat them.　Our clerk and I were
horrified at eating meat without bread, but nevertheless we
accompanied him.　After this repast we many times ate
meat without bread, and bread without meat, and bread
without salt, because it is not usual in the country ; and
bread soaked in water, and pepper, so that we forgot our
first amazement.　In the night they sent us food, and as we
were sleeping in the cloister of the church, for greater

[1] *Sic.*

cleanliness we went to the place where they give, or used to
give, the communion. Whilst we were there with light some
pigeons began to stir ; as soon as we heard them we rushed
to the doors, for the rest was closed, not one escaped us, nor
the young pigeons which we found in the holes : and we
filled a bag with them. Later we returned to halt in this
town, and we were received without their bringing forward
their privileges, that we might not kill the pigeons of the
church, which was now again peopled with them. The
difference which there is between the people of this country
and that of the Barnagais, is in their clothes and dress.
The men wear girt round them some small skirts, some
of stuff, some of tanned leather, like large breeches, also
plaited, like those of the women of our country, and their
extent is not more than two spans ; when they are walking
it seems that they spread them out so that they cover their
nakedness, but if they stoop or sit down, or if there is
wind, it shows. The married women wear very little
covering, and the single women, who have neither husbands
nor friends, have less shame. The beads which other
women wear round their necks these wear girt round their
bodies, and a large quantity of beads over their private
parts, and whoever can get a hawk's bell, or a small bell,
wears it there ; and some of these women (not married)
wear a sheep's skin at their neck, which covers one side and
not more, because they wear it loose, and only one foot and
one fore foot of the sheep is tied and suspended to the
neck. The[1] road which is taken in this country of the
Prester as soon as one arrives from the Red sea, or comes
from Egypt to Çuaquem, is at once to turn one's back on
the North, and travel to the South until arriving at the
gates of Badabajc; this is because a few hours from here
they go in one direction, others in another, asking where

---

[1] This passage appears to have been inserted here by some error of
the printer, and to belong to some other chapter.

the court may be, in a straight line, or to the East or to the West, according to the country where the Prester is staying. At these passages are separated the kingdoms of Amara and Xoa, and because we went about in these countries for six years, sometimes to one part, at others to another, going out of the road and then again returning to it, according as it seemed to us that that was a better arrangement.

Cap. xxxvi.—*Which speaks of the town of Aquaxumo, and of the gold which the Queen Saba took to Solomon for the temple, and of a son that she had of Solomon.*

Amongst these peaks where we were still going, in the parts to the West are wonderful lands and very great lordships, among which is a very good town named Aquaxumo, and it is two days' journey from the town of St. Michael, always between these peaks. We stayed in it for eight months, by order of the Prester John. This town was the city, chamber, and abode (as they say) of the Queen Saba, who took the camels laden with gold to Solomon, when he was building the temple of Jerusalem. There is in this town a very noble church, in which we found a very great chronicle written in the language of the country, and it stated in its commencement how it had been written first in Hebrew, and afterwards put into Greek, and from Greek into Chaldee, and from Chaldee into the Abyssinian tongue, in which it now is, and it begins thus. How the Queen Sabaas hearing related the great and rich works which Solomon had begun in Jerusalem, she determined to go and see them; and she loaded certain camels with gold to give for these works. And on arriving near the city, and being about to cross a lake, which they passed by some bridges,[1] she dismounted and worshipped the beams and said : " Please God my feet

_____
[1] *Pontões.*

shall not touch the timber on which the Saviour of the
world has to hang." And she made a circuit of the lake,
and went to see Solomon, and induced him to withdraw
those beams from there, and she came to the works, and
offered her gifts and said: "These works are not such as
they told me in richness and beauty, because their beauty and
richness has no equal, so that they are greater than what was
related to me, so much so that the tongues of men cannot
tell their nobility and richness, and much I grieve for the
small gift which I brought; I will return to my countries
and lordships, and I will send whatever abounds for the
works, of gold, and blackwood to inlay." Whilst she was
at Jerusalem Solomon had intercourse with her, and she
became pregnant of a son, and remained at Jerusalem until
she brought him forth. After she was able to travel she
left her son, and returned to her country, and sent from it
much gold and blackwood to inlay the works. And her
son grew up to the age of seventeen years, and among the
many other sons that Solomon had this one was so proud
that he outraged[1] the people of Israel, and all the country of
Judæa. And the people came to Solomon and said to him :
"We are not able to maintain so many Kings as you have
got, for all your sons are Kings, especially this one of Queen
Saba; she is a greater lady than you, send him to his mother,
for we are not able to maintain him." Then Solomon sent
him very honourably, giving him the officers that are usual
in a King's household (as I will relate in its place), and
besides, he gave him, in order that he might rest on the
road, the country of Gazaã, which is in the land of Egypt,
and he made his journey to the country of his mother,
where he was a very great ruler. The chronicle says that
he ruled from sea to sea, and that he had sixty ships in the
Indian sea. This book of chronicles is very large, and I
only took from it the beginnings.

[1] *Sobarbava.*

CAP. XXXVII.—*How St. Philip declared a prophecy of Isaiah to the eunuch of Queen Candace, through which she and all her kingdom were converted, and of the edifices of the town of Aquaxumo.*

In this town of Aquaxumo was the principal residence of the Queen Candace,[1] who was the beginning of the christianity of this country. Her birth (as they say) was half a league from here, in a very small village, which now is entirely of blacksmiths. Her commencement of christianity was this. According to what they say in their books the angel said to St. Philip : Rise and go towards the South, by the road which goes from Jerusalem to Gaza in the desert. St. Philip went, and met with a man who was an eunuch, and he was major-domo of the Queen Candace, ruler of Ethiopia. In the country of Gaza, which Solomon had given to his son, this man was the keeper of all the riches of the Queen, and he had been to Jerusalem and was returning to his house, and he was going on a chariot. St. Philip came up to him, and heard him sing a prophecy of Isaiah, and asked him how he understood what he was singing. He replied that he did not know, unless some other man taught him. St. Philip mounted into the chariot, and went on explaining to him that prophecy, and converted him, and baptized and instructed him in the faith. Then the Spirit snatched away St. Philip, and he remained informed. They say that here was fulfilled the prophecy which David spoke : " Ethiopia shall arise, and stretch forth her hands to God." Thus they say they were the first christians in the world. The eunuch at once set out very gaily on the road to Ethiopia, to the house of his mistress, and converted her and all her household, and baptized them in consequence of what he related to them. And the Queen caused all her

[1] Pliny says Candace was the name of many Queens, as Pharaoh was of the Kings of Egypt.

kingdom of Buno to be baptized. This Buno is towards
the east from the town of Aquaxumo, in the kingdom of
the Barnagais, and it is now two lordships. In this town
of Aquaxumo, where she became Christian, she built a very
noble church, the first there was in Ethiopia : it is named
St. Mary of Syon. They say that it is so named because its
altar stone came from Sion. In this country (as they say)
they have the custom always to name the churches by the
altar stone, because on it is written the name of the patron
saint. This stone which they have in this church, they say
that the Apostles sent it from Mount Sion. This church is
very large ; it has five naves of a good width and of a great
length, vaulted above, and all the vaults covered up, the
ceiling and sides all painted. Below, the floor of the church
is well worked with handsome cut stone. It has seven
chapels, all with their backs to the east, and their altars well
placed. It has a choir after our fashion, except that it is
low, and they reach the vaulted roof with their heads ; and
the choir is also over a vault, and they do not use it.
This church has a very large circuit, paved with flag-
stones like gravestones. This consists of a very high
wall, and it is not covered over like those of the other
churches, but it is left open. This church has a large
enclosure, and it is also surrounded by another larger
enclosure, like the wall of a large town or city. Within
this enclosure are handsome habitations of terraced buildings, and all spout out their water by strong figures of
lions and dogs of stone. Inside this large enclosure there
are two palaces, one on the right hand and the other on the
left, which belong to two rectors of the church ; and the
other houses are of canons and friars. In the large enclosure,
at the gate nearest to the church, there is a large ruin,
built in a square, which in other times was a house, and it
has at each angle large stone pillars, squared and wrought.
This house is called Ambazabete, which means house of
lions. They say that in this house were the captive lions,

and there are still some always, and there go before the
Prester John four captive lions. Before the gate of this
great enclosure there is a large court, and in it a large tree,
which they call Pharaoh's fig tree,[1] and at each end of it
there are some very cool platforms of well worked masonry,
merely laid down. Where they reach near the foot of the
fig tree, they are injured by the roots, which raise them up.
There are, on the top of these platforms, twelve stone
chairs, as well made with stone as though they were of
wood, with their seats and rests for the feet. They are not
made out of a block of stone, but each one with pieces of
of stone. They say these belong to the twelve judges
who at this time serve in the court of Prester John. Outside of this enclosure there is a large assemblage of very
good houses, such as there are not in the whole of Ethiopia,
and very good wells of water, of wrought masonry, and also
in most of the houses the before-mentioned ancient figures
of lions and dogs and birds, all well made in stone. At the
back of this great church is a very handsome tank of
masonry, and upon this masonry are as many other chairs
of stone, such as those in the enclosure of the church. This
town is situated at the head of a beautiful plain, and almost
between two hills, and the rest of this plain is almost all full
of these old buildings, and among them many of these
chairs, and high monumental stones with inscriptions. Above
this town there are many stones standing up, and others
on the ground, very large and beautiful, and wrought with
handsome designs, among which is one raised upon another,
and worked like an altar stone, except that it is of very
great size, and it is set in the other as if inchased. This
raised stone is sixty-four ells in length, and six wide; and
the sides are three ells wide. It is very straight and well

---

[1] Mansfield Parkyns calls it a sycamore tree, and says it is remarkable
for the extraordinary circumference of its trunk and the great spread of
its branches, which cast their shade over such a space of ground as
would be sufficient for the camp of the largest caravan.

worked, made with arcades below, as far as a head made
like a half moon; and the side which has this half moon is
towards the south. There appear in it five nails, which do
not show more on account of the rust; and they are like
fives of dice in compass. And that it may not be said, How
could so high a stone be measured? I have already said how
it was all in arcades as far as the foot of the half moon, and
these are all of one size ; and we measured those we could
reach to, and by those reckoned up the others, and we found
sixty ells, and we gave four to the half moon, although it
would be more, and so it made sixty-four ells. This very
long stone, on its south side, and where the nails in the
half moon are, at the height of a man, has the form of a
portal carved in the stone itself, with a bolt and a lock, as
if it were shut up.[1] The stone on which it is set up has an
ell in thickness, and is well worked; it is placed on other
large stones, and surrounded by other smaller stones, and
no man can tell how much of it enters the other stone, or if
it reaches to the ground. There are other stones raised
above the ground, and very well worked ; some of them
will be quite forty ells long, and others thirty. There are
more than thirty of these stones, and they have no patterns
on them; most of them have large inscriptions, which the
country people cannot read, neither could we read them ;
according to their appearance, these characters must be
Hebrew. There are two of these stones, very large and
beautiful, with designs of large arcades, and ornaments of
good size, which are lying on the ground entire, and one of
them is broken into three pieces, and each of these exceeds
eighty ells, and is ten ells in width. Close to them are
stones, in which these had to be, or had been let in, which
were bored and very well worked.

[1] Mansfield Parkyns thus describes it: "The principal obelisk is
carved on the south side, as if to represent a door, windows, cornices,
etc."

CAP. XXXVII.—*Of the buildings which are around Aquaxumo, and how gold is found in it, and of the Church of this town.*

Above this town, on a hill which overlooks much land, and far away, and which is about a mile, that is the third of a league, from the town, there are two houses under the ground, into which men do not enter without a lamp. These houses are not vaulted, but of very good straight masonry, both the walls and the upper part; the walls may be twelve ells high; the stones inside and out are set in the wall so close one to the other, that it all looks like one stone.   One of these houses is much divided into chambers and granaries; in the doorways are holes for the bars and for the sockets of the doors.   In one of these chambers are two very large chests, each one four ells in length, and one and a half broad, and as much in height and inside, and in the upper part on the inner side they are hollowed at the edge, as though they had lids of stone, as the chests also are of stone.   (They say that these were the treasure chests of Queen Saba.)   The other house, which is longer, has only got a portico and one room.   From the entrance of one house to that of the other will be a distance of a game of manqual,[1] and above them is a field.   There were in our company some Genoese and Catalans, who had been prisoners of the Turks, and they affirmed and swore that they had seen Troy, and the granary of Joseph in the Kingdom of Egypt, and that their buildings were very large, but that these of this town were and are, in a great manner, larger, and it seemed to us that the Prester John had sent us here, in order that we should see these edifices, and we had rejoiced at seeing them, as they are much grander than what I write.   In this town, and in its plains,

---

[1] *Mancal*, an unknown game, antiquated in the reign of Don Manuel; the translation of Selves calls it a *juego de herradura*.

which are all sown in their season with all kinds of seed, when there come thunderstorms, and they are over, there do not remain in the town women or men, boys or children, who are old enough, who do not come out to look for gold among the tillage, for they say the rains lay it bare, and that they find a good deal. So they go by all the roads seeking the water-courses, and raking with sticks. Seeing this, and hearing it said how much gold they found, both in the town and in the tilled lands, I determined on making a washing-board, such as I had seen in Portugal, at Foz daronca,[1] and in Ponte de Mucela. When it was done, I began to wash earth, and set up two boards, and did not find any gold. I do not know whether I did not know how to wash, or whether I did not know it when washed, or whether there was not any here: the report was, that there was a great deal. As they say that the church of Aquaxumo is the most ancient, so likewise they hold it to be the most honoured of all Ethiopia : and the offices are well done in it. In this church there are a hundred and fifty canons, and as many friars. It has two head men, one is named *Nebrete*[2] of the canons, which means master of instruction, and the other, Nebrete of the friars. These two heads reside in the palaces which are within the great inclosure and circuit of the church ; and the Nebrete of the canons lodges at the right hand, and he is the principal one, and the most honoured. He does justice for the canons and for the laity of all this country : and the Nebrete of the friars only hears and rules the friars. Both use kettledrums and trumpets. They have very large revenues, and besides their revenues they have every day a collation which they call *Maabar*[3] of bread and wine of the country, when mass is finished. The friars have this for themselves, and the canons also, and this

[1] Arouca, a town in the bishopric of Lamego.
[2] *Nebrete, i.e., Nabrïd,* imposed by hand, the title of the Governor of Axum.
[3] *Maabar* or *Mahabar*, a club, gathering.

Maabar is such, that the friars seldom eat other food than that. They have this every day except Friday of the Passion, because on that day no one eats or drinks. The canons do not make their Maabar within the circuit of the church, and are seldom there, except at fixed hours, neither is the Nebreto in his palace, except at some chance time when he goes to hear causes. This is because they are married, and live with their wives and children in their houses, which are very good and which are outside. Neither women nor laymen enter into the inclosure of this church, and they do not enter to receive the communion. On account of their being married, and that the women do not enter this circuit, they make their Maabar outside, so that their wives and children may enjoy it.

CAP. XXXIX.—*How close to Aquaxumo there are two churches on two peaks, where lie the bodies of two saints.*

Not very far from this town are two hills, one at one end and the other at the other, one to the east and the other to the west. At that which is to the west there is a good bit of ascent, and at the top there is quite half a league of a smiling plain which has some very good villages, and delightful vineyards. On this hill, towards the town of Aquaxumo, and in sight of it, there is a very handsome edifice, it is a tower of very fine masonry: and much of this tower is cast down, and with its masonry a church has been built of St. Michael, to which come many people from the town of Aquaxumo to take the communion on Saturdays and Sundays, on account of its devotion. On the hill which is to the east, on its peak there is another church which is named Abbalicanos, and this saint lies here, and they say that he was confessor of Queen Candace. This church is like an annex of the great church of Aquaxumo, and it is served by its canons. This house and church of Abbalicanos is one of great devotion amongst them, there come to it also many people from the town to hear the offices and take the communion. This church also has a large village at the foot of the hill which is its parish. Further on than this church, about a third of a league, there is a peak which is slender from its base, and appears to mount up to the sky : it is ascended by three hundred steps winding round it. On the top of it there is a very elegant small church of much devotion, which has no more than a small nave, and around it a circuit of well-wrought masonry of the height of a man's breast, and men are afraid to look down over it. There is not more width from this wall to the church than what three men can cover together holding hands. This church has no cloister nor circuit, nor space where it could be made. This church is named Abbapantalian, and his body lies here : it possesses large revenues, and has fifty canons or debeteras, according to their names, and they have a Nebrete like those of Aquaxumo. As the church of Aquaxumo was the beginning of Christianity in Ethiopia, so this one is surrounded by the sepulchres of Saints like Braga in Portugal.

CAP. XL.—*Of the countries and lordships that are to the west and to the north of Aquaxumo, where there is a monastery, named Hallelujah, and of two other monasteries to the east.*

In the country to the west of Aquaxumo, which is towards the Nile, there are extensive lands and lordships, as they say. And in these countries and parts is the land of Sabaim, whence the Queen Saba took her name and title, and where the black wood is found which she sent to Solomon to make inlaid work in the temple. From this town of

Aquaxumo to the beginning of the country of Sabaim there are two days' journey. This lordship is now subject to the kingdom of the Tigrimahom, and a brother-in-law of the Prester John is lord and captain of it: they say it is a great and good lordship. On the north side there lies another lordship named Torate, a country of mountainous ridges; there is a distance of four leagues to these mountains and lordship of Torate. It is on a great and high mountain, and at its foot and on the top of it is a flat space of half a league, with large trees, and a monastery with great revenues (as they say) named Hallelujah, containing many friars. They say that it bears this name, because in the commencement of Christianity in this country, when St. Mary of Syon was built in Aquaxumo, this monastery was built next. They say that they did not know then what they ought to pray or to chaunt, and that there was here a devout father who kept vigils, and commended himself to God at night, and this devout man affirmed that he heard the angels in heaven, who sung Hallelujah, and that from this the custom remained in this country that all the masses commenced with Hallelujah, and so this monastery is called by name Hallelujah. And if in that time that friar was good and devout, now, those who are here, have the reputation of being great robbers. The hill and range on which this monastery stands is entirely surrounded by dry channels, which only have water after the thunder showers for a space of two or three leagues. In another mountain in the same lordship of Torate, is another great monastery, but not so great as that of Hallelujah, and they say that it has good friars, they also say that they are not good friends with the others, because they have a bad reputation. Returning to our road, at a distance of three leagues from the town of Aquaxumo, there is another monastery on another hill, this is named St. John. Further on, a distance of two leagues, there is another monastery which is named Abbagarima. They say that this

Abbagarima was king of Greece, and that he left his kingdom, and came to do penance, and there ended his life in
sanctity. There is behind his chapel a cave very convenient
for doing penance, and they say that he abode there. They
say that this king works many miracles: we came here on
the day of his feast,and there were here more than three thousand cripples, blind men and lepers. This monastery is between three peaks, almost on the side of one of them, and
it seems as though it would fall into the hollow where they
say he did penance. They descend into it by a ladder,and bring
out of it earth like gravel, or soft stone, and they carry it
away and hang it to the necks of the sick in rags. (They say
that some have received health.) I asked about the revenue
of this monastery, the friars told me it had a revenue of sixteen horses, and besides, some endowments of provisions.
It is a small monastery of few friars and small revenues, and
at the foot of it they sow much garlic; there are between the
peaks, large tilled fields, and it has an infinite number of
very good vineyards, they make much raisins of them : they
come in very early, they begin in January and end in March.

CAP. XLI.—*How we departed from the church and houses of
St. Michael, and went to Bacinete, and from there to
Maluc; and of the monasteries which are near it.*

We went away from the Church of St. Michael, with the
country people who carried our baggage, and went to sleep
at a town named Anguelia, at a Betenegnz, which means
a king's house, as I have already said various times. And
already in other towns we had halted in houses like these :
no one uses them, except the lords of the country who at
times hold the authority of the Prester John. They respect
these houses so much that their doors are always open, and
no one touches anything there, nor enters within, except

when the lord is there; and when he goes away nothing remains inside except the open doors, and sleeping couches ready for use,[1] and the place for making a fire. We departed from this place with our baggage, and travelled three or four leagues, and went to sleep on a high hill, and above a large river, which is named Abacinete,[2] and so the country and lordship is named. They said that this lordship belonged to the grandmother of the Prester John; and whilst we were there it was taken away from her, because she was on bad terms with the country. This lordship lies in the kingdom of Tigrimahom, and it is a very populous country in all parts, and fertile, a country of mountains and rivers; all the towns are on heights, and away from the roads: this they do on account of the travellers, who take from them by force whatever they have. The people who carried our baggage made a great fence of thorny bushes for us, and for the mules, which was to defend us from the wild beasts; however, we neither heard nor perceived anything at night. We set out from this place, and went to sleep at a town which is named Maluche, which may be two leagues from where we had slept. This town was surrounded by very beautiful tilled fields of wheat, barley, and millet, the best and thickest we had seen yet. Close to this town is a very high mountain, not very broad at the foot, for it is as broad at the top as it is at the bottom, for it is all scarped like a wall, of sheer cliff, all bare, without any crops or verdure of anything. It makes like three divisions; two at the ends are pointed, that of the middle flat. In one of the pointed divisions, that is, ascending to the summit from the bottom, there is a monastery of Our Lady, named Abbamata. They say that they are friars leading a good life. The order of friars is all one and the same in all the dominions of Prester John. It is all of St. Anthony of the

[1] *Feitos igoacs;* the Selves translation has, *las camas hechas, y por cubrir.*

[2] *Abacinete, i.e., Amba Sancte,* name of a hill.

Wilderness, and from this proceeds another order, which they name *estefarruz*.[1] These hold the others as bad, and say that they burn many on account of there being many heresies among them, such as their not adoring the cross. These are the people who make the crosses which all the clergy and friars carry in their hands, and the laity at their necks, and their opinion is that we have only one cross to adore, and that it is that on which Jesus Christ suffered, and that the crosses which they make, and which other men make, are not to be adored, because they are the work of men's hands; and there are other heresies which they say, hold, and do. Looking at this monastery where it appears in sight, it seems like a league. I wished to go there; they told me not to go, as it was a day's journey, and that they could not go there except by clinging on with the hands, and otherwise it was not possible to go there. On the hill in the middle, which is like a table, there is another house of Our Lady, to which they say much devout visitation is made. On the other peak is a house of Holy Cross; it is a further distance of a league and a half or two leagues. On another hill, which is also scarped, like that of Abbamata, there is another monastery, which is named St. John. There is nothing on the top of this hill but the monastery and houses of the friars, without any verdure, as it appears to sight from below; and its officials live at the foot of the hill in fertile lands, and send thence what is necessary to those who live in the monastery. Already in these lands a great difference is seen from the lands left behind. In the countries and kingdom of the Barnagais, and in the commencement of that of the Tigrimahom, there are many beggars, cripples, blind men, and poor people; in this country there are not so many. The men wear different costumes; so also the women who are married or living

---

[1] *Estefarruz* is probably a misprint of Alvarez for *Estefanuz*, or Stephen.

with men. Here they wear wrapped round them dark coloured woollen stuffs, with large fringes of the same stuff, and they do not wear diadems[1] on their heads like those of the Barnagais. The girls go from bad to worse; there are women of twenty or twenty-five years old, who have the breasts coming to their waists, and their body bare and gaily covered with little beads. Some of the women of full size and age wear a sheep skin suspended to their shoulder, without its covering more than one side. In the parts of Portugal and Spain people marry for love, and on account of seeing beautiful faces, and the things inside are hidden from them; in this country they can well marry on account of seeing everything quite certain.

Cap. XLII.—*Of the animals which are in the country, and how we turned back to where the ambassador was.*

There are in this country tigers and other animals, which at night kill the cows, mules and asses, in the closed towns, which they did not do in the kingdom of the Barnagais which we had left behind. We departed from this place[2] on the 6th of August of 1520, and returned back to where we had left the ambassador, who was lodged by order of the Tigrimahom, and much to his satisfaction, with all the Portuguese who had started with him from Temei, a country in the kingdom of the Barnagais. In the said place a great lord was lodged, by order of the Tigrimahom, in order to protect and provide for the ambassador; and likewise other gentlemen were lodged in towns within sight of this, and many others who accompanied the Tigrimahom. He was lodged in a Beteneguz, and the ambassador was at the distance of a league from that place. On the day that we arrived the Tigrimahom sent to summon the ambassador; and he went

[1] *i.e.*, Fillets.   [2] Maluk.

at once, and all the Portuguese went with him. When we
arrived at the Betencguz where he was, they told us that
he was in the church, he and his wife, to receive the Communion; and this was an hour before sunset, which is the
hour for saying mass on fast days. We went towards the
church, and met with him on the way. Each came on his
mule, with very good state, like great gentlemen as they
are; so they came accompanied by many great lords. This
Tigrimahom is an old man, of a good and reverend presence: his wife came entirely covered up with blue cotton
stuffs; we did not see either her face or her body, because
it was all covered up. As soon as we came up to him, he
asked me for a cross which I carried in my hand, and he
kissed it and ordered it to be given to his wife to kiss it;
she kissed it through her wrapper, and received us with a
good welcome. This Tigrimahom keeps a very large household, both of men and women, and great state, in a great
measure grander than the Barnagais. The ambassador and
those that were with him told us that they had received
great honour and hospitable reception from the Tigrimahom,
both in favour and provisions. It is but a short time that
this Tigrimahom has held this lordship, and as yet, he has
not finished visiting all his lands which are under his orders
and rule, and also those who have the title of kings, as well
as the others underneath them in rank. The Prester John
deposes them and appoints them whenever he pleases, with
or without cause; and on this account there is no ill humour
here, and if there is any it is secret, because in this period
that we remained in this country I saw great lords turned
out of their lordships, and others put into them, and I saw
them together, and they appeared to be good friends. (God
knows their hearts.) And in this country, whatever happens to them, of good fortune or of loss, they say of all of
it, that God does it. These great lords, who are like kings,
are all tributaries of the Prester John; those of this king-

dom in horses, and those of the Barnagais in brocades, silks, and some cotton cloths; and those further on from this place (as they say) are tributaries in gold, silk, mules, cows, and plough oxen, and other things which there are at court. The lords who are beneath these, even though they hold their lordships from the hand of Prester John, pay their tribute to the other lords; and they account for all on delivering it to the Prester. The lands are so populous that the revenues cannot but be large; and these lords, even though they receive their revenues, eat at the cost of the people and the poor.

CAP. XLIII.—*How the Tigrimahom being about to travel, the ambassador asked him to despatch him, and it was not granted to him, and the ambassador sent him certain things, and he gave him equipment, and we went to a monastery, where the friars gave thanks to God.*

As the Tigrimahom was about to set out for other countries we went to take leave of him, and ask him to give us a good equipment for our journey, and to this he answered us saying: that the goods which we were taking to the Prester John he would have them taken to him, and that our own goods which were our clothes, and pepper and cloths for our provisions, that we should take charge of them, and with this he dismissed us and went his way, and we went to where we were lodged. Seeing that we could not travel with so much baggage, we agreed to send again to the Tigrimahom, and Jorge D'Abreu and Mestre Joam went and took to him certain goods, that is to say, a rich dagger and a sword furnished with a velvet scabbard and gilt ends. There came a message that they should carry all our goods, and that in all his lands they should give us bread, wine, and meat to eat. As soon as this message arrived, the same

day we departed, which was the 9th of August. We went
to sleep at some small hamlets, fenced in like those we had
passed from fear of the tigers. On the night that we slept
here, when it was about two hours of the night, a little more
or less, on two men of the country going outside of a yard
the tigers attacked them, and wounded one of them in the
leg. God protected him and we who hastened to him, because certainly they would have killed him, as they are such
pestilent animals. In this country there are villages of
Moors, separated from the Christians; they say that they
pay much tribute to the lords of the country in gold and
silk stuffes. They do not serve in the general services like
the Christians; they have not got mosques, because they do
not allow them to build or possess them. All these countries are great pasture lands, like those left behind, but not
less of tilled land and mountain ridges (not very high), but
rather undulating plains. From these small villages we went
a distance of four leagues to sleep at another small village,
and a little before coming to it we saw on the left hand on
a high hill much green grass and woods, in which is another
monastery of St. John, like the one seen before. They say
that it is a monastery of many friars and much revenue.
Close to the village where we halted is a church of St.
George, a very well arranged building, almost in the fashion
of our churches, small and vaulted, its paintings very well
executed, that is, of apostles, patriarchs, prophets, Elias and
Enoch. Ten priests and friars officiate in it. Up to this
time we have not met with a church ruled by clergy, in
which there are not friars, and in monasteries no priest. In
truth the friars behave more honestly in their habits, and the
priests behave as laymen, except that their lives are more
honest. In the fairs priests and friars are all the same, and
they are the merchants. Across this church of St. George,
towards the east, at the foot of a mountain about a league
from this church, there is a monastery on a river, named

Paraclitos, which amongst us means Holy Ghost. There will
be in it twenty or twenty-five friars, the house is very devout,
and so the friars appear to be. When we came there, they
gave great thanks to God for their having seen Christians of
another country and language who had never come before:
they showed us all their affairs. The house of the monastery
is vaulted and small, and well painted, its cloisters and cells
very well arranged, better than we had yet seen in this
country. It has very good vegetable gardens, with many
cabbages, garlic, onions, and other species of vegetables,
many lemons, limes, citrons, peaches, grapes, figs, common
nuts, and figs of India; many tall cypresses, and many other
fruit trees and plants. After we had seen all, the friars were
at their wits' end, because it was Saturday, and they could
not gather anything to give us, asking us to pardon them,
and that they would give us of what they had in the house.
Then they gave us dry garlic and lemons; last of all they
took us to the refectory, and there gave us to eat boiled
cabbage of the day before, hashed and salted, and mixed
with garlic, without any other sauce, only boiled with water
and salt. They gave us, besides, two rolls, one of wheat,
the other of barley, and a jar of the beverage of the country, which they call *cana*, and it is made of millet. They
gave it all with great good will, and we likewise received it
in the same manner, giving thanks to God as they did. At
a distance of two leagues from this place where we halted,
there is a town named Agroo, where the Tigrimahom has a
Betenoguz, to which we went on various occasions. Here
there is a house of Our Lady, made in a rock, hewn and
wrought with the pickaxe, very well constructed, with three
naves, and their supports made of the rock itself. The principal chapel, the sacristy, and the altar, all is of the rock
itself, and the principal doorway, with its supports, which
could not be better if made of pieces. It has not got side
doors, because both sides are of hewn rock, or of living

rock. It is a beautiful thing, and to be rejoiced at to see, and hear the chaunt in it and the grand tone it gives. Mention of bells may be dispensed with, since they are all of stone, drums and cymbals generally and specially.

CAP. XLIV.—*How we went to the town of Danguqui, and Abefete, and how Balgada Robel came to visit us, and the service which he brought, and of the salt which is in the country.*

On the 13th of August we set out from this place, where we had kept Saturday and Sunday, and went to stop at a town named Dangugui. In this town there is a well built church, its naves very well constructed upon very thick stone supports, well hewn. The patron of this church is named Quiricos, who amongst us is named Quirici.[1] The town is a very good one, situated close to a pretty river, and they say that it has the privilege that no one may enter it on horseback; but on a mule they may. From here we went to sleep at some very bad villages, and we went to sleep without supper and apart, because we were not able to do otherwise. Next day, in the morning, we set out, and went quickly to a town named Belete, where there was a Beteneguz. Whilst we were there a great gentleman arrived named Robel, and his lordship is named Balgada,[2] and so his appellation and title is Balgada Robel. He brought with him many people on horseback, and mules and horses, and led mules for state and drums. This gentleman is subject to the Tigrimahom. This gentleman sent to beg the ambassador to come and speak to him outside of the Beteneguz and of his lodgings, because he could not go to him there without the Tigrimahom's being there; because, as I

[1] Or *Kyriakos.*

[2] *Gada* is an expedition sent from the highlands to collect the salt, *Bâal* means master or chief; *Bâalgada* is a title given to the chiefs of those expeditions, and is a title still used in Ethiopia. like Duke or Count.

have already written, they respect these Betes very much,
which remain with open doors, and no one enters them,
saying that it is forbidden under pain of death for any one
to enter any Beteneguz without the lord being there who
rules the country in the name of the Prester John.   When
this message arrived, the ambassador sent to tell him that
he had come a distance of five thousand leagues, and whoever wished to see him might come to his lodgings, for he
was not going to go out of them. Upon this, the gentleman
sent a cow and a large jar of honey, white as snow and hard
as stone, and sent word that for an interview[1] with the
ambassador he would come to the Beteneguz, and that by
reason of foreign Christians he would be excused the penalty.
On arriving close to the Bete the rain was so heavy that it
suited him to enter inside, and he remained talking to the
ambassador and with all of us about our coming, and of the
christianity of our countries, which are unknown to them.
After that he spoke of the wars that they had with the
Moors, who divided with them the countries towards the
sea, and that they never ceased warring; and he gave a
very good mule for a sword, and the ambassador gave him
a helmet.   We learned afterwards at court, on the many
occasions that we there saw this gentleman, that he was a
very great warrior, and was never free from wars, as they
related to us, and that he was very fortunate.   His lands go
to the south along our road, and on the east lie towards the
Red Sea, and part of them reach the road by which we
were travelling ; and they say it is a great lordship.   There
is in it the best thing there is in Ethiopia, that is the salt,
which in all the country is current as money, both in the
kingdoms and dominions of the Prester and in the kingdoms of the Moors and Gentiles, and they say that it goes
as far as Manicongo.   This salt is of stone taken from the
mountain (as they say), and it comes in the shape of bricks.

---

[1] *Estrevimento*, antiquated.

Each stone is a span and a half in length, and four fingers in width and three in thickness, and so it goes loaded on beasts like faggots. They say that in the place where the salt is collected a hundred and twenty or a hundred and thirty stones are worth a drachm, and the drachm (as I have already said) is worth three hundred reals, according to our account. Then, at a market which is in our road, at a town named Corcora, which is about a day's journey from the place where the salt is got, it already is worth five or six stones less, and so it[1] goes on diminishing from market to market. When it arrives at court, six or seven stones are worth a drachm ; I have seen them at five to the drachm when it was winter. The salt is very cheap where it is got, and very dear at the court, because it does not travel easily. They say that entering into Damute they get a good slave for three or four stones, and that on reaching the countries of the slaves they say they get a slave for a stone, and almost for a stone its weight in gold. We met on this road three or four hundred animals, in herds, laden with salt, and in the same way others going empty to fetch salt. They say that these belong to great lords, who all send them to make a journey each year for their expenses at court. One meets other files of twenty or thirty beasts (these are like those of muleteers) ; in other parts one meets men laden with salt, which they carry for themselves, and others in order to make profit from fair to fair. So it is worth and current as money, and whoever carries it finds all that he requires.

CAP. XLV.—*How we departed, and our baggage before us, and how a captain of the Tigrimahom who conducted us was frightened by a friar who came in search of us.*

We departed from this Betenegus to some very vile places in a mountain named Benacel ; and the next day we

[1] The drachm of gold ; that is, the salt increases in value.

7 2

set out, and our baggage went on in front, and we found it
set down in the middle of a plain where there was much
water. When we arrived, it grieved us to see our goods
thus. Whilst we were thus at our wits' end, there came up
four or five men on mules, and ten or twelve men on foot
with them; amongst them came a friar, and as soon as this
friar came up he at once seized the captain by the head, who
had charge of our baggage, and gave him buffets. We, on
seeing this, all ran up to him to know for what reason he
did that. The ambassador, seeing the captain covered with
blood, laid hold of the friar by the breast, and was going to
strike him, and I do not know whether he did strike him.
I and all those who came up with him carried their arms
ready, and almost at the breast of the friar. It availed him
that he spoke a little Italian, because Jorge d'Abreu was
there who understood it a little; and if this had not been
the case, and I, who saw his hood and said that he was a
friar, he would not have got off well. This matter having
been pacified, the friar told how he had come by order of
the Prester John to cause our luggage to be carried,
and that he had been amazed at that captain, and what he
had done to him he did it on account of the bad equipment
which he was giving us. The ambassador answered that
those buffets had not been given to the captain, but to him,
since he had given them in his presence, and that he felt it
much. All having been restored to peace, the friar said
that he had to go forward on the road by which we had
been travelling, to the house of the Balgada Robel, the
gentleman we had left behind, and that from him and from
his house he would bring mules and camels to carry our
baggage, and that we should go and wait for him at a Beteneguz which was at a distance of half a day's journey from
this place. (This is the friar who is going as ambassador to
Portugal.) We departed on our way, and went to sleep at
a small village where there is a good church; its patron is

Quercos. At night we thought we should have been eaten by the tigers. On the following day we went forward little more than half a league to the Betcueguz which the friar had told us of: this is at a town called Corcora, with very good houses for resting in, and a very good church. Here we remained Saturday, Sunday, and Monday, waiting for the friar. They told us that to the eastward from this place there was a large monastery named Nazareth ; they say it is one of large revenues and many friars, and that there are in it abundance of grapes, peaches, and other fruits ; and they brought us small nuts from it. They say that to the westward, which is towards the Nile, there are great mines of silver, and that they do not know how to get it out, nor to profit by it.

CAP. XLVI.—*How we departed from the town of Corcora, and of the luxuriant country through which we travelled, and of another which was rough, in which we lost one another at night, and how the tigers fought us.*

On the morning of Tuesday, seeing that the friar did not come, we commenced our journey for the space of two leagues up a river which was very pretty with verdure, and trees without fruit ; on either side were very high slopes of mountains, with much tillage of wheat and barley, and beautiful wild olive trees which looked like new olive trees, because they are frequently pruned and cut to allow of wheat and barley growing. In the middle of this valley is a handsome church, house of Our Lady. It has around it small houses for the priests, and twelve cypress trees, the highest and thickest that could be mentioned, and many other trees. Close to the principal door there is a very graceful fountain, and around the church large fields (but all irrigated), which are sown all the year round with all sorts of seed, that is to say, wheat, barley, millet, grain, lentils, peas, beans, tafo, daguza,[1] and as many other vegetables as there are in the country, some sown, others green, others ripe, others reaped, and others threshed. At the head of this valley there is a very high ascent, and before sighting it there is a church which has no other population except a very few houses for the priests; it is a very dry country. In sight of it is an old wall, in which is the form of a portal, as though in former times it guarded that pass, which guards itself by the wildness of the mountain ridge, for the people of the country say that for more than twenty leagues there is not another pass from one side to the other : it fully appears to be so from the many people who flock hither. Descending this mountain by another descent, such as was the ascent, we came at last to a great plain of much extensive tillage of seed crops for all the year (like those behind), and much pasture grass. At the entrance of this plain there is a large and handsome church, its patron Quercos, accompanied by good houses for the priests, almost like an enclosed monastery, and then a Beteneguz, and a large town above it. This plain or valley is about two leagues in length, and half a league wide, and on either side very high mountain ranges. At the feet of the hills, on both sides, there are many small towns and churches in them. Among these churches there are two monasteries, one at one end, the other at the other. One is of Holy Cross, the other of St. John. Both are small, and of few friars, each has no more than ten or twelve friars. In this plain we began to change to a new feature of the country, entering a mountain range not so much high as deep. We passed part of the night separated from one another. In the party where the ambassador went there were four, and I

---

[1] *Dagusa (Eleusine tocusso)*, used for bread, but more for brewing beer. Mansfield Parkyns says (vol. i, p. 265) : "very little 'teff' is grown in this neighbourhood, but chiefly millet *(masho'la)* and *dayousha*".

was with them, in the other there were two, and the baggage was amongst those cliffs, as it pleased God, with one man alone. In the direction in which I was going we saw fire outside of the valleys,[1] and as it was night it seemed to be near, it was more than two leagues off. While we were going in its direction so many tigers followed us that it was a thing not to be believed, and if we approached near any bushes they came so close to us that at close quarters[2] one might have struck them with a lance. In our company there was not more than one lance, all the others carried their swords drawn, and I, who did not bear any, went in the midst of them. Following the fire we arrived close to a wood, and we said, if we enter the wood we shall be devoured by these tigers, let us turn back to the tilled land, and sleep there. So we halted on the cleanest place we found, in the middle of a ploughed field, and fastened the mules all together. The companions, of their goodness, said to me: Father do you sleep, and we will watch over the mules with drawn swords; and so they did. On the next day, at two hours after midday, we all came together again with the ambassador; and even then not all, and we came together in a town which was about two leagues from where we slept, which is called Manadel. This town is one of about a thousand inhabitants, all Moors tributary to Prester John. At one end, as if apart, there live twenty or thirty Christians, who abide here with their wives, and these Christians receive dues as toll. And because I said that the nature of the country had changed, I say that it was two months since we began to travel, and it was always winter, but in this country which we were entering, and where we lost ourselves, it was not winter; rather indeed it was a hot summer. This is one of the countries, that is to say, of the three that I named before in Chapter xxv, where it is winter in February, March, and April, and this country is named

---

[1] Valaras. [2] Maolente.

Dobaa. These lands which have the winter season changed are low lands lying beneath the mountains. The size of this country of Dobaa is five long days' journey in length; I do not know what its width may be, because it enters far into the country of the Moors, so that I could not learn it. In this country there are very beautiful cows, which cannot be numbered or reckoned, and of the largest that can be found in the world. Before we reached this town of Manadeley, on an uncultivated mountain, we heard great shouts: we went up to the bushes and found there many christian people, with their tents pitched, and on our asking them why they were there, they replied that they were entreating the mercy of God that He might give them water, for they were losing their flocks, and were not sowing their millet nor any other seed, with the drought. Their cry was "Zio mazera Christus",[1] which means: "Christ God have mercy upon us." This town of Manadeley is a town of very great trade, like a great city or seaport. Here they find all kinds of merchandise that there is in the world, and merchants of all nations, also all the languages of the Moors, from Giada, from Morocco, Fez, Bugia, Tunis, Turks, Roumys, Greeks, Moors of India, Ormuz, and Cairo, also they bring merchandise from all parts. While we were in this country the Moors, inhabitants of this town, were complaining, saying that the Prester John had by force levied upon them a thousand ouquias of gold, saying that he borrowed them to trade with, and that each year they were to give him another thousand ouquias profit, and that his own thousand should always remain alive. The natives and dwellers in the city said that if it were not for the breeding of flocks they would go away from the country. (Foreigners have nothing to do with this.) They also say that besides this if the Prester John took away from them the Tigrimahom to whom this country belonged he would

---

[1] *Igzio maranna kristos.*

give them another plunderer. So they complain that they
are unable to live (according as they say). In this town a
great fair is held on Tuesday of each week, of as many
things as can be named, and of an infinite number of people
from the neighbouring districts; and it is a fair every day
in the square, for all that merchants require to do.

CAP. XLVII.—*How the friar reached us in this town, and then
we set out on our way to a town named Farso: of the
crops which are gathered in it, and of the bread they
eat, and wine they drink.*

While we were in this town of Manadeley, half forgetting
the friar, there reached us a message that he was coming,
and was bringing mules and camels to conduct us. Immediately some of us went out to receive him with joy and
pleasure, having forgotten our first meeting. As soon as he
arrived we at once departed, and we had not yet gone half a
league, and then after another half league had been traversed
we did not travel further. We went to sleep at a Beteneguz,
which is in a mountain. Next day we travelled a distance
of two leagues, and went to sleep at a large town of
Christians, which may have near a thousand inhabitants: it
is named Farso. There are more than a hundred priests
and friars in the church of this town, and as many nuns:
they have not got a monastery, they lodge about the town
like laywomen. The friars are almost set apart in two
courts, in which are a number of cottages, an unsubstantial
matter, so great is the number of these friars, priests, and
nuns, and the other people who are short of room. In other
churches it is always the custom to give the communion
before the door of the church, and these priests go and give
the communion out of its place, in an open space belonging to
the church, in a tent of silk which they pitch there, very
well arranged, and there they carry on their solemnity of

music with their drums and tambourines, and when they give
the communion it is given as they do in other churches, where
it is the custom to give it at the church door, and in no other
place. Two nights that we slept in this town the nuns
came to wash our feet, and drank of the water after they
had washed them, and they washed their face with it, saying
that we were holy christians of Jerusalem. At this town
there is much tillage of all kinds. Here we saw plots of
coriander, like those of wheat, and no less of a seed which is
called *nug*, which is like pampilhos,[1] and with their heads,
after they are quite ripe and dry, they make oil. Not this
time, but another that we came here, when we had more
knowledge of the country, and the people of the country
had more knowledge of us, I heard inhabitants of this
town say that in that year they had gathered so much crops
of all kinds, that if it were not for the worm, it would have
been abundance for ten years. And because I was amazed,
they said to me: Honoured guest, do not be amazed, because
in the years that we harvest little we gather enough for
three years' plenty in the country; and if it were not for
the multitude of locusts and the hail, which sometimes do
great damage, we should not sow the half of what we sow,
because so much remains that it cannot be believed, so it is
sowing wheat, or barley, lentils, pulse, or any other seed.
And we sow so much with the hope that even if each of
those said plagues should come, some would be spoiled, and
some would remain, and if all was spoiled the year before is
in such manner abundant that we have no scarcity. This
town is almost in a valley, and above it are two hills, and
here we kept a Saturday and a Sunday. We used to go up
to these hills in the afternoons, to see the beautiful herds of
cows that were collected on the skirts of the town, and of
the hills. Those of our company guessed[2] them at fifty

---

[1] *Nug (Guizotia oleifera)*, *Pampilhos*, a plant like *olho de boy.*
[2] *Apodavam.*

thousand cows. I do not say a larger number, and yet the multitude there is cannot be believed. The language of this country is like that we had passed, and here begins the language of the kingdom of Angote, which is named Angutinha, and the country also. This town is the frontier of the kingdom of the Tigrimahom, as far as the Moors who are named the Dobas. After we had passed twice through this district (as I said above), there happened a good thing in it. It has two high hills, and they always have watchmen on them, because further on from this is country of the Moors. There are great plains, although wooded, and they extend quite two leagues, and then are the mountain ranges in which the Moors live. The watchmen saw the Moors come, and they emptied the place and fled away; the Moors came and plundered the provisions which they found, and took away what they could or chose. The watchmen were ashamed of having run away, and communicated with several neighbouring towns to the effect that if they saw them make signals they should come to their assistance, because they had determined to await the Moors if they should return there. These did not long delay returning, the people of the place made their signals, many people flocked to them, and came into the field against the Moors. God was pleased to assist the Christians, who killed eight hundred Moors, and of the Christians there died five. The Christians cut off the heads of all the Moors, and went and stuck them on trees half a league from there, along the great roads by which all people pass, and they sent the shields and javelins of all the dead Moors to the Prester John (this was whilst we were at court). And on our coming on our return from there we found the heads suspended to the trees along the road, as has been said: and we felt fear and disgust at passing under them. In all this country they make bread of any grain, as with wheat, barley, maize, pulse, peas, lentils, small beans, beans, linseed, and teff;

they also make wine from many of these seeds : and the
wine of honey is much the best of all. As the common
people gave us victuals, since the friar found us, by order of
the Prester John, they gave us of this bread, and as it was
not of wheat, we could not eat it, also they brought it at
unseasonable hours, because in all this country it is the
custom to eat only once a day, and that is at night. Besides
this their food is raw meat, and they make a sauce for it
with cow-dung, and that we did not eat : nor of the bread,
unless it was of wheat, or at least of peas. Of the flesh we
ordered our slaves to prepare food for us, until the friar
came to adopt our custom, and to know our wishes, and
endeavoured to give us fowls, mutton and beef, boiled or
roasted, this done by our slaves.

CAP. XLVIII.—*How we departed from the town of Farso, well
prepared, because we had to pass the skirt of the country
of the Moors.*

We set out from this town, and travelled through thick
maize fields, as high as large cane brakes, and we went to
sleep at no great distance, at the foot of a hill close to a
church, because at night we were always away from the
road, and near the towns, on account of the food which they
gave us. Here the friar told us not to scatter ourselves,
and all to keep close together, with our arms ready, and all
the goods in front, because we had to pass a very dangerous
country of Moors, who are always hostile. From this road
which we were now travelling, which is towards the sea, and
towards the South, all are Moors, who are named Dobas,
because the country is named Doba, and it is not a kingdom.
They say that there are twenty-four captaincies, and that
at times twelve of them are at peace, and the others always
at war. In our time we saw them all at war, and we saw
the twelve captains who are used to be at peace at times, all

at the court, for they had made a rising, and were come to make peace. When they came near the tent of Prester John each of these captains carried a stone upon his head, holding it with both his hands. They said that this was a sign of peace, and that they came to sue for mercy. These captains were received with honour, and they brought with them more than a hundred men, and very good led horses and mules, because they entered on foot with the stones on their heads. They may have stayed at court more than two months : they gave them each day beef, mutton, honey, and butter. At the conclusion of peace the Prester John ordered them to be banished from their country more than a hundred leagues, and ordered the captains and people they brought with them to be placed in the kingdom of Damute, with numerous guards. As soon as the people of these captains learned that their lords had been banished they made other captains, and raised the whole country in war. And another time that we were travelling by this road we had to keep Twelfth-day in this country, and it was on a Friday, so we rested Friday, Saturday, and Sunday. At this time, on account of the rising of these captains, the Prester John sent thither many gentlemen, captains of the country, and they went and pitched their camp on a mountain which showed from where we were halting, and we saw the smoke which they made there. The ambassador arranged to send thither two Portuguese to visit those captains and lords, on his part : and they brought back six cows which the captains sent us, and these Portuguese told us that some very great lords were there as captains, and that they had there more than fifteen thousand men, placed in a very large enclosure of thorny bushes, and they name this enclosure *catamar*;[1] and the Portuguese said that they had water outside of the enclosure, and that they did not dare go for it, nor take the horses and mules to drink, except with a

¹ *Cătāma*, a camp.

large force, because if the Moors saw only a small number they rushed upon them and killed them. They also related that every Saturday and Sunday the Moors came and affronted them, because the Christians do not fight on those days. It is said that this war and ill-feeling is with this Prester John, more than with his predecessors, inasmuch as they are tributaries of the Prester. The preceding Presters, until the father of this one who now reigns, always had five or six wives, and they had them from the daughters of the neighbouring Moorish Kings, and from the Pagans; and from the captains of these lordships or captaincies they had one or two, if they found them suitable; and from the King of Dancali another; and from the King of Adel, and the King of Adea. And at the present times known to us there arrived for this David who now reigns, a daughter of the King of Adea, before he had any other wife, and because she had large front teeth, when he saw her he did not like her. And because he had already ordered her to be made a Christian, and she could not return to her father, he gave her in marriage to a great lord; and he did not choose to take any other daughter of a Moorish King, nor of these lordships, and married the daughter of a Christian, and would not have more than one wife, saying that he would follow the law of the gospel. He asks for the tribute from these Kings, his tributaries, which their predecessors were obliged to pay him. They did not bring him this tribute on account of the marriage, and for that reason make this war, which is being continually waged. They also say in this country that these Dobas are such great warriors, that they have a law amongst them that they cannot take a wife without a man's being able to certify that he has killed twelve Christians. No one passes here by this road except in a cafila, which they call a *negada*.[1] This assemblage passes twice a week, once in coming, and another time

---

[1] Or Caravan of merchants.

returning, or to express it better, one goes and the other comes; and there always pass a thousand persons and upwards, with a captain of the *negadas*, who awaits them in certain places. There are two captains, because the negada commences in two parts, and they set out from one end and from the other. These negadas have their origin in two fairs, that is to say, in Manadeley and in Corcora of Angote; and yet, even with these negadas and assemblages, many people are killed in the passage. I know this, because a nephew of mine, a gentleman of the household of the *King* our sovereign, and a servant of the ambassador of Portugal, Don Rodrigo, determined to pass with this negada; and they told us that the Doba Moors had attacked the van, and had killed twelve persons before the people could put themselves on guard. It is a great peril traversing this evil pass, because it is a two days' journey, all through level ground and very large woods, and very high and dense thickets of thorn bushes; and in these two marches, besides that the road is flat and very long, and that they frequently cut them, that is, the thorn bushes near the road, and set fire to them, yet they do not burn, except those that are cut and dried, and some that have withered at the roots, because the thorn bushes which are standing remain in their strength. It is about two leagues from this road to the district of the Dobas, at the commencement of the mountain range, and the ground is flat throughout these thorn thickets. There are in these lands or mountains an infinite number of elephants and other animals, as in the other mountains.

CAP. XLIX.—*How the people of Janamora have the conquest of these Doba Moors, and of the great storm of rain that came upon us during our halt in a river channel.*

The conquest[1] of these Moors of Doba is of a great captain named Xuum Janamora, that is captain of the country. The captaincy is named Janamora, which is a large district, with many people subject to it, and all of it mountainous. They say that they are good warriors, and so they ought to be, for they always keep an eye over their shoulder. In the lands and mountains where they dwell, the Moors come to burn the houses and churches, and carry off the cows from the yards. In this country I saw a priest with poisoned arrows; and I opposed him on account of its being ill done, as he was a priest. He answered me: Look that way, and you will see the church burnt by the Moors, and close to it they carried off from me fifty cows, and also they burned my beehives, which were my livelihood; for that reason I carry this poison,[2] to kill him who has killed me. I did not know what to answer him, with the sorrowfulness which I saw in his countenance, and perceived in his heart. We set out from this halt, and travelled by the said flat road, alongside the hills which are on the side of the Christians, and all peopled by these Janamoras, and we crossed rivers which descend from the said mountains, and close to one of them we went to take our midday rest in some good shade of willow trees. It was very hot, and the sun and day were very bright, and the river did not bring water enough to irrigate a garden. We were divided into two parties, on each side of the water, at speaking distance. During this there began thunder a long way off,

---

[1] Conquest here means maintaining the struggle, or the duty of conquering. Whilst the Moors were still unconquered in the south of Spain, certain parts of their territory were said to belong to the Conquest of Castile, others to the Conquest of Aragon.

[2] *Poçoncha.*

and we said that these were thunderstorms such as there
are sometimes in India. Being in security, without there
being here any wind or rain, and the said thunder having
ceased, we commenced collecting the baggage to set out;
and there was a tent where we dined and reposed ourselves.
The halt having ended, one of our Portuguese, that is,
Mestre Joam, went sauntering along the river up stream,
and immediately returned running, and calling out with
loud shouts: Take care, take care. We all looked in the
direction from which he came shouting, and we saw water
coming, of the height of a lance (without any doubt), and
quite straight and square: and we could not take care sufficiently to prevent its carrying away part of our goods.
And it would have carried away both us and our goods if
we had still been staying in the tent where we had dined.
From me, amongst other things, it carried off a breviary
and a bottle full of wine which I carried for celebrating the
masses; and so, likewise, it carried off a portion from each
of us. From one it took a cloak, from another a hat, from
another a sword; another, in escaping, fell in such a manner, that on the one hand it was a fearful thing, and on the
other a matter for laughter. It pleased God that I had got
the silver chalice put in the skin of a kid and hung up at
the height of a man on the trunk of a willow tree; and a
man of the country ran to it, and saved the chalice, for he
climbed up the willow tree with it, and remained there
until the water went down. This river came from among
very high mountains, among which it had overflowed, and
out of them came this water in a mass. This river brought
down stones as big as barrels of twelve almudes,[1] and from
the noise made by these stones it seemed that the earth was
being overwhelmed, and that the heavens were falling. It
was a thing not to be believed; and as this water came
suddenly, so also it passed away in a short space of time,

[1] Twenty-six almudes make a pipe.

for even this day we crossed over it, and we did not see in
it the rocks which we had before seen, and we saw others
newly come which had descended from the mountains.   We
went to sleep at some poor houses, or near them, where
they received us throwing stones at us, and we slept without supper, and under heavy rains which fell in the night,
with thunderstorms in the flat land, as there had been by
day in the mountains.

CAP. L.—*How we departed from this poor place, and of the
fright they gave us, and how we went to sleep Saturday
and Sunday at a river named Sabalete.*

We set out from this place, we and the Portuguese, because there was nothing to eat, for the country is very
sterile; and we left the friar with all our goods which could
not travel, and we had not got people to carry it.   Before
we started they caused us more fear than we had before,
telling us that, besides the Moors, there were there many
robbers, who went about among the thickets, and killed
travellers with poisoned arrows; and because we had generally seen them carried we had more fear.   So they told us
to go all together, and with our weapons ready.   The road
which we travelled this day was flat, like that behind, and with
larger thickets; the road was wider, because every year they
cut the bushes. We always travelled alongside the mountains,
as we did the day before, and further off from the mountains
of the Moors, because every step we left them further off.
With all this, they said that there was greater danger here,
and that there were wider passages of dry rivers and thick
woods, where bad people might lie in wait.   They also
inspired us with fear, telling us not to sleep on the low
ground, nor to rest near the water, because the country was
very unwholesome, and that we ought to ascend to the high

ground as much as possible. Thus, we travelled without
our baggage all that day, and came to sleep at a large river
named Sabalete, at which river the kingdom of Tigrimahom
ends, and the kingdom of Angote begins. On a very high
hill to the westward of this river is a church of St. Peter,
which is called in our language San Pedro d'Angote ; and
they say that it is the head of this kingdom, and that it is
the church of the kings, and that when this kingdom is
bestowed they come here to take possession of it. And on
the eastern side, on another very high mountain, which is
two or three leagues from this road (and now it is not a
country of the Moors), is a monastery which they say is
large and of much revenue and many friars. However, we
saw nothing of it, except the trees. At this river we remained Saturday and Sunday, and on Sunday night, at the
first sleep, the tigers attacked us, with all the fires we had
burning, and a great part of the mules got loose, and we at
once caught most of them. One mule and an ass escaped,
and we thought they had been devoured. Next day, in the
morning, they came from a village to tell us that in the
night two runaway beasts had come there, and that we
should see if they were ours, and go there and fetch them.
On Monday, the 3rd of October of 1520, we set out on our
way, and travelled for two leagues along a very flat road,
and from that spot the friar, who was now with us with the
goods, took us by some very rough roads over mountains,
to sleep at some pinnacles, saying that the low grounds
were sickly. The goods could not ascend, and remained on
the road. On account of this night's halt, we were all discontented with the friar, and told him not to bring us and
our mules up such mountain ridges ; that we were not afraid
of sickness, and if he did it for the sake of eating, that we
were bringing the goods of the King of Portugal, to provide ourselves withal, and to be able to give him food also.
Here he said that he would not again bring us out of the

road, and that he would go wherever we pleased, and that we should be satisfied. On Tuesday we descended from the said pinnacle, and came back to the road where the baggage had remained, close to a large church of Our Lady. Here we had our midday rest. This church has many priests, and friars, and nuns, and it is directed by the priests. This town is named Corcora of Angote. It is different from Corcora[1] of the Tigrimahom, where on Wednesday of every week there is a great market or fair. At this church we left the camels, with a large part of the goods, because[2] they could not go any further over the rough mountains that we had to pass; and this afternoon we crossed a mountain with great labour, for in many places we went on foot, and with both feet and hands, like cats. We passed this bad road over a mountain ridge, still between other ridges. There are two hills almost level ground, between which lies a valley of great pastures and tillage of all sorts of seeds, which grow all the year round, because we passed by here several times, and we always found wheat just sown, and other wheat springing up, and other in grass, other in the ear, other ripe, and other reaped or threshed on the threshing floor; and so with other seeds of this country, for in the same manner as it is with the wheat, so it is with all other things. This land is not irrigated, because it is almost marshy; and all the land of this nature, or which is capable of irrigation, gives crops all through the year; when one is got in another is sown. In this country, on both sides, on all the slopes, there are an infinite number of towns, and all have their churches; it is a very good country. For a man to know where the churches are, they have around them large trees; by that they are known, even before they are reached.

---

[1] Both these towns of Corcora are in the modern maps.

[2] *Por amor de unas sierras.*

CAP. LI.—*Of the church of Ancona, and how in the kingdom of Angote iron and salt are current for money, and of a monastery which is in a cave.*

On the following Wednesday we travelled (not a long way), and began to descend through a large and beautiful valley and lowland, where there were large fields of millet and beans. This vale is named the country of Ancona. At the head of this vale is a very noble church named St. Mary of Ancona (as they say), of great revenues. This church has many canons, and an Alicanate over them. Besides these canons it has many priests and friars. All the large churches here and further on are named King's churches, all have canons, whom they call Debeteras, and in all an Alicanate, who is like a prior. This church has two small bells, badly made, and they are low down near the ground, and as yet we had not seen any others in all the country that we had gone through. We remained in this town till Thursday, because there is then a great market, which they call *gabeja*.[1] In this country, and in all the kingdom of Angote, iron is current as money. It is made like a shovel, and this shape is of no advantage for anything, except for making something else with it. Of these pieces of iron, ten, eleven, and sometimes twelve, are worth a drachm, which in our Portugal, or in India, would be worth a cruzado (as has been said). Salt also is current as money, because it is current in all the country: here six or seven blocks of salt are worth one piece of iron. From here there lies almost opposite to the westward, a large country named Abrigima: it is a country of very high mountains, and very cold. On the top of this mountain there is much matting grass,[2] and they say that it is very good. I brought some of it to the Genoese who were with us, and they said that they had never seen so good, and that it was better

[1] *Gabya.*   [2] *Esparto.*

than that of Alicante. The provisions of these mountains
are all barley in the low ground, and wheat in the valleys,
the best that can be named among many other good wheats.
The flocks, both cows, sheep, and goats, are very small, as
in the country of Maia, between Douro and Minho, in
Portugal. They call this country Abime raz, it is under
Angote raz, which is the kingdom of Angote. This
country of Abrigima is six days' journey in length, and
three in breadth. They say that after the country of
Aquaxumo became christian with its neighbourhood, this
country followed next after it. In this country the Kings
had their tribunal, as the Queens had in Aquaxumo. Whilst
this country is so sterile, and at first sight sad, there are in
it the edifices which I saw. First, in a very high mountain,
there is a very great cave, and within it is a handsome
monastery, house of Our Lady, named Iconoamelaca,[1] which
means : God gives it plenty; and the spot of land is named
Acate. The house is not so large, as is its elegance. It
has not got large revenues, yet it has a great number of
friars and nuns. The friars have their dwelling above the
cavern, entirely enclosed, and they go down to the monastery
by a single path. The nuns have their dwelling below the
cavern, they are not enclosed, they live upon the slope of the
mountain. All these friars and nuns dig and prune in this
country, and they sow wheat and barley, which they eat, for
the monastery gives them little. The affection which they
bear to this country, and to the monastery, makes them
dwell there. This monastery is inside this cavern, and well
built in a cross, well contained in the cave, so that they go
freely with their procession round the building. In front of
the door of this house there is a wall ten or twelve fathoms
long, and as high as the edge of the cave, and between the
wall and door of the monastery, for there are no churches
within the enclosure of the cave, there is a space of five

---

[1] *Yikun amlak*, may he be Lord.

fathoms, here the nuns stand to hear the offices, and here
they receive the communion. This station of the nuns lies
to the south, because the church lies east and west, and the
station is on the side of the epistle.[1] Above this cave,
descending from the mountain, a river runs during the
whole year, and the water falls on the right hand of this
monastery, near the place where the nuns are, much beyond
the wall which shelters them. The friars, even if they were
much more numerous than they are, would find room in the
cave around the church, although they do not enter it. The
monastery, or body of the church, has three doors, that is,
one principal, and two side doors, as though it were in the
open air, and one is wide. And because I say that it is in
the form of a cross, it is in this manner, namely, of the
form and size of a monastery of San Frutuoso, which is
close to the city of Braga, in the kingdom of Portugal.

CAP. LII.—*Of a church of canons who are in another cave in
this same lordship, in which lie a Prester John and a
Patriarch of Alexandria.*

This monastery before mentioned possesses, at two days'
journey to the west, a large and rich church in another cave;
according to my judgment three large ships with their
masts would find room in this cave. The entrance to it is
not larger than to allow two carts with their side rails[2] to
enter. Above this cave the mountain continues to rise for
quite two leagues. I walked over them, and was near
dying in them from the great ascent, and with the great
cold there was. God protected me. And I was fastened to

---

[1] This passage is not very clear. Selves translates: "the church lies to
the east, and the Epistle is said at the west".

[2] *Fueiros*, projections over the sides of a cart to enable it to carry
more load, side rails, wings, thripples, shelvings.

a cord, and a strong slave to pull it, who assisted me to
ascend, and another behind who drove the mules, because I
did not send them in front for fear of their falling upon me.
We started before morning, and at midday we had not
finished ascending the ground. This church which is in
this cave is very large, like a cathedral, with its large
naves, very well wrought, and well vaulted: it has three
very rich chapels, and well adorned altars. The entrance
of this cave is to the east, and the backs of the chapels are
that way, and if one goes at the hour of tierce[1] there is no
seeing in the church, all the offices are done with lamps.
There are in this church (as they say) two hundred canons
or debeteras, according to their language; I saw an infinite
number, they have not got friars; they have an alicamate, a
very noble prior: he is over all of them, as has been said
before. They say that it has much revenue. These canons
are like well-to-do and honourable men. This church is
named Imbra Christus, which means the path of Christ.
Entering this cave a man faces the chapels, and on the
right hand when one enters are two painted chambers,
which belonged to a King who lived in this cave, and who
ordered this church to be built. On the epistle side are
three honoured sepulchres, and as yet we had not seen
others such in Ethiopia. This principally is high, and has
five steps all around it. The tombs are in this manner.
This tomb is covered with a large cloth of brocade, and
velvet of Mekkah, one cloth of one stuff, and another of
the other, which on both sides reach the ground. It was
covered over, because it was the day of its great festival.
They say that this tomb belongs to the King who lived
here, whose name was Abraham. And the other two
sepulchres are of the same fashion, except that one of them has
four steps, and the other three: and all are in the middle of
the cave. They say that the largest of these two belongs

---

[1] Terza, nine o'clock.

to a Patriarch of Alexandria, who came to see this King,
having heard of his sanctity, and he died here.   The
smallest and the lowest belongs they say to a daughter of
this King.   They also say that this King was a mass priest
for forty years, and that after he withdrew himself he said
mass in this church each day : and this is written in a large
and ancient book, which I saw with my eyes and had in my
hands, quite like a chronicle or life of this King, and they
went over part of it with me during two days that I was
there at leisure.   Among other miracles which they related
of this King, and which they read to me in this book, is
that when he wished to celebrate the angels administered to
him what was requisite, that is, bread and wine, and this
was in those forty years that he was in retreat.   In the
beginning of this book this King is painted with the state
of a priest before the altar, and from a window in the same
painting there comes out a hand with a roll and a little
pitcher of wine, as though it brought bread and wine ; and
so it is painted in the principal chapel.   (I say that I heard
and saw it read in the book.)   And besides that the canons
told me that the stone of which this church was built had
come from Jerusalem, and that it is like the stone of
Jerusalem, which is dark and of a fine grain.   And going
on the mountain above, where my slave led me or assisted
me, at the top of the mountain I found an ancient quarry,
with great excavations and many pieces of stone, and very
large stones with ancient wedges.[1]   I looked at these stones
with great care, and this stone is of the same colour and
grain as that of the church, because I broke off some pieces
of it, and examined it well, and knew that it was the same
stone, and that the stone for the church had been brought
from here, and had not come from Jerusalem as they had
told me.   It is also written in the said book that during the
whole life of this King he had not taken dues from his

[1] *Cunhciras*, not in the dictionaries, possibly for wedge marks.

vassals, and if anyone brought them to him, that he ordered them to be distributed among the poor; and his maintenance was from the great tillage which he used to order to be made. It is also written that to this King it was revealed that there ought not to be any relations of the King in his dominions, that all of them should be shut up, except only the eldest son, the heir, as will be related further on. I saw this church the day of its feast, in order to see that which I had heard of it. There came to it that day fully twenty persons, and all as many as come to it in pilgrimage have to receive the communion. This feast was on a Sunday, and they said mass very quickly, and then they commenced giving the communion at all the three doors of the church, and they finished after nightfall. This I saw because I was at the beginning, and I went away to dinner, and I returned and remained until they finished with torches.

CAP. LIII.—*Of the great church edifices that there are in the country of Abuxima, which King Lalibela built, and of his tomb in the church of Golgotha.*

At a day's journey from this church of Imbra Christo are edifices, the like of which and so many, cannot, as it appears to me, be found in the world, and they are churches entirely excavated in the rock, very well hewn. The names of these churches are these: Emanuel, St. Saviour, St. Mary, Holy Cross, St. George, Golgotha, Bethlehem, Marcoreos, the Martyrs. The principal one is Lalibela. This Lalibela, they say, was a King in this same country for eighty years, and he was King before the one before mentioned who was named Abraham. This King ordered these edifices to be made. He does not lie in the church which bears his name, he lies in the church of Golgotha, which is the church of the fewest buildings here. It is in this manner: all excavated in the stone itself, a hundred and twenty spans in length, and seventy-two spans in width. The ceiling of this church rests on five supports, two on each side, and one in the centre, like fives of dice, and the ceiling or roof is all flat like the floor of the church, the sides also are worked in a fine fashion, also the windows, and the doors with all the tracery, which could be told, so that neither a jeweller in silver, nor a worker of wax in wax, could do more work. The tomb of this King is in the same manner as that of Santiago of Galicia, at Compostella, and it is in this manner: the gallery which goes round the church is like a cloister, and lower than the body of the church, and one goes down from the church to this gallery; there are three windows on each side, that is to say, at that height which the church is higher than the gallery, and as much as the body of the church extends, so much is excavated below, and to as much depth as there is height above the floor of the church. And if one looks through each of these windows which is opposite the sun, one sees the tomb at the right of the high altar. In the centre of the body of the church is the sign of a door like a trap door, it is covered up with a large stone, like an altar stone, fitting very exactly in that door. They say that this is the entrance to the lower chamber, and that no one enters there, nor does it appear that that stone or door can be raised. This stone has a hole in the centre which pierces it through, its size is three palms.[1] All the pilgrims put their hands into this stone (which hardly find room), and say that many miracles are done here. On the left hand side, when one goes from the principal door before the principal chapel, there is a tomb cut in the same rock as the church, which they say is made after the manner of the sepulchre of Christ in Jerusalem. So they hold it in honour and veneration and reverence, as becomes the memory to which it belongs. In the other

---

[1] *Palmo*, measure of four inches.

part of the church are two great images carved in the wall
itself, which remain in a manner separated from it. They
showed me these things as though I should be amazed at
seeing them. One of the images is of St. Peter, the other
of St. John : they give them great reverence. This church
also possesses a separate chapel, almost a church; this has
naves on six supports, that is, three on each side. This is
very well constructed, with much elegance: the middle
nave is raised and arched, its windows and doorways are
well wrought, that is, the principal door, and one side door,
for the other gives entrance to the principal church. This
chapel is as broad as it is long, that is, fifty-two spans
broad, and as many in length. It has another chapel, very
high and small, like a pinnacle,[1] with many windows in the
same height : these also have as much width as length, that
is, twelve spans. This church and its chapels have their
altars and canopies, with their supports, made of the rock
itself, it also has a very great circuit cut out of the rock.
The circuit is on the same level as the church itself, and is
all square : all its walls are pierced with holes the size of the
mouth of a barrel. All these holes are stopped up with
small stones, and they say that they are tombs, and such
they appear to be, because some have been stopped up
since a long time, others recently. The entrance of this
circuit is below the rock, at a great depth and measure of
thirteen spans, all artificially excavated, or worked with the
pick-axe, for here there is no digging, because the stone is
hard, and for great walls like the Porto in Portugal.

[1] *Coruchco*; Selves calls it *coroza*.

Cap. LIV.—*Of the fashion of the church of San Salvador, and of other churches which are in the said town, and of the birth of King Lalibela, and the dues of this country.*

The church of St. Saviour stands alone, cut out of a rock; it is very large. Its interior is two hundred spans in length, and a hundred and twenty in width. It has five naves, in each one seven square columns; the large one has four, and the walls of the church have as much. The columns are very well worked, with arches which hang down a span below the vaulted roof. The vaulted roofs are very well worked, and of great height, principally the centre one, which is very high. It is of a handsome height; most of the ends are lower, all in proportion. In the principal height of these naves there is much tracery, such as . . . . ,[1] or keystones, or roses, which they put on the vaults, on which they make roses and other graceful works. On the sides it has very pretty windows, with much tracery, long and narrow in the middle. Within and without, these are long, like the loopholes[2] of a wall, narrow without and wide within; these are wide both within and without, and narrow in the middle, with arches and tracery. The principal chapel is very high, and the canopy over the altar is very high, with a support at each corner. All this is made from the rock itself. In the other naves they do not deck the chapels and altars with canopies like the high altar in its grandeur. The principal door has at each side many and large buttresses, and the door commences with very large arches, and goes on narrowing with other arches until they reach a small door, which is not more than nine spans high and four and a half wide. The side doors are in this manner, only that they do not commence with so much width, and they end with the width of the principal door. On the outside part of this church are seven buttresses with

[1] *Espelhos.*   [2] *Frechciros.*

arches,[1] which are twelve palms distant from the wall of
the church, and from buttress to buttress an arch, and
above the church, on these arches, a vault constructed in
such manner that if it were built of pieces and soft stone it
could not be straighter nor better constructed, nor with
more work about it. These arches outside may be about
the height of two lances. There is not any variation in the
whole of this rock in which this church stands; it all looks
like one block of marble. The court or cloister which the
church has round it is all worked with the same stone. It
is sixty palms wide at each end, and in front of the principal church door quite a hundred palms. Above this church,
where it should be roofed, there are on each side nine large
arches, like cloisters, which descend from the top to the
bottom, to the tombs along the sides,[2] as in the other
church. The entrance to this church is by a descent through
the rock itself, eighty steps cut artificially in the stone, of
a width that ten men can go side by side, and of the height
of a lance or more. This entrance has four holes above,
which give light to the passage above the edges. From this
rock to the enclosure of the church is like a field; there
are many houses, and they sow barley in it.

The house or church of Our Lady is not so large as that
of St. Saviour, but it is very well constructed. It has three
naves, and the centre one is very high, with large loops and
roses very ingeniously carved in the rock itself. Each nave
has five columns, and upon them their arches and vaults,
very high pitched,[2] and well made. It has, besides, a high
column in the cross of the transept, on which is placed a
canopy which from its fretted work looks as if it were
stamped in wax. At the head of each nave there is a

[1] *Lunas.*   [2] Of the wall of inclosure.

[3] *Revindas, Rerindo, a,* not in any dictionary except the *Diccionario
Portatil* of Santa Rosa de Viterbo, Coimbra, 1825, which says: " Arco,
ou abobeda de meio circulo perfeito que dizem de meia volta em berço".

chapel, with its altar like those of St. Saviour; only it has, besides, altars at each of the doors, which are of the size and fashion of those of St. Saviour. It has six buttresses on the exterior; two on each side are adhering to the wall, and four are distant from it, and well made arches spring from one to the other of them, and upon them are very well constructed canopies, which are very high and like a portico, over the doors. These canopies are all of one size, as broad as they are long. It has a very high and graceful circuit, and behind, as well as at the sides and in front, all round of the height of the church. This church is eighty spans in length and sixty-four in width. This church, also, has in front of its principal door, made out of the rock itself, a large house, in which they give food to the poor; and the way out of the church is through this house to the outside, or they enter the church through it underneath the rock a good distance. On each side of this church, in front of the side doors, are two churches each at its end. This church of Our Lady is the head of all the other churches of this place. It has an infinite quantity of canons, and the church which is on the side of the epistle is as long and as wide as that of Our Lady. It has three naves, and in each nave three columns well wrought of level work. It has not got more than one chapel, and one altar, made like those of other churches. Its principal door is very well worked; it does not face outwards, but to a corridor below the rock, which comes like a path to the house of Our Lady. This corridor comes from a distance; where it begins they ascend to it by fifteen steps of the rock itself. This is a very dark entrance. On the side towards the church of Our Lady, this church has a very pretty side door and two very elegant windows, and behind and on the other side all hewn rock and very rough, without having any work whatever. This church is called the Martyrs, and the church which is on the gospel side of the church of Our Lady, is called Holy Cross. It is small, it is sixty-eight spans in length, it has not got naves, it has three columns in the middle, which appear to have their tops above *(the roof)*, very well made and vaulted; inside all is smooth work. On the side of Our Lady's church it has a very handsome side door and two well made windows; it has a single altar, like others; the principal door is well wrought. It has not got a court nor faces outwards, only to a corridor like a path, which goes outside, underneath the rock, very long and very dark.

The church of Emanuel is well wrought, both inside and out, it is small. It is forty-two spans in length inside, and twenty in width. It has three naves, the middle one very high and with domed[1] vaults: the side naves are not vaulted, and are flat underneath, that is, the ceiling is like the floor of the church. These naves are upon five supports: the breadth and thickness of these supports are of four spans from corner to corner, and the wall of the church has four others. It has very well worked doors, both the side and principal doors, and all of the same size, that is to say, nine spans high, and four wide. It is all enclosed; on the outside there is a space[2] of three steps, which go all round it, except at the doors, which each have a wide court, each with five steps above those which surround the church. It is all of the rock itself, without a piece or fault. This church also has what none of the others have, that is, a choir, to which they ascend by a spiral staircase: it is not large, for a tall man with a span more would knock his head against the ceiling, which is flat, like the floor of the church, and so also over the naves and sides, large as they are; they go to small cells by doors from one to another, and from the choir itself doors open to these little rooms or cells. They do not make use of this choir except for keeping there chests of vestments and church ornaments. These chests must have been made inside this choir,

[1] *Recinda.*   [2] *Curral.*

because they could not enter by any way, I do not know how they could come in even in pieces. The outside walls of this church, also, have what others have not, that is to say, like tiers of walls, one bends outwards and another turns inwards two inches, another, again, turns outwards and another goes inwards, and so it is from the commencement of the steps to the top of the church; and the tier of stone which goes outwards is two spans wide, and that going inwards one span, and in this fashion and width they cover the whole wall, and reckoning up the spans, this wall is 52 spans high. The church has its circuit cut like a wall outside, and inside of the rock itself, and this wall is entered by three good doors like small gates of a city or walled town.

The church of St. George is a good bit lower down than the others, almost separated from the place; it is in the rock, like the others. The entrance to it is under the rock or cliff: there are eight steps to ascend, and when they are ascended one enters into a large house, with a bench which goes all round it on the inside, for outside it is rough rock. In this house alms are given to the poor, who seat themselves on these benches. Entering from this house one comes at once to the church circuit, which is made in the form of a cross. The church also is in the form of a cross, and the distance from the principal door to the chancel is the same as that from one side door to the other, all of one compass. The doors are very well worked outside. I did not go inside, as it was locked. In the circuit of the church, entering from outside, to the right hand, for it is all rough rock, without more than one entrance, there is, at the height of a man or a little more, placed in the wall, a kind of ark full of water. They go up to it by steps; and they say that this water springs there, but it does not flow out: they carry it away for intermittent fevers, and say that it is good for them. All this enclosure is full of tombs, like the other churches. On the top of this church is a large double cross, that is, one within the other, like the crosses of the order of Christ. Outside the circuit the rock is higher than the church, and on this rock are cypresses and wild olive trees. It wearied me to write more of these works, because it seems to me that they will not believe me if I write more, and because as to what I have already written they may accuse me of untruth, therefore I swear by God, in whose power I am, that all that is written is the truth, and there is much more than what I have written, and I have left it that they may not tax me with its being falsehood. And because no other Portuguese went to these works except myself, and I went twice to see them from what I had heard of them. This place is on a slope of the mountain, and from the peak of the mountain to this is a day and a half's journey of descent. This slope or mountain seems to be quite separate from the other mountain, yet it is subject to it, and from this town to the bottom there is still a great descent, and at the end of it a view over four or five leagues, and many great plains which they say are two days' journey distant. (It seemed to me that one could go in one.) They say that there are in these plains other such edifices as those of Aquaxumo, such as stone chairs and other buildings, and that the residences of the Kings were there, like the other buildings of the Queens, and this is in the direction of the Nile. I did not go there, and I relate on hearsay a thing at which I was more amazed. They told me that the works of these churches were done in twenty-four years, and that this is written, and that they were done by Gibetas, that is, white men, for they well know that they do not know how to do any well executed work. They say that King Lalibela ordered this to be done; this name of Lalibela means miracle. They say that he took, or that they gave him, this name, because when he was born he was covered with bees, and that the bees cleaned him without doing him any hurt. They also say that he was not the son of the King, but son of a sister of the King, and that the King died without having a son, and the nephew, the sister's son, inherited the kingdom. They say that he was a saint, and that he did many miracles, and so there is much pilgrimage to this place.

This lordship of Abrigima was given by the Prester John, before our departure, to the ambassador whom he sends to Portugal; and as I say that I came twice to see these churches and edifices, the second time that I came to see them I came with the ambassador, who came to take possession of his lordship. And whilst we were thus going about the country there came to us two *calaces,* which means messengers or word from the King: these calaces said to the ambassador who was taking the lordship of Abrigima, that the Prester John sent to tell him to send him the *gibir,* that is to say, the dues which were owing by his predecessor, for he did not owe anything yet, as he was then taking possession. And what they said was owing was this, namely, a hundred and fifty plough oxen, thirty dogs, thirty assagays, and thirty shields. The new captain gave for answer that he would at once send to know what property was belonging to his predecessor, and that he would pay out of it. In this manner they paid in these kingdoms, as in other places. I have said that those towards Egypt and Arabia pay horses and silks, and so the other lands and lordships pay each their own produce, according to their quality and breed.

CAP. LV.—*How we departed from Ancona, and went to Ingabelu, and how we returned to seek the baggage.*

We departed from the church and fair of Ancona, and having gone a distance of three leagues we reached some villages with all the goods; in these they would not receive

us nor carry our baggage, saying that these villages belonged
to the mother of Prester John, and that they did not obey
any one except her. And they desired to beat the friar who
conducted us, and they did give a beating to one of his men.
We left the baggage here, and went to sleep at a large
town of good houses named Ingabelu. Its situation is on a
hill in the midst of extensive cultivated lands between very
high mountains, the skirts of which are studded with an
infinite number of towns, the largest number and the
greatest that we had yet seen: it seems to me that these
towns exceed a hundred. This town has pretty rivers on
each side of it. They were building here a pretty church
of masonry, of good workmanship ; and that it may not
appear to be a lie that so many towns could be seen from
this Ingabelu, I say that all were not in sight from there,
but we saw them from the mountains by which we passed.
Those which might be furthest off from this town would be
a league and a half. We found in this town an infinite
quantity of fowls, which, if not in a hurry,[1] could be bought
a hundred, if one wanted so many, in exchange for a little
pepper. In this place there are many lemons and citrons :
we remained here Saturday and Sunday. On Sunday night
the tigers sprung into the town, and fell in with a boy and
carried him off. From that place they attacked a large farm
where we were lodging, and there broke loose from us a
mule and an ass, which already once before had escaped at
the river of Sabalete : they got away from the farm house,
the mule jumped into a cow yard and so escaped, and the
ass was devoured. On the morning of Monday the 11th
day of September, we set out from the said town, turning
back to where the baggage had remained, and on the road
we met many people, half peacably inclined, the other half
hostile (these were they who would not receive the baggage),
and their arms were cudgels ; they received us with welcome,

and we did likewise to them, and that night we slept in
their town, and they made amends for the past, for they
gave us very good food. On the following day we set out
on our road, a distance of two leagues or three, and again
slept without our goods. On the Thursday we turned back
again in search of it, and when we found it we still travelled
straight on a good three leagues, all of it crossing mountains
and passing valleys as before, and the whole of it seemed to
be mountains. This Kingdom of Angote is almost all of it
valleys and mountains, and the tilled land has little wheat
and little barley, yet it gives much millet, taffo, and dagusha,
pulse, peas, lentils, beans, many figs, garlic, and onions, and
great abundance of all vegetables. Iron is current as
money in this country, as has been said.

CAP. LVI.—*How the ambassador separated from the friar, and
how those of us who remained with the friar were stoned,
and some captured, and how the ambassador returned,
and we were invited by the Angote raz, and went with him
to church, and of the questions he asked, and dinner he
gave us.*

On Thursday the 14th of the said month of September
our baggage went and stopped at a dry river without any
water at all, and it was about a league from where the
Angote raz was staying: he is the lord of this Kingdom of
Angote. And because it was a dry land, and because the
ambassador had no inclination to speak to the Ras of
Angote, because we had no need of him, he went on before
the baggage a distance of a league and a half, and some of
us went on with him, and others remained with the friar
and the baggage. The friar told us that we should go with
him to a village about a league on one side of the road, and
the baggage remained on the road with the country people

who carried it. As we were travelling, before we arrived at the village, people of the country shouted, and we thought that they were calling people to bring our baggage. But they collected together to shake us, and they took possession of three hills, and we remained in the hollows. On each hill there were quite a hundred men, most of them with slings, and others with their hands threw stones so thickly that they seemed to rain upon us (well did we think of our deaths). There might be in the company of the friar quite forty persons, that is, captains who accompanied him, and his men, and our slaves. There was not one without a blow of a stone, or a wound; I, and a young man who went with us, named Cafu, and who was sick with sores, God was pleased to protect us that we received no stones: but five or six men of the friar, and a captain of Angote, came out with broken heads, and Mestro Joam the same. Not satisfied with wounding, they took prisoners those who were most wounded, and we, those who escaped, returned to sleep at the baggage, without supper. Each one cried out for the bruises from the stones he had received, except myself and the young man of the sores. Friday, in the morning, I set out in search of the ambassador, who was gone on a league and a half. On reaching him they at once got ready; when I related to him the case which had happened to us, he hurried the saddling, mounting, and departure, saying that he would die for the Portuguese. When he and those that came with him arrived at the baggage, we found there the Ras of Angote, who had come to us, and had brought with him a good number of people. When we came up to where he was, the friar who conducted us was with him, the ambassador said to the interpreter: "Tell the Ras of Angote that I do not come to see him nor that friar who is with him, but I come to seek for the Portuguese whom I have lost in his country." Whilst the battle was being related, Mestre Joam arrived, who had remained wounded and a prisoner, he was much covered with blood, and had large wounds on the head, and he said that he had escaped. When a long conversation was ended, which the ambassador, and the Ras of Angote, and the friar, held upon this affair, the Ras of Angote entreated the ambassador that he and I, and our company, should come and stay Saturday and Sunday in his house. The ambassador having consulted with all of us, and it seeming to us good to accede to his entreaty, he granted him the going, and we all went with him, and it might be a league and a half from where we were to his house : and he ordered us to be lodged very well. Here we kept Saturday and Sunday. On Saturday he sent to call us; we came and found him on his dais, his wife and a few people with him : we had no detention on entering, only what takes place in the house of any man. The pomp, presentation, and welcome all consisted in drinking. He had near him four large jars of very good mead, and with each jar a cup of crystalline glass. We began to drink, and his wife and two other women who were with her assisted as well. They would not leave us until the jars were finished, and such is their custom ; each jar held six or seven canadas, and yet he ordered more to be brought. We left him with good excuses, saying we were going away for our necessities.

The following Sunday we went to the church, and there we found the Ras of Angote, who came out to receive us with much good grace. Then he began to talk to me about matters of our holy faith ; he asked to bring apart with me two friars and our interpreter, and the friar who conducted us as a third person ; and they asked me common-place questions.[1] The first was : Where Jesus Christ was born ; what road he

---

[1] *Preguntas d'estrada*, wayside questions. The question about the length of time the Holy Family passed in Egypt was not, however, a simple or purposeless question, as the Abyssinians assert that during that time they visited Abyssinia.

took to Egypt, and how many years he passed there, and
how old he was when his mother, our Lady, lost him, and
found him in the temple; and where he made the water
into wine, and who was there; on what beast he had ridden
into Jerusalem; in what house he had supped in Jerusalem,
and if he had a house of his own there, and who washed his
feet; and what Peter meant, and what Paul meant. Our
Lord was pleased to assist me, that I answered them truly.
Our interpreter told me that the friar who conducted us,
and was there as a third person, told the others that I was
a man who knew much. May God forgive him, but there
was little for me to forget. By reason of what this friar
thus said, they perforce kissed my feet. From what these
friars said of me to the Ras of Angote, he received me with
much good will, and kissed my face. This gentleman, who
is now Ras of Angote, is one of the good priests that there
are in Ethiopia, and at the time of our departure was Barnagais and in gospel orders, who may say mass. At the
end of mass he invited us to come and dine with him, which
dinner we accepted, and the ambassador ordered our dinner
to be taken in as it was; there were very fat roast fowls,
and fat beef boiled with good cabbage : and the ambassador
ordered this to be taken in because their meals are not like
ours. The dinner was in this manner—it should be known
how it is in a great house of one story, which is a Beteneguz : before the raised seat, on which he was seated,
there were many mats spread out; he descended from the
seat, and sat down on the mats, and over the mats they had
put dark sheep skins, and upon them two trays for cleaning
wheat, which they call *ganetas*; these were large and handsome, and very low, they have only a rim of two inches; the
largest of these had sixteen spans circumference, and the
other fourteen. These are the tables of the great lords. We
all sat round with the Ras of Angote : the water came, and
we washed, but no towel came to clean our hands, neither

for putting bread upon, except it was put upon the *ganetas* (trays) themselves; there came bread of different kinds, namely, of wheat, barley, millet, pulse, and taffo. Before we began to eat, the Ras of Angote ordered to be placed before him rolls of that inferior bread, and upon each roll a piece of raw beef, and so he ordered it to be given to the poor who were outside the gate waiting for alms. Upon this we pronounced the blessing according to our usage, at which the Ras of Angote showed much satisfaction. Then came the dainties, and they were these, namely, three sauces or potages, which might well be called sauce of Palmela,[1] one of clove of garlic, and another I know not of what. In these potages there was an admixture of cow dung and of gall, which in this country they consider an esteemed food; and only great personages eat it. These sauces came in small sauce dishes, of a dark clay, and were well made. They put into this sauce the most inferior bread, broken very small, and butter with it. We would not eat of these potages, and the ambassador ordered our victuals to be brought, which he had very well cooked, because we could not eat their viands, neither did they eat ours. The wine was passed round freely.[2] The wife of the Ras of Angote ate close to us, with a curtain betwixt, at a table like ours. She ate her own viands; they also gave her some of ours, I do not know whether she ate them, because the curtain was between her and us. In drinking, she assisted us well. After all the dainties there came a raw breast of beef, and we did not taste it : the Ras of Angote ate some of it, like a person eating cake or other dainties for dessert. So we came to an end of the dinner, and thanks be to God, and we went away to our lodging.

---

[1] *Salsa de Palmela.*　　　　[2] *Era a rodo.*

CAP. LVII.—*How the ambassador took leave of the Ras of Angote, and the friar, with most of us, returned to the place where we were stoned, and from there we went to a fertile country, and a church of many canons.*

On Monday morning we took leave of the Ras of Angote, and the friar who conducted and guided us must needs have us wait for a mule of the Prester John, and an ass with certain baggage, which they had taken from us in the rout of the stone throwing. The ambassador departed with those who had been with him before, and we remained with the friar who had been with him in the hail of stones. On this Monday, near nightfall, they came with the said mule and the ass which had remained there, and the friar at once said that we should start, and that we could still go and sleep where the ambassador was. As it seemed to us it might be so we made ready and departed whilst night was closing in, thinking that we should keep to the road; and he goes and takes us through some bushes, and takes us to where we were stoned, and said he was going to do justice; and there were eight men on mules and fifteen on foot going with us. We went to lodge for the night in the house of one of those chief men who had stoned us, and we found the house and the whole village without people in it. They were all in a mountain which was above the village. We found plenty to eat for ourselves and our mules. As soon as we were in the house those men who came with us left us: certainly we were not without fear, and complained of the friar because he was bringing us to be killed, and because he did not take us on our road. He told us that we came to do justice, and that in the morning we would depart. When morning came he said that we could not go till midday. When we saw this we waited till midday, and when it was midday we required him to start, then he said that we could not go till next day. Seeing these delays, we started and left him. This same day, however, we rejoined the baggage, because it was waiting for us. In the night the friar reached us, because he did not dare to sleep alone among those people who had stoned us, and he brought with him two mules, a cow, and eight pieces of stuff, which they gave him for the blood they had shed. This is their justice, and no other, namely, to take away the goods, which are only mules, cows, and stuffs, from those who can do little. These villages where they stoned us are named, one Angua, and another Mastanho: they said they belonged to the Abima Marcos.

Here we entered into a very pretty country between very high mountains, the feet of which were very thickly peopled with large towns and noble churches. This country is laid out in large tillage fields of all sorts. Here there is an infinite quantity of figs, those of India, many lemons, oranges, and citrons, and extensive pastures of cattle. And on another occasion when I returned here with this friar, who then called himself an ambassador, we came and stayed a Saturday and a Sunday in the house of an honourable debetera, that is, canon, and these two days we went with him to the church: because there were a great number of canons in that church, we asked him how many there might be in it. He told us that there were five thousand three hundred canons, and we asked what revenues they had. He said that they were very little for so many; and we said, since the revenues are so small, why were there so many canons. He told us that at the beginning of that church there were not many, but that afterwards they had increased, because all the sons of canons, and as many as descended from them, remained canons, and the fathers each taught their sons, and so they had been increased in number, and that this happened in the King's churches, and that frequently Prester John diminished them, when he set up a church in a new country, and sent to fetch canons from these churches, as he had ordered two hundred canons to be taken away to the church of Machan Celaco,[1] and that in this valley there were eight churches, and there would be in them fully four thousand canons, and that the Prester took canons from here for the new churches, and also for the churches at court, because otherwise they would eat one another up.

CAP. LVIII.—*Of the mountain in which they put the sons of the Prester John, and how they stoned us near it.*

The above mentioned valley reaches to the mountain where they put the sons of the Prester John. These are like banished men; as it was revealed to King Abraham, before spoken of, to whom the angels for forty years administered bread and wine for the sacrament, that all his sons should be shut up in a mountain, and that none should remain except the first born, the heir, and that this should be done for ever to all the sons of the Prester of the country, and his successors : because if this was not so done there would be great difficulty in the country, on account of its greatness, and they would rise up and seize parts of it, and would not obey the heir, and would kill him. He being frightened at such a revelation, and reflecting where such a mountain could be found, it was again told him in revelation to order his country to be searched, and to look at the highest mountains, and that mountain on which they saw wild goats on the rocks, looking as if they were going to fall below, was the mountain on which the princes were to be shut up. He ordered it to be done as it had been revealed to him, and they found this mountain, which stands above this valley, to be the one which the revelation mentioned, round the foot of which a man has to go a journey of two days; and it is of this kind:

[1] Church of the Trinity.

a rock cut like a wall, straight from the top to the bottom ;
a man going at the foot of it and looking upwards, it seems
that the sky rests upon it. They say that it has three
entrances or gates, in three places, and no more ; I saw one
of these here in this country, and I saw it in this manner.
We were going from the sea to the court, and a young man,
a servant of the Prester, whom they call a calacem, was
guiding us, and he did not know the country well ; and we
wished to lodge in a town, and they would not receive us ;
this belonged to a sister of Prester John. The night had
not yet advanced much, and he began travelling, telling us
to follow him, and that he would get us lodgings. And
because he travelled fast on a mule, and on a small path, I
told one Lopo da Gama to ride in sight of the calacem, and
that I would keep him in sight, and the ambassador and
the other people would ride in sight of me. And the night
closed in when we were quite a league from the road
towards the mountain of the princes, and there came forth
from all the villages so many people throwing stones at us,
that they were near killing us, and they made us disperse in
three or four directions. The ambassador had remained in
the rear, and he turned back, and others who were about in
the middle of the party started off in another direction ; and
some one there was who dismounted from his mule and fled
in panic.[1] Lopo da Gama and I could not turn back, so we
went forward and reached another town, which was still
better prepared, on account of the noise which they heard
behind in the other towns. Here many stones rained upon
us, and the darkness was like having no eyes. In order
that they might not throw stones at me by hearing the
mule's steps, I dismounted and gave the mule to my slave.
God was pleased that an honourable man came up to me,
and asked me who I was. I told him that I was a *guxia
negu:*, that is to say, a king's stranger. This man was very

---

[1] With his knapsack in his hand. *Con la barjuleta en la mano.* Selves.

tall, and I say honourable, because he treated me well; and
he took my head under his arm, for I did not reach any
higher, and so he conducted me like the bellows of a bag-
pipe player, saying, *Atefra, atefra*, which means " Do not be
afraid, do not be afraid". He took me with the mule and
the slave, until he brought me into a vegetable garden
which surrounded his house. Inside this garden he had a
quantity of poles stuck up one against another, and in the
midst of these poles he had a clean resting place like a hut,
into which he put me. As it seemed to me that I was in
safety, I ordered a light to be lit; and when they saw the
light they rained stones on the hut, and when I put out the
light the stone throwing ceased. The host, as soon as he
left me, returned at the noise, and then remained an hour
without coming. Whilst he was away, Lopo da Gama heard
me, and broke through the bushes,[1] and came to me. On
this the host came and said, "Be quiet, do not be afraid",
and ordered a candle to be lit, and to kill two fowls; and he
gave us bread and wine and a hospitable welcome, according to his power. Next day, in the morning, the host took
me by the hand and led me to his house, as far as a game of
ball, where there were many trees of an inferior kind, and
very thick, by which it was concealed as by a wall; and
between them was a door, which was locked; and before
this door was an ascent to the cliff. This host said to me:
" Look here; if any of you were to pass inside this door,
there would be nothing for it but to cut off his feet and his
hands, and put out his eyes, and leave him lying there; and
you must not put the blame on those who would do this,
neither would you be in fault, but those who brought you
hither: we, if we did not do this, we should pay with our
lives, because we are the guardians of this door." Lopo da
Gama, I, and the calacem then at once mounted and rode

---

[1] *Farou na silceira; Rompicudo por una curamada*, Selves.

down to the road, which was below us, a good league off,
and we found that none of our party had passed by; and
vespers were over, and yet we had not come together.

CAP LIX.—*Of the greatness of the mountain in which they put
the sons of Prester John, and of its guards, and how
his kingdoms are inherited.*

The manner they have of shutting up these sons of the
kings. Until this King David Prester John, all had five or
six wives, and they had sons of them or of most of them.
By the death of the Prester, the eldest born inherited;
others say that he who appeared to the Prester the most
apt, and of most judgment, inherited: others say that he
inherited who had the most adherents. Of this matter I
will say what I know by hearing it from many. The King
Alexander, the uncle of this David, died without a son, and
he had daughters, and they went to the mountain and brought
out from it Nahu his brother, who was father of this David.
This Nahu brought with him from the mountain a legitimate
son, who was, they say, a handsome youth, and a good
gentleman, but of a strong temper. After that Nahu was in
the kingdoms, he had other wives, of whom he had sons and
daughters, and at his death they wished to make king that
eldest son who had come from the mountain with his father;
and some said that he was strong in temper, and would ill-
treat the people. Others said that he could not inherit
because he had been born as in captivity, and outside of the
inheritance. So they set up as king this David who now
reigns, and who at that time was a boy of eleven years of
age. The Abima Martos told me that he and the Queen
Helena made him king, because they had all the great men
in their hands. Thus it appears to me, that beyond primo-
geniture, adherence enters into the question. Other sons

of Nahu, who were infants, remained with the eldest who
had come from the mountain with his father, and they took
them all back to the said mountain, and so they do with all
the sons of the Prester from the time of that King
Abraham until now. They say that this mountain is cold
and extensive, and they also say that the top of it is round,
and that it takes fifteen days to go round it ;[1] and it seems
to me that may be so, because on this side, where our road
lay, we travelled at the foot of it for two days; and so it
reaches to the kingdoms of Amara and of Bogrimidi, which
is on the Nile, and a long way from here. They say that
there are on the top of this mountain yet other mountains
which are very high and contain valleys : and they say that
there is a valley there between two very steep mountains,
and that it is by no means possible to get out of it, because
it is closed by two gates, and that in this valley they place
those who are nearest to the king, that is to say, those who
are still of his own blood, and who have been there a short
time, because they keep them with more precaution. Those
who are sons of sons, and grandsons, and already almost
forgotten are not so much watched over. Withal, this
mountain is generally guarded by great guards, and great
captains; and a quarter of the people who usually live at the
court are of the guards of this mountain and their captains.
These captains and guards of the mountain who are at court,
lodge apart by themselves, and no one approaches them, nor
do they go near others, so that no one may have an opportunity of learning the secrets of the mountain. And when
they approach the door of the Prester, and he has to receive
a message or speak to them, they make all the people go
away, and all other affairs cease whilst they are speaking of
this.

[1] In the preceding chapter it was said to be two days' journey in
circumference.

Cap. lx.—*Of the punishment that was given to a friar, and also to some guards, for a message which he brought from some princes to the Prester; and how a brother of the Prester and his uncle fled, and of the manner in which they dealt with them.*

With regard to the matter of these princes, I saw this: they brought here a friar who was about thirty years old, and with him quite two hundred men. They said that this friar had brought a letter to the Prester John from one of the princes of the mountain, and these two hundred men were guards of the same mountain. They flogged this friar every two days, and they also flogged these men, distributing them in two parties. On the day they flogged the friar, they flogged half of the guards, and they always began with the friar, then all the others were always in sight of one another, and each time they put questions to the friar, Who gave him that letter, for whom, and if he had brought more letters, and what monastery he belonged to, and where he had become a friar, and where he had been ordained for mass? The wretched friar said that it was sixteen years since he had come out of the mountain, and that they had then given him that letter, and that he had never returned there, nor had dared to give the letter except now; that sin had caught him (and this might be the truth, because in this country they are not accustomed to put in a letter the year, nor the month, nor the day). To the guards they did not put any other question, except how had they let this friar get out. The manner of flogging is this: they throw the man on his stomach, and fasten his hands to two stakes, and a rope to both feet, and two men both pulling at the rope; there are also two as executioners to strike one at one side and the other at the other; and they do not always strike the flogged man, many blows fall on the ground, because if they hit him every time, he

10

would die there, so severe is the flogging, and of this
company I saw a man taken away from the flogging, and
before they could cover him with a cloth he died. Immediately they informed the Prester John of it, because these
justices are done before his tents, and he ordered the dead
man to be taken back to where he had been flogged, and those
who were to be flogged afterwards he ordered to put their
heads on the feet of the dead man. This justice lasted two
weeks, for this regularity of flogging the friar every two
days never ceased, and half the guards after him; except
Saturdays and Sundays, on which days justice was not
done. It was the common fame and report through all the
court that this friar had brought letters to the Portuguese
from the princes of the mountain that we might take them
out of it, and we were innocent of this, and I believe the
friar was in the same case.

But in the days and time that we were there, a brother
of the Prester John, a youth (as they said) of sixteen years
of age, fled from the mountain, and came to the house of
his mother, a queen, who had been wife of Prester John,
and on account of the pain of death that here falls on
whoever takes in a prince from the mountain, the mother
would not take in her son, but had him arrested and taken
to Prester John.[1] They said that he asked his brother
why he fled, and that he answered that he was dying of
hunger, and that he had not come except for the purpose
of relating this to him, since no one would bring this
message to him. They said that the Prester John dressed
him richly, and gave him much gold, and silk stuffs, and
ordered him to return to the mountain. They also said
generally in this court that he only fled in order to go away
with the Portuguese. With regard to this individual who

---

[1] This is the worst trait of Abyssinian character to be found in any
of the accounts of that country; and instances of similar conduct are
only to be found in Russia.

thus fled and was sent back to the mountain, when we, and
this ambassador who is going to Portugal, were at Lalibela,
where the rock churches are, and he was going to take
possession of the lordship of Abrigima, which Prester John
gave him, there came that way a calacem with many people,
and he brought as a prisoner this brother of the Prester;
and he and his mule were covered with dark cloths, so that
nothing of him appeared, and the mule only showed its eyes
and ears. The messengers said that this man had run
away in the habits of a friar in company with a friar, and
that this friar, his companion, had discovered him the day
on which they left the lands of Prester John, and had caused
him to be arrested, and so the friar himself brought him a
prisoner. They did not allow any person to approach or
speak to this brother of Prester John, except two men,
who went close to the mule. Everybody said that he would
die, or that they would put out his eyes. I do not know
what became of him. Of another we heard say (and he is
still alive) that he had attempted to fly from the mountain,
and that in order to get away he had made himself into a
bush, that is, covered himself with many boughs; and some
cultivators who were at their tillage saw the said bush
move, and went to see what it was, and finding a man they
took him prisoner, and the guards, as soon as they had him
in their power, put out his eyes. They say that he is still
alive, and that he is an uncle of this Prester John. They
relate that there are in this mountain a great multitude of
these people, and they call them Ifflaquitas, or sons of this
Israel, or sons of David, like the Prester John, because all
are of one race and blood. There are in this country (as
they say) many churches, monasteries, priests, and friars.[1]

---

[1] See Major Harris for an account of the imitation by the King of
Shoa of this custom of shutting up the King's relations.

CAP. LXI.—*In what estimation the relations of the Prester are held, and of the different method which this David wishes to pursue with his sons, and of the great provisions applied to the mountain.*

In this country Prester John has no relation of his own, because those on the mother's side are not held or reckoned or named as relations; and those on the father's side are shut up and held to be dead, and although they marry and have children, as they say that they have an infinite number of sons and daughters, yet none of them ever comes out of the mountain, except, as has been mentioned before, if the Prester dies without an heir, then they bring out from it his nearest relation, and the most fit and proper. It is said that some women go out to be married outside, and they are not held to be relations, nor daughters nor sisters of the Prester, although they are so: they are honoured so long as their father or brother lives, and as soon as these die they are like any other ladies. I saw, and we all saw, at the court, a lady who was daughter of an uncle of this Prester, and although she still went about with an umbrella,[1] she was much neglected. We knew a son of hers who was as illtreated as any servant, so that in a short time his lineage died and remained without any mention of being related to the king. This King David Prester who now reigns, had at our departure two sons; they said that he gave them large settled estates or dotations[2] of large revenues assigned to them. They showed to me in what part one of them had extensive lands. But the general voice was that as soon as the father should close his eyes, and that one of them should be made king, that the others would go to the mountain like their predecessors, without

1 *Esparavel*, a parasol or umbrella, apparently a mark of rank.
2 *Morgados ou contos*.

taking anything with them except their bodies. I also heard say that the third part of the expenses of the Prester were made for these princes and Iflaquitas, and that this Prester dealt better with them than his predecessor had ever done; and that, beside the large revenues which were appropriated to them, he sent them much gold and silks and other fine cloths, and much salt, which in these kingdoms is current as money. And when we arrived and gave him much pepper, we learned for certain that he sent them the half of it; and he sent word to them to rejoice that the King of Portugal, his father, had ordered a visit to be paid to him, and had sent him that pepper. We also knew for certain, and by seeing it in many parts, that Prester John has in most of his kingdoms large tillages and lands, like the King's lands[1] in our parts. These lands, or king's patrimony, are ploughed and sown by his slaves, with his own oxen. These have their provisions and clothes from the king, and they are more free than any other people, and they are married, and they proceed originally[2] from slaves, and they intermarry. Of all the tillage that is near the mountain, most of it goes there, and the rest to monasteries, churches, poor people, and principally to poor and old gentlemen who once have held lordships and no longer hold them: and he twice ordered some of this bread to be given to us Portuguese, that is to say, once in Aquaxumo five hundred loads, and another time another five hundred in Aquate, and of this tillage he has nothing for himself, neither is any of it sold, and all is spent and given, as has been said.

---

[1] *Reynenguos*, private estates of the King.   [2] *Deab inicio*.

CAP. LXII.—*Of the end of the kingdom of Angote, and beginning of the kingdom of Amara[1], and of a lake and the things there are in it, and how the friar wished to take the ambassador to a mountain, and how we went to Acel, and of its abundance.*

We return to our journey and road.[2] We went along the mountains and by a river, and above it a very pretty country, with much millet and other grains of the country, and yet they had not wheat. There was much population on the skirts of the mountains on either side of the river, and coming to the end of the valley, we left the river, and began to find a country of thickets and stones : not mountainous, but of small valleys, and other lands of much wheat, barley, and the other vegetables which the country produces. Here the kingdom of Angote ends, and the kingdom of Amara begins. Here towards the East, and in the kingdom of Amara, there is a great lake where we halted, and this lake or lagoon is quite three leagues long, and more than a league wide. This lake has in the middle a small island, on which is a monastery of St. Stephen with many friars. This monastery has many lemons, oranges, and citrons. They go to and from this monastery with a boat of reeds, with four large calabashes,[3] because they do not know how to build boats. These which I call reeds are bulrushes[4] with which they make mats in Portugal. This boat or ferrying is conducted in this manner : they take four pieces of wood and place them around those bulrushes, which are well arranged, and other four planks upon the bulrushes at right angles to the others, and they separate them well, and at each corner they place a great calabash, and so pass over on it. This lake does not run except in winter with the excess of water : they say that it pours out at

---

[1] Amhara.
[2] See Cap. 57, p. 139.
[3] *Cabaça.*
[4] *Boinhos.*

two ends. There are in this lake very large animals which they call in this country *gomarras*;[1] they say that they are sea horses. There is also a fish, properly a conger, and it is very large. It has the ugliest head that could be described, and formed like a large toad, and the skin on its head looks like the skin of dog-fish:[2] the body is very smooth like the conger, and it is the fattest and most savoury fish that could be found in the world. This lake has large villages all round, and all of them come down to the water. It is said that there are round this lake fifteen Shumats or captaincies, all within a space of two or three leagues. There are around good lands of wheat and barley. Of these lakes we saw many in this country, and this is the largest I saw.

From here we travelled quite four leagues through bushes and muddy places, a country of much millet, and well watered. At the end of the journey and much overtired, the friar wished to take the ambassador to some very high mountains to halt and sleep. The ambassador answered him, that he had not come to go all round countries, but to travel by straight roads; and that with regard to food, that he brought enough to buy it, either with gold or silver, or pepper, and cloths of the King of Portugal, which his captain-major had given us, and that on the roads where we halted outside the towns they brought us provisions, if he, the friar, did not take them by force from those that brought them, and from fear of him they did not bring them. We remained on the road halted in the open air, and the friar with his men went up the mountain; and at midnight he sent us bread and wine. Friday we set out from the place where we slept thus, and the friar did not come nor any message from him, nor people for the baggage. When we had gone the distance of a league, a servant of the friar reached us, and said that we should not go beyond the first town which was a good one for halting at Saturday and

---

[1] *Gumari*, a hippopotamus.   [2] *Lixa squatina.*

Sunday : and this we did. As soon as we arrived at this
first town, and saw that it was good, we did not wish to pass
it. This town is named the Acel; it is situated on a small
hill between two rivers and is good land, there were here
many millet fields, and all other grain crops and wheat. It
is a very good town, and they hold a great fair in it.
Beyond one of the rivers there is a large town of Moors,
rich with great trade of slaves, silks and all other kinds of
merchandise. It is like the town of Manadeley in the
territory of Tigrimahom. The Moors of this place also say
that they pay to the Prester very heavy tribute like the
others. Here there is great intercourse between the Christians and Moors, because the Christians and Christian
women carry water to the Moors and wash their clothes.
The Christian women go to the town of the Moors, which is
separate and alone, from which we formed a bad opinion.
We stayed Saturday and Sunday in a field at the foot of the
town, where our people were all night with their lances,
keeping off the tigers which fought with us energetically,
that is to say, with the mules, and our people did not sleep
all night. Here there were disputes between Jorge d'Abreu
and the ambassador about a very small matter.

On Monday we travelled over flat country between mountains which were very populous and much cultivated, for a
distance of two leagues. We ascended a very high mountain without cliffs or stones or bushes, all taken advantage of
for tillage ; and on the summit of this mountain we passed
our midday rest, separated from one another, on account of
the quarrels which had taken place in Acel, at the foot of
some small bushes. From this place one could see much
land at a great distance ; there sat down with me ten or
twelve respectable men, and the interpreter was with us, and
the talk was about the height of this mountain on which we
were, and of the many countries we saw. They showed me
the mountain where the princes were, and which I have

mentioned before; it seemed to be three or four leagues from here: its scarped rock, like that further back, ran to such a length towards the Nile, that we could not sight the end of it. And the mountain where we were was so high that that of the princes seemed to be commanded by it. Here they related to me more fully the numerous guards and restrictions over these princes, and the great abundance they had of provisions and clothes. And because from here one could discern a very extensive view as far as the eyes could see towards the West, I asked what countries went in that direction, and if they all belonged to Prester John. They told me that for a month's journey in that direction were the dominions of the Prester; after that, one entered mountains and deserts, and after them very wretched people, very black and very bad. In his opinion, these lasted for a distance of fifteen days' journey, and when these were finished, there appeared white Moors of the kingdom of Tunis. (And I am not surprised, because it is from Tunis that the Kafilas come to Cairo and to this country of the Prester.) They bring white burnooses, but not good ones, and other merchandise. They also told me that on this mountain was divided the country of the millet from that of the wheat, and that further on we should not find more millet, but wheat and barley.

CAP. LXIII.—*How we came to another lake, and from there to the church of Macham Celacem, and how they did not let us enter it.*

Here we travelled for three leagues on level roads, always on this mountain height, all through fields of wheat and thin barley. We met with another lake like the former one, although not so large, and yet it was about a league in length, and half a league in breadth. This lake has a small

stream flowing out of it, and no water entering it except
that from the hills when it rains. It seems to be of great
depth, surrounded by strong rushes. We went to sleep in
a great field of grass, where the mosquitoes were near
killing us. These fields are not taken advantage of except
for pasture, as they are rather marshy, and the people do not
know how to draw off the water at the feet of the mountains
from the tilled lands. There were many and large towns,
and much tillage of wheat and barley. From here we took
our road through very large valleys, and yet they had very
poor cultivation of wheat and barley; some were yellow,
as though dying from the water, and others which were
dying of drought, and so we were confused with the
perishing of these crops. We began to enter here into a
country where by day there was great heat, and at night
great cold. In this country ordinary men wear round them
a strip of ox-hide; these ordinary persons are nearly all of
them, and very few are the special ones: and the women
likewise wear a cloth a little bit bigger than that of the men,
and here cover what they can of what God has given them;
the rest shows. The women wear their hair in two parts or
in two lengths; with the one the hair comes down to the
shoulders, with the other it is brought over the ears to the
top of the head. They say that these lands belong to the
Prester's trumpeters. A little apart from the road there is
on the right hand side a large grove at the foot of a mountain, and there there is a large church of many canons; it is
said that it was built by a king who lies there. Passing
through great mountain ranges this day, we went to sleep
outside of all of them at the entrance of some beautiful
plains. On the 26th of September in the morning we
travelled through these plains a distance of a league; we
arrived at a very large church, which is named Macham[1]
Selasem which means the Trinity. We came later to this
church with the Prester John to transfer there the bones of

---

[1] *Makana Selase*, place of the Trinity.

his father. This church is surrounded by two enclosures, one of a well built high wall, and another of palisades of strong wood. This which is of palisades is outside, and of the circumference of half a league. We were going very joyfully to see this church which the friar vaunted very much, and we slept here to carry out our desire, but we did not see it because they did not let us enter, and it was in this way. When we were a good crossbow shot from the stockade enclosure, there came to us men in great haste telling us to dismount; this we did at once, knowing that it is their custom to dismount when they are near churches, and out of reverence for this which is a great one, it appeared to us that they dismounted further off. Going on foot and arriving close to the door of the wooden enclosure, there were there a great many men who would not let us go in. Not only us, but also the friar who brought us, for they put their hands on his breast, saying that they had not leave to let us come in. It did not avail us to say that we were Christians, the tumult was so great, that it almost came to a fight. We went away from them, and mounted and went our way : and when we were already a good way from the church, they came running after us, asking us to turn back, and that they would let us enter, as they now had got leave. Then we did not choose to turn back, so this time we did not see the church or its construction. The plain in which this church stands and its situation are as follows : its enclosures are on an open hill, and all round is a plain ; on one side it is a league in extent, in another direction the plain extends two leagues, in another three, and in another direction below, which is towards the south, four or five leagues : it is a wonderful country, there is not a span that is not made use of, and sown with all sorts of seed, except millet, which they have not got. This plain has fresh crops all the year round, one gathered in and another sown. At the back of this church runs a pretty river, open and without

any trees, and water comes from it to irrigate a great part
of the tilled lands. Other conduits of water descend from
the mountains, so that these fields are all irrigated. In
these plains there are many large houses standing apart, like
farm houses, and there are small villages, and in them
churches, because, though there is a king's church, the cultivators are not deprived of churches.

Cap. LXIV.—*How the Presters endowed this kingdom with
churches, and how we went to the village of Abra, and
from there to some great dykes.*

We continued our journey through these plains, which
appeared as I have described, and issuing from them, that
is, from those we had seen, we entered into others still
wider, and yet not so well provided with tillage : they
appeared to be soaked with water like marshes ;[1] there are
great pastures in them, and also great lakes, and from
them overflow the waters which make the marshes. There
are very many herds, both cows and sheep (there are no
goats here). There are very many villages distant from
the road, and in all of them churches. We travelled
through these plains quite ten or twelve leagues towards
the East,[2] where they showed us a great church, which they
said was of St. George, in which lies the grandfather of
this Prester John (I will speak of it). When we were in it
they said that the former kings coming from the kingdoms
of the Barnagais and Tigrimahom, where their origin was,
increasing their dominions in these countries of the gentiles,
and coming through the kingdom of Angote to this kingdom of Amara, made a great stay and residence in it. And
they made in it a great establishment of churches for their
tombs, and endowed each one with large revenues. To that

---

[1] *Breylos* for *brejos.*　　　　　　　　[2] ? West.

church which King Nahu built, the father of this Prester
who now lives, he ended by giving as an endowment the
whole of this kingdom, without one span remaining which
does not belong to churches, and he ended by giving it to
the church of Macham Selasem, and he began and his son
ended. These churches of the kings do not prevent those
of the cultivators, which are in infinite number. A man
may travel fully fifteen days through the lands of Macham
Selasem, and there is not in all this kingdom a single
monastery that we saw or heard speak of, after all the
number of them in the countries left behind, but all are
churches of canons, and those of the cultivators of priests.
This kingdom now has no lordship; it used to have its title,
and it was Amara tafila, which means King of Amara, like
as also Xoa tafila means King of Xoa. There was this lordship here until the remains of Nahu were removed to the
church of Macham Selacom, at which the Portuguese were
present; then the going and confirming the dotation to the
church was concluded, and the Prester set aside the Amara
tafila that there was till then, and gave the lordships to the
churches, that is to say, to the ancient ones as they had
held them. As his father had left them to this church of
Macham Selasem, all the canons and priests of these
churches and of all the others of the other kingdoms and
lordships left behind, and further on, serve the Prester in all
services except in wars. And the administration of justice
is all one, both of canons and of priests and friars. So the
friar who conducted us bore himself with one and all, as to
carrying our baggage, and so they one and all obeyed him,
(as has been said) and he ordered priests and friars to be
flogged. Going through these great plains, when nothing
else appeared in sight, it seemed to us that we were now at
sea[1] and out of the mountains. We came to stay Saturday
and Sunday, which was the last day of September, at a

¹ *Mareados.*

small village of Our Lady, very poor and ill kept, close to
which church towards the east commence most wild mountains and deep fosses descending to the greatest abysses
men ever saw; nor could their depth be believed, like as the
mountains where the Israelites live are scarped from the top,
so are these. Below they are of great width, in some
places of four leagues, in others five, in others about three.
(This in our opinion.) They say that these dykes run to the
Nile, which is very far from here, and higher up we know
well that they reach the country of the Moors; they say
that in the parts of the Moors they are not so precipitous.
At the bottom of these dykes there are many dwellings and
an infinite number of apes, hairy like lions from the breast
upwards.

Cap. LXV.—*How we came to some gates and deep passes
difficult to travel, and we went up to the gates, at which
the kingdom begins which is named Xoa.*

On Monday the 1st of October 1520, we travelled on our
road through level country of lakes and large pastures for a
distance of three or four leagues, all along these dykes, and
we went to sleep near them where we had to cross these
depths. Tuesday morning we began to travel for half a
league, and we arrived at some gates on a rock which
divided two valleys,[1] one to the right, the other to the left
hand, and so narrow near the gates that they might hold
one cart and no more; with small buttresses, between which
the gates shut and close from slope to slope. Going through
this gate one enters at once as into a deep valley, with
shale[2] on either side raised more than the height of a lance,
as if the edge of the sword had made this, these slopes, and
this valley. The height of these walls has a length of two

---

[1] *Valuras.*   [2] *Piçarra.*

games of quoits[1] of such narrowness that a man cannot
go on horseback, and the mules go scraping the stirrups
on both sides, and so steep that a man descends with
his hands and feet, and this seems to be made artificially.
Coming out of this narrow pass one travels through a loop-
hole[2] which is about four spans wide, and from one end to
the other these clefts are all shale; it is not to be believed,
and I would not have believed it, if I had not seen it: and
if I had not seen our mules and people pass, I would affirm
that goats could not pass there in security. So we set our
mules going there as if one was sending them to destruction,
and we after them with hands and feet down the rock,
without there being any other road. This great roughness
lasts for a crossbow shot, and they call these here *aqui afagi*,
which means death of the asses. (Here they pay dues.)
We passed these gates many times, and we never passed
them without finding beasts and oxen dead, which had come
from below upwards and had not been able to get up the
ascent. Leaving this pass, there still remains quite two
leagues of road sufficiently steep and rocky, and difficult to
travel over. In the middle of this descent there is a rock
hollowed out at the bottom, and water falls from the top of
it (there are always many beggars in this cave). Thus we
descended fully two leagues until reaching a great river
which is named Anccheta, which contains many fish and very
large ones. From here we travelled, ascending for quite a
league, until reaching a passage which sights another river,
at which are other gates which now are not used; and yet
the gates are there still. Those who pass these dykes and
clefts come to sleep here, because they cannot go in one day
from one end to the other. At this halting place[3] the friar
who conducted us committed a great cruelty, as though he
were not a Christian, or had done it to Moors. Because a

---

[1] *Joguos de malham.* Selves translates: "*juegos de herraduras.*"

[2] *Espinguam.* Selves calls it *cuchilla.*   [3] *Meijoada.*

Xuum or captain of some villages which are on a hill above
the place where we were resting, did not come up so quickly
with the people who lived there, he sent some men of his,
and those who carried our baggage, to go and destroy for
them some great bean fields which they had by the side of
their houses.   These men who went there brought to where
we were more than a *moio*[1] of beans, which were their provisions in this country, because in these valleys they have
nothing except millet and beans.   It was a pity to see such
destruction ; and because we opposed him, he said that such
was the justice of the country, and also each day he ordered
many of those who carried our baggage to be flogged, and
he took from them mules, cows, and stuffs, saying that so
should be treated whoever served ill.

On Tuesday the 2nd of October we took our road through
many steep rocks (as before) between which we passed very
narrow and bad paths, and dangerous passes ; both on one
side and on the other scarped rock, a thing not to be
credited.   We reached the other river, a good league from
where we slept ; this river is great, and is named Geman ; it
also contains much fish.   They say that both these rivers
join together and go to the river Nile.   We began to travel
and ascend as great cliffs as we had descended the day before.
In this ascent there will be two leagues ; at the end of it
are other gates, and another pass such as from aqui afagi.
These gates are always shut, and all who pass through them
pay dues.   Neither above nor below is there any other way
or passage.   Outside of these gates we went to sleep at a
plain which is about half a league from the gates.   Already
when there, nothing showed of the dykes, clefts, and cliffs
which we had traversed ; on the contrary, all appeared to be
a plain on this side and on the further side, without there
being anything in the middle, and there were five long
leagues from one set of gates to the other.   The kingdoms

[1] *Moyo, modius*, measure of sixty alqueires, or bushels.

of Amara and Shoa are divided by these gates and ravines. These gates are called Badabaxa, which means new land. In these ravines and cliffs there are numerous tribes of birds, and we could not determine where they breed, nor how they could bring up their young without their falling down from the rocks : because whoever saw it would not judge otherwise than that it was an impossible thing, according to its greatness.

Cap. lxvi.—*How the Prester John went to the burial of Janes Ichee of the monastery of Brilibanos, and of the election of another Ichee, who was a Moor.*

On Wednesday, the 3rd of October, we travelled through plains not very far removed from the edge of the rocks and ravines, and we went to sleep on the rock itself opposite the monastery which is named Brilibanos.[1] I saw the Prester John go to this monastery three times. The first was to the burial of the head[2] of the monastery, who was named Janes, in our language Joannes, and the title of his prelacy was Ichee.[3] This Ichee of this monastery is the greatest prelate there is in these kingdoms, exclusive of the Abima Marcos, who is over all. And the Prester also went in the month in which they hold the funereal memorial which they call tescar.[4] He also went there at the end of forty days after the death of the said Ichee to choose and appoint another. They said that the deceased was a holy man, and that in life he had worked miracles, and therefore the Prester went to his burial and funereal memorial. There was among us a Portuguese, a native of Lisbon, by name Lazaro d'Andrade, who was a painter, and he lost his sight; the Prester sent to tell him to go to the tomb of this deceased man, and to wash with good faith, and that

[1] Probably *Debra Libanos*.   [2] *Maioral*.
[3] *Ichage* is the chief monk of Ethiopia.   [4] Misprinted *testar*.

11

he would receive health : he went there and returned as he
went. He whom they made Ichee was also held to be a
man of holy life, and he had been a Moor. As he was
much my friend, he related to me all his life, and told me
that when he was in his sect he heard a revelation, which
said to him : You are not following the path ; go to the
Abima Marcos, who is head of the priests of Ethiopia, and
he will teach you another path. Then he came to the
Abima Marcos, and related to him what he had heard, and
the Abima Marcos had made him a Christian, and had
taught him, and held him as a son : and therefore the
Prester took this friar who had been a Moor for governor
of this monastery, and he bears the name of Jacob. This
Jacob also acquired the Portuguese language, and we both
understood one another very well, and he wrote in his own
handwriting the Gloria of the Mass, and the Creed, and
Paternoster, and Ave Maria, and Apostles' Creed, and the
Salve Regina, and he knew it in Latin as well as I did.
He also wrote out the Gospel of St. John, and all very well
ornamented. This Jacob now remained Ichee in this monastery. Ichee means prior or abbot, and in the Tigray
language, which is in the kingdoms of the Barnagais and of
Tigrimahom, they say Abba for the principal father; and for
the prior of the cloister who is below him, they say that
there was (as I have before written) in this language a
prior of the cloister who is called Gabez.[1] In the time
when this happened, it was not when we were travelling,
but another time when the court came here and stayed at a
distance of a league and a half from the said monastery in
a very large plain, because the monastery lies in the very
deep ravine where we passed through the gates.

Returning to our journey; Thursday and Friday, we also
travelled through plains, and not at any distance from those
ravines ; and we came to stop at some small houses almost

[1] *Gabāz* is a prior in Aksum. There is a Gābāz in every church, but
there the title means the chief of the vestry.

under the ground. They make them in that way on account of the winds; because it is all a plain without any shelter, they also make the cattle folds underground, that the cows may be sheltered from the wind. Here there live dirty and ill clad people, they breed numerous cows, mares, mules, and fowls. Around these hamlets were the strongest and best crops of barley that we had yet seen, but there were few of them. In the tilled fields, in many places they sow three or four bushels[1] of seed in a tillage, and at the distance of a crossbow shot from there a similar quantity, and so the land is divided,[2] and all the villages had their sowed land scattered. There were not as much as six alqueires of sowing for any one cultivator or inhabitant, though the land is the best that could be mentioned, because there is no one to put it to profit. There are many birds in these plains, such as storks, wild ducks, water fowl, and birds of many kinds, because there are many lagoons, and no one knows how to catch them. This mountain is named Huaguida.

CAP. LXVII.—*How we travelled for three days through plains, and of the curing of infirmities and of the sight of the people.*

Monday, the 9th of October, we travelled through plains like the preceding ones, both of grass and tilled land, and we went to sleep at a place named Anda. Here we ate barley bread very badly made. So also we travelled on Tuesday through plains like those of the days before, and we slept close to some small villages. On Wednesday we now fell in with better land and tillage of wheat and barley, that is, crops all the year round, one gathered and another sown. This country is called Tabaguy; it is a very populous country, with large towns and great breeding of all sorts of

[1] *Alqueire.*   [2] *Cingida.*

11 2

animals. There were in this country many sick people, as of fevers, and all is left to nature, for they do not apply any other remedy, only if they have a headache they bleed the head itself: and if they have a stomach ache or pain in the back or shoulders, they apply fire, as to the beasts. For fevers they do not apply any remedy. On this Wednesday we had sight of the tents and camp of the Prester John, and we went to sleep off the road, as we were accustomed. On Thursday we travelled a short distance, and also we travelled little on Friday, and went to stay Saturday and Sunday at a small town which has a new church not yet painted, because all are painted, but not with good work. This church is named Auriata,[1] which means of the apostles, and they said that it was a king's church. The tents are about three or four leagues from here, and from this town it is little more than half a league to the church where the Abima Marcos was lodged. On this Saturday and Sunday that we remained here there came to us three mariners, who had fled from our fleet in the port of Masua, and the friar who conducted us learning that the mariners had come to see us, was in great ill humour at it, saying, that it was not the usage of the country, when strange people came, for them to have conversation with any one before speaking to the King; and with this ill humour he returned to his tent and to his lodging. This same Saturday the friar went to see the Abigima Marcos, and brought to us from there a tray of raisins and a jar of very good grape wine. On the following Sunday one of the said mariners came again to see us, and because the friar had complained the day before of his coming, the ambassador told the mariner to go first and speak to the friar, and to tell him that he did not come for any bad purpose, but only from the great friendship that he had always had with us. The friar when he saw him ordered him to be seized

---

[1] *Hawaryat* means apostles, and is thus used in the name of a church.

and arrested, and they wanted to put him in irons if the ambassador and we had not gone to take him out of their hands, and with rough words, and above all the said friar said very complainingly that we were not to speak to any one until we had spoken to the Prester John, because such is their custom when new people arrived.

CAP. LXVIII.—*How a great lord of title was given to us as a guard, and of the tent which he sent us.*

On Monday, the 17th of October, we set out, thinking that we should this day reach the court and camp, because we had gone to halt at a league from it. Then it seemed to us that they intended to take us there next day very early. While we were in this hope, there came to us a great lord, who is called by title Adugraz, which means chief major domo, he said that he was come to protect us and give us what we had need of. This gentleman told us to mount at once and come with him. We got ready, as it appeared that he was going to take us to the court: he took a turn backwards, not by the road we had come by, but he turned with us round some hills and we returned back more than a league, he telling us not to be in any ill humour, as the Prester was coming in that direction where we were going, and indeed six or seven horsemen were going in front of us on very good horses, skirmishing and amusing themselves, and a great many mules. They conducted us behind some hills, and the gentleman lodged himself in his tent, and ordered us to be lodged near him in our poor tent, such as we had brought for the journey, and ordered us to be provided with all that was necessary, and we were much put out of the way;[1] and the Prester was coming to halt near where we were. On Wednesday in the morning they brought us a large round

---

[1] *Desriados.*

tent, saying that the Prester John sent us that tent, and
that nobody had a tent such as that except him, and the
churches, and that his tent belonged to him when he was on
a journey. So we remained till Friday without knowing
what we were to do. The captain who guarded us and the
friar warned us to look well after our goods, as there were
many thieves in the country, and the Franks[1] who were in
the country also told us so : they further told us that there
were agents and captains of thieves, and that they paid
dues of what they stole.

CAP. LXIX.—*How the ambassador, and we with him, were
summoned by order of the Prester, and of the order in
which we went, and of his state.*

On Friday, the 20th of October, at the hour of tierce, the
friar came to us in great haste, for the Prester John had
sent to call us, and that we should bring what we had
brought for him, and also all our baggage, as he wished to
see it. The ambassador ordered all that to be loaded which
the captain-major had sent for him, and no more. We
dressed ourselves and arranged ourselves very well, God be
praised ; and many people came to accompany us. So we
went in order from the place we started from as far as a
great entrance, where we saw the tents pitched in a great
plain, that is, certain white tents, and, in front of the white
ones, one very large red tent pitched, which they say is set
up for great feasts or receptions. In front of these pitched
tents were set up two rows of arches covered with white
and red cotton cloths, that is, an arch covered with red and
the next with white : not covered but rolled round the arch,
like a stole on the pole of a cross, and so these arches were
continued to the end ; there may have been quite twenty

---

[1] Franks : who these were is explained in Cap. 72.

arches in each row, and in width and height they were like
the small arches of a cloister. One row may have been
apart from the other about the distance of a game of quoits.[1]
There were many people collected together; so many that
they would exceed twenty thousand persons. All these
people were in a semi-circle, and removed a good way off
on each side; the smartest people were standing much
nearer to the arches. Among these smarter people were
many canons and church people with caps like mitres, but
with points upwards of coloured silk stuffs, and some of
them of scarlet cloth : and there were other people very
well dressed. In front of these well-dressed people were
four horses, that is, two on one side and two on the other,
saddled and caparisoned with rich brocade coverings ; what
armour-plating or arms were underneath I do not know.
These horses had diadems high above their ears, they
came down to the bits[2] of the bridle, with large plumes on
them. Below these were many other good horses saddled
but not arrayed like these four, and all the heads of all of
them were on a level, making a line like the people. Then,
in a line behind these horses (because the crowd was much
and thick), there were honourable men, who were not
clothed except from the waist downwards, with many thin
white cotton cloths, and crowded, standing one before the
other.[3] It is the custom, before the King and before the great
lords who rule, to have men who carry whips of a short stick
and a long thong, and when they strike in the air they make
a great noise, and make the people stand off. Of these a hundred walked before us, and with their noise a man could not
be heard. The people riding horses and mules, who came with
us, dismounted a long way off, and we still rode on a good
distance, and then dismounted at about a crossbow-shot
from the tent, or the distance of a game of mancal. Those
who conducted us did us a courtesy and we to them, for we

---

[1] *Malham.*   [2] *Mossos.*   [3] Not translated by Selves.

had been already taught, and this courtesy is to lower the
right hand to the ground. In this space of a crossbow-
shot there came to us fully sixty men like courtiers or mace-
bearers, and they came half-running, because they are
accustomed so to run with all the messages of the Prester.
These came dressed in shirts and good silk cloths, and over
their shoulders or shoulder, and below, they were covered
with grey skins with much hair on them ; it was said they
were lion skins. These men wore above the skins collars of
gold badly wrought, and other jewels and false stones, and
rich pieces round their necks. They also wore girdles of
silk coloured ribands, in width and weaving like horse-
girths, except that they were long and had long fringes
reaching to the ground. These men came as many on one
side as on the other, and accompanied us as far as the first
row of arches, for we did not pass these. Before we arrived
at these arches, there were four captive lions where we had
to pass, and in fact passed. These lions were bound with
great chains. In the middle of the field, in the shade of
these first arches, stood four honourable men, among whom
was one of the two greatest lords that are in the court of
the Prester, and who is called by title Betudete.[1] Of these
there are two, one serves on the right hand, the other on the
left hand. They said that he of the right hand was at war
with the Moors, and he of the left hand was this one here.
The other three who stood here were great men. Before
these four we did as did those who conducted us. On
reaching them we remained a good while without speaking
to them, nor they to us. On this there came an old priest,
who they say is a relation and the confessor of the Prester,
with a cloak of white Indian cloth[2] of the fashion of a bur-
noose, and a cap like those of the others who stood apart.
The title of this man is Cabeata, and he is the second
person in these kingdoms. This priest came out of the

---

[1] *Bitwaddad*, because he was liked, a favourite.   [2] *Cacha.*

said tent which would yet be two casts of quoits from the arches. Of the four men who were with us at the arches, three went half way to receive him, and the Betudete, who was the greatest lord of them, remained with us; and when the others came up he also advanced three or four steps, and so all five came to us. On reaching him, the Cabeata asked the ambassador what he wanted and where he came from. The ambassador answered that he came from India, and was bringing an embassage to the Prester John, from the captain-major and governor of the Indies for the King of Portugal. With this he returned to the Prester, and with these questions, and ceremonious courtesies, he came three times. Twice the ambassador answered him in the same manner, and the third time he said, I do not know what to say of it. The Cabeata said: Say what you want and I will tell it to the King. The ambassador replied that he would not give his embassage except to his Highness, and that he would not send to say anything except that he and his company sent to kiss his hands, and that they gave great thanks to God for having fulfilled their desires and having brought Christians together with Christians, and for their being the first. With this answer the Cabeata returned and came back directly with another message, when the above-mentioned persons went to receive him as before: and on reaching us he said that Prester John sent to say that we should deliver to him what the great captain had sent him. Then the ambassador asked us what he ought to do, and that each of us should say whatever he thought of it. We all said that we thought that he should give him what was sent. Then the ambassador delivered it to him piece by piece, and, besides, four bales of pepper which were for our own expenses. When it was received it was all carried to the tents, and all afterwards brought back to the arches where we were. And they came and stretched the tent cloths which we had given on the arches, and so with the other stuffs. Having set everything in sight of the people, they caused silence to be made, and the chief justice of the court made a speech in a very loud voice, declaring, piece by piece, all the things which the captain-major had sent to the Prester John, and that all were to give thanks to the Lord because Christians had come together with Christians, and that if there were here any whom it grieved, that they might weep, and any that rejoiced at it, that they might sing. And the great crowd of people who were near by gave a great shout as in praise of God, and it lasted a good while; and with that they dismissed us. We went to lodge at the distance of a long gunshot from the tents of the Prester, where they had already pitched the tent which they had sent us, and there we remained and also the goods which remained to us.

CAP. LXX.—*Of the theft which was done to us when the baggage was moved, and of the provisions which the Prester sent us, and of the conversation the friar had with us.*

When our baggage came and was brought we began to see by experience the warning which was given us of thieves, because on the road they had taken by force from a servant who attended us, four tinned copper vessels, and other four of porcelain, and also other small kitchen articles, and because the servant had attempted to defend himself they had given him a great wound in one leg. The ambassador ordered him to be taken care of (of these pieces none appeared again). As soon as we were lodged the Prester John sent us three great white loaves, and many jars of mead and a cow. The messengers who brought this said that Prester John sent it, and that they would give us immediately fifty cows and as many jars of wine. The follow-

ing Saturday, the 21st day, he sent us an infinite quantity
of bread and wine, and many dainties of meat of various
kinds, and very well arranged : and the same happened on
Sunday, when, among many other dainties, he sent us a calf
whole in bread, that is to say in a pie, so well dressed that
we could not get tired of it.   On Monday the friar came to
us to say that if the ambassador would give all the pepper
to the Prester John, that he would order food to be given to
him and to his company, as far as Masua. And they ceased
giving us food, neither did the fifty cows nor the jars of
wine come.   In the meantime they prohibited all the
Franks who were in this country from speaking to any of
us : and also they told us not to go out of our tent, that
such was the custom of all those who come to this court,
until they had had speech with the king not to go forth
from their tents.   We well knew later that such was their
custom, and on account of this prohibition they kept prisoner a Portuguese, nicknamed the Sheep, who came to
speak to us on the road, and one of the Franks, saying, that
they came to tell us the things of the court. This Sheep ran
away one night with his chains from the custody of a
eunuch who guarded him, and came to our tent. Next
morning they came to fetch him, but the ambassador would
not give him up, but sent the factor and the interpreter to
go and ask the Betudete from him, why he ordered Portuguese to be put in irons, and had them so ill-treated by
slave eunuchs. The Betudete answered, saying : who had
bid us come here, that Matheus had not been to Portugal
by order of the Prester John, nor of Queen Helena ; and
that if the slave had cast irons on the Portuguese, that the
Portuguese should in turn cast them on the slave, and that
this was the justice of the country.

CAP. LXXI.—*How the Prester moved away with his court, and how the friar told the ambassador to trade if he wished, and how the ambassador went to the court.*

On Tuesday, 24th of October, while we were hoping that they would send to call us to speak to the Prester, he set out on a journey with his court to the place he had come from, which might be a distance of two leagues. The friar came, saying on his own part, that if he wished to go to where the King had changed his quarters, that we should buy mules on which to carry our goods; also telling the ambassador that if he wished to buy and sell that he might do so. The ambassador replied to him that they had not come to be merchants, but they came to serve God and the Kings, and to bring Christians together. Up to this time they had said that buying and selling was a very bad thing, and this they were doing to prove the intentions of our people. On the following Thursday the ambassador ordered me and Joam Gonzalvez, the interpreter, to go to the court and to speak to the Betudete and the Cabeata. We went and we told him those things which had been said by the friar to the ambassador, and the said friar went with us. We did not speak to the Cabeata, and we spoke to the Betudete in this manner. First we said that the friar had come to tell the ambassador to buy and sell, and that they gave him licence for that, and that the ambassador was much amazed at this, because neither he nor his father, nor his mother, nor ancestors bought or sold, nor had such a business; and the same was the case with the gentlemen and persons who came with him, and who had never been so accustomed: and that the ambassador and those that came with him were servants in the house and court of the King of Portugal, and that they served the Kings in honourable services and in wars, and not in mer-

chandise; and besides the friar had told him to give all
the pepper that remained to the Prester John, and that he
would order food to be given him as long as we remained
and until we reached the port of Masua, from which we had
set out. And to this the ambassador said that it was not
the custom of the Portuguese to eat and drink at the cost
of the feeble and poor people, but to eat and drink, and pay
with gold and silver: and because money was not current
in these kingdoms, on that account the captain-major of the
King of Portugal had given him, besides much gold and
silver, much pepper and stuffs for their expenses, that of
this pepper which he had brought for his expenditure he
had already given four bales to the Prester, and the rest he
kept for what has been said: and, besides, that the friar
had told him that if he wished to come to the court he
should buy mules for his baggage. With regard to this he
sent to say that for the present he did not require mules,
nor to move from where he now was, and that when he had
to depart he would buy mules. To this the Betudete answered that the Prester had already ordered ten mules to be
given, and had they not given them? We replied that we
had not seen any such mules, only that this friar had given
in the journey three tired mules to three men that came on
foot. To the other matters he gave us no answer, but spoke
of things that were irrelevant, as, for instance, whether the
King of Portugal was married, and how many wives he had,
and how many fortresses he had in India, with many other
questions beside the purpose. We also told the Betudete,
on the part of the ambassador, that if the Prester wished to
listen to his embassage, that he should say so, and if he did
not choose that to no other person would he give it; and that
if he wished to have it in writing, that he would send it. To
this he answered, that we should wait, and that we should
soon have an answer. So we returned without any conclusion. Up to this time they had always forbidden the Franks

who were about the court to speak to us, or to come to our tent; and if they came to see us, it was very secretly, and the friar was always by with us as a guard.

CAP. LXXII.—*Of the Franks who are in the country of the Prester, and how they arrived here, and how they advised us to give the pepper and goods which we brought.*

Because many times I mention Franks, I wish to say that when Lopo Soarez, captain-major and governor, went from India and came to Jiddah with a large fleet, in which I also was, there were in the said place of Jiddah sixty Christian men captives of the Turks. These Christians were of many nations. These who are at the court say that they were all waiting for the favour of God and the entry of the Portuguese into Jiddah to join with them; and, because the fleet of Lopo Soarez did not make the land, they remained there. A few days after that, sixteen of these white men, with as many other Abyssinians of this country of the Prester, who were also there prisoners, stole two brigantines, and fled to go in search of the said fleet. Not being able to fetch Camaran, they made Masua, which is close to Arquico, the country of the Prester. They landed at the said port and abandoned the brigantines, and went to the court of the Prester, where they were doing them great honour, more than to us up to the present time, and they had given them lands, and vassals who provide them with food. These are the Franks, and most men of these nationalities are Genoese, two Catalans, one of Scios,[1] another a Basque, another a German; all these say that they have already been in Portugal, and they speak Portuguese and Castilian very well. They call us also Franks, and all other white people, that is to say, Syrians, which is Chaldea and Jerusalem; and the people of

---

[1] *De Xio*, a Greek.

Cairo they call Gabetes.[1] On Sunday, the 29th of October, there came to us two of the said Franks, saying that they came in consequence of an agreement amongst themselves with respect to what they had heard say about us, namely, that the people of the court said that the pepper and all the goods that we brought belonged to the Prester John, and that the captain-major had sent it to him, and that since we would not give it him, so we should not find favour with him : and they were of opinion that it would be well to give this pepper that we had brought and all the other goods, because otherwise we should not have leave to return, because this was their custom, never to allow any one to return who came to their kingdoms : and that they would sooner have pieces and stuffs than cities or king-doms : and that this was their opinion. Upon this we held council, and, with the opinion of the ambassador and of ourselves, we all agreed to give to the Prester four out of the five bales of pepper that we still had, and to keep one for our expenses. We also decided to send him four chests covered with hide,[2] which were among the company, in which came clothes, and this because we thought that he would be pleased with them, and that we should obtain favour. Then, on Monday, the 30th of October, the Franks came to us very early with many mules and men-servants of theirs to carry our baggage. The ambassador, with all of us, determined to send the said present of pepper and chests, and that I, with the clerk and factor, should convey it, and that the ambassador, with the other people, should go later in the afternoon. We set out with the said pepper and chests, and going along the road we met a messenger, who said he was bringing us the words of the Prester ; and he dismounted to give them to us, and we dismounted to receive them, because such is their custom to give the King's

[1] Copts. They still call white people Copts ; see M. Parkyns.
[2] Encoiradas.

words on foot, and for them to be heard on foot. He told us that the Prester John ordered that we should come at once to the camp. We said that the ambassador was coming presently after us, and that he should return with us in order to give us the means of being able to present a service which we were conveying to his highness. He said he would do so, and moreover asked what we would give him for himself; because this is their custom always to beg. We contented him with words, with the intention of giving him nothing. He conducted us before a great enclosure of a high hedge, within which were many tents pitched, and a large long house of one storey thatched with straw, in which they said the Prester sometimes remained, and this man said that he was there. Before the entrance of this hedge there were a very great many people, and those like-wise said that the Prester was there. We dismounted a space further off (according to their custom) and thence we sent to say that we wished to present a service to his high-ness. There came to us an honourable man saying, almost with ill-humour, how was it the ambassador had not come. We answered him that it was because he had not got mules or people to carry his goods, and that now he would come because the Franks had gone for him. We asked this man to tell us how we could present this pepper and chests to his highness; he told us not to take care for anything, that anyhow the ambassador should come, and when he had come and when he was summoned he would take the pre-sent. This man then ordered us to be shown where our tent should be pitched when he came, and the ambassador delayed very little.

CAP. LXXIII.—*How they told the ambassador that the grandees of the court were counselling the Prester not to let him return, and how he ordered him to change his tent, and asked for a cross, and how he sent to summon the ambassador.*

This day we learned that the Prester was not within this hedge enclosure, and that he was not in the tents nor in the houses that were there, and that he was higher up in other tents which could be seen from there on a hill, and which was about half a league from these tents. We did not see or hear anything more this day; we only pitched our tent in the place which they had assigned to us, which was not very far from the hedge enclosure on the right hand side. The Franks who were at the court came to our tent, and they told us that the grandees of the court were opposed to us, and that the friar was putting it into their heads to counsel the Prester not to allow us to return, nor to go out of his kingdoms, because we spoke ill of the country, and that we should speak more evil of it if we went out of it: and that it had always been the custom of this kingdom not to allow foreigners who came to it to go away. We had suspicions of this from what we had heard, and what these had told us; and from what we knew already of Joam Gomez and Joane, a Portuguese priest, who had come here, sent by Tristan de Acunha, in the company of a Moor, who is still alive, and dwells in Manadeley. And they did not suffer these Portuguese to depart, because they said it would cause their death if they went away. And so one Pero de Covilhan, also a Portuguese, who went away from Portugal forty years ago, by order of the King, Don Joam, may he be in holy glory, and he has been in this country for thirty and odd years. There is also a Venetian whom they call Macoreo in this country, and who says his name is

12

Nicolas Brancaliam; it is thirty-three years since he came
to this country. Also one Thomas Gradani, who has been
here fifteen years, without any of them being allowed to go
away. These go about the court, and there were others
who died, without being allowed to depart. They say, for
their excuse, that whoever comes to seek us, has need of us,
and it is not in reason that they should go away, nor that
we should let them go. We did not now find this Pero
de Covilham at court, and they tell us that he is in his
house close to the rocky gates which we passed. On Tuesday, the last day of October, the Prester John came from
the tents above, where he was staying, to the enclosure tents
and house where we were. When he passed he saw our tent
standing not very far from his, and he at once sent a man
to the ambassador to tell him to order his tent to be moved,
as the place where it was was sickly. We were on the spot
which they had assigned to us the day before. The ambassador said in answer, that he had not got anyone to shift
his tent or his baggage, and that people should come to
shift it to wherever his highness commanded. This day, in
the evening, there came a message from the Prester asking
whether the ambassador had, or whether any of his suite had,
a gold or silver cross, to send it to him to see it. The ambassador said that he had not got one, neither was there
one in his company, and that one he wore he had given
to the Barnegais; and with this the page went away. He
returned immediately saying that we should send any we
had got. We sent one of mine of wood, with a crucifix
painted on it, which I always carried in my hand on the
road, after the custom of the country. He sent it back at
once saying that he rejoiced much that we were Christians.
The ambassador then ordered word to be sent to Prester
John by the page who brought back the cross, that he still
had for the expenses of himself and his company a little
pepper, and that he wished to give it to his highness, and

also four chests for keeping clothes, and that when he sent
they could take to him this pepper and the chests. Then
the page went with this message, and returned at once,
saying that the King did not want the pepper nor the
chests, and that he had already given the cloths which they
had presented to him to the churches, and most of the
pepper to the poor, and also that he had been told that the
captain-major of India had given to the churches all the
stuffs which the King of Portugal had sent for him. The
ambassador answered that whoever had told him such a tale
had not told him the truth, that all the things were still
together, and that the servants of Matheus must have told
that story that the cloths were given to the churches. And
because I knew all that had happened with regard to the
cloths which the King of Portugal sent to his highness, I
answered: That it was true that in order that these cloths
which the King had sent should not be damaged, and also
to serve God and honour the churches, I had assisted to
hang them up in the principal church of Cochym, which is
that of Holy Cross, on the principal feast days; and that
when the feasts were ended, I had helped to take them
down, fold them and put them by, and this had been done
to serve God and honour the feasts, and also that the cloths
might not be injured and eaten by moths : and on this
account they might have told him that they had been given
away to the churches, but such was not the truth. When
this answer had gone, another messenger arrived to say
that the Prester ordered that the ambassador should come
there at once with all his company and people (this might
be about three hours after sunset). We all began quickly
to dress ourselves in our good clothes to go whither we
were summoned. When we were dressed, another message
came that we were not to go : so we all remained like the
peacock when he makes a wheel and is gay, and when he

12 ²

looks at his feet[1] becomes sad : as pleased as we were at going, so sad were we at remaining.

CAP. LXXIV.—*How the ambassador having been summoned by the Prester, he did not hear him in person.*

On Wednesday, the 1st day of November, about one or two hours after nightfall, the Prester sent to call us by a page. We got ready and went. On reaching the door or entrance of the first enclosure of the hedge, we found there porters who made us wait more than an hour in great cold, with the sharp wind that was blowing. Where we stood we saw in front of the other hedge enclosure many lighted candles, and men held them in their hands. And as we stood thus at this entrance, because they did not allow us to pass, our men fired off two firelocks. There came at once a message from the Prester asking why we had not brought from the sea many firelocks. The ambassador answered that we had not come for war, and on that account we had not brought arms, only three or four firelocks, which the men carried for their amusement. Meantime there came five of the principal men, among whom was an Adrugaz, to whom we were consigned when we arrived, and he made us turn back. When he came up to us with a message from the Prester, they made their accustomed courtesy, and we did so with them, and we began to advance ; and we might have walked five or six paces, and we stood still, we and they. These five men were in front of us in order, as in a row, and at the end of them were two men with lighted candles in their hands on both sides. These messengers, who thus guided us, commenced to say, each one separately : *Hunca hiale huchiu abeton*, which means : What you commanded, sire, here I bring it. And each one said these

---

[1] Selves translates, " when he lowers it ".

words quite ten times, one ending another began, and so
they all went on. They continued saying this until we
heard a cry from within, said by a company, and they said
thus, in a very loud voice—louder than those outside whom
we were following : *Cafaciaha*, which means, Come inside ;
and we walked a little farther on. They again stood still,
and we with them, and they again said the same words as
before, until from within they answered like the first time.
Of these pauses they made quite ten from the first entrance
to the second, and each time that from within they said :
Cafacinha (because it was the word or permission of the
Prester), those who conducted us, and we with them, bowed
our heads, and put our hands to the ground. Passing the
second entrance those who guided us began to say another
chaunt, it was this : *Capham hia cainha afranguey abeto,*
which means, The Franks whom you commanded here, I
bring them, sire. And this they said as many times as the
former words ; and they waited for an answer from within,
which was the first, namely : *Cafazinha;* and so with many
pauses we reached a dais, and before it were many lighted
candles which we had seen from the first entrance, and they
counted them, and there were eighty of a side, in very good
order, and that those who held them might not get out
of line they held in their hands before them some very long
canes, across them breast high, and so the candles were all
in order. The said dais was in front of the long one-storied
house, which was mentioned before. This house is set up
on thick piles of cypress wood, and the beams,[1] which are
above the piles, are painted with poor colours, and on them
are planks which descend from the top to the bottom. With
regard to level it is not all well-constructed, and above it is
covered with a thatch of this country which they say lasts a
man's life. At the entrance of this house, which is at the
upper end of the house, four curtains were suspended, and

---

[1] *Sonares.* Selves has *traves.*

one of these which was in the middle was of brocade, and
the others of fine silk. In front of these curtains on the
ground was a large and rich carpet, and there were two
large cotton cloths, hairy like carpets, which they call
basutos[1] (this is their word), and the rest full of coloured
mats, for no part of the floor appeared; and also it was from
one end to the other full of lighted candles, like the others
we had seen outside. While we were quiet, from within the
curtains there came a message from the Prester John, saying, without any other preliminary, that he had not sent
Matheus to Portugal, and although he had gone without his
permission, and the King of Portugal had sent by him
many things for him, and what had become of them, and
why did they not bring them as the King of Portugal had
sent them, and those things which the captain-major of
India had sent him, they had already given them? The
ambassador replied that if his highness would hear him, he
would give him an explanation of everything, and he began
at once to say that what the captain-major had sent he had
already given, and besides he had given him what he
brought for his expenditure. And with respect to what the
King of Portugal had sent, on account of the death of
Duarte Galvam, the ambassador who died at Camaran, and
those who were killed at Dalaka, for one of them was
the factor, interpreter, and presenter of the articles which
were sent; and on account of the winds having been contrary, and that they could not fetch the port of Masua, and
returned to India, and the captain-major who was then in
India when he left Portugal, the King thinking that his
ambassadors, Duarte Galvam and Matheus, were already at
this court of his highness, had only sent him to the Red Sea
straits to conquer Moors, and to learn about his ambassador
whom he had sent : and, therefore, they had made ready to
go to Jiddah, not being certain of being able to make the

[1] *Básúto* means carded cotton.

port of Masua, as on a former occasion they had not made it, so they had not brought the stuffs and things which the King of Portugal had sent him, which things were in India together and preserved; and they only brought Matheus, in order if they should be able to make any port of Abyssinia to land him there, and afterwards send the goods which the King had sent with his first embassage. And because God was pleased that they should make the port of Masua which is in his hands, although it was in the power of the Moors, the captain-major determined to send to him Don Rodrigo with these articles which he had already presented to him, and he had come in company with Matheus, only for a visit, and to learn the road for the time when an ambassador should come from the King of Portugal, and that Matheus had died at the monastery of Bisan. In reply to this answer, there came another question, that three had been killed in Dalaka, and how had Matheus escaped? To this it was answered that Matheus had escaped because he had not gone on shore from the caravel. The ambassador still requested him as a great favour to hear him, and he would know the truth, and that he would also give him in writing that which the captain-major had ordered him to say verbally, besides what was in the letter, and that from both sides he would learn the truth respecting the King's ambassador, and of the visit sent to him by the captain-major. Messages went and came without any conclusion, and so they dismissed us on the following day, and he sent us much bread and wine and meat, and two men, who said they had to take charge of us, and give us every day bread, wine, and meat, and all that we required. This was forgotten, and some days we were very ill provided.

CAP. LXXV.—*How the ambassador was summoned another time, and he took the letters he had brought, and how we asked leave to say mass.*

At night on Saturday, the 3rd day of November, the Prester John sent to call us, and we went at night. On reaching the first door or entrance and waiting a little, there came a message to say that we should fire with the muskets, and that they should not carry balls, so as not to do any mischief. A little after that they ordered us to enter, and we advanced with pauses as on the former occasion; and on arriving between the doors and curtains where we were before, the dais in front of it was richly decked out, both the sides and front, with brocades, and there were smarter people on both sides, all in a semicircle with drawn swords in their hands, and placed as though they were about to slash one another. There were two hundred candles lighted on each side in a row, like those of the other day; and when we arrived messages began at once to go and come through the Cabeata and a page who is called by the name of Abdenago, who is the chief and captain of all the pages. This man brought his messages with a drawn sword in his hand. The first message which came was, How many we were, and how many firelocks we had brought? And upon this came another: Who had taught the Moors to make firelocks and bombards, and whether they fired with them at the Portuguese, and the Portuguese at them, and who was most afraid, the Moors or the Portuguese? Each of these questions came by itself, and each had its answer; and as to the fear of the bombards, since the Portuguese were strengthened in the faith of Jesus Christ, they had no fear of the Moors; and if they had had fear they would not have come from such a distance, and without necessity, to seek them. With respect to making firelocks and bombards,

that the Moors were men who had knowledge and skill
like any other men. They asked if the Turks had got good
bombards, the ambassador replied, that they were as good
as ours, but that we were not afraid of them, because we
were fighting for the faith of Jesus Christ, and they against
it. He asked who had taught the Turcs to make bombards.
The answer was given as for the Moors, that is to say,
that the Turks were men, and had the wit and knowledge
of men, perfect in all respects excepting in the faith. After
this he sent to say that they should play with sword and
shield, and the ambassador ordered two men of his suite to
come out. They did it reasonably well, and yet not as well
as the ambassador desired that the affairs of the Portuguese
should be conducted: and as the Prester sent to ask for
others to come out, the ambassador proposed to Jorge
d'Abreu that they should both go out; and they went out
with their own swords and targes,[1] and they did it very well,
as was to be expected from such men who had been brought
up and trained in war and arms. At the end of it all the
ambassador sent to tell the Prester John that he had done
that to do him service, and that otherwise he would not
have done it, even though they gave him fifty thousand
crowns,[2] for any other prince, unless he were commanded
to do it by the King of Portugal his sovereign, under whose
obligation he was. And he begged His Highness to hear
him, and learn what the captain-major of the King of
Portugal had ordered him to say, and to dismiss him, that
he might be able to join the fleet at the time of its arrival,
so as not to cause expense without profit. An answer came
that we had now just arrived, and had not seen even a
third part of his dominions, that we should rest, and that
the captain-major would come to Masua, and he would send
him a message, and that then we should go away; and that
they should make a fortress in Masua and in Suaquem, and

¹ *Cofos.*   ² *Cruzados.*

in Zeila, and he would send all the provisions necessary for them, because the Turks were many and we were few, and besides this, by having a fortress in the Red Sea, it would be easy to make a journey to go to Jerusalem. The ambassador answered that these were the desires of the King of Portugal, and that he still begged of him to give him a hearing, and if he determined not to hear him, that he would send him the captain-major's letter, and likewise he would send him in writing that which the captain-major had bade him say. He ordered that all should be turned into his own writing and language, and that they should send it all to him: and the ambassador did so, and sent to ask him to look at it all and give him his dismissal. After this, Prester John sent to ask that they should sing to a musical-instrument,[1] and dance, and they did so. When the dance was over we spoke to him and said that as we were Christians, that they should give us leave to say mass according to our custom, according to the Church of Rome. He immediately sent us a message that he well knew that we were Christians, and that since the Moors who were bad and vile said their prayers after their fashion, why should not we follow ours, and that he would order what was necessary to be given to us, and so he directed us to return to our lodging. When we arrived there they followed us with three hundred large loaves and twenty-four jars of wine; the person who had it brought said that they had given him thirty jars, and that on the road those who carried them had diminished them by six.

---

[1] *Manicordio*, also written *monocordio*.

CAP. LXXVI.—*Of the questions which were put to the ambassador by order of Prester John, and of the dress which he gave to a page, and also whether we brought with us the means of making wafers.*

On the following Sunday there came to our tent many messages from Prester John to the ambassador, and all were about the arms which the King of Portugal sent him, and whether he had sent them to India. The ambassador told him that the arms, and all the other things which the King had sent would arrive this year which was coming, and that the captain-major would bring them or have them sent, and that so he had sent word and written in his letters. On this day he sent to ask if we had brought the means of making corbam, that is to say, the host. We answered that we had : and he desired that they should be shown to him. I at once took to him the instruments, which were very good, and in which was an image of the crucifix very apparent and well made. I did not remain long, for he at once ordered them to be returned. On this day he sent for us to go and show him how the white armour was fitted which the captain-major had sent him ; they went to fit them where he could see it. He also sent to ask for the swords and cuirasses which the ambassador had in his company ; all was sent to him, and he then sent to ask whether the King of Portugal would send him some of those arms ; he was told that he would send him as many as were necessary. This day in the afternoon he sent as much bread and wine as on the former occasion, and when it was quite night a page came to our tent with a message, and the ambassador dressed him up entirely as a Portuguese, with a shirt with a collar embroidered with gold, a jacket,[1]......a cap with gold

---

[1] *Pelote de usteda*; not mentioned by Selves : a jacket or tunic without sleeves.

points, silk drawers,[1] light shoes,[2] gaiters, and shoes, and so he went away very joyfully and those who came with him. On the following day in the morning the said page returned with the jacket and nothing else, saying that the Prester had scolded him for taking the said clothes, and besides that he begged for a jacket of Portuguese cloth, upon which to put the armour: the ambassador gave this also, and as to the jacket which the page brought and left, the ambassador told him that the Portuguese were not accustomed to give and take back. So he carried away the jacket, and did not bring it back again.

CAP. LXXVII.—*How the Prester John sent to call me, the priest Francisco Alvarez, and to take to him wafers and restments, and of the questions which he asked me.*

Then on Monday, at the hour of vespers, the Prester sent to summon me, Francisco Alvarez, to bring to him wafers, as he wished to see them. I carried eleven wafers very well made (and I did not carry them in a box, because I already knew the reverence with which they respect them, that is to say their own which are only a roll, and these had a very neat crucifix). I carried them in a very good porcelain, covered over with tafeta. He saw them, and (according to what they told me) he rejoiced greatly at seeing them, and again ordered that they should bring the instruments in order to compare their opening with the figure on the wafers: and also that I should show him all the other things with which we say mass. I brought to him the full vestments, the chalice, corporals, altar stone, and cruets. He saw all, piece by piece, and ordered me to take it and unsew the altar stone, which was sewn up in a clean cloth,

---

[1] *Ceroules.* Selves has *çaraguelles.*
[2] *Cervilhas.* Selves has *Xervilletas.*

and I unsewed half of it, and had it again covered up. This altar stone was very smooth and square and well made on the upper part, the lower part was little squared, and of the nature and fashion of the stone. They returned it to me, saying that since there were such good workmen in Portugal how had they made this thus rough? I answered that the upper part was very well made and smooth and square and well wrought, and that below it had a good foundation : they still said that it was not well, that the things of God ought to be perfect, and not imperfect. When it was night they told me to go to the tent and to enter it. I entered, and they placed me in the middle of the tent, which was spread with carpets for a space of two fathoms from where the Prester John was. He then bade me dress myself as if to say mass ; and I dressed myself in his presence, first putting on my surplice which I had brought with the vestments. When I was dressed he asked me who had given us that habit, whether it was the apostles or any other saints. I answered him that the church had taken it from the passion of Jesus Christ. He told me to tell him what each of the pieces signified. I at once commenced with the surplice, saying that it was the habit of the clergy, and putting on the amice, I said that it denoted the linen or cloth with which they covered the eyes of Jesus Christ ; and putting on the alb, I said that it signified the shirt which our Lady had made for her Son, for which the knights of Pilate had cast lots : and that the girdle signified the chastity and purity of the priests ; and that the maniple denoted a small cord with which they tied the hands of Jesus Christ. Here the Prester spoke with his mouth, and the interpreters told me that he said that we were good Christians since we thus esteemed the Passion of Christ. Coming to the stole, I told him that it signified the great cord which they fastened to Christ's neck when they led Him hither and thither ; and the mantle signified the vesture which they put upon Him in derision. Here he again spoke, and the interpreters told me that he said that we were true Christians since we had got the entire Passion. He again spoke to the interpreters, and they said that he bade me take off the vestments, and tell him over again what each piece denoted. On divesting myself I commenced with the mantle and concluded with the amice, and there remained only the surplice upon me. He told me to dress another time, and to explain as before, and so I again explained to him, beginning with the amice and ending with the mantle. Here he affirmed with a very loud voice that we were Christians who possessed all the Passion entirely; and he said to us that since I said that the Church had taken this from the Passion of Jesus Christ, which then was this Church, because two were at the head of Christendom, the first, Constantinople in Greece, and then Rome in Frankland. I replied to him that here there was only one Church, and although at the beginning Constantinople had been the head, it had ceased to be so, because the head of the church was where St. Peter was, by reason of what Jesus Christ had said: Tu es Petrus, super hanc petram edificabo ecclesiam meam. And when St. Peter was at Antioch there was the church, because there was the head, and as he came to Rome it remained and always will be the head. And this Church, ruled by the Holy Spirit, ordained what was necessary for saying mass; and besides I affirmed more of this Church, telling him that in the articles of our faith, which the apostles had composed or declared, the apostle St. Simon said: I believe in the Holy Catholic Church. And in the great Creed which was composed at the Council of Vierapollos,[1] three hundred and eighteen bishops who agreed against the heresy of Arius say: "Et unam sanctam catolicam et apostolicam ecclesiam." They do not say I believe in the churches, but only in the Catholic and Apostolic Church: this is the holy

_____
[1] Of Nice. Selves has Niceno.

Roman Church in which is St. Peter, upon whom God founded his Church, as he says, and St. Paul a chosen vessel, and teacher of the nations. So it is called Catholic and Apostolic, for in it are all the apostolic powers which God gave to St. Peter, and to all the apostles to bind and to loose. They answered me that I gave good reason for the Church of Rome, but they said that the Church of Constantinople was of Mark, and that of Greece was of Joannes, Patriarch of Alexandria.[1] To this I replied that his reasoning assisted mine, because St. Peter was the god-father and master of St. Mark, and he had sent him to those parts: and thus, neither Mark nor Joannes could make houses except in the name of him who sent them, and thus their houses were members of the head which sent them, to which all the powers were given. And after that, not so long ago, that St. Jerome, and many other saints, separated themselves, and ordained separation from the world with hard lives to serve God, and that these separations they did not nor could not carry out without authority of the apostolic Church, which is that of Rome. How could they make churches to the prejudice of the great head, unless they were built and made for Jesus our Lord. They agreed fully to this, and the interpreters said that the Prester was much pleased. Then they asked me whether the priests were married in Portugal, I told them they were not. They also asked me whether we held to the council of Pope Leon, which took place at Viera;[2] I answered, Yes, that I had already spoken of it, and that there the great creed was composed. They asked me how many bishops were with the Pope there; I said I had already told them there were three hundred and eighteen. Then they said that at this Council it was ordained that the clergy should

---

[1] Selves renders this: "the church of Greece had been founded by the Apostle St. John at Ephesus, and that of Alexandria by St. Mark the Evangelist.   [2] The Council of Nice.

marry, and that the Council was sworn, how then did we not marry. I replied that of this Council I knew nothing, except that in it the Creed had been made, and it had been ordained that Our Lady should be called Mother of God. Then they told me that many things were there ordained and sworn, which Pope Leon had broken, and that I should tell them what these were. I answered that I did not know of them, but it seemed to me that if he had broken any of them, they would be such as touched the heresy which was extensive at that time, and that he would approve those which were necessary and profitable to the faith, and that otherwise he would not have been approved and canonized as a saint, as he was. Again they returned to the marriage of priests, saying that the apostles were married. I replied to them that I had never read in a book, nor had heard say that the apostles, after going in the company of Jesus, had had wives, or had been married; and that although St. Peter had a daughter, he had her of his wife before he was an apostle of Jesus Christ; and St. John the Evangelist was at the marriage of Cana in Galilee, where was Our Lady and Jesus Christ her son; and afterwards St. John the Evangelist left this marriage and followed Christ our Lord, and was a virgin: and also that I had read and heard tell that after the death of Christ the apostles and disciples zealously preached the faith of Jesus Christ until their deaths, and did not weary in it, and preached chastity; and thus the Roman Church in truth established and ordained that no priest should have a wife, so as to be more pure in their consciences, and not take up their time with wives and children, flocks, tillage, and property. They replied to this that their books ordered that they should marry, and that so St. Paul had spoken. They put a great many other questions to me whilst I was still in my vestments, and last of all they asked me if we had the song of the angels when Christ was born. I answered, Yes;

and they asked if we said it in the mass. I said, Yes
we did. They then asked me to say the beginning of it.
I then began, "Gloria in excelsis Deo". They told me to say
it chaunting it; I then sung two verses of it. Then they
asked if we had the Credo: I replied that I had already
quoted it. Then they asked me to say something in chaunt,
and I sung two other verses. Then they asked me to say
some recited, and I said the Gloria and the Credo. There
was there an interpreter, and also the friar who guided us
on the road. This friar had been in Italy, and knew some
little Latin. The Prester asked him if he understood, and
he replied that he did, and that I had said the Gloria and
Credo like them, and that the only difference was in the
language. The interpreter who was there also told me that
at each question and answer which I gave, chiefly with
regard to the portions of the vestments, the Prester said
that we had got all the matters of the Passion, and that we
were Christians, as though as yet he had doubted it. Here
the Prester asked me why we did not say mass according
to our use; I told him that we did not say it because we
had not got a tent for a church. The Prester said that
next morning he would send for a tent, and would order it
to be given to us, and that we might say mass every day.
Then he bade me divest myself of my vestments, which I
had worn up to this time, and to tell him again what each
piece signified. I told it him like the first time, and he
gave us our dismissal; and it was past midnight when we
went away; and all the evening was employed in what has
been related, without an idle moment.

CAP. LXXVIII.—*Of the robbery which took place at the ambas-*
sador's, and of the complaint made respecting it to Prester
John, and how we were robbed, and how Prester John sent
a tent for a church.

This night which I thus passed with the Prester, towards
morning of the following day a great robbery of the ambassador took place in the tent where we lodged : from it they
carried off two cloaks and two rich jerkins, seven shirts, and
a cap, all good pieces, and other less valuable pieces ; and
they took them all from a leather bag as large as a trunk,
in which he kept his clothes.   They carried off from Manuel
de Moraes another leather bag with all that he had ; and
from one of the Franks whom we found here they took seven
pieces of cloth, which he had brought the day before to be
kept.   They estimated the robbery done that night at two
hundred cruzados.   On the morning that this happened,
the ambassador requsted me and the factor and the clerk to
go to the tent of the Prester to make a complaint, and ask
justice of him for the great robbery committed against him.
That night, whilst we were close to the tent with the pages,
taking this message of the complaint we came to make, and
to ask justice, since the ambassador had made prisoner one
of the thieves who committed the robbery, a woman came
crying out and demanding justice, saying that the night
before the ambassador of Portugal and his company, by
means of an Arab, who knew the language of the country,
had by force robbed her of her daughter, and taken her to
the tent where they lodged, and had done what they pleased
with her, and because her son had complained of their stealing his sister and forcing her they kept him a prisoner with
the Arab who had deceived and carried off the said girl, and
they accused him of having committed a great robbery.   Thus
we found ourselves waylaid and robbed and we and the

woman having been heard, one answer was given to all, that is, that justice should be done, and that we might go in peace.

On this day, during the night that we were making this complaint, the friar who was with me the night before in the presence of Prester John, came with a rich tent, already half worn, saying that the Prester sent it for us to say mass, and that it should be pitched at once, because the next day was the great feast of the archangel Raphael, and that we should say mass on this feast, and likewise every day, and pray to God for him. This tent was of brocade and Mekkah velvet, lined inside with fine stuffs of Chaul; so that the tent would have been a splendid one if it had been new, and it was still good. They said that four years ago the Prester had taken it in the camp of the King of Adel, who is the Moorish King, lord of Zeila and Barbara; and so the Prester sent to say that we should bless the tent before saying mass in it, lest there should have been any sin of Moors in it. It was at once pitched that night, and in the morning we said mass in it; there came to it as many Franks as had been at the court these forty years, and also some men of the country.

CAP. LXXIX.—*How the Prester sent to call the ambassador, and of the questions he put to him, and how he sent to beg for the swords which he had, and some pantaloons, and how they were sent.*

On Thursday, the 8th day of November, Prester John sent to call us, and we went at once. The ambassador decided on ordering the chests and loads of pepper to be sent which he had already promised him. When we arrived at the entrance of the first enclosure, they detained us with cold inquiries, and all about the negroes who were prisoners on account of the robbery done to the ambassador : and such was the discussion and inquiry that they bade us let go the negroes without any conclusion or remedy for the theft : and finally he ordered three hundred loaves, and thirty jars of wine, and certain dishes of meat from his table to be given us, and so we returned to our tent. They sent another time to call us, and after we had gone, we were a long time engaged with questions, among which was whether the ambassador came by order of the King of Portugal, or of his captain-major, and whether, when the captain-major had come to Masuwa, he had killed all the Moors, or whether any of them had already returned there : and why we did not travel from the sea to Damute, which was nearer ; and, why, if we were servants of the King, we did not wear crosses on our shoulder, that is on the skin, for it is the custom of all the servants of the Prester to have a cross on the right shoulder, both the great lords and small people : and after that, that we should give him the pepper which we had for our provisions for the road. The ambassador replied that we should eat much gold and silver and stuffs, all of which we had brought from the King of Portugal ; and so he replied to each of the questions as was fitting ; and, moreover, he requested him to give him leave and dismissal for our journey. Upon this there came a reply, that we were not to fear, that we should soon have leave to depart. The ambassador answered : What fear could we have, being in the presence of his highness and in his court, kingdoms and lordships, and all of us Christians. With this we were sent to our lodging.

On the Friday next following Prester John sent the swords which he had got. The ambassador sent to tell him that if they seemed good to him he should take them, and the ambassador would take it as a favour that he should make use of them. An answer was sent that if he took them, the King of Portugal would say that he took from his

people the swords which they stood in need of. Again the
ambassador sent to tell him to be pleased to take them, and
that they had many in the fortresses in India belonging to
the King, and in his factories, and that the King would be
glad that His Highness should use the arms of his vassals.
While this message was going, they came on the part of
Prester John to beg for some pantaloons, and the ambassador sent him some of his own and others of Lopo da
Gama, and sent him word that the pantaloons and clothes
and swords, and other pieces which he had seen, and knew
were in the possession of the ambassador and his companions, were all at his service, and he would do him a
favour in sending for all that seemed good to him, because
if he made use of his things the captain-major and King of
Portugal would give the ambassador and his companions
recompenses for this. This day he made many inquiries
which were replied to, which are not written to avoid pro-
lixity.

Cap. LXXX.—*How Prester John sent certain horses to the
ambassador for them to skirmish, and how they did it,
and of a chalice which the Prester sent him, and of questions which were put, and of the robbery in the tent.*

On Tuesday, the 12th[1] of November, Prester John sent
five very big and beautiful horses to our tent, desiring the
ambassador to ride with four others on those horses, and come
and skirmish before his tent. It was already nightfall, and the
ambassador, as it seemed, was not much pleased, because it
was not after his fashion ; and our people clung together,
because at one time they said do this, and at another do
that : and having finished we went to our tent, and the
Prester sent us three jars of wine. On the next day the

---

[1] This date does not agree with the preceding one, which would
make it Monday.

Prester sent to the ambassador a chalice of silver gilt, strong and well made after our fashion, both the foot and the vase. On the foot it had the twelve Apostles, and round the vase an inscription in well-made Latin letters which said : *Hic est calix novi testamenti :* and a message to say he sent it for us to drink to him. This chalice had not got a patena, nor did they understand the inscription ; and the fashion of the chalice was not like theirs, because their chalices are of very wide cups, little less than a porringer, of considerable depth, and they take the sacrament from it with a spoon. This day the Prester sent to ask many questions, and to say many things, among which was, How long was it since we had taken Zeila; that he wished to go there by land, and that his people would meet with and see the people of the King of Portugal, but that we should know that for two days' journey there was no water, and what remedy was there for this. To this we answered that we had come from Portugal five or six months without taking water, because there was nowhere to get it, and that notwithstanding this it came in abundance, and so it could be carried for these two days on camels, as there were many in the country. On the following day, which was the 14th of the said month, the Prester sent two pieces of little value, namely, a small reading-desk of gilt wood for the altar of our church, and a pitcher made of wood for washing our hands or pouring water on them. This day he sent to tell us to send him the names of all of us in writing, and they were taken at once. He again sent to ask what was the meaning of Rodrigo, and what Lima meant, and so on of all the other names and surnames ; we explained it all to him in writing. When it was near dawn of the next day another robbery was committed in the tent of the ambassador like the former one. While he was lying in the tent, six or seven men took from Jorge d'Abreu's pillow a cloak which had cost him forty cruzados, and besides two bales of cotton

stuffs of our property : and no measures were taken as to
this. They say that it is true that there is here a captain of
thieves, and that this man has the charge of pitching the
tents of Prester John, and that he and his men do not
receive anything for their labour, except what they steal.
This day Prester John sent a saddle all worked with blood-
stones.[1] This, besides, being very heavy, was very badly
made, and already used : he said he gave it for riding upon :
then there came a question asking what thing of this
country the King of Portugal would be most pleased with,
if he would be pleased with eunuchs, or with something
else. The ambassador sent to say that Kings and great
lords esteemed more the things which other Kings sent
them, than the value of them.

Cap. LXXXI.—*How the Prester sent to show a horse to the
ambassador, and how he ordered the great men of his
Court to come and hear our mass, and how the Prester
sent to call me, and what he asked me.*

In the morning of the following day, which was the 15th
of the said month, Prester John sent a caparisoned horse to
show the ambassador : the caparison was of plates, and he
asked whether there were such arms in Portugal. An
answer was sent him that the King of Portugal had sent to
him by Duarte Galvan, an infinite number of arms, amongst
which were caparisons for horses all of steel, and these were
in India, and that the King would send him as many as he
pleased.

The next Saturday following Prester John ordered the
lords and grandees of his Court to come and hear our mass,
and likewise on the following Sunday, when there were many
more than on the Saturday, who were present at the mass

[1] *Alaquequa*, Selves translates *lazos*.

and baptism which we performed : and according to what
appeared to us from their demeanour, and what was told us
by the Franks that we found in the country, and also the
interpreters who attended us, they were astonished and
very much praised our services, saying that they found
fault with one thing only, that was that we did not give the
Communion to all that were at mass, and also to those that
we baptised. They had their answer, which was that we
did not give the Communion except on certain festivals in
the year, and to those who had confessed their sins ; and
those who had been baptized, although at that moment they
were pure, were ignorant,[1] and did not understand with
what reverence and veneration they ought to receive the
body of the Lord ; and those who received this Sacrament
had to be of full age, and that their ignorance did not
suffice. They replied that this was a good reason, but that
their usage was that as many priests and deacons, and also
other lay people as were in the church, all were communicants, also every child that they baptize, whether big or
small, at once receives the Communion. And since those
who said this were great lords, and church people, I answered them that their custom did not seem to me good,
because among the many who were at church at mass there
might be mortal sins in one or in some of them, and that
our Lord Jesus Christ[2] said that whoever received His body
unworthily received the condemnation of his soul : and as
to the newly baptized, our Lord Himself said that he who
believed and was baptized shall be saved, and he who does
not believe shall be condemned ; so the ignorant, and those
who were not brought up or indoctrinated in the faith,
would have little belief, and those of tender age, their
ignorance would suffice for them. On that account it seemed
to me bad to give the Communion to such, so long as they
were not brought up in, nor indoctrinated in the faith, nor

¹ *Bouçacs, boçal.*   ² Selves has corrected this to St. Paul.

had the age and capacity for holding and believing so deep
a mystery. All those who were there present praised this,
and said that the Prester would rejoice to hear it.

On Monday, the 18th of the said month, the Prester sent
to call me to ask many questions, and I answered him as
God assisted me, to some of them, I do not know, and to
some of them, it is thus. The first was, How many prophets
prophesied the coming of Christ? I answered him that
in my judgment all spoke of it, that is of His coming, and
some of the Incarnation, others of the Life, others of the
Passion and Death, and others of the Resurrection, so that
all redounds of Christ. He bade them ask me how many
prophets there were? I replied that I did not know. Upon
this came the question : How many books each prophet had
made? I replied that it seemed to me each prophet had
made one book in chapters, because we did not read book
the first, second, or third, of Jeremiah nor of Daniel, nor of
the other prophets, but so many hundred verses of each
book. They asked me how many books St. Paul wrote? I
said that he wrote after the manner of the prophets, and it
appeared to me to be one book only, and that he made it in
chapters, because he wrote to many parts, as to the Romans,
and to those of Corinth, those of Ephesus, to the Hebrews,
and to other nations, and that he would capitulate it all
in one book. They asked me how many books the Evangelists made? I answered them likewise, and that I had
never read more than one beginning to the book of each
Evangelist, and that it did not say book the first or second,
and that there could not be more than one book in chapters,
except St. John who wrote the Apocalipsis; this would make
two books. Then there came another question asking me to
say all the books of the Prophets, Apostles, and Evangelists
of the Old and New Testaments, how many books were there
in all ? I had already heard that among all there would be
eighty-one books, and for what I had heard, I answered

that there were eighty-one, but that with regard to this answer and the other answers, I did not affirm anything positively, because for six years I had been navigating, and 1 had not books with me, and the memory would break down. The answer came that I had a good memory, and that my replies were the truth, although I had given them as opinions.

CAP. LXXXII.—*How the Ambassador was summoned, and how he presented the letters which he had brought to Prester John, and of his age and state.*

On Tuesday we were all summoned, that is to say, the ambassador and those who were with him; we went and remained before the first gate or entrance a good three hours, it was very cold and quite night. We entered through the enclosures as before on two occasions that we entered them. There were many more people assembled than on any of the other times, and many with arms, and more lighted candles before the doors; and they did not detain us there long, but soon bade us enter with the ambassador, nine Portuguese, beyond the curtains. [Beyond these curtains we found others of still richer texture, and they bade us pass these also. Having passed these last we found a large and rich dais of very splendid carpets. In front of this dais were other curtains of much greater splendour, and whilst we were stopping before them they opened them in two parts, for they were drawn together, and there we saw Prester John sitting on a platform of six steps very richly adorned.] He had on his head a high crown of gold and silver, that is to say, one piece of gold and another of silver placed vertically, and a silver cross in his hand ; there was a piece of blue tafetan before his face which covered his mouth and beard, and from time to time they lowered it and the whole of his face appeared, and again they raised it. At his right hand he had a page with a flat silver cross in his hand, with figures pierced in it with a graving tool : from where we stood it was not possible to make out these figures on the cross, but I saw it later, and saw the figures. The Prester was dressed in a rich robe of brocade, and silk shirt of wide sleeves which looked like a pelisse. From his knees downwards he had a rich cloth well spread out like a bishop's apron, and he was sitting as they paint God the Father on the wall. Besides the page with the cross, there stood on each side of him another, each with a drawn sword in his hand. In age, complexion, and stature, he is a young man, not very dark. His complexion might be chestnut or bay,[1] not very dark in colour, he is an elegant man of middling stature, they said that he was twenty-three years of age, and he looks like that, his face is round, the eyes large, the nose high in the middle, and his beard is beginning to grow. In his presence and state he fully looks like the great lord that he is. We were about the space of two lances distant from him. Messages came and went all through the Cabeata. On each side of the platform were four pages richly dressed, each with lighted candles in their hands. When the questions and answers were ended, the ambassador gave to the Cabeata the letters and instructions of the captain-major put into their language and characters; and he gave them to the Prester, who read them very speedily, and said as he read them : If these letters are from the captain-major, how do they speak for the King of Portugal ? The ambassador gave him for answer: How could the captain-major write without speaking for the King his sovereign, whose captain-major he was in the Indies. Here the questions ceased, and he again said, that, besides giving many thanks to God for this favour which had been granted to him in

---

[1] *Maçaã baiones.*

seeing those whom his predecessors had not seen, neither
he had imagined that he should see, his wishes were that
he should rejoice if the King of Portugal would order forts
to be built in Masua and Suaquem, because he was afraid
that the Turks our adversaries would make themselves
strong in the said places; for if such should be the case
they would rout him, and us Portuguese, and that for those
said places he would give all the stores and men and provisions that might be necessary: but it appeared to him that
it would be better to take Zeila, because it was better
supplied with provisions, and by taking that city everything
would be secure, because supplies went thence to Aden,
and to Jiddah and Mekkah and all Arabia, as far as Tor
and Cairo. There was a reply to this, saying that there
was no obstacle[1] to taking Zeila nor all the other towns,
because where the power of the King of Portugal reached,
the towns became unpeopled, and they did not wait even
for the shadow of the ships; and also that Zeila was outside of the strait, and Masua and Suaquem were within
the strait; and when a fortress was constructed in each of
these towns, from thence they might conquer Jiddah and
Mekkah, and all the other places as far as Cairo, and the
navigation would be defended from the Rumys and Turks
who are in Zebid. This seemed good to the Prester, and
he again said that he would give the provisions and all that
was necessary for this expenditure and fleet. The ambassador said that His Highness should name where and
through whom they should have these provisions. The
Prester replied that he would give orders to those who
were to provide them, and should afterwards remain as
captain in the fortress wherever it was built. The ambassador said that a fortress could not remain without a
captain, and that if His Highness thought it would be for
his service, that he would ask the captain-major to leave

---

[1] *Detença.*

him here to be captain. And so we took leave with good words, and we went away contented, and chiefly with the sight of him.

CAP. LXXXIII.—*How I was summoned, and of the questions which they put to me respecting the lives of St. Jerome, St. Dominick, and St. Francis.*

On the following day, the 20th of November, I was summoned by the Prester, and he asked me many questions, among which was that I should tell him what were the lives led by St. Jerome, St. Dominick, and St. Francis, and what sort of men they were, and what country they were natives of; because, in the letter of the captain-major, it was mentioned that the King of Portugal had established houses of these Saints in the places which he had taken; that is to say, in Manicongo, in Benim, and in the Indies. I replied to him, but not consecutively, that St. Jerome had been Patriarch of Jerusalem and a native of Greece or Slavonia; that St. Dominic was a native of Spain, of the bishopric of Osma; and St. Francis a native of Italy; and I gave a long account of their orders, as I knew of them, and also referring to the book in which I had their lives; and I spoke much to him of the great houses of these blessed Saints which there are in Frankland; and that from them had proceeded many other saints on account of the holy lives they led. He then told me through the interpreter to show him the lives of these saints, since I said that I had them. Then they put forward another question, which they had already asked me before, namely, since we were Christians and they also, how was it that there was difference between them and us who doubted of the Churches of Antioch and Constantinople and that of Rome; and that each followed its business like Rome and Antioch, and that Antioch had anciently been the head until the Council of Pope Leon, at which were three hundred and eighteen bishops? I replied that I had already before told His Highness that there was no doubt that Antioch in Greece had been the head, and that St. Peter had been for five years bishop in it, and that later for twenty-five years he had been bishop in Rome, and this would prove to be the truth by the saying of Christ which said : "Upon thee, Peter, will I found my Church"; and that St. Peter and St. Paul had suffered in Rome, and their bodies lie there, where the true Church is. To this, there was no further reply. Then they came to another matter, namely, whether we did all that the Pope commanded. I told them we did, and that so we were obliged to do by the article of our own holy faith in which we confess that we believe in the Holy Mother the Church, which is the Catholic Faith : and the Pope is the Church, and he whom he binds shall be bound, and he whom he looses shall be loosed, and not only the living, but also the dead, from the pains of Purgatory. Upon this, they answered me : That if the Pope ordered anything which the Apostles had not written, that they would break it; and if their *abima* were to order it, that they would burn it, that is, the order. I answered them, that we observed whatever the Pope ordered, because he is the head of the Church, and as his title is Holy Father, so he orders nothing except holy things taken from the Books of the Prophets, from which the Apostles took the same, and from the text of the gospels which the four evangelists wrote; and also from those books of the Holy Mother Church, from which the holy doctors take the things which are necessary, and which lie dispersed in them, and which for simple persons are difficult to understand, if the Holy Father, with his learned men, were not to declare and teach them, because he and his learned men are illuminated by the Holy Spirit. As also the Holy Father, Cardinals, Archbishops, Bishops,

Patriarchs, and other rectors of the Church are preachers and proclaimers of their holy faith, of whom the country of the Prester was greatly wanting, for if there were any learned men in his country, they are so for themselves only, and not in order to proclaim, declare, and teach others, and they should know that everything was not declared nor written in the books, but on many heads, only by figures and parables. And so wrote St. John, in the twentieth chapter of his gospel, that Jesus Christ did many signs and miracles in the presence of his disciples which are not written in the books. Still, upon this they told me that we were not bound to observe what the Pope ordered, but only the Council of Pope Leon, which was all of the Apostles. I answered them, that I knew nothing else of the Council of Pope Leon, except what I had already told them; that is, that in it it was established and ordained that Our Lady should be called Mother of God, and also that they made the great creed: and that by the Apostles we are obliged to hold and believe all the things belonging to the Church of Rome; and they taught us to believe in the Holy Mother Church, which is the Catholic Faith, which is not more than one Church, that is, the Roman, in which St. Peter is the head, and his successors in his chair succeed him in the power which Christ gave him when he said to him : " I give thee the keys of the Kingdom of Heaven." And, although in other times Constantinople was a head, it changed to Rome because there was the truth. Then came the answer that my reasoning seemed to him to be good. They came again with another question, asking why there were not in Ethiopia nor in their country and lordships as many saints and sainted women as in Italy, and that in Germany and in Greece there were many saints ? I replied, that it appeared to me that in those parts there had ruled many Emperors and their lieutenants who were Pagans and cruel men, and that the Christians who had been converted to the faith of

Jesus Christ were so constant in the faith, that they preferred to die for Christ rather than worship idols and follow
a bad sect; and on that account it seemed to me that there
were many martyrs in those parts, and so many confessors
and virgins, because, seeing the constancy and fortitude of
the martyrs, and hearing the many and great preachings
which, since the ascension of Christ until now, there have
always been in Frankland, they would always follow the
true faith, and thus there were there many saints, men and
women. Upon this came an answer, that what I had said
was true, and that he rejoiced to hear it so clearly put; but
that I should send him word if I knew how long it was
since this country of Ethiopia belonged to Christians and
had been converted to the faith of Jesus Christ. I sent to
tell him that I did not know, but it seemed to me that it
would not be a long time after the death of Christ, because
this country was converted by the eunuch of Queen Candace,
who was baptised and instructed in the faith by the Apostle
St. Philip; and that the Apostle St. Matthew had also
arrived in these parts, but that I did not know whether
this country had again belonged to Gentiles or to other
nations. The answer came, that only the country of Tigray, which is in Ethiopia, had been converted by this
eunuch, and the rest had been won and converted by arms,
as he did every day; and the first conversion of Queen
Candace was ten years after the death of Christ, and since
that time until now Ethiopia had always been ruled and
governed by Christians, and therefore there had not been
martyrs here, neither had it been necessary, and that many
men and women in their kingdom led holy lives and went
to Jerusalem and died saints; and he wished me to show
him next day the lives of St. Jerome, St. Francis, and St.
Dominic, and Quirici, whom they call Quercos, and the life
of Pope Leon.

CAP. LXXXIV.—*How the lives of the said Saints were taken to him, and how he had them translated into his language, and of the satisfaction they felt at our mass, and how Prester John sent for us and clothed us.*

On the following day, Thursday, the 21st of the said month, Prester John sent for my *Flos Sanctorum*, telling me to send it with the lives of the before-named saints marked. I sent him the book with the lives of those saints marked, and they soon sent back the book, and with it came two friars who said that the Prester ordered them to write the name of each saint in their writing over each figure, and also the pictures of the Passion of Christ: and as to the pictures of the Passion, they were to put where and how each subject had happened, and as to the lives of the saints they put their names. Having taken away the book, it was again sent back with the friars, and a message that they were to put from what country each saint was, and where he suffered, and what life each had led; and this for all the saints in the *Flos Sanctorum*. We did what he commanded with respect to those saints, and found out where they lived, and were born, and where they died, and other particulars. On the following Friday, the said friars came with the book to extract the lives of the before-mentioned saints. We spent several days in drawing them up, as they were long, and it was a very laborious task to translate our language into theirs. Besides these lives, we compared some lives of other saints which they possessed with those of our *Flos Sanctorum*; they were those of St. Sebastian, St. Antony, and St. Baralam;[1] of this St. Baralam they had the life, but not his feast day, and they inquired of me very earnestly for his day; I found myself in sore straits, because I did not find it in any calendar, and I came upon

---

[1] St. Barlaam, November 19.

it later in the calendar of an almanack, and when I told them the day, they at once ordered it to be put down in their books, and the day to be observed. I did not venture to go there without taking the calendar book with me, because they used to ask for the day of some saint, and wanted me to tell it to them at once off hand.

On Sunday, St. Catharine's day,[1] Prester John sent some canons and priests of the principal clergy of his house to hear our Mass, which we used to sing on Saturdays, Sundays, and feast-days. They were there from the beginning to the end. The interpreter told us that these men said that at this office they had heard a Mass not of men but of angels; and at all that we said, there was present a Venetian painter, who said that his name was Nicolas Brancaliam, a resident in this country of more than forty years (and he knew the language of the country well); he was a very honourable person, and a great gentleman, although a painter. He was like the herald[2] of these canons and priests, and told them what was being done in the Mass, such as the " Kyrios", the " Gloria", the " Dominus robiscum", which meant " calamclos", which means " the Lord be with you"; and so of the epistle and gospel and all other things. This man was herald, and they said that he was a friar before he came to this country. These canons and priests spread the fame of this office of Mass throughout the district, and said they never expected to see such another, and they complained of nothing else except that one priest only said the Mass, and that the communion was not given to all that were there. I gave the answer which I have before related in another chapter; it seemed to me that they were satisfied with the answer, and from this time forward many more came to our Mass.

On this Sunday, the Prester sent a very good horse to

---

[1] 25th November is St. Catharine's day.

[2] Or fugleman.

the ambassador, at which some of our company murmured, as though it grieved them. Also on this Sunday, and at such hours that we were already asleep, the Prester sent to call us. We went and entered with the formalities of other occasions, and we arrived before the first curtains; there they gave us rich garments, and they bade the ambassador enter beyond the curtains, and there they gave him his dress : then they bade us all enter (for we were now dressed) before the presence of the Prester where he was upon the platform, with the state of the former time. And then many things took place, among which the first was, that the Franks might go away in peace, and the ambassador and his company, and that one Frank of those who were here at first, and who was named Nicolas Muça, should remain, and that he would write by him ; and that he had to write with letters of gold, and that he could not write immediately, so that the ambassador should go on slowly at his own pace, and the Frank would carry the letters to him. The ambassador replied that he would not go away without an answer, because thus he could not give a good account of himself, and that he would wait as long as His Highness ordered, but withal he entreated His Highness to dismiss him in good time, so that he might meet with the fleet of the captain-major in Masua. The Prester answered with his own words, that he was pleased, and asked the ambassador whether he would remain at Masua as captain. The ambassador said that his wish was to go and see the King of Portugal his sovereign, but that in this he would do whatever His Highness commanded, because the King of Portugal and his captain-major would hold that to be for his service ; and with that he sent us to our tents.

CAP. LXXXV.—*Of the sudden start which Prester John made for another place, and of the way in which they dealt with the ambassador respecting his baggage, and of the discord there was, and of the visit the Prester sent.*

On Monday, the 25th of the said month, in the morning, they told us that Prester John was going away to another place (as in fact he did go), and it was in this wise. He mounted a horse and set out with two pages, and no other people; he passed in sight of our tent, caracoling with his horse. There was a great tumult in our quarter, and cries of: the Negus is gone, the Negus is gone, and this throughout all the district: everybody started off after him as hurriedly as he could. Before his departure orders were given to give us fifty mules to carry flour and wine, and of these they did not give more than thirty-five for the said flour and wine, and the fifteen to carry our baggage, and also they sent us certain slaves. Of these fifteen mules and slaves, the ambassador took what he wanted, saying that all was his. We were put in charge of an honourable gentleman named Ajaze Rafael. Ajaze is a title of lordship, Rafael is his name: this person was a priest, and another great captain was told to watch over us. They said that they would send and give us two cows each day.

On Tuesday we set out on our journey after the court, we may have gone quite four leagues, and we did not reach the place where the Prester was. On Wednesday we travelled and reached the court, and we took up our quarters in a large plain close to a river, which might be half a league from the King's tent. When we were settled there came to us an honourable friar, who is the second of those of Prester John, and he is the head and captain over the scribes of Prester John, that is of the scribes of the Church characters. This man is Nebret of the friars of Aquaxum, and he told the ambassador that his lord sent him to learn how we had come, and how we were, and he also told us that they would give us everything that he ordered to be given us. The ambassador answered that he kissed His Highness's hands for this visit, and that we had come very well, and that they had given him all the things which His Highness had ordered. Upon this Jorge d'Abreu said that he should not say that, for that they had not given all the mules, and those that they had given were one-eyed or blind, and the slaves were old and worth nothing, and that such as they were everything was for the ambassador, that he had taken it without giving anything to any one. The ambassador replied that he should not say so, that all the mules and slaves and other things were perfect. Jorge d'Abreu answered: If they gave perfect mules and slaves and other things, you have got them, and to you they give mules and horses, and to the others they give nothing, henceforward it must not be so. All this passed before the friar who had come to pay a visit; and when he went, the ambassador said to Jorge d'Abreu : For God's sake do not let us cause discontent, let us make ready for our journey, for there are mules in abundance, some have been given us, and others will be given. After this they got into such discussions that they took to swords and lances, and I with my crozier in the midst making peace, for these acts seemed to me evil. There were a good number of blows and thrusts, but there was only one small wound, which was given to Jorge d'Abreu ; and the said Jorge d'Abreu and Lopo da Gama went out of the tent, and the rest remained within it.

CAP. LXXXVI.—*How the Prester was informed of the quarrels of the Portuguese, and entreated them to be friends, and what more passed, and of the wrestling match and the baptism we did here.*

The friar who came to pay a visit and who came at the beginning of these quarrels made mention of them to the Prester, and afterwards on Friday morning there came a message from Prester John to say that the mules and slaves that he had ordered to be given to carry our baggage, he had not ordered them to be given up to us, but that we should give them in charge to an *azmato* who had to conduct us, and that we should now give in charge to him the mules and slaves, and he would have charge of them, and of conveying our baggage, and that he well knew that neither the ambassador, nor those that came with him, were merchants to undertake to convey baggage or goods, nor to load it or carry it, and that if they gave over the mules and slaves to the person he sent, the ambassador and his people would not have any other trouble than to travel, and that the azmate would take care to have our baggage carried. Then they gave over the mules and slaves to the person sent by the Prester. When this was done, the Prester sent for the ambassador and all of us, and we went at once. The first message that came from within was to say : why do you quarrel; and that he entreated us to be friends. The ambassador answered that this was not the first time, because these two men, that is, Lopo da Gama and Jorge d'Abreu were much opposed to him and to the service of the King of Portugal, for which he came, and that he begged His Highness to order them to keep apart from his tent and company. Whilst this answer was going, there came another message to beg that we would be good friends. The ambassador sent word that he was not going to be his friend, nor should he go in his company; and many other things passed. During this they told us to sit in a green field of long grass; and we having sat down in a great heat, we arose with great cold, because the stay there was from ten o'clock until night; and in like manner Jorge d'Abreu and Lopo da Gama were called there. So messages came and went to them, as to us, and what they were I do not know, because we were very far from one another. It was already quite dark and very cold as we were without food, and the ambassador sent word to the Prester to give us leave, for it was not usual to keep such persons day and night without necessity, and without food in the cold fields. Then they gave us leave and we came to our tent, and Jorge d'Abreu and Lopo da Gama went by order of the Prester to the quarters of the great Betudete. A message was sent after us to the ambassador asking him not to take ill the stay in the field, that he had done it in order to hear both sides, and that his desire was not to annoy him, but to give him satisfaction and send him away with joy: he also sent to ask if he had here any good wrestlers; the ambassador, however, excused himself as it was night. When we were in the tent there came large presents of bread and wine and meat, and messages repeating that we should not be angry at the delay they had made.

On Sunday, the 2nd day of December, of the said year 1520, in the afternoon, our Portuguese painter, named Lazaro d'Andrade, was standing near the King's tent, and was invited to wrestle, and he wrestled; and in the beginning of it they broke one of his legs. After this breakage, Prester John gave him a dress of rich brocade, and they brought him to our tent on men's shoulders. On Monday, the next day, Prester John sent to ask the ambassador if he had other wrestlers to send them to wrestle with his, and as it seemed to the ambassador that there were here others who were invited for this purpose, who might go

and avenge the painter, he sent there two chosen wrestlers,
namely a servant of the ambassador named Estevan Palharte, and one Ayras Diz, who came with the clerk of the
embassy. When they were at the wrestling, Ayras Diz
entered first to wrestle with the man who broke the
painter's leg, and he broke his arm, so he at once returned
to our tent with his broken arm. Estevan Palharte did not
wrestle, because he found himself alone and was afraid.
This wrestler who broke a leg and an arm is a page of the
Prester, and is named Gabmaria, which means servant of
St. Mary, and he had been a Moor; he is a strong broad
shouldered man, and they say he is a man who is cunning
with his hands, in working silk and gold, and making
fringes,[1] tassels, and cloths. This day there came a message
to the Prester from his Betudete who was in the war, saying
that he was sending to him thence much gold and slaves,
and the heads of some great men who had been killed
there, and that he had had a great victory over the enemy.
Whilst we were in this plain and district of the Prester,
there were some Franks in their tents, and the wife of
one of them named mestre Pedro Cordociro, a Genoese,
happened to be delivered, and when the child was eight
days old, he requested me to baptize it. As it was a child
born in the country and at court, and so few days old, for
they do not baptize male children except after forty days,
I was not willing to baptize it without letting Prester John
know of it, because the many others that I had baptized
were our slaves of ten and twelve years of age. I went
to the tent of the Prester and sent to tell him how they
required of me baptism according to our custom, and that
His Highness should give his orders what I was to do.
A message came at once that I was to baptize it and give
it all the sacraments as is done in Frankland and in the

---

[1] Firos, an ornament for coifs.

Roman Church, and to allow to come to the baptism and
sacraments as many of the people of the country as wished
to be present: and he ordered oil to be given me. I
celebrated this baptism on the 10th of December, there
came to it many people of the most honourable and principal people at Court. At this baptism we held a cross
uplifted, because such is their custom. I officiated as
slowly as I was able. The people who were present were
astonished, according to their gestures and what was said
by the Franks and our interpreters who understood them;
and the Court people said that this office was ordained by
God, and they went away as much comforted as if they
had eaten good viands, and they very much praised our
offices both baptism and mass, because we officiated very
deliberately, and they seemed to them more perfect than
their own.

CAP. LXXXVII.—*Of the number of men, horse and foot, who
go with the Prester when he travels.*

We departed from this place, turning back by the road
by which we had come. The people who continually go
on the road with the Court is a thing scarcely credible:
for certainly the distance between each place of encampment is three or four leagues, and the people are so many
and so close together that they look like a procession of
Corpus Domini in a great city, without diminution in any
part of the road. The people are of this kind; the tenth
part of them may be well-dressed people, and the nine
parts common people, both men and women, young people,
and poor, some of them clothed in skins, others in poor
stuffs, and all these common people carry with them their
property, which all consists of pots for making wine, and
porringers for drinking. If they move short distances,

these poor people carry with them their poor dwellings, made and thatched as they had them; and if they go further they carry the wood of them, which are some poles. The rich bring very good tents. I do not speak of the great lords and great gentlemen, because each of these moves a city or a good town of tents, and loads, and muleteers, a matter without number or reckoning. I do not know what to say of those on foot. We Portuguese and the Franks often talked of these mules, because in the winter that is coming, as is reported, for many lords go to pass the winter at their lands, the Court cannot move with less than fifty thousand mules, and from that upwards, the number may reach a hundred thousand. There are very few horses, and the led mules are twice or thrice as many as the others, these are not reckoned in the number of mules. Of the horses many are very handsome, and as they are not shod, they soon founder, so they do not travel upon them: neither do I reckon these, therefore I say very few horses. If the Prester travels far, the villages remain full of foundered horses, and afterwards they take them away at leisure. I do not reckon the mules with packs; the male mules serve as well for the saddle as the female; they serve in one manner only, those that are saddle mules for the saddle, and the pack mules for packs. There are also a quantity of ponies[1] for packs, but they founder like the horses. There are many asses which serve better than the ponies, and many pack oxen, and in many districts camels which carry large loads, these in the flat lands.

[1] *Sendeiros Galegos.*

CAP. LXXXVIII.—*Of the churches at Court, and how they travel, and how the altar stones are reverenced, and how Prester John shows himself to the people each year.*

Prester John rarely travels in a straight direction, nor does anyone know where he is going. This multitude of people travels along the road until they find a white tent pitched, and there they settle down each in their own places. Frequently Prester John does not come to this tent, but sleeps in the monasteries and large churches which are in the country. In the tent which is thus pitched they do not neglect to make solemn observances of instrumental music and chaunts, yet not so perfect as when the lord is there : moreover, the churches always travel with the Court, and there are thirteen of them. They travel by the straight road, although Prester John goes off the road. The altar stone or stones of all the churches are conveyed with much reverence, and are only carried by mass priests, and always four priests go with each stone, and four others outside of these to do them reverence ; they carry these stones on a trestle[1] raised on men's shoulders, and covered with rich cloths of brocade and silk. In front of each altar or stone, for all go together, walk two deacons, with thurible and cross, and another with a bell ringing it. And every man, or woman, who is going on the road, as soon as he hears the bell goes off the road, and makes room for the church ; and if he is riding a mule he dismounts and lets the church go by. Also, whenever the Prester travels with his Court, four lions always go before him, these too travel by the straight road, and they go bound with strong chains, that is to say, with two chains, one behind and one before, and many men conduct them ; to these also people give up the road, but it is from fear. We travelled on our road, with various halts, till the 20th of December, when we

---

[1] *Padiola*, a hand-barrow.

stopped at the great gullies which have the gates, where we passed in coming,[1] and there they gave us quarters in large fields, when Prester John's tents were pitched. They at once began to make a very high platform in one of the tents for Prester John to show himself on Christmas-day, because he generally shows himself three times a year, that is, once at Christmas, another time at Easter, and another on Holy Cross day in September. They say that he makes these three exhibitions of himself because his grandfather, the father of his father, who was named Alexander, was kept by his courtiers hidden for three years when dead, and they were masters of his kingdoms and lordships : for up to that time no one of the people ever saw their king, and he was not seen except by a very few of his servants and courtiers ; and at the request of the people the father of this David showed himself these three days, and so does this one. They say that if he goes to war, he goes uncovered in the sight of all, and even when travelling, as will be related further on, where we saw him.

CAP. LXXXIX.—*How Prester John sent to call me to say mass for him on Christmas-day, and of confession and communion.*

Whilst we were thus a good way off from the tents of Prester John in our tents, and our church pitched close by, we said mass every day. On the vigil of Christmas, already midday or more, Prester John sent to call me, and asked me what festival we made next day. I told him how we celebrated the birth of Christ, and he asked me what solemnity we observed. I told him the manner which we followed with respect to that, and how we said three masses. He said that they did all as we did, but that they did not say more than one mass, and of the three masses that we

[1] See Chapter lxv, p. 160.

were used to say, he asked me to say one for him, whichever I wished.   I replied that I would say whichever His
Highness commanded.   Then he told me to say the mass
of tierce, that he would be very glad to hear it, and also
the office we were accustomed to use.   He ordered that our
church tent should at once be brought close to his tent.   It
was brought and he ordered two tents to be taken away
from his tent, and our church to be pitched at the principal
entrance of his tent, so that there would not be more than
two fathoms between the church and the tent : he also said
that at cock-crow he would send to call us to come to the
church, that so his priests chaunted, and that we were to
do everything as we were accustomed to do in our country,
as he wished to hear us.   When our church tent was thus
pitched we at once sung in it vespers and compline, which
the Prester heard inside his tent, and I say that he heard
them, because we saw him there, as it was so close as has
been said.   Then we went to our tents, and as soon as the
cocks crew, he summoned us, and we went six of us who understood church matters and could sing well: these were, Manuel
de Mares, a servant of the Marquis of Vilareal, and player
on the organ, Lazaro d'Andrade, painter, a native of Lisbon,[1]
Joan Escolar the clerk of the embassy, mestre Joam, Nicolas Catelam, and mestre Pedro a Genoese.   I took there
as many books as I had got, although they were apart from
the feast, but only to make up a number, because they are
much given to asking for books ; and I opened them all
upon the altar, and we began our matins as well as we were
able, and certainly it appeared that our Lord assisted us
and gave us grace.   At the commencement Prester John
sent twenty candles, as he thought we had few, for we had
not got more than four candles.   We prolonged these
matins a good deal with prose, hymns and canticles which
we introduced, for we could not do anything else, as we had

_____
[1] From this it appears that his leg-bone was not quite broken.

nothing prepared and marked out, and we sought what
could be best chaunted or intoned.   I continued the matins
in their order whilst the others sung, and in all this office
as long as it lasted, Prester John never moved from the
edge of his tent, which as I have said was close to the
church.   Two messengers never ceased coming and going
to ask what we were singing, whenever they heard a change
in the sound of psalms, hymns, responses, prose, or canticles.   I feigned what I did not know, and told them they
were books of Jeremiah, which spoke of the birth of Christ;
and so of the psalms of David, and other prophets.   He was
pleased and praised the books.   When our service, which
was rather long, was finished, there came an old priest who
had been and they say still is the master of Prester John,
and asked us if we had finished, or why we were silent.   I
told him we had finished.   He replied that he would have
rejoiced if the service had reached to next morning, and it
had seemed to him that he had been in paradise with the
angels.   I told him that until mass we had no other office,
and that I wanted to hear the confessions of some who
wished to receive the Lord's body.   Then there came
another message to ask where confession was to be made :
when it came I was already hearing confessions upon a
drum which they had sent to strike for matins, and this old
priest having come with this message, and finding me
already seated and hearing confessions, lit a blazing torch
and placed it in front of me as if for them to see me from
the tent ; and he sat down on the ground close to me with
his elbow on my knees, and the penitent on the other side ;
and he did not rise from that place until I had heard two
persons in confession, and the morning became altogether
light.   At the end of this, this honourable priest said :
would that God were pleased that the Neguz should give
me leave to remain with you for all my life, for you are holy
men and do things completely.   This priest went away

and soon returned, saying that Prester John desired me to
hear confessions, that he wished to see our mode, which
they had related to him, for hearing confessions. I sent
word that it was getting late for saying mass at the hour
which His Highness had ordered. He sent to tell me to
go on confessing, and to say mass when I chose or was able
to do so, for he would not hear any other mass this day
than ours. I returned again to hear confessions on the
drum where he could well see me sitting dressed in my
surplice, and the penitent with his hat on his head, kneeling,
with as much decorum as was possible. When this confession was finished, I sent to tell him that we would say
mass as it was getting late. He said that whenever we
pleased, for he was not weary with seeing and hearing, and
was ready to hear mass. We got ready for our procession
with the cross raised up, and a picture of our Lady in our
hands, and all with lighted tapers and two torches near the
cross. And as we made or began our procession inside
the circuit of our church tent, the Prester sent to say that
he saw the procession well, but that we should make it
outside the *mandilates* of his tent, that is to say, the curtains which surround his tents, so that all the people might
see it, and he sent fully four hundred tapers of white wax
from his tents for us to carry lighted in our hands, beginning with the Portuguese and white men, and going on
with his people as far as the tapers went. Thus we did
it with as much decorum as we were able. When the
procession was finished, which was very late on account of
the great circuit we made, we began our aspersions of holy
water, and went to sprinkle Prester John with it, which
could be thrown upon him without stirring from the
church : there were with him, as they said, the Queen his
wife, the Queen his mother, who is Queen Helena, and the
Cabeata and other courtiers. Inside our church were all
the great men of the Court that there was room for, and

those that could not find room stood outside, because from the altar as far as the Prester's tent all was clear down the middle in order that His Highness might see the office of the mass. All remained thus until the end, and we gave the communion to those that had confessed, with great reverence (according to our custom) they on their knees with their napkins in their hands divided in two rows, so that they might be seen from the Prester's tent. On ending, with the cross uplifted, we returned to sprinkle holy water on Prester John, because it is the custom of the two churches which are nearest his tents, that is the churches of our Lady and Holy Cross, to sprinkle him with holy water every day at the end of mass: and they cast this water from a distance of more than two games of ball; and they throw it in this manner. One like a deacon goes with the priest who says the mass, and carries a pitcher in his hand, and pours water into the priest's hand, and the priest only makes a sign with his hand and the water towards the tent. We sprinkled it with hyssop in his face. The Franks and interpreters, and chiefly Pero de Covilham, who now was with us, and all who understood the language of the country, said that the people very much praised our customs and offices, and said that we did them with great devotion, and principally the communion, which was administered with great purity. The Prester also sent to say that our services seemed to him very good and very complete.

Cap. xc.—*How the Prester gave leave to go to the ambassador and the others, and ordered me to remain alone with the interpreter, and of the questions about Church matters, and how we all sang compline, and how Prester John departed that night.*

When all was concluded, that is to say procession, mass, and communion, the Prester desired the ambassador and all the Franks to go and dine, and that I should remain alone with one interpreter. Remaining alone, the old priest came and said that Prester John said that we observed Church matters very well, but what reason had we for allowing laymen to come into the church the same as the clergy, and that also he had heard tell that women entered it? I answered that the church of God was not closed to any Christian, and that Christ was always with arms open for every Christian who approached and came to him, and since he received them in glory in Paradise, how should we not receive them in church, which is the road' to the church of Paradise. With respect to women, although in former time they did not enter into the Sanctuary,[1] the deserts of Our Lady were and are so great, that they had sufficed to make the feminine gender deserving to enter into the house of God. And as to ministering at the altar, that men in orders ministered. They came to say that my reasons seemed good to him, but he wished to know why, as I was the only priest, and he who carried the thurible was not a priest, how it was he carried it, because the incense ought to go in the hand of a priest, and of no other person? I answered that the person who served as a deacon was a *zagonay*, what they call of the gospel, and that his office was to carry the thurible. There came another message asking if we had that in a book, as our books were better than theirs, because our books contained all things. I answered that our books were very perfect, because since the time of the apostles we had always had learned men and doctors in the holy mother Church, who never did, nor now do, anything else but compile and bring together those things which are scattered about in the Holy Scriptures, both by the prophets, apostles, or evangelists, and by Jesus Christ our Saviour. They again told me that they had eighty-one books of the Old and New Testaments, had we

---

[1] *Sancta sanctorum.*

15

any more? I told them we had the eighty-one books, and
more than ten times eighty-one drawn from those, with
many declarations and perfections. They said they well
knew that we had more books than they had, on this account they desired that I should tell them of books not
seen by or known to them. Thus they kept questioning
me, without the two messengers ever ceasing to go and
come, nor I able to sit down, but only to lean upon a staff
until the hour of vespers; and if these questions and
answers had to be written down, two hands of paper would
not suffice, neither could memory retain them for the haste
they made. Some answers went and other questions came,
each in their own fashion, and in much disorder, because
they were not all questions from Prester John, for some
were from his mother, and others from his wife, and also
from Queen Helena. I answered as God helped me, I was
in such a state of weakness and hunger that I could not
endure it, and instead of an answer, I sent to ask His
Highness to have pity for an old man, who had neither eat
nor drunk since yesterday at midday, nor had slept, and
could not stand for weakness. He sent to say, that since
he rejoiced to converse with me, why did not I rejoice too.
I replied that old age, hunger, and weakness, did not allow
of it. He sent to say that if I wished to eat he would send
it to me, that he had already sent a great deal to eat to our
tent, and if I wished to eat there I might go, or if I wished
to eat here he would order food to be given me. I told
him I wished to eat at our tent, to rest myself: then they
gave me leave. While I was on the road, a page reached
me half dead with running; when I heard him come, I
thought it was my sins come to make me turn back. He
told me the Prester sent him to beg me to send back the
hat I had on my head, and to pardon him, and not be
angry at having been so long without eating, and as soon
as I had eaten to come back at once, as he wished to learn

more things from me. On reaching our tent I was seized with a giddiness, that the sight left my eyes, and I became quite cold. An hour and a half had not passed before he sent to call me, and as it was already late, those who knew church matters went with me, and we sung compline, only because there was no place at our tent, and when compline was finished, there came a message to strike our church tent, because Prestor John was going away that night, as in effect he did do, in order to pass the bad passages without anyone knowing of it. While we were lying sleeping in our tent, a little more or less than midnight, we heard a great tramping of mules and people passing close to us, and then we heard say that the Noguz was travelling; and as it seemed to us that we should be left without people, we made ready quickly; and when we arrived at the first pass, there was no remedy for it, and our people made way for us with their lances, and we travelled thus that day with lances in front and lances behind, and we in the middle, not allowing anyone to come among us; because otherwise we should never have got together again. We went and found the King's tent pitched in the middle of the ravines in sight between the meadows, where I before related that the friar ordered the beans to be pulled out, and there slept all the people who were able to pass, and we did not sleep much, for before midnight we heard say that the Negus was travelling, and we went after him at once : and we got out of the bad passes before morning. We heard say that in this night there died in these passes, men, women and many mules, asses, ponies, and pack oxen ; we found many dead. This is the pass which is named Aquia fagi, which means death to asses, by which we passed in coming. It was certain that a great lady died this night, and with her a man who led her mule by the halter, and two who went close to her, and the mule, all of them went over a rock, and were dashed to pieces before they reached the bottom : it could not be otherwise, because the cliffs are, as I before said, something incredible : and whoever sees them, they appear to him more like hell than anything else. So we made our journey without observing the octaves of Christmas, which they do not observe in this country. And I before said that the Court did not finish moving in four or five days; here they spent more than three weeks in getting through these gates, and the baggage of the Prester was more than a month passing every day.

CAP. XCI.—*How the Prester went to lodge at the church of St. George, and ordered it to be shown to the people of the embassy, and after certain questions ordered me to be shown some rich umbrellas.*

On the 28th of December of 1520, we came to a place on the road where we saw a church which we had seen in coming, but did not go to it, which is named St. George. They pitched the tent of the Prester below the church, and we in our place, which was already assigned to us; and next day, very early, they sent to call us, and tell us to go to the said church. When we were there, he ordered it to be shown to us, and we saw it very well. It is a large church, with all the walls painted with pictures of subjects and very good stories, well proportioned, made by a Venetian whom I mentioned before, named Nicolas Brun-caliam, and his name is on these pictures, and the people here call him Marcoreos. This church has all its outer parts which are within the covered circuit (which is like a covered cloister) hung with rich curtains, pieces of brocade from top to bottom, plush, velvet, and other rich cloths and stuffs. When we arrived within the gate of the outer circuit which is uncovered, and intended to enter the

covered circuit, they ordered the curtains to be drawn,
and the principal door appeared, which is all plated with
plates, which at first sight looked like gold, and so they
told us that it was : yet we saw that on the contrary it was
all leaves gilt and silvered, and the gilding was very well
applied, both to the doors and windows. In seeing these
things, the Cabeata, who is a great lord, went with us to
show them; the Prester was there within his curtains, and
he saw us and we him when we passed before his curtains.
From thence he sent to ask what we thought of that
church and its paintings. We said we thought it beautiful,
and that it looked entirely like something belonging to a
great sovereign and king. He being pleased, sent to say
that his grandfather had ordered the building of this
church and was buried there; he also asked whether in our
country we had churches lined with wood like that, or with
what wood were they made. Our answer was that this
church was very good as we had already said, but that our
churches were of stone vaults, and in those that were of
wood, the wood was covered with gilding and blue, and the
pillars were of great pieces of marble and other splendid
and valuable things. He replied that he well knew that
our things were rich, great, and perfect, because we had
good masters. The covered circuit of this church is erected
upon thirty-six wooden pillars, very high, and as thick as
the masts of galleys : they are cased with wood, and on the
wood are paintings like those on the walls : so that it is a
regal building, and the people of this country think well of
it and reckon it as very great.

This same day, in the afternoon, Prester John sent to call
me, and asked me what I thought of that church, and I
gave him my opinion, adding what all had said with truth :
he asked me about more lives of saints. I answered what I
knew ; he also asked me about our church ceremonies, and
I gave him answers according to my knowledge. When

these questions were ended, which took place near his tent, and I was dismissed, they brought down from the church four large and very splendid umbrellas, at which I wondered and was astonished, because I had seen many large and splendid ones in India, but never had seen any of this sort. They went to tell the Prester how I was astonished at the umbrellas, for which reason he sent for me back again, and there were before his door the Franks who from the first had been at his court, and I went back to where they stood. Upon this the umbrellas came, and they ordered them to be shewn to me, and told me to look at them well, and to say what I thought of them. I said in answer that they seemed to belong to a great king, and that in India there were many large and splendid umbrellas, but that I had never seen such as these. He then ordered that they should plant the umbrellas on the ground in the sun, and to tell me that when he travelled, and wished to rest, either he or the queen his wife, they set up one of these umbrellas, and they rested under their shade, or ate if they required. I sent to say that the umbrellas were such in greatness and splendour that His Highness could well repose under the shade of any of them. Then there came another message to ask if the King of Portugal had got any such umbrellas. I said that the King of Portugal did not use umbrellas with a pole, but that he used shades[1] of the fashion of that on my head, trimmed with brocade or velvet, or satin or other silk, with cords and tassels of gold, of the fashion that pleased him, and that if he wished to repose when he travelled he had many palaces and great houses, and shady places and gardens where he rested, with many infinite adornments which dispensed with umbrellas, and that it seemed to me that these umbrellas of the Prester were more for state than from the necessity of shade. There came another message, that I spoke the truth, and that these umbrellas had be-

---

[1] *Sombreira*, the same word is used for umbrellas or hats.

longed to his grandfather, and had remained in this church, and that he was ordering them to be sent as a loan to another church to which we were going. These umbrellas were of so great a circumference that ten men could very well be under the shade of each of them. After I had given my answers to the best of my ability, he sent to ask if I would like to drink wine of grapes or of honey, or çauna, which is of barley. I sent to ask that they should serve me with wine of grapes, and that the wine of honey was hot, and the çauna cold, and not fit for old men; that it should be wine of grapes or honey, whichever His Highness commanded. He sent a second time to tell me to declare which I wished for: I sent word I wished for grape wine. He sent me four jars of wine of honey, telling me to invite the Franks of old standing who were near the tent, and present at all these conversations. So he did not choose to send the grape wine which I asked for. We drank several times, and the rest we sent to our tents.

CAP. XCII.—*Of the travelling of Prester John, and the manner of his state when he is on the road.*

On the 29th day of the said month Prester John sent to say that we were not to travel, but to go as we should be directed. So we did; and his travelling was in this manner. In the days that had passed no one knew where he was going, and the people took up their quarters wherever they found the white tent pitched, and we settled down each one in his place, according as it had been before ordained, that is to say, on the right hand or on the left, far or near: and at the said tent ceremony was observed as though His Highness was there, but not so perfect as when he is there: for it is easy to know whether he is there or not, and that by the service of the pages and other things. Up to this time sometimes he remained behind us, sometimes he went on before, as he pleased. [Now he began to travel in this manner, that is, bareheaded, with a crown on his head, surrounded by red curtains behind and on the sides, in good quantity, full and high : he goes in the bay,[1] and those who carry the curtain go outside, and carry it raised up with poles. There go with him inside the curtain six pages whom they call 'legamonchos', which means pages of the halter, and they go in this manner. The mule carries a rich headstall over the bridle, and this headstall has at the chin two ends with thick tassels[2] of silk : and with these ends or tassels go two pages, each on one side, who lead the mule as if by a halter ; two others go, one on each side, with their hands on the neck of the mule, and two others behind them in a similar manner, with their hands on the mule's haunches, or on the hinder pummel of the saddle. In front of the Prester go twenty pages on foot, of the principal ones, and in front of these pages go six horses very handsome and richly caparisoned : with each of these horses are four men, very smart and well dressed after their fashion. These four men lead each horse, two at the headstall like the Prester's mule, and the other two with their hands on the saddle, one on each side. In front of these horses go six mules saddled and very well furnished, and with each one four men, as with the horses. In front of these mules go twenty gentlemen of high rank dressed in their cloaks, and we the Portuguese went in front of these gentlemen, for there they assigned to us our place.] No other people—horse, foot, or mule—approach for a great distance ; and if there are any going in front, there are always runners galloping their horses as long as they do not tire ; and if they founder, they take others, and make the people go apart from the road a long way off, so that no one shows. The Betudetes go with the men of the guard a long way off from the road, one on one side, and the other on

---

[1] Or hollow.   [2] Enxarafas.

the other : and they go at the distance of at least a musket
shot; where there are plains, at times, they go at a distance of
half a league or more, sometimes a league, according as the
land lies. If the road is rocky and shut in by cliffs, so that
it is not possible to pass except all by the same road, one of
the Betudetes goes forward half a league, and the other
remains as far behind ; the one that goes forward is he of
the right hand side, and he of the rear of the left hand side.
There go with each of these Betudetes more than six thousand men. Also there go, as I have before said, four lions
bound with strong chains, led before and behind. So also
travel the churches, with much honour and reverence, as has
been related. There is another thing which the Prester
always brings wherever he goes, and he does not move
without it—that is, a hundred jars of mead, and each jar
contains six canadas.¹ These jars are black, like jet, very
well made, stoppered with clay and sealed with a seal. Nobody, even though he should be a great lord, approaches
these to ask for or take anything without leave from the
Prester. There also they carry another hundred closed
painted baskets full of bread. These go behind the Prester
at no great distance; men carry these things on their heads.
They go one in front of the other—that is to say, one jar,
then one basket; and behind them come six men who go
like officers of the King's table. When they reach the
Prester's tent they put it all inside, and he grants of it to
whom he pleases.

Cap. xciii.—*How the Prester went to the church of Macham
Selasem, and of the procession and reception that they
gave him, and what passed between His Highness and
me respecting the reception.*

We came to pass Saturday and Sunday, the last days of
December, in a meadow, with all the Court. On Monday we

¹ A *canada* equal to three pints.

all set out together, the Prester going in his curtain, as on
the former days. On the first day of January 1521, we
came and stopped at another large church, which they did
not let us see on our first coming. Its dedication is Macham
Selasem, which means the Trinity. Before we arrived at
this church, the Prester travelling bareheaded (as has been
said) with his crown on his head and a cross in his hand as
always, and inside his curtain, and we in front of him as on
the previous days—quite a league before we arrived at this
church, the Prester ordered eight saddled horses, very large
and handsome, which are prized in this country, to be
brought, and had them sent to the Portuguese that they
might ride them and skirmish before him; and so they did.
At the distance of a quarter of a league before reaching the
church, an infinite number of people came to receive him,
in this manner. The people could not be reckoned, the
crosses were innumerable, clergy and friars exceeding
twenty thousand divided into bands, as there were many
monasteries and churches, and thus they accompanied their
crosses. The friars must have been from a distance, because
in this kingdom of Amara there is no monastery, nothing
but great churches, and tombs of kings. There would be
among this clergy fully a hundred mitres, that is high caps;
and there were here sixty-four umbrellas, these could easily
be counted, because they were high above the people, and
were large and rich, but not so much so as those of the
church of St. George, which the Prester ordered to be
shown to me. All these umbrellas belonged to the churches
in which the kings lie buried, and they leave them there
when they die. This great multitude of people thus
assembled together, although a great number of them were
of the Court, yet a great part belonged to churches and
monasteries and had come for this reception. The business
which had to be done was that many people of the country
came to see the Prester who was travelling with his head

uncovered, as they had never seen him. As soon as we arrived at the church, and prayers were ended, the Prester went to his tent; and before we set out from that place he sent to call me, and he also sent word to the ambassador and his company to go to their quarters. He sent to ask me what I thought of this reception, and whether such were made for the King of Portugal. I replied that for the King of Portugal they made great receptions and festivals; but that I had never seen a reception or assembly of so many crosses and mitres, nor so many people together at once; and that his reception appeared to me so good that no better could be made in the world: and that it also seemed to me that wherever a man should relate this outside his kingdoms and lordships, he would not be believed unless it were on account of the great fame which His Highness enjoyed in Christendom and in all the world; and that this would more oblige the giving credit to such a thing. To this came the reply that the people were yet much more than they appeared to be, because they were naked people, and did not look as numerous as they were, and that our people were clothed and smart, and even though they were few they seemed to be many; and that I might go in peace to my quarters with the ambassador. I found him still on the road. When I reached him there came another message from the Prester, to say that this church was new, and that as yet they had not said mass in it; and that it was the custom for as many as entered it to make an offering; and that the ambassador should give his arms, and that I should give the hood which I had on my head, and likewise that each should give the piece which he had to bestow. By this we knew that he was delighted and rejoiced much at our opinion.

CAP. XCIV.—*Of the fashion and things of this church of the Trinity, and how the Prester sent to tell the ambassador to go and see the church of his mother, and of the things which happened in it.*

The following day the Prester sent to call us and conduct us to the above-mentioned church, and he was already in it. This church is large and high, and the walls are of white stone hewn masonry, and with good tracery on the walls. However, they do not fix the upper woodwork upon the walls, because they could not support it, from not being linked and bound one with another, that is to say the stones and corner stones, but they are laid one above another, without any going all through the walls: though, at first sight it looks well to anyone who does not know what is inside. It has the principal door lined with plates of metal like that of the church of St. George, which we left behind us; and in the midst of this plating are stones and false pearls well set. On the top of the wall, over the principal door, are two effigies of our Lady very well made, and two angels of the same fashion, all done with the paint brush, and they say that they were painted by a friar, who learned by himself, and I saw this friar. The church has three naves in the body of the church raised on six supports. These supports are of masonry in pieces. A third nave outside, which is closed and covered in like a cloister and almost like part of the church, is raised upon sixty-one high wooden props, like very tall masts; upon these props rests the woodwork, almost flat, of very thick planks. There were suspended all round the tower sixteen curtains that could be drawn, of the length of the stuffs, which were all very rich brocade, and each curtain was of sixteen pieces of stuff. The Cabeata went about showing us these things. When we had seen all, the Prester sent to ask what we thought of

these things, works and stuffs. We answered that it seemed
to us very good, and that it looked as it should do, seeing to
whom it belonged. Then he asked if they could send him
lead to cover this church. The ambassador said that everything that His Highness might wish for, the King of
Portugal would send to him in abundance, as His Highness
would see, because all metals were in his possession. From
this place we set out with the Prester to his tents, he in his
curtain, and we on our mules, without any more ceremonies.
The tents were close to another church of the same form as
this, only that it was smaller. When we arrived and dismounted close to the tent, the Prester sent to tell the
ambassador that we should go and see the church of his
mother, which was close to the tents. We went there, and
certainly it is well made for its size. Here they told us not
to find any fault with it, because the Prester's mother was
so fanciful that if we found any fault with it, or said that it
was not so good as that of her son, that she would order it
to be thrown down and to be constructed afresh. When we
had seen this church, and while we were still in it, the
Prester sent to say that, since we had much gold in Portugal,
why did we sell rich stuffs to the Moors for gold? The
ambassador replied that the expenses of the King of
Portugal and of his captains and fleets were so great, on
account of the many wars they continually waged with the
Moors, in many parts, that if they did not trade, they would
not be able to endure them, especially as these expenses and
wars were a long way off from the kingdom of Portugal,
from which succours had to come; and as they went so
much by sea they carried with them merchandise, and to
some they sold and from others they took, and by this
means they supplied a part of the expense. To this there
was no answer, but he then sent word to show us in the
church two large door curtains, very rich with figures, and
he asked where those stuffs were made. He was told that

all those were made in Christendom, and not in any other
part. Upon this he sent to ask if they would send him
many of those, and he would send much gold. The
ambassador replied that if His Highness wrote to the King
of Portugal, that he would send him as many as he wished
for. At this they came with another rejoinder saying, what
had we brought him? The ambassador answered that he
had brought him that which he had given him, that is to
say a valuable sword, and a gold-mounted dagger, and two
cannons with their chambers and balls and powder, and
four cloths for hanging on walls, and some handsome
cuirasses, and that this had been given him by the Captain-
major of India, and that he did not send these things
except as a sample; and that if it pleased him he should
write to the King of Portugal, and he would send him as
much as he desired. They came with another addition,
saying, that it was the custom of all those who had sent
ambassadors to these countries to send many goods, and so
they had always done to his predecessors, and that we had
come and had brought nothing. The ambassador replied
to this, that it was not the custom of the King of Portugal
and of his captains, when they sent embassies or messages
to other kings and great lords, to send any presents, except
out of friendship: rather, on the contrary, all those sent
things to him to make him their friend: and if the captain-
major of India had sent him those presents, he had sent
them to serve him, and not on account of any such custom;
nevertheless, the King of Portugal had sent to the Prester
by another ambassador who died in Camaran, more than a
hundred thousand cruzados in goods, and he had sent them
as to a brother, and not from custom or obligation. With
regard to what His Highness said, that the King of Portugal had sent him many things and that they had not presented them, he had already many times sent to tell him
that he would see by the captain-major's letters what he

had sent him ; and how what the King of Portugal had sent
had remained in India, and also he could know by the
factor and clerk who came with them, because the affairs of
such sovereigns are conducted by factors and clerks. And
although they sent factors, the Portuguese were not accustomed to act falsely, but to deal with great truth in all that
was charged or commanded to them, and he had told him
the truth several times, and if he chose to believe it he
might believe it, and if not, let it be as His Highness commanded. And His Highness should know that the ambassador had come by order of the great captain-major of the
King of Portugal who governed the Indies, and the manner
in which he had come had been such as was usual for going
to all kings and emperors : and that His Highness should
not send to say to him that which was not usual among the
Portuguese, but rather should dismiss him, for he wanted
to go because the time had arrived. The Prester sent to
say that if we had come in the times of the preceding kings
that they would not have done us any honour such as he
had done us, unless we had brought them much goods.
The ambassador replied that, on the contrary, many injuries had been done to us in his countries, and robberies,
stealing whatever we had, and that there did not remain to
us clothes, nor the goods we had brought for our maintenance, and that if we died in this country we should
all go to Paradise as martyrs, on account of the affronts
which we had met with and experienced, for already they
had attempted three or four times to kill us in his countries, and that we endured all with patience, for the love of
God, and of the King of Portugal, to whom we belonged :
and that the King of Portugal had done other honour to
Matheus, because he said he was the Prester's ambassador.
Withal he entreated him to despatch us, that we might go
and give an account of that which we had been commanded,
because the Portuguese were not accustomed to lie, but to

do and speak truth. To this came an answer that neither
the Portuguese nor the ambassador told lies, but that
Matheus had been a liar, and that he well knew the honour
which had been done to him by the King of Portugal, and
his captain in India, as soon as he arrived there, and that
we should not be angry, and we should soon be despatched,
with much satisfaction to ourselves, and that we should go
in peace to dine.

CAP. XCV.—*How Prester John sent to tell those of the embassy
and the Franks to go and see his baptism, and of the representation which the Franks made for him, and how
he ordered that I should be present at the baptism, and
of the fashion of the tank, and how he desired the Portuguese to swim, and gave them a banquet.*

On the 4th day of the month of January Prester John
sent to tell us to order our tents, both that of the church
and our own, to be taken from this place to a distance of
about half a league, where they had made a large tank of
water, in which they were to be baptized on the day of the
Kings, because on that day it is their custom to be baptized
every year, as that was the day on which Christ was baptized. We took thither a small tent for resting in and the
church tent. The next day, which was the vigil of the
day of the Kings, the Prester sent to call us, and we saw
the enclosure where the tank was. The enclosure was a fence,
and very large, in a plain. He sent to ask us if we intended
to be baptized. I replied that it was not our custom to be
baptized more than once, when we were little. Some said,
principally the ambassador, that we would do what His
Highness commanded. When they perceived that, they came
back again with another message to me, asking what I said
as to being baptized. I answered that I had been already

baptized, and should not be so again. They still sent word that if we did not wish to be baptised in their tank, they would send us water to our tent. To this the ambassador replied that it should be as His Highness ordered. The Franks and our people had arranged to give a representation of the Kings,[1] and they sent to tell him of it. A message came that it pleased him, and so they got ready for it, and they made it in the inclosure and plain close to the King's tent, which was pitched close to the tank. They gave the representation, and it was not esteemed, nor hardly looked at, and so it was a cold affair. Now that it was night they told us to go to our tent, which was not far off. In all this night till dawn a great number of priests never ceased chaunting over the said tank, saying that they were blessing the water, and about midnight, a little earlier or later, they began the baptism. They say, and I believe that such is the truth, that the first person baptized is the Prester, and after him the Abima, and after him the Queen, the wife of the Prester. They say that these three persons wear cloths over their nakedness, and that all the others were as their mothers bore them. When it was almost the hour of sunrise, and the baptism in fullest force, the Prester sent to call me to see the said baptism. I went and remained there till the hour of tierce, seeing how they were baptized ; they placed me at one end of the tank, with my face towards Prester John, and they baptize in this manner.

The tank is large, the bottom of it in the earth, and it is cut very straight in the earth, and well squared ; it is lined with planks, and over the planks waxed cotton cloth is spread. The water came from a rivulet through a conduit, like those to irrigate gardens, and it fell into the tank through a cane, at the end of which was a bag that was full ; because they strain the water which falls into the tank ; and it was no longer running when I saw it : tho

[1] Adoration of the Magi.

tank was full of blessed water, as they said, and they told
me that it contained oil.   This tank had five or six steps at
one end, and about three fathoms in front of these steps
was the dais of Prester John, on which he sat.   He had
before him a curtain of blue tafetan, with an opening of
about a span, by which those who were baptized saw him,
because he was with his face to the tank.   In the tank
stood the old priest, the master of the Prester, who was
with me Christmas night, and he was naked as when his
mother bore him (and quite dead of cold, because it was a
very sharp frost), standing in the water up to his shoulders
or thereabouts, for so deep was the tank that those who
were to be baptized entered by the steps, naked, with their
backs to the Prester, and when they came out again they
showed him their fronts, the women as well as the men.
When they came to the said priest, he put his hands on
their head, and put it three times under the water, saying
in his language, "In name of the Father, of the Son, and of
the Holy Spirit": he made the sign of the cross as a blessing, and they went away in peace. (The "I baptize thee", I
heard him say it.)   If they were little people they did not
go down all the steps, and the priest approached them, and
dipped them there.   They placed me at the other end of the
tank, with my face looking to the Prester, so that when he
saw the backs, I saw the fronts, and the contrary way when
they came out of the tank.   After a great number of baptized persons had passed, he sent to call me to be near him;
and so near that the Cabeata did not stir to hear what the
Prester said, and to speak to the interpreter who was close
to me : and he asked me what I thought of that office.   I
answered him that the things of God's service which were
done in good faith and without evil deceit, and in His
praise, were good, but such an office as this, there was none
in our Church, rather it forbade us baptizing without necessity on that day, because on that day Christ was baptized,

so that we should not think of saying of ourselves that we
were baptized on the same day as Christ; also the Church
does not order this sacrament to be given more than once.
Afterwards he asked whether we had it written in books
not to be baptized more than once. I replied, Yes, that we
had, and that in the Creed, which was made at the Council
of Pope Leon, with the three hundred and eighteen bishops,
about which at times His Highness had questioned me, it
was said: "Confiteor unum baptisma in remissionem pecca-
torum." Then they said to me that such was the truth, and
so it was written in their books; but what were they to do
with many who turned Moors and Jews after being Christians and then repented, and with others who did not
believe well in baptism, what remedy would they have ? I
answered : For those who do not rightly believe, teaching
and preaching would suffice for them, and if that did not
profit, burn them as heretics. And so Christ spoke, and
St. Mark wrote it: "Qui crediderit et baptizatus fuerit sal-
vus erit, qui vero non crediderit condemnabitur." And as to
those who turned Moors or Jews, and afterwards of their
own free will recognised their error, and asked for mercy,
the Abima would absolve them, with penances salutary for
their souls, if he had powers for this, if not, let them go to
the Pope of Rome, in whom are all the powers. And those
who did not repent, they might take them and burn them,
for such is the use in Frankland and the Church of Rome.
To this there came the reply, that all this seemed to him
good, but that his grandfather had ordained this baptism
by the counsel of great priests, in order that so many souls
should not be lost, and that it had been the custom until
now ; and he asked if the Pope would concede to the Abima
to hold these powers, and how much it would cost him, and
in how much time could they come. I answered him that
the Pope desired nothing except to save souls, and that he
would esteem it fortunate to send to him, the Abima, with

such powers, and that it would only cost him the expenses
of the journey, which would not be much, and also the
letters of his powers: and that they could go and come
through Portugal in three years : and by the road of Jerusalem, that I did not know it. To this there came no
answer except that I might go in peace to say mass. I said
it was no longer time for saying mass, that midday was
long passed. So I went to dine with our Portuguese and
the Franks.

This tank was all closed in and covered over with
coloured tent cloths, so well that more could not be said,
and so well arranged, with so many oranges and lemons,
and boughs suspended and so well disposed, that the
boughs, oranges, and lemons appeared to have grown there,
and that it was a well ordered garden. The large tent
which was over the tank was long and ....,[1] and
above covered with red and blue crosses of the fashion of
the crosses of the order of Christ. This day, later in the
afternoon, Prester John sent to call the ambassador and
all his company. The baptism was already ended, and
His Highness was still within his curtain where I left him.
We entered there, and he at once asked the ambassador
what he thought of it. He replied that it was very good,
although we had not got such a custom. The water was
then running into the tank, and he asked if there were
here Portuguese who could swim. At once two jumped
into the tank, and swam and dived as much as the tank
allowed of. He enjoyed greatly, as he showed by his looks,
seeing them swim and dive. After this he desired us to
go outside and go to one end of the enclosure or circuit;
and here he ordered a banquet to be made for us of bread
and wine (according to their custom and the use of the
country), and he desired us to raise our church tent and the
tent we were lodging in, because he wished to return to

[1] *De comecira*, omitted by Selves.

his quarters, and that we should go in front of him because he was ordering his horsemen to skirmish in the manner in which they fight with the Moors in the field. So we went in front of him, looking at the said skirmish. They began, but soon there came such heavy rain that it did not allow them to carry out the skirmish which they had begun well.[1]

CAP. XCVI.—*How I went with an interpreter to visit the Abima Mark, and how I was questioned about circumcision, and how the Abima celebrates the holy orders.*

Next day after the baptism I went to visit the Abima Marcos, whom as yet I had not spoken to, nor seen, except at the baptism, when he was half dead with the cold, and I could not speak to him there. He rejoiced greatly at my visit, and would not give me his hand to kiss it, but rather wished to throw himself on the ground with demonstrations of kissing my feet. When we were seated both together on a bedstead, the beginning of our conversation was to give thanks to God for bringing us together. Then he began to speak of the great pleasure he had received from what they had related to him of what I had said on several occasions, and from what he had seen had passed with me at the baptism, and from the great clearness with which I had spoken the truth in the presence of the Prester, which he would not believe from him, the Abima, because he was alone; and that if he had a partner or two, who would assist him in speaking the truth, he would withdraw the Prester from many things and errors, in which he was with his people. Upon this there came in a priest of his, a white man, son of a Gibete, that is, a white man born in this country. This one asked why we were not circumcised, since Christ had been so. I answered that it was true that Christ had been circumcised, and that he chose it

[1] Selves has abridged this chapter considerably.

in order to fulfil the law which was in force at that time, and in order not to be accused before the time of being a breaker of the law : and afterwards it had been commanded to cease circumcision. This priest next said that he was the son of a Frank, and that when he was born his father would not have him circumcised, and when he was already twenty years old and his father had died, he had gone to bed entire, and in the morning found himself cut smaller : how would that be since God no longer would have circumcision. I answered him that it would be a great lie, because although God had not forbidden circumcision, yet he would not be sufficiently worthy nor so holy, that God should have wrought a miracle for him, and from imperfect to make him perfect : and if it was so as he said, that he went to bed entire and found himself cut, the devil must have cut him to make a mockery of him. The Abima, with as many as were in the house, were seized with much laughter, and the Abima rejoiced much; and this priest, from this time forward became much my friend, and came every day to our mass, and was very friendly with the Portuguese. The Abima sent for wine and fruit, and sent with me to our tents much bread and wine and a cow. On the 8th day of January the Abima Mark conferred orders, and I went to see their manner of giving them, and it is as follows. They pitched a white tent in a large plain without inhabitants, where there were quite five or six thousand people to be ordained. The Abima arrived upon a mule, and I with him, as I came in his company, and many others who came with him. In the midst of these people he made a speech from his mule in Arabic, which one of his priests translated into Abyssinian. I asked the interpreter that I brought with me what the Abima said. He told me that he said if there was anyone here who had two wives or more, even though one was dead, that he was not to become a priest, and that if he did become a priest, that he excommunicated him, and held him to be accursed by the curse of God. Having made this speech he went to sit on a chair in front of the said tent, and before him sat three priests on the ground with several books in their hands, and others which ruled the office; and they made all sit down, as many as were to be ordained, squatting,[1] that is to say, upon their heels. This in three very long rows, and each row ended at the three priests who had the books. And there they examined them a very short examination, for each one did not read more than two or three words: then they go to one who stands behind these with a vase of ink and a stamp like a seal, and he puts this stamp on the flat of the right arm. Then they rose from where they came, and went to sit in the middle of the plain in a clump, in which sat all those that had been examined, and there were very few who did not pass. When this examination was ended, the Abima went into the tent and sat on the said chair. This tent had two entrances, and they put all the examined persons in a line, one before another, and they passed before the Abima, entering by one door and going out by the other: when they passed before him, he put his hand on their head, and said words which I did not understand, and so there did not remain one for whom this ceremony was not done. Here he took a book in his hands and read a piece for himself, and held a cross in his hand, and made with it the sign of the cross over them. This ceremony being concluded, a priest who was with the Abima went out to the door of the tent, and read from a book something like an epistle or gospel; then the Abima said mass, which was not more than as much as one might say the psalm *Miserere mei Deus* three times. And he gave the communion to these priests, who were two thousand three hundred and fifty seven, all mass priests: because the mass priests are ordained by themselves, and the

[1] *En cocras*, for *en cocaras*.

deacons by themselves on another day: and the Abima told me that the deacons were ordained in all the orders as far as deacon, like St. Stephen. And later I saw men ordained *zagonais* and priests of the mass all in one day, and this several times, because he conferred orders almost every day, and always in great number, because they come to him from all the kingdoms and lordships of the Prester, for there is no other who ordains these priests. They are not put down in a register, nor do they carry a letter, or other certificate of their orders; and as to the number which I named, which was 2,357, I did not count them, but I asked the person who had the charge, and he told me this number, and certainly it seems to me that it would be true. As to the orders of *zagonais*,[1] I will relate where I saw them and was present at them.

CAP. XCVII.—*How the Prester questioned me about the ceremony of holy orders, and also how I went to the lesser orders which they call zagonais, and what sort of people are ordained.*

On the following day, 9th of January, Prester John sent to call me, and as soon as I arrived, there came a message to say that they had told him that I had been to see how they made his priests, and what did I think of it? I answered that I had seen two things, which if I had not seen, even though another should have told them to me with an oath, I should not have believed, and which would not be believed from me, although I should affirm that I had seen them, as I did see them. One was the multitude of clergy and crosses at the reception of His Highness, and the other was the great number of priests that I had seen ordained together; and the office seemed to me very good, but what did not seem to me good was the great indecency with which those priests came who were ordained; and so I had

---

[1] Deacons, from *diaconos*.

seen the order of the Church transgressed in the ordaining of those priests. Then there came a message that I should not be astonished at any of these things, for, as to his reception, there had only come to it the priests of the churches of his ancestors which were in those districts, and that these wore mitres, and hats, and crosses, which his ancestors had left them ; and that the clergy who had been ordained were very few for what there usually are, as there are always about five or six thousand ordained ; and now there were few because they did not know that the Abima was coming : and he asked me to tell him what indecency I had seen and what breach of the commands of the Church. I answered that it seemed to me very indecent and a very shameful thing that priests who were ordained for the mass, and were to receive the body of the Lord, to come almost naked and showing their nakedness, and that Adam and Eve as soon as they had sinned saw that they were naked and covered themselves because they had to appear before the Lord : and these had to receive him : and also that a friar had come entirely blind, how was he, who never had eyes, to be made a priest for the mass : also another entirely paralysed of the right hand, and four or five who were paralysed in the legs : these also they made priests, and a priest had to be sound in his limbs. The answer came, that he rejoiced much that I looked at all things and spoke of what did not seem to me right, so as to amend them. As to the priests that were naked he would see to that. With respect to the cripples, that I should speak to Ajaze Raphael, who was present on the occasion. This Ajaze Raphael was the honourable priest and great gentleman to whom we were entrusted when we came to the Court. Then I went to dine with him in his tent, and before we dined he sent for a book, which, according to what they read in it, must have been a sacramental of their fashion, and he read in it that a priest had to be

complete, as I had said. I told him that the book spoke
the truth, and that a priest had to be complete in age,
judgment, learning, and limbs : and that those that I saw
and had called cripples were wanting in some of their limbs;
firstly, the blind man who had never seen, how could he
know learning, or administer the sacrament ? The Ajazo
answered, that I had good reason if our books spoke thus.
I said that they did so, and at great length. He asked
me what such as these would do if they had not alms
from the church. I answered that in this country I did
not know, but that in our country such as these, being
given to the church, might serve and would have alms in
the churches and monasteries, and such as the blind would
be organ blowers and bell ringers, and do other things
which there are there, and which there are not in this country. And if they did not serve in monasteries or churches,
that the Kings of the country had in their cities and towns
large hospitals, with much revenue, for the blind and cripples, and sick and poor. The Ajazo answered, that this all
seemed very good, and that the Prester should know it,
and would be much pleased.

On the 10th day of the said month of January the Abima
made deacons. They do not examine for this office, and
they make deacons of children in the lap who cannot yet
speak, and, to the age of fifteen years, when they are still
unmarried, and if they are married, they cannot be deacons.
Those who are going to be mass priests, as soon as they are
deacons they get married, and, when married, are ordained
for the mass; because if they got ordained for the mass
before being married, they could not afterwards be married
or have a wife. The children who can neither speak nor
walk, are carried by men in their arms, because women cannot enter into the church, and their lamentations resemble
those of kids in a yard without the mothers, when they are
separated and are dying of hunger, because they finish the

office at hours of vespers; and they are without food because they have to receive the communion. The little
children of such age we know that they cannot read, and of
the bigger ones there are but few who can read, and the
ceremony with regard to them is this. The Abima is seated
on a chair in the church tent, and these deacons pass before
him in a line after he has said a short prayer, and when
they pass thus, he cuts a lock of hair from the head of each;
then he takes the book and again reads a prayer; they come
another time and he gives them keys to touch, and they
open the door of the tent or only put their hands to it.[1]
Also they put a cloth on their head, and each of these things
they do in turn ; and he gives them small earthenware pots
(to touch),[2] for there are no cruets there; and they return
another time and he puts his hands upon their heads; and
between each of these things he always prays a little, and
the little ones come in arms, as has been said. Then they
follow with their mass, and at the end of it they give the
communion to all of them, and it is an amazing thing the
danger of the little ones, for even by force of water they
cannot make them swallow the Sacrament, both on account
of their tender age, and their much crying. This office
having been concluded, the Abima begged me to come and
dine with him at his abode, and when I was there he asked
me to give him my opinion of that office, as I had been
present, and had seen it well, and the Prester had sent
to tell him to talk to me about the said office, because
he would find in me good reason. Then I told him what I
had said to Ajaze Rafael of the enormity and indecency of
the priests and cripples and blind men who had come to be
ordained. He answered, that the Prester had already sent
him word of this, and of what had passed about it, and of

---

[1] This passage is not clear. Selves has, "They put their hands on the
church door as though opening and shutting it."

[2] From Selves.

what ought to be done, and also he had sent him word of what the Ajazo had said, but he asked me about the zagonais whom he had just made. I said to him that his services seemed to me very good, but that to ordain children newly born, and great ignorant boys, did not seem to me well, neither should it be done in the house of God. He answered that God had brought us to this country to speak the truth, and that he only did that which he was commanded, and that the Prester ordered him to make zagonais[1] of all the children, and that they would learn, because he was very old, and he did not know when they would have another Abima, and that this country had already been twenty-three years without an Abima, and that it was not very long ago that they had sent two thousand ounces of gold to Cairo in search for an Abima: and on account of the wars of the Sultan[2] with the Turk, they had not sent him, and they had taken the gold, and that now God had brought us to this country for us to speak the truth, and that this country might quickly be provided with an Abima, because his life as Abima was short. After these two times of going to see how orders were conferred, I went an infinite number of times later to see them, for they were given nearly every day, and also on Sundays, for they did not wait for the four seasons, nor Lent. If some day they desisted from conferring them, then at once some came to me and made friends with me without my knowing them before, and they entreated me for the love of God to speak to the Abima, and ask him to confer orders, as they had nothing to eat: and if I went to ask it of him at vespers, at that time he ordered the tent to be pitched in order to confer them next day; and certainly I never asked it but what he did it, for he had a very good will towards me; and all the things which I said to him he used to do them as though I had been his equal in dignity.

---

[1] *Que zagonassem*, literally *to zagonise*.   [2] Of Egypt.

CAP. XCVIII.—*How long a time the Prester's country was with-out an Abima, and for what cause and where they go to seek them, and of the state of the Abima, and how he goes when he rides.*

How this country was for twenty-three years without an Abima : they say that after the time when the Abima died in the time of the great grandfather of this Prester, who was named Zeriaco, the father of Alexander, the grand-father of this king, and father of his father Nahu, for ten years after the death of the said Abima, the Prester would not send for another, and he said he did not choose that an Abima should come from Alexandria, and that he should not come from Rome, for he did not choose it, and he would rather lose his countries than have a reverend father from the country of the heretics : and he died also at the end of ten years that the country had been without an Abima : and his son Alexander, grandfather of this Prester, had re-mained in the same opinion for thirteen years without choosing to send for an Abima, until the people complained, saying that now there were neither priests nor zagonais to serve the churches, and that the servants being lost, the churches would be lost, and that when the churches were lost the faith would be lost. Therefore, seeing this, Alex-ander sent to Cairo to seek for an Abima from the Patriarch of Alexandria who was there, and he sent him two, so that one should succeed the other, and both were alive in our time. Whilst we were here the Abima Jacob died, who was to succeed this one who is now living ; and he told me that he had been fifty years in the country, and that he had come as white as he now was, and he was then of the age of sixty-five years, and that he was getting to the age of one hundred and twenty and odd years. That the Prester who sent for them was most Christian, and that soon after they

had come, the Prester John by his command had ordered that
Saturday should not be kept, and that they should not do
other erroneous ceremonies which they used to do, and that
they should eat pig's flesh and all other meat, although it
had not had its throat cut. When this had begun to be
done at the Court and its neighbourhood, not very long ago,
there came to this country two Franks, who are still living in
it, that is to say, one Marcorco, a Venetian, and after him
Pero de Covilhan, a Portuguese; these, when they arrived,
before they were at Court, began to keep the usages of the
country which are still kept in some parts, that is, to keep
Saturdays, and to eat like the people of the country. Some
priests and friars who pretended to know something of the
Bible seeing this, came to the Prester and complained of
the two Abimas, principally of the Vicar, and saying, What
thing is this? these Franks who have now come from Frankland, each one from his own kingdom, and they keep our
ancient customs, how is it that this Abima, who came from
Alexandria, orders things to be done which are not written
in the books? and on this account the Prester had given
orders to return to the former usages. This the Abima related to me, giving great thanks to God for our arrival, and
because the Prester had seen and heard our mass, and was
much pleased with all our offices, and Church matters, and
he, the Abima, hoped in God that by our coming, and others
who should come after us, this country would return to
the truth, and he did not pray to the Lord for anything
else but to grant him life until he should see in this
country a ruler of the Church of Rome, and to hear tell
that the Latin mass was celebrated in the house of Mekkah
which belongs to Mahomed; and he trusted in God that it
would soon be, because the Abyssinians had a prophecy that
there would not be more than a hundred Popes in their country, and that then there would be a new ruler belonging to
the Church of Rome, and that the Abima would complete

the hundred; and also he held it to be a prophecy that the Franks from the end of the earth would come by sea and would join with the Abyssinians, and would destroy Jiddah and Tor[1] and Mekkah; and that so many people would cross over and would pull down Mekkah, and without moving would hand the stones from one to another and would throw them into the Red Sea, and Mekkah would remain a razed plain, and that also they would take the great city of Cairo, and upon that there would be great differences as to whose it should be, and the Franks would remain in the great city.

The manner of this Abima in his person and state is in this wise. I will relate how he was in his tent, for I never saw him more than once in his house. He is always seated on a bedstead, such as the great people of this country are accustomed to use, and he has a curtain over the bedstead: he wears a white cotton robe of fine thin stuff, and in India from whence it comes it is called cacha: he has an upper garment which does not seem like a good cloak for rain,[2] nor like a church cloak, he has a hood like that of a cloak for rain, it is of camlet of blue silk. On his head he has a large turban, also of blue stuff, and, as I have said, he is a very old man, small and bald. He has a beard like very white wool, thin and of middling length, for in this country the clergy do not use to wear beards. He is pleasing in his speech, and rarely speaks without giving thanks to God. When he goes out to the King's tent, or to confer orders, he goes on a mule well caparisoned and accompanied by many both on mules and on foot. He carries a cross in his hand, and at his side they carry three crosses on poles raised higher than him. With respect to this I told him that these crosses ought to go in front of him. He told me that the cross which he carried in his hand was most excellent, and that no others had to go before it. He carries before him

---

[1] Tero.　　　　　　[2] Bedem.

through all the country wherever he goes two tall umbrellas with long supports, like those of the Prester, but not rich ; there also go before him four men with whips, who make the people withdraw on each side where he goes on the roads. The country is covered with children and youths and priests and friars who follow after him shouting, each in his language. I asked what they shouted, they told me that they said : My lord make us priests or zagonais, and may God grant you a long life.

CAP. XCIX.—*Of the assembly of clergy, which took place in the church of Macham Selasem when they consecrated it, and of the translation of the King Nahum, father of this Prester, and of a small church there is there.*

Saturday, the 12th day of January, there was a great assemblage of clergy in the said church, and all the night they were engaged in much chaunting and sounding of instruments, and they said that they were consecrating the church. Mass had not yet been said in this church, for it was said in another small church which was close to this, in which was buried the father of this Prester ; and he wished to remove him to the large church which he had ordered to be built and had commenced in his lifetime, and which his son had finished ; and they said that it was thirteen years since he died. On the Sunday, when it was morning, they said mass in this church. This church already has, at its beginning, four hundred canons with large revenues, and they have increased as the others did, and they have not enough to eat. On the 15th of the said month we were all summoned, and they told us to go to the said church, where there were more than two thousand priests, and as many zagonais ; these were together before the principal entrance to the church, and inside the circuit, which is almost part of it. The Prester was within his curtains upon the space above the steps of the principal entrance, before him were the before mentioned clergy, and they made a great office, with singing, and instruments, and dancing, and leaping. When a great part of the office had been performed, the Prester sent to ask what we thought of it. We replied that things done for the service of God in His name, all seemed good to us, and certainly they did a service that was agreeable to see as a thing done in praise of God. Soon he again sent to ask which seemed to us the best mode, this or ours, and which pleased us most, we were to say which, and that they would take. Here we answered that God would be served in many ways, and that this office seemed to us good, and that also ours seemed to us good, because all was for God, and the one and the other were done with one object, namely, to serve God, and obtain merit before Him. Then there came another message, that we were not to keep anything back in our hearts, and to send and tell him the truth. Then we sent word that we had already said the truth, and that we kept back nothing in our hearts; and so we remained there until the end of the office. This being ended, they ordered all the people to go out of the church, and all the clergy, and we also with them, and they sent to place us on the north side, and told us to remain quiet there. The clergy and people all went to the small church, where the father of this Prester was buried, and there entered it, as many as it would hold. Whilst we remained thus, not knowing why we had been sent to this place, there passed between us and the great church all the clergy and people in a very well ordered procession, and they brought the remains of the father of the Prester, and carried them to the great church; and there came in this procession the Abima Marcos, who was very much fatigued, and two men supported him under the arms on account of his great age. Moreover, there came

17

in it the Queens, that is, the Queen Helena, mother of the Prester, and the Queen his wife; and each of them with her black parasol for mourning, because, before, they had white parasols. All the people also were covered with black cloths, and wept and uttered loud cries, saying: *Abeto, abeto*, which means, "O Lord, O Lord". They said this so dolefully, that we, standing where we were, all wept. The bier in which the remains came was under a canopy of brocade, closed in with curtains of satin. So they placed the bier and canopy in the church, in the cross part, where we stood with the people who could not enter the church. We came to this office at sunrise, and we went away by night with torches.

CAP. c.—*Of the conversation which the ambassador had with the Prester about carpets, and how the Prester ordered for us an evening's entertainment and banquet.*

On the 17th of January, Prester John sent to call us, and we all went with the ambassador, both Portuguese and Franks; and as soon as we arrived near the tents, the Prester sent to ask how much carpets of twenty palms cost in Portugal. The ambassador sent him word that he was not a merchant, nor were those who came with him, and that he did not know for certain what they cost. They again came to say that a carpet of twenty ells had been brought from Cairo for four ounces of gold. The ambassador replied that it seemed to him that in Portugal it would cost twenty ducats. Then they came with another question, whether there were in Portugal carpets of twenty or thirty ells? The ambassador sent word that there were. Then they returned to ask whether, if the Prester sent gold to the captain-major, he would send him those carpets, and if he would send him enough to carpet the whole of that

church? The ambassador sent word that he would send
him enough for a thousand such churches. Another time
he sent to ask, if they would send those carpets if he sent
the gold? They answered him that whatever His Highness
sent to ask for from the King of Portugal, or his great
captain, all should be sent him in perfection, as his Highness would see from the things that he might have need of.
He ceased about the carpets, and sent to ask if there was
anyone in Portugal who could read the Arabic character
and the Abyssinian character? They answered that all
interpreters were to be found in Portugal. He sent word
that he well believed that there would be such in Portugal,
but at sea who would read those letters? They replied
that at sea there were a great many Arabs and Abyssinians who continually sailed in the ships of the King of
Portugal; and that the Moors carried off Abyssinians from
their country, and went to sell them in Arabia and Persia,
and in Egypt and India, and to the Portuguese. And the
Portuguese, whenever they took Moors prisoners, happened
to find among them many Abyssinians. At once they freed
them, and clothed and treated them very well, because they
knew they were Christians; and that we had brought here
George the interpreter, whom His Highness knew well,
who had been rescued from captivity from a Moor of Ormuz,
and he could tell His Highness how he got there. The
Prester then ordered him to be asked how he went from
these countries to Ormuz. He replied that a man who was
a Moor and had become Christian deceitfully, had sold him
to the Moors, and they carried him to Ormuz, and he had
remained there until the father Francisco Alvarez, who
came there, took him out of captivity, and did and still
does to him many favours: and so also to the other Abyssinians that they take from the Moors who keep them as
captives. Upon this he sent to ask if we wished to eat:
we replied that we kissed the hands of His Highness, and

17 *

that we had already eaten. Then he had us conducted to a
tent which had never been pitched till then. It was pitched
behind the great church, inside the circuit; it was a large[1]
tent; above it was covered with crosses of Christ, just
like that which was over the tank the day of the baptism.
The whole of this tent was carpeted, and it was large like a
reception room, and he sent to tell us that for his sake we
should enjoy ourselves there and talk of our affairs. Whilst
we were in conversation they brought to us much to eat
and drink of various viands, among which were many fowls,
or their skins, and they were stuffed with their own meat
without bones, minced and pounded with spices: these
skins of fowls had nothing wanting except the necks, and
the legs below the knees, and they had nothing broken, so
that we could not determine how or whence they had ex-
tracted the meat from inside, or the skin from the meat.
This dainty was very good. There also came large earthen
pots with boiled meats and other viands of divers kinds,
done in their fashion : what was boiled was done with much
butter, and the roast well roast. There were also many
jars of wine, among which was one very large jar of clear
glass (for the others were of black earthenware), and with
this jar was a large gilt glass cup, and another cup of
silver, enamelled with four large stones which looked like
sapphires, placed in a square on this cup, which was large
and beautiful. After this repast, the Prester sent to request
us to sing and dance after our fashion, and to enjoy ourselves. Then our people began to sing songs to a harp-
sichord which we had here, and afterwards dance and
country songs. There were with us certain pages and
others, and we heard others outside, as though the Prester
were there, and also those who were with us affirmed that
he was there, and that nothing indecorous ought to occur
among us. For this evening they sent us twenty-five large

[1] *Comprida de comicira.* See page 244.

white candles and a candlestick of iron, and a large tray on which to set the candlestick, and it had as many places for holding candles as there were candles, for they sent them according to the number. We were at this entertainment quite till midnight. Seeing such hours we sent to ask leave to go, and they gave it us. We went to our quarters, and the morning did not delay long, for it was very late.

CAP. CI.—*How the Prester sent to call the ambassador and those that were with him, and of what passed in the great church.*

On the following day, 18th of January, the Prester sent to call us to go to the said church. We went, and he ordered us to be placed before his curtains, where he was before, on the top of the steps which make a courtyard before the principal door : and there we stood. We mounted two rows of the steps, and there were in the church much more clergy than the other time when the remains of his father were removed. All these clergy did nothing but sing, dance, and jump, that is to say, leaping upwards. When we had been a good while at this feast, he sent to ask us if they sang like that in our country. We answered no, because our singing was very slow and quiet, both the voice and the movement of the body, and that they did not dance or leap. Upon this he sent to ask whether as that was not our custom we thought theirs bad. We sent word that the service of God, in whatever manner it was done, seemed to us good. When this office was ended, they began to walk round the church with twenty-five crosses, and each priest who carried a cross carried a thurible, because they carry the cross in the left hand almost like a staff, and the thurible in the right hand. Others carried thuribles without crosses, and they expended incense without stint. On the steps where we stood there were two basins of brass, very large, gilt, and wrought with a graving tool, and full of incense, and at each turn they took they cast off rich vestments and cloaks made according to their custom; and also some of those who sang and danced had such vestments. There were in this office many mitres made in their fashion. They told us to move from the place where we stood to another side of the church, on the side of the epistle; and in that part, at the transept door, were the Queens, the mother and wife of the Prester, each with her white parasol. Whilst we were in front of them, where they assigned to us to stand, they sent to ask of what metal were the patens and chalices in our country. We replied that they were of gold or of silver. They came to ask why we did not make them of any other metal. We answered that the regulations forbade their being of other metal, because other metals are dirty and produce rust and verdigris and other impurity. Still they came with another message to know whether we did this from economy or if there was there much gold and silver. They had for answer that it was done for cleanliness and to do what the regulations ordered, and that if they did it out of economy they would not make them of gold and silver, but would make them of tin or lead or copper, which were metals of low price. Here we knew why the Prester put these questions, because he had moved from his curtains inside the church, and had come to the umbrella of his wife, which was stuck in the cross entrance: and he also sent to ask how many chalices each church had in Portugal? We answered that there were monasteries and churches there which had two hundred, and no church, however poor, had less than three or four chalices, and upwards. He sent to ask what was the name of the church or monastery which had two hundred chalices? We told him that many possessed that number, principally a monastery named Batalha. He sent to ask why it was called Batalha? We said because the King of Portugal had won a battle there, and had ordered this monastery to be built, and the patron of it is our Lady : and because he had a monastery in the kingdom of Amara, for that reason he asked this question, and in this kingdom there is no other called Battle, because in former times a Negus had there conquered certain Moorish kings, and had built this monastery in honour of our Lady. He sent to ask how many kings lie buried in Batalha? We told him that four lay there and one prince, and several Infantes, and that other kings lie buried in other rich monasteries, and cathedral sees in the kingdom of Portugal, in splendid tombs. Upon this he sent to tell us to go and say our mass because midday was approaching, which was the hour at which we used to say it.

CAP. CII.—*How the ambassador and all the Franks went to visit the Abima, and of what passed there.*

On the 29th of January, the ambassador with all the Franks, both the Portuguese and those that were here before, went to see the Abima Marcos at his quarters, because as yet the ambassador had not spoken to him. We found him, as I had gone to find him, in his house. The ambassador attempted to kiss his hand, but he would not give it, and gave him the cross which he always holds in his hand to kiss, and also to all those that accompanied him. When the ambassador was seated, he told the Abima how he came to visit him on behalf of the great captain of the King of Portugal, and that he should pardon him for not having visited him sooner, and that he had not visited him, because they had not given him an opportunity to visit anybody. The Abima answered that he should not be surprised at that, as it was the custom of this Court that they did not

allow any foreigner to go to the house of any person, and
that the Prester did not do this but the great people of the
Court who were bad did it; and that the Prester was a good
and holy man.   The ambassador said to the Abima that the
great captain sent him to kiss his hands, and that he commended himself to him in his prayers, and he entreated him
to strengthen Prester John, so that he should have courage
to join his people with those of the King of Portugal to
destroy Mekkah, and cast out from it the Moors and the bad
sect of Mahomed.   The Abima answered that he would do
as much as was in his power, and that Prester John was
already encouraged not only to destroy the house of Mekkah,
but to take the holy house of Jerusalem ; and so they found
it in their writings that the Franks would join with the
Abyssinians, and would destroy Mekkah and would take
the holy house : and he always had prayed to God to show
him the Franks, and that God had fulfilled it for him, and
for this he gave Him great thanks ; and that here was the
Portuguese Pero de Covilham, who spoke the language
between us and them ; and that many times he had said to
him : Cide[1] Petrus do not be vexed, for in your days the
people of your country will come to this country and to
these kingdoms : and now you have to give thanks to the
Lord.   The ambassador further said to the Abima that the
King of Portugal had been informed of His Holiness by
Matheus his brother, and by other persons, and therefore
he sent to entreat him to make the Prester be strong and
constant in this enterprise, as was to be hoped from such
men as they were.   The Abima answered that he was not
holy, but was a poor sinner, and Matheus was not his
brother, but he had been a merchant and a friend of his,
and that going on his journey with a lie, it had been ordained
by God that he should afterwards do such great service and
profitable work ; and as to encouraging the Prester, it was

_____
[1] *Sidy*, Sir, Arabic.

unnecessary, for he was so strong and strenuous in the Christian faith, and so strenuous for the destruction of the Moorish State, that more so he could not be; and that he, the Abima, had told him of the greatness of the King of Portugal, and of the great name he has in Cairo and all Alexandria, and that he ought to give many thanks to the Lord for making him a friend and acquaintance of so great a king as is the King of Portugal; and that the Prester had much information about this, and was very joyful on that account : and the Abima still trusted in God, that he should see the great captain of the King of Portugal in the fortresses of Zeila and Masua, which would be built for the service of God. Many other things having passed he gave us leave, and we went away.

CAP. CIII.—*How Pero de Covilham, Portuguese, is in the country of the Prester, and how he came there, and why he was sent.*

I have sometimes spoken of Pero de Covilham, a Portuguese, who is in this country, and have quoted him, and will not desist from quoting him, as he is an honourable person of merit and credit, and it is reasonable that it should be told how he came to this country, and I will relate the cause of it, and what he told me of himself. Firstly, I say that he is my spiritual son, and he told me in confession, and out of it, how thirty-three years had passed that he had not confessed, because he said in this country they do not keep the secret of confession, and he only went to the church and there confessed his sins to God. Besides, he related to me the beginning of his life; first, that he was a native of the town of Covilham' in the kingdoms of Portugal, and in his youth he had gone to Castile to live with Don Alfonso, Duke of Seville, and at the beginning of the wars between

Portugal and Castile he had come with Juan de Guzman, brother of the said Duke of Seville, to Portugal. This Don Juan had given him to Don Afonzo, King of Portugal, as a groom,[1] and he soon took him as his squire, and he served in that capacity in the said wars, and went with the king to France. When king Don Afonso died he remained with king Don Joan his son, whom he served as squire of the guard until the treasons, when the king sent him to go about Castile, because he could speak Castilian well, in order to learn who were the gentlemen who had gone there. On his return from Castile, the King Don Joan sent him to Barbary to buy woollen cloths[2] and to make peace with the King of Tremezen; and returning he was again sent to Barbary, to Muley Belagegi, he who sent the remains of the Infante Don Fernando.[3] In this journey he carried goods of the King Don Manuel, who was then Duke, to buy horses for him, because the King Don Joan intended to give him an establishment, and one Pero Afonso, a veterinary, an inhabitant of Tomar, was going to inspect the horses. On this arrival coming from Barbary, it was ordained that one Afonso de Payva, a native of Castel Branco, should come to these parts, and he waited for Pero de Covilham to come together. When he came, the King spoke to him in great secrecy, telling him that he expected a great service of him, because he had always found him a good and faithful servant, and fortunate in his acts and services; and this service was that he and another companion, who was named Afonso de Payva, should both go to discover and learn about Prester John, and where cinnamon is to be found, and the other spices which from those parts went to Venice through the countries of the Moors: and that already he had sent on this journey a man of the house of Monterio, and a friar named frey Antonio, a native of Lisbon, and that they both

---

[1] *Mozo d'espolas.*   [2] *Alambeis; almayzales,* Selves.
[3] The Constant Prince.

had arrived at Jerusalem, and that they had returned thence, saying that it was not possible to go to those countries without knowing Arabic, and therefore he requested Pero de Covilham to accept this journey and to do this service with the said Afonso de Payva. To which Pero de Covilham answered, that he regretted that his capacity was not greater, so great was his desire to serve His Highness, and that he accepted the journey with ready willingness. They were despatched from Santarem on the 7th of May of 1487; King Don Manuel, who was then Duke, was present, and gave them a map for navigating, taken from the map of the world, and it had been made by the Licentiate Calçadilha, who is Bishop of Viseu, and the doctor mestre Rodrigo, inhabitant of Pedras negras, and the doctor mestre Moyses, at that time a Jew, and this map was made in the house of Pero d'Alcaçova; and the King gave four hundred ducats[1] for the expenses of both of them, which he gave out of the chest of the expenses of the garden of Almeirim, the King Don Manuel, then Duke, being present at all this. The King Don Joan also gave him a letter of credence for all the countries and provinces in the world, so that in case he saw himself in danger or necessity, this letter of the King's might succour him:[2] and in the presence of the Duke he gave them his blessing. Of the said four hundred ducats they took a part for their expenses, and the rest they placed in the hands of Bartolomeu, a Florentine, for it to be given to them in Valencia. Setting out, they travelled and arrived at Barcelona on the day of Corpus Domini: and they changed their route from Barcelona to Naples, and they arrived at Naples on St. John's day, and their journey was given them by the sons of Cosmo de Medicis; and from there they passed to Rhodes; and he says that at this time

[1] *Cruzados.*

[2] See Gaspar Correa's account of King John's scouts in *Vasco da Gama's Voyages*, pp. 8-11.—Hakluyt Society.

there were not more than two Portuguese in Rhodes, one was named frey Gonzalo, and the other frey Fernando, and they lodged with these. From here they passed to Alexandria in a ship of Bartolomeu de Paredes: and in order to pass as merchants, they bought much honey, and they arrived at Alexandria. Here both the companions fell ill of fevers; and all their honey was taken by the Naib of Alexandria, thinking that they were dying, and God gave them health, and they paid them at their pleasure. Here they bought other merchandise and went to Cairo. Here they remained until they found some Moghreby Moors of Fez and Tremecem, who were going to Aden, and they went with them to Tor, and there they embarked and went to Suaquem, which is on the coast of Abyssinia; and thence they went to Aden, and because it was the time of the monsoon, the companions separated, and Afonso de Payva went to the country of Ethiopia, and Pero de Covilham to India, agreeing that at a certain time they should both meet in Cairo to come and give an account of what they had found to the King. And Pero de Covilham departed thence and came to Cananor, and thence to Calicut, and from there he turned back to Goa, and went to Ormuz, and returned to Tor and Cairo in search of his companion, and he found that he was dead. Whilst he was about to set out on the way to Portugal, he had news that there were there two Portuguese Jews who were going about in search of him; and by great cleverness they heard about each other, and when they had met, they gave him letters from the King of Portugal. These Jews were named, one, Rabbi Abraham, a native of Beja, the other, Josef, a native of Lamego, and he was a shoemaker. This shoemaker had been in Babilonia, and had heard news or information of the city of Ormuz, and had related it to King Don Joan, with which news, he said, the King had been much pleased. And Rabbi Abraham had sworn to the King that he

would not return to Portugal without seeing Ormuz with
his own eyes. When the letters had been given and read,
their contents were, that if all the things for which they
had come were seen, discovered, and learned, that they
should return and welcome, and they should receive great
favours : and if all were not found and discovered, they
were to send word of what they had found, and to labour
to learn the rest ; and chiefly they were to go and see
and learn about the great King Prester John, and to
show the city of Ormuz to the Rabbi Abraham. Besides
the letters, these Jews made requisitions to Pero de Covilham that he should go and learn about Prester John, and
show the city of Ormuz to Rabbi Abraham. Here he at
once wrote by the shoemaker of Lamego, how he had
discovered cinnamon and pepper in the city of Calicut,
and that cloves came from beyond, but that all could be
had there ; and that he had been in the cities of Cananor,
Calicut, and Goa, all on the coast, and to this they
could navigate by their coast and the seas of Guinea,
coming to make the coast of Sofala, to which he had
also gone, or a great island which the Moors call the
island of the moon ; they say that it has three hundred
leagues of coast, and that from each of these lands one
can fetch the coast of Calicut. Having sent this message
to the King by the Jew of Lamego, Pero de Covilham
went with the other Jew of Beja to Aden, and thence to
Ormuz, and left him there, and returned thence and
came to Jiddah and Mekkah and El Medina, where lies
buried the Zancarron,[1] and from thence to Mount Sinai.
Having seen all well he again embarked at Tor and went
as far as outside the strait to the city of Zeila, and thence
travelled by land until he reached Prester John, who is very
near to Zeila ; and he came to the Court, and gave his letters

---

[1] The leg-bone, supposed by popular superstition in Spain to be
buried in the great mosque of Cordova.

to the King Alexander, who then reigned, and he said that he received them with much pleasure and joy, and said that he would send him to his country with much honour. About this time he died, and his brother Nahum reigned, who also received him with much favour, and when he asked leave to go he would not give it. And Nahum died, and his son David reigned, who now reigns; and he says he also asked him for leave and he would not give it, saying that he had not come in his time, and his predecessors had given him lands and lordships to rule and enjoy, and that leave he could not give him, and so the matter remained. This Pero de Covilham is a man who knows all the languages that can be spoken, both of Christians, Moors, and Gentiles, and who knows all the things for which he was sent; moreover he gives an account of them as if they were present before him.

Cap. CIV.—*How Prester John determined to write to the King and to the Captain-major, and how he behaved with the ambassador and with the Franks who were in his country, and of the decision as to departure.*

I return to our journey, or history of us who were in the tent in which they gave us a banquet. From this time forward Prester John's scribes did not cease from writing the letters which we were to carry for the King of Portugal and his captain-major: and they spent a long time over them, because their usage is not to write one to another, and their messages, communications, and embassages, are all by word of mouth. With us they began to acquire the manner of writing, and when they were writing, all the books of the epistles of St. Paul, of St. Peter, and St. James were present, and those that they esteemed as the most lettered studied them, and then began to write their letters in their Abyssinian language, and other letters in

Arabic, and also others in our Portuguese language, which the friar who had guided us read in Abyssinian, and Pero de Covilham turned them into Portuguese, and Joam Escolar, the clerk of the embassy, wrote them, and I, who, by order of the Prester, assisted in arranging the language, and it is very laborious to translate the Abyssinian language into Portuguese: thus the letters were made for the King our Sovereign in three languages, Abyssinian, Arabic, and Portuguese; and likewise for the captain-major; and all of them in duplicate, that is to say, two in Abyssinian, two in Arabic, and two in Portuguese. And they go by two ways, that is to say, one in Abyssinian, one in Arabic, and one in Portuguese, in one bag of brocade, and three others of the same sort in another little bag: so also those for the captain-major go in two little bags. These letters are all written on sheets of parchment. On Monday, the 11th of February of the year 1521, Prester John sent to call the ambassador and all that were with him, and also the Franks who had come before. While we were a good space in front of the doors of his tent, the Prester sent to the first arrived Franks rich cloths of brocade and silk, that is to say, damask, of which three pieces came, and besides he sent thirty ounces of gold to be divided amongst all, and they were thirteen, so that each had two ounces and four to be divided amongst all. We, seeing how well they did for those Franks, who had come to them as runaways, thought that they would do better for us, and we made sure that they had prepared for us dresses of brocade. Messages were going and coming, and during this his great Betudete, who is the lord of the left hand wing, came and brought to me a cross of silver, and a crozier wrought with inlaid work, saying that the Prester sent it to me as the title and possession of the lordship which he had given me. Having received the cross and crozier we again sat down. As all the messages which went and came were about friendship between the ambassador and Jorge d'Abreu, again another time a message returned that the ambassador should be a friend to Jorge d'Abreu, and that we should all travel together as we had come. The ambassador replied that he was not going to be his friend, nor to travel where he was, but rather he begged of His Highness to keep him at his Court two months after his departure, because he sought to kill him. Upon this a message came that the Prester ordered thirty mules to carry our baggage, and that eight of these should be given for the baggage of Jorge d'Abreu, and those who were with him; and saying, besides, that he sent thirty ounces of gold for the ambassador, and fifty for those that accompanied him, and that Jorge d'Abreu, and those that were with him, were to have their share of it: and that he sent a hundred loads of flour, and as many horns of mead for the road; and that we were to be entrusted to certain captains, who would conduct us from one country to another as far as the sea; that is to say, each one through his own lands: and that they were not to annoy or injure the cultivators who were poor, for we had told him that when we came, they destroyed the people of the country: and these captains were to give us all that was necessary. Then we were entrusted to the sons of the Cabeata, because we had to travel a good deal through the lands of the Cabeata, which are of the church of the Trinity, to which the remains of the Prester's father were removed. And this church had from its beginning four hundred canons, and a son of the Cabeata is "licancte", which means the office which Caiaphas held when they brought Christ before him, that is to say, high priest or judge that year. And the Cabeata is head in this church, and in the other churches of this kingdom, which all belong to the kings, and his title and style means head over the heads. And this head remains over all like a bishopric.

CAP. CV.—*How the Prester sent to the ambassador thirty ounces of gold and fifty for those that came with him, and a crown and letters for the King of Portugal, and letters for the Captain-major, and how we left the Court and of the road we took.*

This day, in the afternoon, there came to our tent thirty ounces of gold for the ambassador and fifty for us: and with them came a large crown of gold and silver which belonged to Prester John; and its value is not so great as its size. It was brought in a round basket lined inside with cloth and outside with leather. This crown was presented by Abdenagus, page and captain of the pages, and it was stated by him that Prester John sent that crown to the King of Portugal, and to tell him that a crown was never removed except from father to son, and that he was his son, and he took it off his head and sent it to the King of Portugal, who was like his father, and that he sent it as a present; and as a crown was a precious thing, by it he presented and offered all favour and assistance and succour of men, gold, and provisions which might be necessary for his fortresses and fleets, and for the wars he might please to make against the Moors in these parts, from the Red Sea as far as the Holy House.[1] And because the dresses did not come which we knew were already made, some of our people murmured, and those who had brought these things heard it, and said that Prester John was much vexed with the ambassador because two days before he had ordered to strike and cudgel close to his tent a Portuguese who was named Magalhães, and who had betaken himself to Jorge d'Abreu; and that he was also vexed because he would not be friends with Jorge d'Abreu, and that he was despatching us with much reserve, and that we were not

[1] Jerusalem.

18

to expect dresses, nor anything else, and that we should lose much for what has been related.

On Tuesday, the 12th of February, which was our Shrove Tuesday, the friar who had guided us came, and he brought the letters for the King and for the captain-major, for as yet they had not been delivered to the ambassador, nor did the Prester send an ambassador. The letters came in this manner; before those which were for the King were in two bags, and now they changed them into three, because there were three of each language, and they had separated one of each language, and had made three bags; and for the captain-major there were two bags, as there were before, and all were of brocade. All five came placed in a basket lined with cloth inside and with leather outside. Then he took out the bags and showed that they were closed and sealed, and having shown them, again put them into the basket, and sealed its fastenings, and said to the ambassador that we might go whenever we pleased as we were entirely despatched. The ambassador replied to the friar that he wished to speak again to the Prester John before his departure, if His Highness should be so pleased. The friar and those that came with him said that the Prester had gone away that morning early, which we knew was true, and they said that he was very discontented with the ambassador because he so illtreated men, and because he would not be a friend of Jorge d'Abreu, and for other things which he kept to himself, and that we might depart in peace, and that mestre Joam and the painter should remain in the country; as in effect they did remain. Seeing that we were thus despatched, we began to make ready to start as soon as we could, and the friar came with the thirty mules they were giving us for the journey, and with many horns in which to carry wine for the journey. When they promised them we thought that they would give them full of wine, and they came empty, and they said that the Prester said that notwithstanding that they did not drink wine during Lent, since it was our custom to drink it, that the gentlemen who conducted us would give it to us, that so it had been ordered. With respect to the mules, they at once set aside eight for Jorge d'Abreu and his companions, and also his share of the horns. Upon this some of us went to the market to buy what they wanted for the road, and on this account we were giving up our departure till another day, as it was already late, when so great a wind fell upon us that it broke the tent ropes, and the whole of it came to the ground. When we saw this and how we were left in the open, all of us that were there began to call out : "Come, come, let us be going, since they send us, let us go in peace." So we set out from the Court this day, which was our Shrove Tuesday, and went to sleep in a field a distance of a league from the Court. There came with us and in our company Pero de Covilham, with his wife and some of his sons, and the friar came with Jorge d'Abreu, almost like his guard, and they took up their quarters apart from us.

On Ash Wednesday, in the morning, we commenced our journey, and while travelling, a son of the Cabeata passed by us, who was going to give us what was necessary in the lands of his father or of his church, through which we had to travel several days ; and there also passed by Abdenago, the Captain of the pages, who had brought us the crown, because when we had done with the lands of the other gentlemen, we were to pass through his. We went to take up our quarters at the foot of a high hill, which had upon it a church of St. Michael, and we remained in a cultivated field, and at the end of it the above-named gentlemen took up their quarters, and we did not know of their being there till after we had settled ourselves. Jorge d'Abreu and the friar were in their company, and what was necessary for our supper came from there. Then in this second night of our journey, sin began to excite

18 *

fresh quarrels : for Joan Gonzalvez our factor began to
quarrel with one Joan Fernandez, whom he had brought,
or whom the Captain-major had given him, to be his assis-
tant with the goods that were entrusted to him, in such
sort that they said that he struck him with a stick. When
this quarrel began we made peace again as well as we could,
and the ambassador favoured Joan Fernandez, and he left
the factor and went in company with the ambassador. The
following day we travelled on our road in parties, that is to
say, Jorge d'Abreu and the friar in one party, and we with
the son of the Cabeata in another party, and we were well
provided with all that was necessary every day. When
we were in the kingdom of Angote, close to a monastery
of the Abima Marcos, the lands of the Cabeata having been
left behind, and we had almost entered those of Abdenago,
sin got into the head of Joan Fernandez, and he went and
waited for the factor who was going alone with the goods,
and with a lance belonging to the ambassador, and gave him
two lance thrusts, one in the hand and another in the breast.
That in the hand wounded his fingers, and that in the
breast, God was pleased that it struck him on a rib, and
did not go through it.   And as we were going rather
divided, and here there were two roads, some of us were on
one side, and others on the other; and when we came
together they called me to confess him, and another man
to cure him ; we found him half dead ; God was pleased to
give him health with the care that was taken of him. Joan
Fernandez ran away and met with the ambassador, and
those who were coming after him shouted loudly to take
him prisoner, that he had killed the factor ; and he was arrested ; and the factor shouted and said that the ambassador
had killed him with the favour he had shown and the lance
he had given to his servant, or the man who had been
given to him for his service. Abdenago had gone on to
his lands where we expected to go and sleep, and with these

quarrels we did not go. We remained by a great river, as its appearance showed it to be in the winter and season of thunderstorms, for at this time it contained very little water, and there we slept, with the said Joan Fernandez a prisoner and his hands tied behind him. The ambassador ordered all to watch and guard that prisoner, and he begged me to remain near the factor, and so we lay down together with our heads on one saddle, and it seems we slept. Meantime there was not wanting someone who let loose the prisoner, and he ran away to Jorge d'Abreu, who was lying down in the same river bed lower down than us. Then the ambassador's fear became doubled. The next day we travelled and found Abdenago, who was coming in search of us, and we went with him and Jorge d'Abreu and the friar in their party and by another road, all through the lands of Abdenago : so he travelled with us through his lands and those that were not his as far as Manadeley.

CAP. CVI.—*Of what happened in the town of Manadeley with the Moors.*

When we arrived at this town of Manadeley, a town entirely of peaceful tributary Moors, as has been before related, we passed by this town and went to take up our quarters at some springs beneath some large trees ; and because the people of the country do not care for water nor shade, but only for the heights where there is sun and wind, Abdenago passed on to a hill and sat down in a tent of his own, and we remained at the said springs. And some of our people turned back to the town to buy what they wanted ; among them was a servant of the ambassador's named Estevan Palharte : and, as it appeared, he got into a quarrel with a Moor in such a manner that the Moors broke two of his teeth, and some of our people coming up to his assistance they took one of them and struck him on the head with stones, so that he was brought to our tent half dead. However, on learning this, Abdenago came up and ordered those Moors to be made prisoners whom he found to be in fault. And because this day it soon became night, on the following day he sent to call us, and we went to where he was and got the Moors prisoners; that is to say, two of them; and he bade us all sit down on the ground and on the grass; and he also was seated on the ground with his back leaning against his chair. Thither they brought the prisoners and he gave them their trial, and put questions to them: and on account of what he found against them, he ordered them at once to be stripped and severely flogged, and to be asked from time to time: What will you give? They began by promising one ounce of gold—two—three. They again flogged them and asked: What will you give. At last they arrived at giving seven ounces. This they gave soon, and this gold was given to the two wounded men: and the two Moors were then made prisoners and sent to Prester John. I will now at once relate what happened to them. We travelled forward on our road as far as the town of Barua, where we stayed on first coming from the sea, and when we had been there already some days, there came a message from Prester John, and with the message came one of the Moors who had been flogged, and the head of the other Moor, and the messenger said that he had brought this message: That the Prester had examined into the fault of those Moors, and the injury which they had done to the Portuguese, and he had cut off the head of the one he had found to be in fault, and he sent it to us, in order that we might be certain of the truth, and know that it was that man; and that as to the other he did not find him to be guilty, but he sent him also, and if we thought that he was guilty, we should do what we pleased with him, either kill him, or let him go free, or make him a captive. We all held a council over this, and the ambassador asked what we thought we ought to do with this Moor. This was what was said by those of us who were in this matter: I spoke for all of them because I knew their wishes; and I said that since the Prester sent to say that he found him to be without fault, that neither ought we to blame him; and that if we did any justice upon him, they would hold us to be cruel men without mercy; and that if we let him go and sent him to his country, the Prester would consider that as good. All those that were there said the same; and the ambassador said that was not his opinion, but that he should take him as his slave; as in effect he did, and ordered him to be loaded with chains, and he kept him thus ten days; and the Moor escaped with all the chains that he wore.

CAP. CVII.—*How two great gentlemen from the Court came to us to make friendship between us, and committed us to the captain-major.*

When we left this town of Manadeley, on the way to Barua, as has been said, we travelled through many countries, and Abdenago with us, as he had been ordered to do, and the friar with Jorge d'Abreu. We arrived at a district which is named Abacinete, a large town, and captaincy of people who were not tender hearted, for here at times they wished to throw stones at us, and in effect they did do so. This town is at one end of the kingdom of Tigray. When we were in our quarters there came to us two great lords of the Court, one of them was the Adrugaz, to whom we were at first entrusted at Court, as has been said already many times in this book; and the other was by title the Gragela, and by name Arraz Ambiata, who later was

Barnagais, and was Betudete. When they came to us they at once spoke of how Prester John had remained much discontented because the ambassador would not be friendly with Jorge d'Abreu before His Highness, when he begged it of him; and that which had not been done, he now sent to entreat that it should be done, and that they should become friends, and not keep apart before the captain-major, as it appeared to be a very unseemly thing; and also the others who had fought on the road, that they should be friends. Then we made them become friends and meet together. Upon this the said lords gave to each of us his mule as the Prester had ordered. They further said that they had come to present us before the captain-major, and also to see and visit him in the name of Prester John, inasmuch as the Barnagais, who was lord of this country, and other lords, had remained at the Court. When friendship had been established, and the said mules had been given, we all travelled, returning as far as Barua, where we remained until the time of the monsoon had passed, during which they[1] were to come for us. When the time had passed, Don Rodrigo the ambassador did not choose to order any provisions to be given to Jorge d'Abreu, nor to those who were with him. And one day that he sent to ask it of him by Joan Fernandez, who wounded the factor, the ambassador wished to have him beaten, but he ran away. Upon this Jorge d'Abreu sent to ask me to come to a church, and there he told me to tell the ambassador to order provisions to be given for him, and those that were with him. I told him, and soon after returned with the answer that the ambassador said that he would give them to him, but that for those who were with him he would give nothing, as they were traitors to the service of the King of Portugal. Jorge d'Abreu answered, that for himself he did not want it, but for those who were with him, and that if he did not

---

[1] The Portuguese fleet.

choose to give it that he would take it, and so we separated.
Jorge d'Abreu went to the Adrugaz and Grageta to make
a complaint to them. At this, those lords sent to call us,
and they called all of us, and not to their houses which
were large and good, but to a field in front of a church.
When we were all assembled, the Adrugaz made a speech
to the ambassador, asking why he treated his countrymen
so ill, and saying that since he did not give them of that
which was given for them, he would sell the horse and
mules to maintain them, and this was not usual among
grandees, and that he should consider how much displeasure
Prester John would feel at his so ill treating his company;
and that if he would treat them in another way, he himself
would be treated differently, and would be more pleased
than he was; and he entreated him to give them their own,
and not break the friendship which he had already promised
to keep with Jorge d'Abreu. The ambassador replied that
he was not going to give it him, and they were traitors to
the service of the King of Portugal for which he came.
Jorge d'Abreu said that if he did not order it to be given
him that he would take it: and so we arose all of us in a
bad humour, and each one went to his quarters. As it
seemed likely to the factor that Jorge d'Abreu would
attack him and take his goods, because he had said that he
would take it if a provision was not given him, he went to
sleep at the ambassador's quarters, which were some
houses of a gentleman, good and strong according as they
are in this country. Whilst we, the clerk of the embassy,
and my nephew and I, were lying in bed, late in the night
we heard shouts of, " Come this way, go that way", and
then musket shots; and running up, the clerk and I (my
nephew remained behind as his eyes were suffering), we
saw them knocking down the houses with rams, and firing
musket shots, and it seemed to us that those that were
inside must be dead, so great was the noise. So we went

running to the houses of the Barnagais, where the said
lords were lodging, to tell them to come to our assistance ;
and because the houses had two doors, one at each end,
as we entered by one door, the ambassador and his companions entered by the other, and they were bringing with
them the crown and letters of Prester John, and what
goods they could, and one of the ambassador's men came
wounded by a musket shot in the knee, which made four
or five wounds, as they had given others besides that with
the bullet.[1]   The ambassador and his men had gone out by
a back door which the house had, and which the others did
not know of.   These lords then sent at once to arrest all
the others, and the clerk and I went with the people that
the lords sent on this errand.   We found them still occupied
in knocking down the house, thinking that they had caught
the people inside.   Here they began to ill-treat them with
thumps and cudgelling, for they had no more powder, nor
withal to defend themselves, and they were all carried off
before these noblemen.   They were further ill-treated, and
it was ordered that they should be taken to another town
near this named Gazeleanza, where they were to remain
without going out, and they set guards to keep them.
Many days passed after this, and because they could not
see them,[2] and also because it is the custom of this country
that no grandee can leave the Court without licence, nor go
to the Court without being summoned to it; these lords,
Adrugaz and Grageta, did not know what to do with us,
and did not dare to leave us nor to take us away, nor to
return themselves, neither could they make peace between
us, and at length they took counsel and decided to send us

<hr>

[1] Selves translates: "one was wounded in four places by a gun which
must have been loaded with slugs."

[2] This passage is very obscure ; it either means that the lords had not
seen Jorge d'Abreu and his companions, or that they did not wish to
see them.

back to the Court, and expose themselves to any punishment which he might please to give them for this.

CAP. CVIII.—*How they took us on the road to the Court, and
how they brought us back to this country.*

These noblemen, seeing that the time had gone by for
them[1] to come for us, and also that there could be no peace
between us, as has been said, took the determination to
send us back, and we began to travel, we and the Franks
who were coming with us. On arriving at the town of
Abacinen, before mentioned, the first town, at once the
people put themselves on guard not to receive us, and so
many friars came down from a mountain that they seemed
like sheep, and all brought bows and their weapons, and it
was like a field battle, and there were wounded on both
sides. Nevertheless, the field remained in our possession,
and we took up our quarters in the town : and those of the
place on the mountain, and the men belonging to these
lords treated the town like a town of Moors, and plundered
everything, both wheat and barley, fowls, capon, sheep,
and household furniture, and whatever they found. From
this place we departed and travelled our journey in parties,
that is to say, Jorge d'Abreu and those that were with him
and the friar together, and we with the ambassador and
his people, and the Adrugaz and Grageta. Thus we travelled till we reached Manadeley, where they wounded our
men, and here we found the Moor who ran away from the
ambassador, and yet he was but little afraid of him. When
we had passed this town about half a league, we met the
Barnagais, who came from the Court and brought a message
for the noblemen and for us what we were to do. We all
placed ourselves in a tilled field at the foot of a big tree, as

---

[1] The ships of the captain-major.

many as there was room for there. These noblemen were
much reproved by the Barnagais for having brought us
without leave, and he also bawled a good deal at the ambassador and at Jorge d'Abreu: and he told the ambassador
at once to give up to him the crown of the Prester, and
the letters which he was carrying for the King of Portugal
and the captain-major. Between the ambassador and Jorge
d'Abreu some very ugly words passed. Then the Barnagais told the others to continue on their way to the
Court, and there they would have their punishment. He
then gave us captains to conduct us separately as we came.
So we travelled with him as far as his lands, through the
heavy rain which now fell. Those who went with the ambassador's party he took with him to the town of Barua,
where the quarrel happened, which is the chief town of his
kingdom, and he put Jorge d'Abreu and his company in
Barra, which is the chief town of the captaincy of Ceivel,
all belonging to the Barnagais. The Barnagais himself
settled in the town of Barra, and he said that he did it in
order not to be annoyed by the ambassador: and the distance from one town to the other may be three leagues and
a half or four. At this time we were very ill provided
with all things; Jorge d'Abreu and his companions were
better provided than we were: and our hunting and fishing
was of great advantage to us, for we had a river and hunting ground.

Cap. cix.—*In what time and day Lent begins in the country
of Prester John, and of the great fast and abstinence of
the friars, and how at night they put themselves in the
tank.*

In this country of Prester John Lent begins on Monday
of Sexagesima, which is ten days before our Lent, and after
the day of the Purification they observe three days of severe

fast, generally, clergy, friars, and laymen. They say that
they observe the fast of the city of Niniveh, and they assert
that there are many friars here who in these three days do
not eat more than once, and do not eat bread but only herbs,
and they also say that most of the women do not give milk
to their children more than once a day. The general fast
of Lent is almost bread and water, because even though
they should wish to eat fish, in that country they have not
got it. In the sea and in the fresh water, where there are
rivers, there is much fish, and yet here there is very little
skill in catching them, although some little, but not much, is
caught for the great gentlemen. The general food during Lent
is bread : at this time there are no vegetables here, for they
have not got them except when it rains, from their want of
skill, because there is plenty of water for gardens and
orchards and other good works, if they would choose to
make them. In most of the monasteries the friars have got
some cabbages like the kind called "orto", which they keep
taking the leaves off (this all through the year), and they
eat them. In the districts where there are grapes and
peaches, these come in Lent, because they begin in February and finish at the end of April, so that those who have
them have something to eat. What they generally eat is
cardamine seed, which they call *caufa*, and they make with
it a sauce and call it *tebba*, and they soak their bread in it,
and it is very hot. They do the same with linseed, which
they also eat in sauce, and call it *tebba;* and so they prepare mustard and call it *cenafiche*. These three sauces are
the general food of Lent : and they do not eat milk or
butter, nor drink wine of grapes or honey. The general
drink is a beverage made of barley, which they call *çanha*,
and they also make it of Indian corn[1] and of another
grain called *guza ;*[2] they also make it of darnel. They do
not drink this when it is fresh because it brings a man to

---

[1] *Milho zaburro.* [2] *Guza,* probably *dagusha.*

the ground, and when it is cold and settled, this is the best drink here. There are many friars who do not eat bread in Lent, and others in the whole year, and others who in all their lives do not eat it, and I will relate what I saw of this. When the ambassador and I were going on the road to the court, in a district which is called Janamora, a friar came to us to go in security from the robbers: and he travelled with us for more than a month, and because he was a friar I kept him near me. This friar brought with him six or seven novices who were going to be ordained, and he carried four large books to sell: he carried the books on a mule. He lodged with me in my tent, and the first day at night I called him to eat, as it was his supper hour; he excused himself, that he did not want to eat; upon this, the novices came with water-cresses,[1] and they gave them a boiling without salt or oil, or anything else, and they ate those cresses without any other addition. I asked the novices about this, and they told me they never ate bread. And because I had often heard say that there were many friars here who did not eat bread, and I doubted this, I watched this friar and looked after him night and day: the whole day he was close to me like my groom, and at night he slept near me on the ground in his habit as he wore it by day; and always, in all this time that this friar was with me, I never saw him eat anything but herbs, that is to say, water-cresses, mallows, water-parsley, where they found them, nettles, and if we passed near any monastery, he sent there to find a cabbage, and not finding herbs, the novices brought him lentils in a gourd of water newly grown with the sprout just out; he ate of those, and I ate them, and it is the coldest food in the world. This friar travelled with us more than a month, and at the court he was in our company three weeks without eating anything except what has been mentioned. Later, I saw this friar in the town of Aquaxumo, where Prester John

[1] *Agriones.*

sent us to for eight months : as soon as he knew that I was
there, he came to see me and brought me a few lemons ; he
was wearing a habit of leather without sleeves, and his arms
were bare ; and we embraced. I succeeded in putting my
hand under his arm, and I found that he was girt with an
iron girdle four fingers broad, and I took the friar by the
hand and brought him into my room ; and I showed that to
Pero Lopez, my nephew, and besides we also found that
this girdle was lined[1] on both edges on the side towards
the skin with points of the size of those of a saw for sawing
wood, not sharpened (and all this out of Lent). This friar
considered himself aggrieved by this, and he never visited
me again, and on my account he went away from that town :
later I saw many of these. We also heard tell of many
friars here, who, during the whole of Lent, did not sit down,
and always remained on foot. I heard that there was one
in that condition at a distance of two leagues from where
we were in a grotto. As it was Lent, I rode and went to
see him, I and others, and we found him standing in a
tabernacle of wall the size of himself. This tabernacle was
made like a box without a covering, much plastered with
clay and dung : and this tabernacle was already old, and
others had been there before ; and where the hips reached
there was a ledge,[2] and the walls were thinner by three
inches ; and where the elbows reached, for each of them
there was another such recess ; and in front was a stand in
the wall with a book. This friar was clothed with a haircloth woven with the hair of oxtails, and underneath it he
had another such iron girdle as that of Aquaxumo. He
showed it us of his own will, without our asking him, or
knowing that he had got it. In another grotto near this
one lodged two friars, young boys who supplied him with
food of herbs. These grottoes had been long used for these
purposes,[3] because there were tombs in them. This friar

---

[1] *Revinda.* [2] *Releixo.* [3] *Pendenças.*

became much our friend after this visit, and came to see us often after Lent.

In the town of Barua, during another Lent, we saw two friars in the outer part of the church of that town, in similar tabernacles, one on one side, and the other on the other. They ate the same kind of herbs and sprouted lentils. I used to visit them frequently, and they showed that they rejoiced much at my visitation : and if any day I did not go to visit them, they sent to visit me. These were in their habits ; I do not know whether they wore a haircloth or a girdle underneath. I asked if they went outside from there ; they told me how they visited one another, and yet they did not sit down; and one of them, the one who showed most friendship towards me, said that he was a relation of Prester John. They remained in this abstinence until Easter ; and came out at the mass of the resurrection. We also heard that on the Wednesdays and Fridays in Lent many slept in water up to their necks ; and we could not believe it : when we were in Aquaxumo, we heard that we might see this in a great tank, which I have already mentioned when I spoke of this place, and that there was a great function there during Lent. Joam Escolar, clerk of the embassy, and Pero Lopez, my nephew, went one night to this tank, and they came back amazed at the multitude of people who were there, all in the water up to the neck. These were canons and wives of canons, and friars and nuns, because there are here many of all orders, as has been said. Hearing of this wonder on Thursday, I went in the morning to this tank to see how they were : and I found the tank full of stone resting-places along the edge, where it was shallow a stone, and as it increased in depth so the stones increased one above the other, as they sit upon them with the water up to their necks. As they told me that in this place and in the neighbourhood there are at this season hard frosts and cold at night, and after this, seeing Pero de Covilham at a place called Dara, I told him what I had seen. He told me that since he had seen it he had not any doubt about it, and that I should know that this was general in all the country of Prester John, and that here there were many who not only did not eat bread amongst people, but who abode in the large forests, and in the greatest depths and heights of the mountains, where they find any water, and where living people never come. Close to this Dara are some ravines of very great depth, like those before mentioned, and these are without inhabitants in the plains or flat ground. A great river falls into these ravines, and so great is the fall, that the water becomes broken up in the air, and when it reaches the bottom it seems rather a mist than water. Pero de Covilham showed to me in that ravine a grotto, which was scarcely perceptible, and he told me that a friar abode there who was esteemed as a saint, and below this grotto there seemed to be a garden, because something green showed. And on one of the slopes of this ravine he showed me a long way off where had died a white man, who was unknown, and who had lived fully twenty years in that solitude, in another grotto, and they did not know the time of his death, only not perceiving him on the mountain, they went to look at his abode or grotto, and they found it closed up from inside with a good wall, so that no one could enter it or come out of it. They informed Prester John of it, and he ordered that this grotto should not be opened.

Cap. cx.—*Of the fast of Lent in the country of Prester John, and of the office of Palms and of the Holy Week.*

The general fast of Lent for most of the friars and nuns, and also some of the clergy, is to eat every second day and always at night. Sundays are not fast days. Some old women also, who are in a way withdrawn from the world, keep this fast; and they say that Queen Helena fasted every day in the whole year, and only ate the said three times a week, on Tuesday, Thursday, and Saturday. In the kingdoms of Tigray, which are those of the Barnagais and Tigrimahom, the people in general during Lent eat meat on Saturdays and Sundays, and in these two days of Lent they kill more cows than in all the year, and more if they should marry their first or second wife on the Thursday before Shrove Tuesday; and they marry on that day because they hold that after marriage they may eat meat for two months, in whatever time of the year it may be, and so those who marry in these two kingdoms eat meat and drink wine, and eat butter all through Lent. I saw this in the kingdom of Barnagais, and heard of it in that of Tigrimahom; and because I say, or a second wife, let it not be supposed, or let it appear that all have more than one wife, because generally they have one as has been said; and whoever has plenty to live upon has two or three, and they are not prohibited to them by the secular justice, but only by the Church, which casts them out, and they are not capable of any benefit, as has been said. I have seen with my eyes, on the above-mentioned Thursday, married men, friends of mine, who brought other wives to their houses, and used and enjoyed this evil privilege. In this district was the commencement of Christianity, and in all the other kingdoms they hold these to be very bad Christians for this bad custom of theirs. In all the rest of the country and other kingdoms and lordships the fast is kept throughout Lent by great and small, men and women, boys and girls, without any breach, and they do almost the same at Advent. On Palm Sunday they celebrate their office in this manner. They begin their matins a little after midnight, and keep up their singing and dancing with all their images and pictures uncovered until it is quite daylight: and at the hour of prime they take the branches which each holds in his hand into the church or to the principal door, because neither women nor laymen come inside. The clergy then enter the church with the boughs, and there sing a great deal and very hurriedly, and they come out with the cross and with the palms, and give to each person his branch, and then they make a procession round the church, with the palms in their hands, and returning to the principal entrance, there go inside the church six or seven, as we go in, and they close the door, and he who has to say mass remains with the cross in his hand; they also sing both inside and outside, as we do; that is to say, in that manner, for their language is not ours, and they say mass according to their custom, and give the communion to all. In holy week mass is not said, except on Thursday and Saturday. It is usual to give salutations among one another, principally the grandees, when they meet once in the day to kiss one another on the shoulders, both together on the right shoulder, and the other remains on the left hand side; and during holy week they do not give this salutation of peace to those they meet, nor do they speak, but pass one another as if they were dumb, and without raising the eyes. And a man of fashion does not dress in this week in white clothes, all go dressed in black or blue. They abstain during this week from all work, and every day they celebrate long offices in the churches (but not with tapers, as we do). On Thursday, at hour of vespers, they perform mandato[1] ; that is to say, the office of washing feet, and all the people assemble in the church, and the superior of the church sits on a three-legged stool, with a towel girt round him, and a large basin of water before him, and beginning by washing the feet of the clergy, ends with all of them. When this is finished they begin their chaunt, and they chaunt all the night, and the clergy, friars, and zagonais do

---

[1] Maundy, from the words of Christ, "*Hic est mandatum meum*".

not go out of the church any more, and do not eat or drink till Saturday after mass. On Friday at midday they very much decorate the church with hangings, according to their circumstances, because some of them are hung with brocades, coarse brocade, and crimson, and others with whatever they have got, or are able to get. They put their hangings principally before the chief entrance, because that is the station of the people : and before the door they put on the hangings a paper crucifix, that is to say, a print,[1] and above it a small curtain, with which it is covered. They sing all night, and all day they read the passion ; when that is concluded, they draw the curtain from off the crucifix, and when it is uncovered they all cast themselves on the ground, and prostrate themselves, and give one another buffets, and they knock their heads against the walls, and also strike themselves with buffets and thumps. This lamentation lasts quite two hours. When this is over, two priests go to each door of the circuit which leads to the churchyard, and in all the churches there are three doors ; at each door are two priests, one on each side, and each has in his hand a small scourge with five straps, and all, as many as were standing before the principal church door, go out through these doors stripped from the waist upwards. Passing through them they stoop, and those who stand with the scourges keep striking them as long as they are still. Some pass quickly, and receive few strokes ; others wait, and receive many. Old men and old women will remain half an hour, until the blood runs, and then they sleep in the circuit of the church, and when it is midnight they begin their mass, and all receive the communion. On Easter at midnight they begin their matins, and before morning make a procession. When dawn breaks they say mass, and keep all this week until Monday of the Sunday after Easter,[2] so they make sixteen days of observance, that

[1] De molde.   [2] In albis.

is, from Saturday before Palm Sunday to the Monday after Sunday after Easter.[1]

CAP. CXI.—*How we kept a Lent at the Court of the Prester, and we kept it in the country of Gorage, and they ordered us to say mass, and how we did not say it.*

We happened to keep a Lent at the Court of Prester John, which we kept at the extremity of a country of pagans, who are named Gorages, a people (as they say) who are very bad, and of these there are no slaves, because they say that they sooner allow themselves to die, or kill themselves than serve Christians. This district in which the Court was situated is outside of the Gorages. As it appears, and as the Abyssinians say, these Gorages dwell underground. All the Court and we were encamped above a great river, which ran through great ravines, and on each side was a plain like that of Çarnache dos alhos[2] in Portugal; and in all parts of the river there were an infinite number of dwellings placed in the cliffs, one above the other, and some of them very high, which had no more door than the mouth of a large vat, through which a man could easily pass, and above these doors, an iron in the stone to which they fastened cords so as by them to know the house; and so they kept them now because in these dwellings many of the lower people of the Court were lodging, and they said that they were so large inside that twenty or thirty persons could find room inside with their baggage. And there was on this river a very strong town, which, on the side towards the river, was a very high scarped rock, and on the side towards the land a very high cave, which had fifteen fathoms in height, and six in width, and on both

---

[1] *Pascoela.*

[2] *Çarnache dos alhos,* two leagues from Coimbra.

sides it stood over the river, and inside this cave on both sides there were everywhere dwellings like the above-mentioned; and inside the circuit were small houses of walls and thatched in which Christians now live, and they have in it a very good church. The entrance to this town is of stone, and low, with many turns, so that it seems that neither mules nor cows could enter there; yet they enter into a large portion of it, for the space of the third of a league. Up the stream there is a great rock scarped from top to bottom, and quite at the top it is level. There is nearly in the middle of this rock a monastery of our Lady, and they say that there was the palace of the king of that country and kingdom of Gorages. This rock faces to the rising sun, and they ascend to this monastery by a movable ladder of wood : and they say that they raise it every night from fear of the Gorages, when the Court is not here. After that[1] the ascent is by stone steps to the left hand, and a corridor runs past fifteen cells for friars, all which have windows over the water, and very high; further on are their pantries and refectory, and store rooms for provisions. Turn-ing to the right hand by a dark path a man reaches broad daylight, and the principal door of the monastery, which is not made of the rock itself, only it seems that in ancient times it was a great hall, and the form is of a church with screens :[2] it is very light and spacious, because it has many windows over the river, and there are few friars. Many people of the Court used to come here to receive the communion, as they have much devotion for this house and its friars, because they say that they lead good lives, and suffer much injury from the bad neighbours they have. As the people of the Court and the Court are encamped in such a situation that the left wing, which belongs to the great Betudete, is towards these Goragues, there were few

---

[1] *I.e.*, the termination of the wooden ladder.

[2] *Paredinhas.*

days that it was not said : " Last night the Goragues killed fifteen or twenty pesons of the people of the great Betudete ;" and they took no measures for this, because it was Lent, and on account of the rigid fast no one fights from the debility and weakness of their bodies, for the fast must not on any account be broken. During holy week, near to Easter, Prester John sent to tell us to be ready to say mass near his tent as he wished to hear it. I sent to tell him that I was ready, and that we were all ready, but that we had no tent, as one that they had given us had become rotten with the rains, and was quite worn out. He sent to say that he would give a tent and order it to be pitched, and also would send to call us for us to be ready and come with all our arrangements. When it was a little past midnight he sent to call us, and we went at once, and they conducted us before the king's door, which we found in this state. A great part of the fence enclosure was broken and removed, from the great tent of the Prester as far as the church of Holy Cross, and on each side facing one another were more than six thousand lighted candles in very good array, and the length of the lines might be a musket shot, and from face to face of those who held the candles the distance might be fully two games of ball, one in front of the other, and it was all smooth ground. There were more than five thousand persons behind these who held the candles, and those of the candles remained like a wall,[1] and they could not be broken because they had before them canes fastened together, and they held the candles upon them in array. Before the tent of the Prester four gentlemen were riding and caracolling their horses ; and they placed us near them. Upon this Prester John came out of the tent upon a black[2] mule like a raven, the size of a large horse, which the Prester holds in great estimation, and this mule always travels when the Prester travels, and if he does not ride

---

[1] Seto.   [2] Macho murzelo ; mulo morzillo.—Selves.

upon it ho goes on a litter.   And ho came out in this manner, namely, in a cloak[1] of brocade which almost reached to
the ground, and the mule was also caparisoned and covered
over ; the Prester had his crown on his head and a cross in
his hand, and there were on each side two horses with their
haunches almost in a line with the head of the mule, but
not near, for they went a good distance apart ; these horses
were so caparisoned and adorned and covered with brocade,
that with the light it seemed that they were sewn up in
gold ; and they had great diadems on their heads, which descended to the bits, and large plumes set in the diadems.
As soon as the Prester came out, the four who before that
were caracolling their horses between the candles went out,
and did not show here again; and when Prester John passed,
those who had come to call us placed us behind him, without any one else coming there or passing before the candles,
only twenty or thirty gentlemen who went on foot a good
bit in front of the Prester.   Thus we arrrived at the church
of Holy Cross, where the Prester went to hear the office of
the resurrection, and here he dismounted and entered the
church, and at once went inside his curtain, and we remained at the door.   Soon after, an immense number of
clergy came out from inside, and a great many more joined
them who were outside, for there was not room for them in
the church, and a great procession was ordered, and they
put us at the head of it, with the most honoured dignities of
the church, so we walked until the procession returned to
the church ; and as many as it would hold entered it, and the
rest remained in the plain, and they bade us enter, and we
were near the curtain till mass was finished.   When they
were going to give the communion Prester John sent to say
that we should go and make ready to say our mass, as the
tent was pitched for us, and that he was coming soon.
We went with those who had called us and always had
<hr>
[1] *Hopa*, a cloak without sleeves.

accompanied us, and they conducted us to a black tent close
to that of the Prester, and we, seeing the black tent, said :
"They have pitched this tent for us as a mockery." Then the
ambassador said : "Padre, you will do well not to say mass,
because this is done to put us to the proof." I answered
him : "Neither do I wish to say it, let us go to our tents :"
and this was when dawn was breaking. We went to our
tents, which were in the grove close to the river. Then
there came two pages in a great hurry over the rocks to call
us, and they called us with anger. We were discussing
about not going ; however, we went and arrived at Prester
John's tent as the sun was rising. At once there came
a message from inside, asking, Why we had omitted to
say mass on so great a feast ? I answered, that I did not
choose to say mass on account of the great affront which
had been offered—not to us, but to God and his holy resurrection, as they had pitched a black tent for us to say mass
in, such as they do not pitch, except for horses and vaga-
bonds.[1] They returned with another message, asking what
tent they were to pitch. I answered that, it must be a
white one, to represent the splendour of the resurrection,
and the purity of Our Lady, and that a red one might well
do, as it would represent the blood which Christ shed for us,
and that which the apostles and martyrs had shed for him.
With this they went away and returned, saying, that we
should send and tell him who were the persons who had
pitched the tent, and we should see the justice which he
would order to be done. We replied that we did not
know who had pitched the tent, neither did we ask him to
do justice on any one, as this had not been done to us, but
to God, and it grieved us more than any one else, because
we could not say mass on so great a feast. They then

---

[1] *Humiziados*, Selves translates *enfermos*, sick people. Homiziados
are persons hiding on account of some crime they have committed.

returned, asking that we should have patience, and that
he would punish those who had pitched the tent, and that
we should go to it, since it was not to say mass, but to dine.
We held council whether wo should go to it or not, however
we went, and they sent us a very good meal of many good
viands, and good wines, among which were grape wines of
good flavour, and very red.   Pero de Covilham was with us
during all that passed that night and day, and he told us at
the dinner that he felt such great pleasure such as he had
never felt in this country, nor had expected to feel, that we
had not said mass in this tent, and at the answer which we
had given; and that all this had only been in order to test.
the estimation we had for the things belonging to God and
the Church, and that now they would hold us in esteem as
good Christians.   All this Lent we were very well provided
with food and drink, and plenty of grapes and peaches
which there are in this district.   At the end of the dinner
there came to us the old priest who performed the baptism,
and he said that Prester John sent him to say that since to-
day we did not say mass, that we should anyhow say it next
Sunday, and that he would order a good tent to be given,
and that we should celebrate offices after our fashion and
usage for the soul of his mother, who had died a year ago,
and that they would then do her teskar, that is to say, memorial service.   All this we did according to our custom.

CAP. CXII.—*How Don Luis de Menezes wrote to the ambassador
    to depart, and how they did not find him at Court, and
    how the King Don Manuel had died.*

Sunday, the octave of Easter, when they told us to say
mass, was the 15th of April.   We said the office and mass
for the mother of the Prester John.   We went very early
and found a large new white tent pitched, with its curtains

of silk hung in the middle according to their usage, and very near to his tent. The friar who is now going as ambassador with other clergy is here, and we at once sung a nocturn for the deceased and said mass. Before the mass was finished there arrived two packets of letters which Don Luis de Meneses sent to us ; he had come for us and was remaining at Masua. The packets had come by different roads and both messengers arrived together. There came in these packets letters to Prester John begging him to send us at once. Having seen our letters we found in them that we should set out at once and come to him to Masua by the 15th of April, as he could not wait longer : both because the monsoon did not allow of it, and because he was required in India. These fifteen days had finished this day when the letters were given to us : and in them came the news how the King Don Manuel had died. On this account we were all half dead, and we at once held council as to whether we should be silent about it, or should tell it : it was agreed that we ought not to keep it secret, because the Prester knew the news of India more quickly than we did, by the Moorish merchants who were continually coming from there: and that it was better that he should learn it from us than from others. As it is their custom in mourning to shave the head with a razor, and not the beard, and to dress in black clothes, we began to shave each other's heads, and to dress in mourning. During this our food came, and those who brought it seeing the work we were engaged in, set the food down on the ground and without speaking returned and told it to the Prester. He at once sent two friars to know what had happened to us. The ambassador said that someone should answer the friars, as he could not for weeping. I declared to them what was the matter, according to the usage of the country, and with their words, saying : "Tell His Highness that the stars and the moon have fallen, and the sun has grown dark and lost its brightness, and we

have no one to cover or protect us ; we have neither father
nor mother to care for us, except God, who is the Father of
all : the King Don Manuel our Sovereign has departed from
the life of this world, and we remain orphans and unpro-
tected." We commenced our lamentation, and the friars
went away. In that hour proclamations were made that all
the shops should be shut where bread and wine and other
merchandise were sold, and also that all the offices should be
closed ; and this shutting up lasted three days, during which
no tent was opened. At the end of three days he sent to
call us, and the first word he spoke was : " Who inherits
the kingdoms of the King my father ? " The ambassador
said, " The Prince Don Joam his son." Hearing this he said
"*Atesia, atesia*", that is to say, " Do not be afraid, for
you are in a country of Christians, and as the father was
good the son will be good, and I will write to him." Then
we explained to him how they were waiting for us at the
sea, and that also they wrote to his Highness to say that we
begged his leave to go away, and that now we did not seem
to be doing well[1] in his country. He told us to go and eat,
and that next day they would commence despatching us, and
that we should translate the letters which came for him into
his language. And as we already knew the nature of his despatching, on the Sunday that they gave us the letters, we
at once despatched Aires Diaz, a Portuguese of our company, and with him an Abyssinian, to go with our letters to
the said Don Luis de Meneses; and on the following day we
took the letters to the Prester in his language, and he at
once departed to another place with his Court, and we with
him. As we were travelling on the road they asked me
who was carrying for me the church tent. I replied that
the tent was not mine, and that I had not the care of
it, that we had said our mass, and the tent had remained as we found it. They told me that I had done

_____
[1] Obscure : perhaps the words. " to stay longer". have been omitted.

wrong, that the Prester did not take back anything he had
given, and that the tent with its curtains was worth more
than a hundred ounces of gold, and that if Prester John
ordered mass to be said, and that we told him that we had
got no tent, he would be angry. Withal we travelled three
days, and as soon as we took up quarters we requested our
leave and to be despatched. They told us not to have any fear,
that he had already ordered his measures. With all our importuning he ordered that Joan Gonzalvez our factor should
go with his and our letters on the way to the sea, and he at the
same time gave him a very good mule and rich dresses and
ten ounces of gold. He ordered that he should go at once,
and he set out immediately with two servants of the Prester.
We remained, and however much we importuned the Prester
and made requests to him, he kept us waiting yet a month
and a half, and at the end of that time he gave us rich
dresses, and to four of us he gave gold chains with
their crosses, and to each he gave a mule, and to me he gave
a mule from his own stables, the pace of which was flying;
and he gave for all of us eighty ounces of gold and a hundred loaves for the road, and he gave us his blessing. We
did not travel long before we got a message from our people
whom we had sent to the sea, that Don Luis had been gone
a long time; and we knew well that we should not find him
because the monsoon did not allow of it; nevertheless, we
arrived, and we found much pepper and cloths which he left
for our maintenance, and letters for us and for the Prester.
Then there was a council among us what we should do with
that pepper : and although the opinion of some was that we
should take up quarters and eat it, since Don Luis in his
letters ordered that in no way should we go away from the
sea coast, because next year at all events they would come
for us, others thought that only one or two of us should go
to the Court to take the letters to the Prester, and to ask
him for justice for the death of four men who had been

killed at Arquiquo. And with this opinion of most of us it was agreed amongst us that we should send half the pepper to Prester John and the other half should remain for our maintenance, and that the factor and I should carry it; and I was to go to read to him the letters and have them translated into his language; and this having been settled in one day that the departure should be next morning. On that morning the ambassador came to me, saying, " Padre, I wish to give you another companion to go with you to the Court." When I said, " Let it be as you command", he replied to me : " Should you be pleased with my company, it is I that intend to go with you, and we will take all the pepper." And because I opposed him, saying that nothing would remain for the other people to expend, he said that still he would go and carry all the pepper. He did this expecting great favours and to obtain them all himself. So the ambassador did not choose but to carry all the pepper to the Prester; and we set out at once. I went only to carry the letters to the Prester and to translate them into his language. We set out for the Court on the 1st day of September, and we travelled at a slow pace, with mules and loads; and we reached the Court at the end of November, and found the Prester in a Kingdom which is named Fatiguar, which is on the edge of the Kingdom of Adel, to which kingdom and sovereignty belong Barbora and Zeila ; and the king is great and powerful. They say that he is esteemed and looked upon as a saint among the Moorish Kings because he continually makes war upon the Christians; they also say that he receives supplies from the King of Arabia and the Sheikh of Mekkah, and from other Moorish Kings and lords he receives horses and weapons for this purpose ; and that he sends every year large offerings to Mekkah of many Abyssinian slaves that he captures in the wars : and also he makes presents of those slaves to the King of Arabia and to other princes. Now with respect to the place or plain where

we reached the Prester and where we found him, it is as
they say one day's journey from the first market town in the
Kingdom of Adel ; and there are eight days' journey from
that market to Zeila. This kingdom of Fatiguar, what we
saw of it, both on entering and leaving it, is all more plain
than mountain, that is to say there are small and low hills
all made use of for much tillage of wheat and barley ; and
also much cultivated ground and fields, also sown with the
above-mentioned grain ; there is also great breeding of all
cattle, cows, sheep, goats, small mares and mules bred from
she-asses. There is a great view of this country, and it
seems like a great hill, not a mountain nor of rocky cliffs,
but all wooded and cultivated land. They say that there
are many monasteries and churches in it, and that it is a
very rich country. There is on the highest part of it a lake
of an extent of four leagues, from which there came to the
Court an infinite quantity of fish, and oranges, lemons, and
citrons, and Indian figs. Pero de Covilham told me that
this hill was of a circumference of eight days' journey round
its foot ; and he also made the conjecture of the size of the
lake at four leagues. When the Court left this plain in
which we were, we travelled two days and a half until we
reached the foot of the hill, and having approached near, it
seemed much higher and more fruitful, as it was said to be.
There come forth from it many streams, which contain much
fish. We travelled across the foot of this hill a day and a
half, and then left the hill and kingdom of Fatiguar, and
entered that of Xoa ; where we presented the pepper and
the letters translated into Abyssinian, and we got no answer
whatever. Prester John was going this road to make some
partition of lands between himself and his sisters, that is
to say, two who were sisters both of father and mother, because his father had five wives. And these partitions were
of the lands and property which had remained after the
death of his mother. Here we remained four days, and in

those they sorted the lands, which were divided into three parts, which Pero de Covilham said were lands of more than ten days' journey. And the Prester gave to each of his sisters her share, and one part for himself, and he then ordered his part to be divided into two, and he gave them to his two infant daughters; and cows, mares, sheep, and goats which covered the hills and fields and valleys, all were in the same partition, and they were divided in the same way as the lands. The Prester would not travel from this place and go to other partitions, as the lands were many and far apart, and he gave orders that they should be divided like these, and that his share should be divided between his daughters. We heard say that the gold and silk of this division was uncounted; and as to the silks, they said that the Prester ordered that his share should be given to the churches and monasteries which were situated in the lands which had belonged to his mother. We travelled to the town of Dara, where Pero de Covilham showed me the thickets in which the friars led a rigid life, and the white man died in the grotto which they found walled up.[1]

CAP. CXIII.—*Of the battle which the Prester had with the King of Adel, and how he defeated Captain Mahomed.*

I return to the relation of what I heard of the Kingdom of Adel and of a great captain there was in it, and of the death which he died (and this I heard from many and above all from Pero de Covilham). It was most certain that there was in this Kingdom of Adel a great Moorish captain who was named Mahfudi,[2] whom the people of this Court still sing of when they travel. They say that this captain entered the lands of the Prester during every Lent for twenty-five years, because during Lent the great fast breaks the people's

---

[1] See chapter cix.   [2] *Mahfuz.*

strength and they are not able to fight. He entered so far
into them that many times he reached to a distance of twenty
leagues. One year he would enter the kingdom of Amara
or of Xoa, another the kingdom of Fatignar, and he entered
sometimes at one place sometimes at another. He began to
make these incursions in the lifetime of King Alexander,
who was uncle of this king, and he continued them during
twelve years of his life ; and because he died without children, Nahum his brother, the father of this king, succeeded
him, and Mahfud did the same during his time. This David
who now reigns, commenced to reign at the age of twelve
years, and until he was seventeen years old Mahfud did not
cease these incursions and warfare during Lent. They say
that he made such great incursions and forays that in one he
carried off captive nineteen[1] Abyssinians, and that he sent
them all as an offering to the house of Mekkah, and as
presents to the Moorish kings : and they say that there they
become great Moors, because they escape from the great
severity of the fast, and enter into the abundance and luxury
of the Moors. He also carried off a great multitude of
all sorts of flocks. On the twenty-fourth year of his incursions, on his entry into the kingdom of Fatignar all
the people fled and took refuge in the before-mentioned
hill, and Mahfud followed them ; and they say that he
entered the hill and burned all the churches and monasteries there. I have before related that in all the countries
of the Prester there are chavas, who are men at-arms,
because in these kingdoms the cultivators do not go to
the wars, and that there were in these kingdoms many
chavas, and those who took refuge on the hill were cultivators and chavas, that is, men-at-arms who had fled.
Mahfud took them all prisoners, and he ordered the cultivators to be separated from the men-at-arms, and he
ordered the cultivators to go in peace, and to sow for next

---

[1] This figure, xix, is probably a misprint.

ceived or ill informed, and if any one had told him so, that he had not told him the truth; and that if he judged of it by looking at the map of the world, that he would not acquire a right knowledge of the countries, because Portugal and Spain are in the map of the world as things that are well known, and not as things requiring to be known : and that he should look in the map how the cities and castles and monasteries were, and also how Venice, Jerusalem, and Rome were, like things well-known and in small spaces, and let him look at his Ethiopia, how it was an unknown thing, very large and much spread out, full of mountains, and lions and elephants and many other animals, and also many mountain ridges, without the map showing any city, town, or castle; His Highness should know that the King of Portugal, by means of his captains, was powerful enough to defend and guard the Red Sea against all the power of the great Sultan and of the great Turk, and to make war upon them even to the holy house; and that he had made greater conquests in the parts of Africa with the King of Fez and Morocco, and many other kings, subjugating all the Indies and making all their kings his tributary subjects, as His Highness well knew from the adversaries of the King of Portugal, who were the Moorish merchants from India trading at his Court. To this there did not come any answer, and there was another question, and he dismissed us, sending to us plenty to eat and drink; and so he did every day whilst we went with the Court.

Four or five days after the map of the world, the Prester sent to call us, and he sent to say that he wished to write to the Pope of Rome, whom they name Rumea Negus lique papaz : which means the King of Rome and Head of the Popes : and he desired that I should write the beginning of the letter, because they were not accustomed to write, and did not know how to write to the Pope.

Don Rodrigo the ambassador answered that we had not come to write, nor was there any one among us who could write to the Pope. I said that I would tell him the beginning, and after that they could continue with whatever he had in his heart to write or to request. There came a message that we should go and dine, and afterwards come back, the friar and I, and that I should bring all my books to prepare the letters; and so we did. When we came we found all those whom they hold to be most learned, assembled together with many books; and they at once asked me for my books. I replied that books were not necessary, but only to know the intentions of His Highness, and by that we should be ruled. Then a man who was the principal one there in rank and learning, and whose title is Abuquer, which means chief chaplain, told the Prester's intention to the friar, and he told it to me. Then I set to writing and shortly made a small beginning, which was at once taken in my handwriting to His Highness, and was brought back at once, and in that hour we put it into their language and sent it back again. There was no delay with it, for the page came back at once, saying that the king was much pleased with the writing, and amazed because it had not been taken out of books : and he ordered that it should at once be written in clean writing and in two letters; and he ordered that his learned priests should study in their books the most they could to search for what more could be put in the letters. *When the friar and I were coming to our tents, the ambassador came out and said to me: " Padre, I regret very much what I said to-day to Prester John that there was no one among us who knew how to write to the Pope, because he will hold us for men of little knowledge, I entreat of you to put all your efforts in this, and do for him all you know." I answered him, " that whether it was strong or weak, it was done to the best of my knowledge, and that he would see here what I

found without any inhabitant. The Prester came up to the doors of this palace and with his lance struck the doors three times, and he did not choose that anyone else should strike them, nor enter nor approach them, that it might not be said that he went to plunder, and that if he had found the king there, or many other people, he would have been the first to enter in person, because he was going in fair and open warfare; and since he found nobody, nobody should enter. So they turned back again. This battle was in the month of July and they asserted that it was on the same day that Lopo Soarez destroyed and burned Zeila,[1] at which destruction I was present: and the Moors who were taken prisoners there said that the chief captain of Zeila was with the King of Adel in wars with the Negus of Ethiopia. Several times the Prester ordered us to be shewn four or five bundles of short swords with silver hilts, not very well made, saying that they had taken all those and others in the war with the Sultan of Adel, and also the tent which he gave us of common brocade and Mekka velvet was taken in that war, and belonged to the king himself, and on that account he had sent to tell us to bless it before saying mass in it, in case the Moor had sinned in it. The head of Mahfud was going about the Court of the Prester more than three years before that passed in our going or arrival in it; and every Saturday and Sunday and days of observance, the common people and boys and girls made great festivity with it, and at this day it is about the Court, and it seems to me that it will be there for ever, so enamoured are they of it. Gabri Andreas (as I have said) is a friar and a very honourable person, and a gentleman of great revenues, and (according to fame) he is very eloquent, and is a friend of the Portuguese, and he understands Church matters well, and enjoyed talking about them. He has not got more than half his tongue, and the end cut off, because King Nahum ordered it to be cut off because he talked a great deal.

---

[1] Neither Barros nor G. Correa give this date.

CAP. CXIV.—*How the Prester sent us a map of the world which we had brought him, for us to translate the writing into Abyssinian, and what more passed, and of the letters for the Pope.*

While we were at the town of Dara, Prester John sent us a map of the world, which we had brought to him four years ago, and which Diogo Lopez de Sequeira had sent him, with a message that if the letters on the map said what the countries were that we should put his letters at the foot of them that he might know what these countries were. We at once set to work, the friar who is going to Portugal and I, he wrote and I read, and beneath our writing he placed theirs. And because our Portugal is mixed with Castile in a small space, and Seville is very near Lisbon and near to Corunna, I put Seville for Spain,[1] and Lisbon for Portugal, and Corunna for Galicia. When the whole of the map was finished and nothing remained they took it away. The following day he sent to call the ambassador and all of us that were with him, and immediately in the first conversation he sent to say that the King of Portugal and the King of Castile were sovereigns of few lands, and that the King of Portugal would not be strong enough to defend the Red Sea from the power of the Turks and Rumys; and that it would be well if he was to write to the King of Spain that he should order a fortress to be built in Zeila, and the King of Portugal should order one to be built in Masua, and the King of France order one to be made in Suaquem; and all three, with the forces of the Prester, would be able to guard the Red Sea and take Jiddah and Mekkah and Cairo, and the holy house, and go through all the countries they chose. The ambassador replied to this that His Highness was de-

[1] Or Seville belonging to Spain, etc., etc.; Selves translates : " I told him to write Spain under Seville, Galicia under Corunna, and Portugal under Lisbon."

year much wheat and barley against he came, so that he and
his people might find enough to eat for themselves and their
horses. And he said to the men-at-arms: " Knaves who
eat the king's bread, and guard his lands so ill, all of you
to the sword ;" and he ordered fifteen men-at-arms to be
killed ; and returned with a great troop, and without any
opposition whatever. Prester John being greatly vexed at
this, principally at the burning of the monasteries and
churches, ordered spies to go into the kingdom of Adel to
learn in what part this Mafudo would determine to enter.
And he learned how the king of Adel would enter in person,
and Mahfud with him, and great forces, and that they
would enter this same kingdom of Fatiguar and that they
were coming out of Lent in the time when the wheat and
barley were young to destroy them all, and during Lent
would go to another part. On knowing this, Prester John
determined to wait for them on the road, and they say
that he was much opposed by all his people and by the
grandees of the Court, who said that he was a youth of
seventeen and that it was not well that he should go to
such a war, and that the Betudetes and captains of his kingdoms were sufficient there. They say that he said that he
needs must go in person to avenge the injuries which had
been done to his uncle Alexander and to his father Nahum,
and to himself for six years, and that he trusted in God to
avenge it all. So he set out with his people and Court
without ordering men to come from distant lands, so as not
to be heard of; and they say that he travelled day and
night, and one night before dawn he went and pitched his
camp over where the first fair of the kingdom of Adel is held,
one day's journey from where we found the Prester when we
brought him the pepper. They say there is here a great
pass which the King of Adel had passed the day before,
and he was encamped about the distance of half a league in
the Prester's country, and off the road : and the Prester was

encamped in the country of Adel. When it was clear daylight they saw each other, and they say that as soon as
Mahfud saw the camp of the Prester, and saw the red tents
which are only pitched for great festivals or receptions, he
said to the King of Adel, " Sire, the Negus of Ethiopia is
here in person, to-day is the day of our deaths, do what you
can to save yourself, for I shall die here." They say that
the king escaped with four horsemen, and of these four one
was the son of a Betudete, who was with the King of Adel,
and is now with the Prester in his Court, because here they
think nothing of joining the Moors and becoming Moors, and
if they wish to return, they get baptised again, and remain
pardoned and Christians as before. This one gave the
account of what took place among them. As soon as the
King of Adel had put himself in safety, which was very
early in the morning, Prester John, as they relate, who
did not know of the king's flight, ordered that all should
receive the communion and commend themselves to God,
and get their breakfasts, and make ready : and at the hour
of tierce they began to set their battle array, and go out
to fight with the Moors, leaving their tents pitched. They
say that as soon as the Moors saw them in motion, Mahfuz
came out to speak to the Christians, asking if there was
among them any knight who was willing to fight with him
to the death. A friar of the name of Gabri-Andreas came
forth for this purpose, and he killed Mahfuz, and cut off his
head. He is still alive and is a man who is much honoured
at the Court. There was then a general onset on the Moors,
who had nowhere to escape, because the Prester's tents
were pitched opposite the principal pass, and the other pass
which was further off, by which the king had fled, was
already taken possession of. When the Moors were routed
and killed, Prester John returned to his tents to rest, and
the following day he marched into the kingdom of Adel until
he arrived at a rich palace of the King of Adel, which he

had done". As soon as he saw it he rejoiced much (according to what he showed), and the minute[1] of the letter which I drew up goes in a separate letter and is smaller; it begins " Blessed Holy Father".* They employed three days in preparing the other letter, and they spent fifteen days in making a small gold cross, which weighs a hundred cruzados, and which is also going to the Pope.

Cap. cxv.—*How in the letters of Don Luis it was said that we should require justice for certain men of his who had been killed, and the Prester sent there the Chief Justice of the Court, and Zagazabo in company of Don Rodrigo to Portugal.*

In the letters which Don Luis de Meneses sent to Prester John, he made a complaint and required justice for four Portuguese whom the Moors had killed in the town of Arquiquo, a port of the Red Sea and in his country; which justice and vengeance he had not chosen to execute or take by himself, because it was in the Prester's country, and that he desired to serve His Highness and not annoy him. We had asked this justice many times, and had for answer that he regretted very much that the captain-major Don Luis had not taken vengeance, and killed all the Moors that were in the town of Arquiquo, and that he valued more one Portuguese than all the Moors and negroes that were in his country : and that since he (Don Luis) did not choose to take vengeance himself, that he would order justice to be done : and he ordered the Chief Justice of his Court to come before us in front of his tent, and he sent to tell him by the Cabeata that he was to go with us to the sea, and to take prisoners all the Moors, Turks, Rumys, and Christians, whom he should discover to have been in

---

[1] *Menuta.*   * All this passage is omitted by Selves.

the town of Arquiquo at the time that they killed these
men of Don Luis de Meneses. And those that he found
guilty of the said death, or in not having arrested those
who had killed, and who had raised the brawl, he was to
give them up to any captain-major who came from Portugal,
and he might kill them or do justice as he pleased; killing,
beheading, or taking them as captives, either Christians or
Moors, Turks and Roumys; but that the Portuguese were
not to complain any more of this justice, but to take it for
themselves. In this town, and in these days, Prester John
determined to send an ambassador to Portugal, for up to
this time he was not sending any one. He sent to call the
ambassador and me, and he said, that he had determined to
send a person with us to the King of Portugal, in order
that his desires might have effect quicker, his representative being there; and he asked if we thought that Zagazabo
would be sufficient for this journey, inasmuch as he could
speak our language, and had already been to our countries.
We answered that Zagazabo was quite sufficient for this
journey, and for being the envoy of His Highness, because
he was a man who got on well with us, and we with him,
and that he had no need of an interpreter: and that now
His Highness was doing what he ought to do, because on
his return he would give more belief to what his own countrymen saw and heard of foreigners, than to what foreigners
said of themselves. They then decided that we should
have him for our companion. The following day he sent us
dresses, and thirty ouquias[1] of gold, and a hundred loaves
for the road. Still we waited a great deal later, and the
cause (according to what the ambassador himself told us
later) was because the determination of Prester John was
tardy, this detention was necessary as the ambassador was
not yet despatched, until he had given him the things
which he had to carry for his journey and himself, that is

[1] *Ouquia*, a gold coin worth twelve *cruzados*.

an old friar, who was very venerable and the head of the others, and they flogged him in the above mentioned manner, and they did not once touch this friar. When they had done with him they brought another friar who might be a little more than forty years old, and he looked respectable, and they flogged him like the others, and this one was touched twice. When it was over I asked the cause of it, and what sin the friars had committed. Then they related to me that the friar who had been last flogged had been married to a daughter of the Prester, that is of Alexander, uncle of this David, and he had separated from her, and he had married a sister of this Prester, who did what she pleased, and the husband did not dare to meddle with this from fear of the Prester, and also because in this country the faults of women are not looked at with much surprise, and he left this second wife and returned to the first. And Prester John ordered that he should return to his sister. When this order came he did not choose to do it, and went and became a friar: and on this account the Prester ordered these friars to come before the Chief Justice for him to see whether this man was rightly a friar. He judged that he had lawfully taken the habit, and because he had judged thus the Prester had ordered him to be flogged. And the Padre or guardian had been flogged because he had given the habit to the other. And the third man was flogged because he had received the habit; and they commanded him at once to leave the habit and to return to the Prester's sister. With this we remained without being heard this time, nor till fifteen days later, on account of things which happened in the monastery, which I will relate.

CAP. CXVII.—*How, after the death of Queen Helena, the great Betudete went to collect the dues of her kingdom, and what they were, and how the Queen of Adea came to ask assistance, and what people came with her on mules.*

It might be eight or nine months after the death of Queen Helena, who reigned over the greater part of the kingdom of Gojame, that still as many as newly came to the Court, went to weep before her tent, which still remains pitched in its place ; and we also did this when we came. After her death Prester John sent the great Betudete to the said kingdom of Gojame to collect the *Gibre*[1] which is paid to the King each year as dues, and in these days the said Betudete arrived with the gibre, which amounted to three thousand mules, three thousand horses, and three thousand basutos— these are some cloths which the great people have upon their beds, they are of cotton and fleecy like carpets and not so close worked, and as to price, those that are least valuable are not less than an ouquia, and they are worth from two, three, four up to five ouquias ; besides thirty thousand cotton cloths of small value, which are worth two of them a drachm, and sometimes less. They also said that they brought thirty thousand ouquias of gold ; it is already known that an ouquia weighs eleven cruzados. At the presentation of this gibre, I saw with my eyes all the gold which came covered up on trays,[2] and they said that it was a great quantity, and it all came in this manner. The Betudete in front, stripped from the waist upwards, and with a crown wound round his head, like the head gear of a Castilian muleteer,[3] and when within hearing from where he could be heard at the Prester's tent, he said three times, with a very small interval between each cry, " Aalto," which in our language is like Sire : and they answered him from within the tent twice in their lan-

---

[1] Tribute.　　　　　　　　　　　　[2] *Garcia.*

[3] Or such as is still generally worn by the Aragonese peasants.

parts those who went in the service of kings, not only themselves, but moreover their servants, factors, majordomos,
property, revenues, and lordships were much favoured and
guarded. And so it was hoped that His Highness would
favour his ambassador and order justice to be done, and
that he should be restored to his lordship. At once there
came an answer saying, who was the person that had caused
us vexation, and had taken the lordship of the said Zagazabo. We replied that it was Abdenaguo the head of the
pages who had ordered this act of force to be done by his
stewards and factors, and that we asked His Highness to
give us judges above suspicion, and that he should order
the pages to carry to him any message that might be
necessary upon this business. Soon four pages came to us
saying that their lord commanded them that whatever thing
should be requested of him by us in this business, that
they were to do it with free will and without fear of anybody. The judges in this suit were the Ajazo Duragote
and the Ajazo Ceyte, to whom we were to address ourselves.
We went to them soon, and they appointed a time that
such an hour of the sun we should come to such a place.
We went, and there were present the representative of
Abdenaguo and the ambassador in person: and they argued
on both sides, and brought forward reasons until a conclusion was come to verbally, because here there is no
writing in the tribunals, and all was verbal, and the sentence is given verbally. The judges concluded with the
sentence that the land and fief[1] which Zagazabo claimed
was very small, and that it was subject to another land of
great extent and of a great lordship of which Abdenaguo
was the lord, and that it was of right that the great wind
enters in all the land; and thus the entry could not be
taken away from Abdenaguo, great lord as he was. Then
we went away to complain, having remained struck down

---

[1] *Gulto.*

by this sentence. We complained to the King. He sent to tell us to go to our quarters, and not to be vexed, that all would turn out well, and that next day we should go and plead to the Chief Justice, and he would do us justice. With that we went away. Next day we went to wait for the Chief Justice in the road to the Prester's tent: he received us with good will, saying that he had already received the king's instructions for the despatch of our business, and that we were to wait at the tent of justice, as he was going to speak to the king, and that then he would despatch us. All the same we went further on with him as far as where he separated from the people to go and speak to the king. While we remained thus expecting our despatch from the good will we had seen in him, when he came out from the tent there came out with him two pages, who accompanied him to the place where they flog men, and there they called the executioners, and they had him stripped and thrown down and tied, as I have already described, that is they threw him down on his stomach and made fast his hands to two stakes, and his feet tied together with a leather cord, and two men to pull at it, and he was bare from the waist upwards. There were two executioners on each side of him, and most times they strike the ground with the scourge. And when orders come from the king to strike, the blow reaches the bones, and of these blows they gave him three. Reckoning this time, I have seen the Chief Justice flogged three times, and after that, two days later, return to his office, because they do not hold it to be a dishonour; rather they say the king is fond of him, because he remembers him, and a short time after does him favours and bestows lordships. And when they now thus flogged the Chief Justice, there were there sixty friars, all clothed in new yellow habits according to their usage. When they had done flogging the Chief Justice, they took

to say, clothes and gold for his expenses. Also we waited
for the Chief Justice who had to go with us, as has been
said. After all we set out without them, saying that we
would go on at a slow pace: this was because we had often
seen his despatch. So we went away and they caught us
up on the road, each in their turn, and we travelled until
we reached Barua, which is near the sea, where our quarters
were, which is the chief town of the country of the Barnagais. We did not find any news of the Portuguese
coming to the port, and we all waited together until the
monsoon had passed. During this time the Chief Justice
arrested three or four gentlemen, and one Xumagali who
was at Arquiquo at the time they killed the men. This
Xumagali was soltam,[1] Xumagali means a small gentleman,
like a gentleman without lands. This one was arrested,
because at that time he was justice, and he did not do his
duty, and one Gabri Jesus was arrested because he came
there and did nothing; and Arrais Jacob was arrested,
because at that time he ruled the country of the Barnagais;
and one Dafela, who is a great lord, was arrested because
some Moors and Turks took refuge in his lands, and he did
not make them prisoners, though he knew that they were
at the death of Don Luis de Meneses' men who were killed
at Arquiquo. These four were great gentlemen, and all
five were sent as prisoners to the Court by the Chief
Justice, and no one went to accuse them. Although they
were ill treated, they became free. As soon as the Chief
Justice arrived at Court, and gave news to the Prester that
the Portuguese had not arrived, and that we remained
without a remedy, the Prester at once sent a Calacem,[2]
ordering us to go to the town of Aquaxumo, where, as I
before said, we had been, and where had been the dwellings
of the Queens of Saba and Candacia. There they ordered

---

[1] Sultan, apparently the title of a magistrate of Arquico.
[2] A king's messenger.

us to be given five hundred loads of wheat, and a hundred cows, and a hundred sheep), and a hundred jars of honey, and another hundred of butter; and for his ambassador who came with us, twenty loads of wheat, and twenty cows, and twenty sheep, and twenty jars of honey, and as many of butter.

CAP. CXVI.—*How Zagazabo the ambassador returned to the Court, and I with him, for business which concerned him, and how they flogged the Chief Justice and two friars, and why.*

Whilst we were in this town of Aquaxumo there came a message to the ambassador of the Prester that a small lordship belonging to him had been taken from him; then he begged me to go with him to the Court to ask for justice. I went, and we discovered there that his adversary was the principal page of Prester John, who was Abdenaguo, captain of the pages, because there is no service here, but what it has one person over all the others. As all the messages went to the Prester through the pages we had no remedy in putting in our word, so then we sought succour from an Ajaze, who is a great lord; and although he was a great friend of Abdenaguo our adversary, yet for the sake of justice he made known to the Prester how we had come and for what. Then there came a message asking me what I had come to Court for. I gave an account of all, and said that the injury and unreasonable thing done to Zagazabo, was done rather to the King of Portugal and to us Portuguese than to him, since he was absent from his land and lordship for the service of the King of Portugal and the company of us Portuguese, by the order of His Highness, and that his land should be confirmed to him, and not usurped and forcibly taken from him : and that in our

guage, " Who are you ? " He, in their language, replied, "I who call, am the smallest of your house, and am he who saddles your mules and puts the head stalls on your baggage mules, I serve in what other business you command, I bring to you, Sire, what you commanded me." All this was said three times, and when that was done, the voice from inside said " Pass on, pass forward." And he went on and made his bow before the tent and passed on. Behind him immediately came the horses, one behind the other, each horse had a man or boy at the halter. The foremost thirty were saddled, they were reasonably good, but of the others that followed behind, the best was not worth two drachms, and many of them were not worth a drachm ; I saw them later given for less, and these would be quite three thousand. After these sorry nags came the mules after the manner of the nags, that is thirty good ones saddled, and all the others small young mules, but better than the nags. There were male and female mules of a year and over, and two year old and three, and none more than that except the saddled ones ; for none of the others were fit for riding. These would be quite three thousand, and they passed by as had done the Betudete and the little horses. After the mules came the basutos, and each man carried a basuto, for he could not carry more from their great volume. After the basutos came the cloths, each man with a bundle of them ; they said that each man carried ten cloths, and there would be quite three thousand men with the basutos, and three thousand with the cloths, and all these were from the said kingdom of Gojame, who were obliged to bring the gibre.[1] Behind the cloths came three men, each with a trencher[2] on their heads, of those in which they eat : they were covered with large green and red cloths of tafetan. Behind these trays came all the men of the Betudete, and they passed in turn as did the Betudete. They said that the gold went in

[1] 12,000 men in all. [2] *Garcia.*

those trays; and they ordered him to go to his quarters with
all the gibre, and so he did. Ten days from prime till after
vespers were spent in this passing by of the dues. It was
fifteen days since a Moorish Queen had come to this Court;
she was the wife of the King of Adea, and sister of one that
came to be the wife of the Prester John, and he rejected
her because she had two large front teeth, that is to say,
long ones. And he married her to a great lord who was
Barnagais, and now is Betudete.[1] This Queen came to the
Prester to ask him for assistance, saying that a brother of
her husband had risen against her and was taking the kingdom. This queen came quite like a queen, and brought with
her fully fifty honourable Moors on mules and a hundred
men on foot, and six women on good mules; they are not
very dark people. She was received with great honour, and
the third day of her arrival was called and came before the
tent of the Prester, and she came with a black canopy.[2]
She was dressed twice that day, once at the hour of prime,
and the other time at hour of vespers : both dresses were
of brocade and velvet and Moorish shirts from India. They
said that the Prester sent word to her to rest herself and
not be vexed, and that he would go as she desired, and that
he was waiting for the Barnagais and the Tigrimahom, and
as soon as they came he would at once set out. Eighteen
days after this Queen's arrival, she received dresses. On
the following day Tigrimahom arrived, and the day after that
Barnagais arrived. Both brought the gibri which they are
obliged to pay to the king, and with them came the *chauas*
of their lands, that is the men-at-arms; and also many lords
came with them. When these lords were assembled, before
they presented their gibris, Prester John commanded that
the Betudete should come and present the gibri of Gojamo
which had already passed before him, as has been said. As
this was on Friday, and the holydays of Saturday and Sunday

---

[1] See chapter xlviii, p. 110.   [2] *Esperard*, should be *esparard*.

were following, the Betudeto came on Monday following with the gibri, and with the same formalities as before; and this in the presence of Barnagais and Tigrimahom and many other gentlemen who had come with them. He spent the whole day, from morning till night, in presenting it and its reception. The following day, after the hour of prime, Barnagais began to give his gibri, and he began with very handsome horses; there were a hundred and fifty, and what with running and making them jump, he passed the day without doing anything else. The day after they said that he presented many silks and much thin stuffs from India; I did not see him present these, as I was unwell. When this was presented the following day very early, Trigrimahom began to present his gibri. He also began with horses, which were two hundred, larger and more handsome than those of the Barnagais, because they came from a less distance; and of one set and of the other most came from Egypt, and others from Arabia. This day nothing was done but horses. The next day they presented more silks than ever I had seen together, and the whole day passed in presenting, counting and receiving. On the following Tuesday, at the hour of midday, Balgada Robel, a great gentleman, subject to Tigrimahom, came to present his gibri separately. It was thirty horses, all from Egypt, the size of elephants, and very fat, each horse with a Xumagali, that is a gentleman without title, and eight of these Xumagali were dressed in some very good cuirasses of ours, and some of them placed on velvet, and others on soft leather and gilt studs. These eight wore some of our helmets on their heads. Balgada Robel was counted among these eight, and the twenty-two all wore coats of mail with full sleeves and fitting close to the body. All the thirty carried two azagays and several knives like Turks: and all had small red caps with large ends, which fluttered in the wind. Before them came two little negroes dressed in red and yellow livery, each upon a camel covered with the same livery, and sounding kettledrums. As soon as they reached near the tent of the Prester, they set aside the horses at one end and did not cease from their music and the Xumagalis from skirmishing : they did it in such a way that the Prester ordered other horses to be brought of those given by the Barnagais and Tigrimahom, that they should play also. This lasted till sunset. This Balgada Robel is a gentleman to whom on our coming Don Rodrigo gave a helmet, and sold him a sword for a mule. They said that he was always fighting with the Moors, and so he has at Court the reputation of a great warrior and good knight.

CAP. CXVII.—*How assistance was given to the Queen of Adea, and how the Prester ordered the great Betudete to be arrested, and why, and how he became free, and also he ordered other lords to be arrested.*

Of the chauas, that is the men-at-arms, who came with the Barnagais and Tigrimahom and the gentlemen of their company, Prester John sent fifteen thousand with a gentleman of the title of Adrugaz, already mentioned several times in this book, to go immediately to the Kingdom of Adea and establish the King in peace in his kingdom, and the Queen of Adea was to go more at leisure. The Queen and the Adrugaz set out immediately, and they said that they had more than a month's journey through the Prester's country before reaching the Kingdom of Adea. When this Queen had departed, on the following day the King ordered the arrest of the Betudete who had brought the gibri of Gojame. He also ordered that the other Betudete, who was named Canha, should be arrested, and so he ordered with respect to Tigrimahom. They were all made prisoners in one day, and early in the morning he set out and all the

Court with him, and we in our turn: the Prester's ambassador and I were at a river feeding the mules, and there passed by this Betudete who brought the gibri, and he said to me "Abba baraqua," which means "Father give me a blessing." I answered "Izi baraqua," which means "God bless you." This Betudete was accompanied by fifteen gentlemen on mules, and we mounted and went on in his company. As soon as I approached him he took my hand and kissed it, and again asked for my blessing, saying, "What do you think of this; do they thus make prisoners of great men in your country?" I replied that in my country, if great lords were arrested for small matters or for the anger of the King, they gave them their own houses for prisons, and if it was for great things they were prisoners in large castles and prisons. He, with tears which ran down the whole of his face, again said to me: "Father, pray to God for me, for I shall die of this." And I continued encouraging and consoling him to the best of my ability until in the afternoon he separated from us, and all those who came with him, both on mules and on foot, were none of them his men. On the following day we again met, and he began again with me as the day before, and I with him; he always begging me to pray to God for him, as he would die in that prison. And the restraint under which he was consisted of a very slender chain a fathom long, just like a chain for holding dogs, and a small thin ring at the wrist, and he carried the chain itself in his hand, and those who accompanied him were all guards. We arrived one Thursday where the king's tents were pitched, and they say that that night Prester John ordered that they should bring to him the Betudete, and those who guarded him brought him; and two of the Betudete's sons were that night in his company. When he was before the door of the tent, the Prestor from within sent pages to bring the Betudete behind the tent, as he wished to speak to him in person, and the guards

and his sons were to wait, withdrawn a little from the door
of the tent. There they waited until morning, when the
Prester travelled, and all of us with him, without there being
any news of the Betudete, whether he was dead or alive;
nor what had become of him. The two sons who went with
him to the door of the tent, and three who had remained at
home, all grown men and great gentlemen, and good knights
(according to report), made great lamentation with all their
servants and those of their father, for he had a household
like that of a great king. Then the Prester ordered that
the Betudete's sons should travel alone, without their servants or those of their father, and so it was. I saw them
all five travelling without a groom or anybody; stripped
from the waist upwards, and without their black fleecy sheep
skins on their shoulders, and from the waist downwards they
had black cloths, and their mules were covered with black.
Their people and those of their father travelled separately,
and in mourning, and all on foot, with their mules saddled
in front of them. On the following Tuesday we came to stop
at the entrance of the Kingdom of Oyja, and here were pre-
parations[1] to celebrate the feast of the Kings,[2] which they
name *tabuquete*, and they celebrate baptism, as has been
related above. Here these sons of the Betudete, as soon as
it is morning, go from house to house, that is, to the houses
or tents of the great men, as others are used to do, to search
for news of their father, if he is alive or dead, or what had
become of him, or what was expected to happen to him.
They did not find any news until the end of fifteen days,
when those came who had carried him to the Kingdom of
Fatiguar, to a mountain which they say is at the edge of the
Kingdom of Adel, and which is very high, and deep in the
middle, and it has only one entrance; and they say that
inside this mountain there are great herds of cows, and that

---

[1] *Corregido;* Selves has, *la corte...estaba aderezado.*

[2] January 6, Twelfth Day.

anyone who newly enters there does not last more than four or five days, and soon dies of fevers; and that they had left him there without any person to serve him except the Moors, who would keep him there till he died. With this news the lamentation was greater than at first. Then they began to say through the Court that the Prester had given him this death because he had to do with his mother; and such had been the report when she was alive; and they say that he had a son of her; also that the Prester did not choose to kill him in the lifetime of his mother that she might not be more defamed than was already the case. As this began to be muttered about, proclamations were soon made throughout the Court that no one was to speak of the Betudete under pain of death. This report soon died out, and three months later, when we were near the sea in the country of Tigrimahom, there was news that the Betudete had not died, and that his sons, with the aid of the King of Adel, had rescued him, and that from Adel they were making much war upon the Prester. In these countries proclamations were made that no one was to speak of the Betudete, and they ceased. Then fresh news arose that the Prester had ordered the beheading of twenty Moors who guarded the Betudete, and of two of his own servants, because they had spoken to him, and the Moors because they had given them an opportunity for so doing; and this we learned was the truth. It was also said that the Prester wished to pardon him since God had given him life for so long a time in such a dangerous place, and because he missed him, for he was a man of great mind and a warrior.

CAP. CXIX.—*How the Tigrimahom was killed, and the other Betudete deposed, also Abdenago from his lordship, and the ambassador[1] was provided for, and Prester John went 'in person to the Kingdom of Adea.*

As soon as we had arrived at the place where we were to keep the feast of the kings or *tabaquete*, before it was reported where the Betudete was, on the next night Prester John ordered the Tigrimahom to be taken away, neither was it then known where he had been taken to. The following day they sent to take away all that he had got in his tents, and for three days they did not cease to take away, and count and deliver up common silks, and camlets and good cloths of India. We found ourselves there six white men, that is to say, I, and another Portuguese, and four Genoese, and to each of us the Prester ordered to be given six cloths, that is, three camlets and three pieces of Indian stuffs. Many days did not pass before it was said that Prester John had ordered the Tigrimahom to be taken to the Kingdom of Damute to a very high mountain, which had only one entrance, and that one was artificial, and above it was uninhabited and very cold, and that there they sent men who were to die. And where we heard in the country of Tigrimahom news that the Betudete had escaped, that was untrue; but we found there certain news that the Tigrimahom had died in the said mountain, and had died of hunger and cold. In those days when we were at the Court, the other Betudete, who had been arrested, was deposed from his office, and Arraz Anubiata, who was Barnagais, was made Betudete. And they made Balgada Robel Tigrimahom, he who came with thirty well-equipped horses. There was a great rumour and talk at the Court about the death of Queen Helena. They said that since she had died

_____
[1] The Prester's ambassador.

all of them would die great and small, and that while she
lived, all lived and were defended and protected; and she
was the father and mother of all, and if the king took this
road, his kingdoms would become deserts.   When the
tabuquete or baptism was ended, without the ambassador or
I making further requests as to our claims, because we did
not venture on account of the great affairs which we saw
going on, the Prester sent to call us, and took away from
Abdenago, our adversary, the great lordship which he held,
and he bestowed on his ambassador both the land which we
were claiming and that lordship which he had taken away,
and so he dismissed us well satisfied.   Before our departure
a message arrived from the Adrugaz that they had gone
with the Queen of Adea to the assistance of her husband,
and that the people would not obey him, and wherever he
went all ran away and took refuge in the mountains, and
that His Highness should send more men.   His Highness
determined to go there in person, and to take the queen his
wife to a place where we had already been with him, which
is in the Kingdom of Orgabija, on the edge of the said
Kingdom of Adea, and there to leave the queen and his
children and all the Court.   So he did, and there went with
him some Portuguese, namely, Jorge d'Abreu, Diogo Fernandez, Afonso Mendes, and Alvarenga, and five or six
Genoese.   When they returned they said that as soon as
the Prester had entered the Kingdom of Adea all the people
came in, obeying him as their sovereign, and withal he did
not desist from going forward to very near Magadoxo; and
they said that it was a very fruitful kingdom, very wooded,
so much so that they could not travel without cutting trees
and making roads.   They also said there were there plenty
of provisions, and great breeding of herds, and many and
very large animals of different sorts.   They say that there
is in this kingdom a great lake like a sea, which cannot be
seen across from side to side, and they say there is

in it an island, in which in a former time a Prester John had ordered a monastery to be built, and had put in it many friars, although it was a country of Moors. Pero de Covilham related this, and now these Portuguese and Genoese who went there say that the friars of that monastery nearly all died of fevers, and some few remained in another small monastery out of the island, and near the lake, and so they found them. And that on this occasion Prester John ordered many monasteries and churches to be built, and left there many priests and friars, and many laymen to inhabit and dwell in that kingdom. When the kingdom was pacified they came back to where they had left the Court. They say that this kingdom pays tribute of cows in great number, and which we saw at the Court. They say that they come from there as large as great horses, and white as snow and without horns, with large hanging ears.

CAP. CXX.—*Of the manner in which the Prester encamps with his Court.*

The method which is followed in encamping the Court of the Prester. It is always encamped on a plain, for otherwise they would not find room, and the Prester's tents are pitched on the highest ground of the plain, if there is any. The back of the tents is always placed to the east and the doors to the west; four or five tents are pitched together; all belong to the Prester, and they surround them all with curtains, which they call *mandilate;* these are woven like a chess-board, half white and half black. If he is going to remain several days they surround these tents with a large fence, which will make a circumference of half a league. They say that they make in this enclosure twelve gates; the principal one is to the West, and apart from it, at a good distance, are two gates, each on its own side, and one of

these serves for the church of St. Mary, which is to the
north, and the other serves for the church of Holy Cross,
which is to the south. Beyond these gates which serve for
these churches, almost at a distance equal to what there is
between them and the principal entrance, are two other
gates on each side, and that which is to the south serves for
the tents of the queen mother of the Prester, and that which
is to the north serves for the pages' quarters. There are
guards at all these gates, but I did not get behind to see,
for they let no one pass there; only they say that in the
whole there are twelve gates, and I know for certain that
there is one gate at the back, because it serves for the kitchen
pages; for I saw it from a distance, how the pages brought
and carried the viands. These gates are made when the
tents are surrounded by a fence, and when they are not enclosed, there will only be the tents surrounded by curtains,
which they call *mandilate*, as has been said. Behind the
tents, quite a crossbow shot or more, are pitched the tents
for the kitchens and the cooks, divided into two parts,
because there are the cooks of the right hand and of the left
hand. When the food comes from these kitchens, it is in
this manner (according as I saw it in a district called Or-
gebeia, from being on some hills close to the kitchens, for
in other parts the tents were pitched on such level ground
that there was no means of seeing). They came with a
large canopy of tafetan, as it seemed, red and blue, of six
pieces in length. This canopy was raised like a pallium on
canes, which in this country are very good, and they make
with them the shafts of lances. Under this pallium came
other pages who carried viands in large trays which were
made like trenchers for cleaning wheat in, except that they
are very large, and in each they brought many little round
dishes[1] of black earthenware, in which were the meats of
their fowls and small birds, and many other things, and

---

[1] *Escudilhinas*, for *escudellinhas*.

white food, which are made more of milk than of anything
else; and also little pipkins, black like the dishes, with
many other dainties and broths of different kinds. These
viands that I speak of which came in these trays, I do not
say that I saw them when they brought them, because they
were far off from where I stood; but I saw them when they
sent them to us, for they came in the same trays as they
came from the kitchens and without the canopy, and the
little pipkins were still covered with their lids, and closed
with dough; and the trays which they sent us came full
without showing that they had been moved; and for this I
say that so they come from the kitchens. All these victuals
in which spices of ginger or pepper can be put, they put so
much in them, that we could not eat them from their much
burning. Among these tents of the kitchens and cooks, or
almost behind them, is the Church of St. Andrew, and it is
called the cooks' church. In this part of the camp where
the kitchens are, and behind them, nobody goes.

CAP. CXXI.—*Of the tent of justice and method of it, and how
they hear the parties.*

In front of the gates of the tents or fence, if there is one,
there is always a space of quite two crossbow shots, and a long
tent is always pitched there, which they call *cacalla;* this is the
court of justice or tribunal. Nobody passes on a mule or
on horseback between the tent of the tribunal and the Prester's tents; this is from reverence for the king and his
justice, and all dismount. This I know, because they fined
us there because we entered on mules, and we were excused
as foreigners, and warned that this should not happen to us
again. Inside this tent of *cacalla* no one abides, only there
are in it thirteen plain[1] chairs of iron and leather, and one

Mouchas for *mochas,* without horns, or points, or, in the case of
chairs, may be arms.

of these is very high, it would reach to the breast of a man, and the other twelve are like ours that we usually set at a table. These chairs are brought out every day, and are placed six on one side and six on the other, and the tall one like the cross table of a friars' refectory. The commissioners[1] or judges who hear the parties do no sit in them, these chairs are only for ceremony, and they sit on the ground and on the grass if there is any,[2] as many on one side as on the other. There they hear the parties who are litigating, each one of his own jurisdiction, because as I said that the cooks are divided into those of the right hand and those of the left hand, so they are all. The hearing is conducted in this manner. The plaintiff brings his action and says as much as he pleases without anyone speaking, and the accused answers and says as much as he pleases, without anyone hindering him. When he has finished, the plaintiff brings his reply (if he wishes it), and the accused also with his reply if he chooses, without anyone disturbing them. When they have finished their arguments by themselves or by their representatives, there is there a man standing, who is like a porter, and he repeats all that these parties have said, and having finished relating it all, he then says which of the parties spoke best in his opinion, and which of them has justice on his side. Then one of those who are sitting like commissioners, the one nearest the end, does like the porter, that is, he relates all that the parties had said, and then says which he thinks has justice. And in this manner follow all those who are sitting. They rise to their feet when they speak, and then it comes to the turn of the Chief Justice, who has been attentive to what has been said by the others and to their opinion; and so he gives his sentence if there is no proof required. If there is to be proof, they give a delay according to the distance, and all verbally, with-

[1] *Desembargadores.*

[2] See chapter cvi, p. 278, where the Abdenago acted in this way.

out writing anything. There are other things which the Betudetes and Ajazes hear, and they hear them standing because they are in front of the Prester's tent, between this *cacalla* and his tent, and as they hear the party or parties, so they go at once to the Prester with what has been said; they do not enter his tent, but only inside the *mandilate* or curtain, and from there make their speech, and so return to the parties with the decision of the Prester: and sometimes they spend a whole day with these goings and comings, according as the facts and suits may be.

CAP. CXXII.—*Which speaks of the manner of the prison.*

In front of this tent or house of justice which is named *cacalla*, at a good distance from both parts, both that of the right and left hand, there are two tents or houses like prisons, with chains, which are called *manquez bete*, in which are the prisoners of each of the parts, both of the left and right hand, and they are guarded and bound in this way: according to the act and suit so is the imprisonment and also the guards. The prisoner gives food to the guards who keep him, and pays them for their time as long as he is imprisoned, and whoever has chains or fetters on the feet, when they order him to come before the tent of the Prester where they hear the prisoners, those guards who keep him carry him in their arms; two give each other their arms, and the prisoner goes sitting on their arms with his hands on their heads, and the other guards all round with their weapons. So they go and come. There is here another kind of imprisonment. If I require that a man be arrested, I am obliged to give him food as long as I accuse him, and also to the guards who keep him; and this I know because it happened to some of us Portuguese, who asked for an arrest for some mules which they had been robbed of, and because they did not send to give food to the prisoners and guards, they in turn required that they should be set free. And of another Genoese, I know by seeing it, that they stole a mule of his, and the thief confessed that he had stolen it, and that it was no longer in his possession, nor had he anything with which to pay for it. They adjudged him to be a slave, and the Genoese seeing that he was a powerful man, who could rob or kill him, sent to the devil both the mule and the slave.

———————————

CAP. CXXIII.—*Where the dwellings of the Chief Justices are situated, and the site of the market place, and who are the merchants and hucksters.*

In front of these tents of the prison there is great traffic, and in a straight line from them are the tents of the two Chief Justices, each one on its own side, and between them is a church, which is called the Church of the Justices. In front of this church are the lions, a considerable distance away from the church, and they are four in number, and they always bring them wherever Prester John goes. After another large space from the lions there is another church; it is called the Market Church, that is of the Christians who sell in it, because the greater part of the sellers are Moors; and the principal merchants of stuffs and large goods are Moors, and the Christians sell low priced things, such as bread, wine, flour and meat; and the Moors can sell nothing to eat because in this country they do not eat anything which the Moors make, nor meat which they kill. This market must be in front of the tent of Prester John, but not in a place where it can be seen from the door, and sometimes it happens that the plain is so great and without break of level ground[1] that the market is very far off; and the least distance at which the market can be placed is half

———

[1] *Sem tresposta.*

a league, and at times nearly a league, or even more. Although the court changes its place as often as it chooses, they always follow this mode of encampment. From the king's tent to this market all is open space in the middle, that is, there is no tent in it, only the two churches, that is, that of the justices and lions, and that of the market; and these churches and lions are a long way off from other tents.

Cap. cxxiv.—*How the lords and gentlemen and all other people pitch their tents, according to their regulations.*

Near to the two churches which are near the tent of the Prester, but in the outer part, are two tents for each church, one very clean and good, in which they keep the church furniture, the other a smoky tent, in which they make the corban or host; all the churches are in this manner. In front of these churches next come other large long tents of high pitch;[1] these are called *Balagamija*, in which they keep the stuffs and treasures of the Prester, and these on both sides are all of brocade, as has been said; and these tents of *Balagamija* are always guarded, and the captains and factors of them are eunuchs. In front of these tents of the wardrobe, on either side, are the tents of the pages, and further on are the tents of the Ajazes, who occupy a space like a town, with their tents and those of their people; further in front and further off are the tents of the Betudetes, and each one occupies as much as a town or city; these lie almost outside like guards. On the right hand, also outside like a guard, are the quarters of the Abima, which by themselves form a district town; and many foreigners come to his quarters, because they receive from him favour and protection. The Cabeata is more to the inside than the Abima, and they said that his quarters,

[1] *Comicrias* for *cumiciras*, summit, point of a building. See pp. 244, 260.

that is, those of his office, were close to the church of St.
Mary, because this office always goes to a friar; and because
he is a priest and has a wife he cannot be close to the church,
and they gave him quarters close to the Abima. Returning
more to the inside, follow gentlemen in their places, and
after them come other respectable people, and after these
come people like winesellers, bakers who sell and supply
food, and also there are women. At the end of these, and
now near to the market, are the quarters of the smiths on
both sides[1], and each set of smiths form a large village.
Men who come from outside to buy and sell and do business
encamp further off, and they greatly extend the camp, which
always occupies two large leagues.

Cap. cxxv.—*Of the manner in which the lords and gentlemen
come to the Court, and go about it, and depart from it.*

The mode which the lords and gentlemen follow in coming
to or going away from the Court is this, namely: no great
lord of lands, if he is in them, can come out of them, nor set
out for the Court by any means without being summoned
by the Prester; and being summoned he cannot omit coming
for any cause. And when he sets out from the land of
which he is the lord, he does not leave in it either wife or
children or any property, because he goes away with the
expectation of never returning, since, as has been said
before, the Prester gives when he pleases, and takes away
when he pleases; and if he happens to take it away, from
that moment they take from him whatever they find belonging to him in the lordship; that is to say, the lord who
comes to succeed him in his place. For this reason they
carry everything away with them without leaving anything,
or at least without putting it in another lordship. When

[1] *I.e.*, of the open space going to the market.

a lord approaches near the Court with great show he takes
up quarters at least a league from the Court, and there he
often remains a month or two months without moving from
there ; and they treat them as if they were forgotten as long
as the Prester chooses. They do not however desist whilst
thus forgotten from entering the Court and speaking to
other lords, but not with an array, nor with clothes, but with
two or three men, and stripped from the waist upwards, and
with a sheep skin over their shoulders ; and so they return
to their tents until they have permission to enter. When
they get this permission, they enter with great array, and
sounding kettledrums, and encamp in their station, which is
already ordained for each. When he encamps he still does
not appear clothed as he made his entry, but walks about as
before his entry, naked from the waist upwards, although at
his entry he came clothed and with pomp. Then they say
generally : Such a one is not yet in the favour of the sovereign, for he still goes about stripped. As soon as he had
any speech of the Prester, he at once comes out dressed,
and then they say : Such a one is in the king's favour.
Then it is divulged and said why he was summoned, and
sometimes and frequently they return to their lordships, and
at others not. If they return to them they are despatched
more quickly ; and if they are taken from them, they let
them go five, six, and seven years without going away from
the Court. By no manner of means can they go from the
Court without permission, so obedient are they, and so much
do they fear their king ; and much as they used to be accompanied by many, so now are they neglected, and they go
about on a mule with two or three men, because the many
who used to accompany them belonged to the lordships that
have been taken from them, and they transfer themselves to
the new lord ; and this we used to see every day.

CAP. CXXVI.—*How those who go to and come from the wars approach the Prester more closely, and of the maintenance they get.*

If such gentlemen are summoned for wars, as we saw happen many times, their entry is not delayed, but they come in at once. As they come with a body of men, so they enter from their march. With regard to these, they do not observe what I mentioned, that people do not enter between the *cacalla* and king's tent on mules or on horseback. These who come for wars come up to the king's tents, and show themselves off close to them, and they skirmish and sport and show their method of warfare, as they think best to please the king. This we saw an infinite number of times. These men who go thus to the wars do not remain two days at the Court, because their ordinances are to call a hundred thousand men, if they want as many, to assemble in two days, so as they arrive they are sent off. Because here there is no pay to be given, and every man brings with him what he is to eat, which consists of flour of parched barley, and that is a good food, and parched peas or millet. This is their maintenance for the wars, and the cows, they find them where they go; and if it is the season of . . . . .[1] wheat, that is the principal provision for war of those people.

CAP. CXXVII.—*Of the manner in which they carry the Prester's property when he travels, and of the brocades and silks which he sent to Jerusalem, and of the great treasury.*

The manner in which Prester John travels has been before mentioned, as we saw him travel; now I will only relate

[1] *Cerolho.* This passage is omitted in Selves' translation. *Cerolho* might be a misprint for *scrolho*, late, tardy.

how his stuffs and property travel, which are in the Balagamija, and which are beyond reckoning. All silk stuffs go in
square osier baskets ; they will be four spans[1] long, and two
or two and a half wide, they are covered with leather of raw
cowhide with the hair on ; from each corner comes a chain
to go over the lid, which has an iron ring in the middle
through which they pass these chains, and in them a padlock. Thus these baskets go locked, and both those containing silks and those with thin Indian stuffs, and men
carry them on their heads, more than five or six of them.
And between a certain number of these carriers are guards.
And since every year the silks and brocades increase in
number, both those that are paid to him and those that he
buys, and so many are not expended, neither can they carry
them all on a journey, he orders every year some to be
put in hollows in the earth which are arranged for that purpose. We knew of one as our road passed by there, and
close to some gates which have already been mentioned, and
which are named Badabaje, at the great ravines which I
spoke of before. And at this hollow there are many guards,
and all the merchants who pass there pay dues for toll. In
the same way that the stuffs travel, the treasure also travels
in smaller baskets covered with leather, and also locked like
those of the stuffs, only that they have over their leather
covering and chains and padlock, another cowhide put on
fresh and sewn with straps of the hide, and it dries there
and becomes strong. These treasure baskets are in very
great quantity, and travel with numerous guards, and they
say that every year he puts many of these also into hollows
in the earth or in grottos, because he cannot carry the increase of each year. This hollow, which we knew of, is a
league from the house of Pero de Covilham, and he used to
tell us that the gold which was in this hollow was enough
to buy the world, because every year a large sum was put

[1] *Palmos.*

in, and they never took it out again. As to the silks and brocades, Pero de Covilham said that they often took them out to give them to churches and monasteries, as was done three years before our arrival, when Prester John sent large offerings to Jerusalem of the silks and brocades from the grottos, on account of the multitude he possessed; and that there were many of these excavations or grottos of the same kind as that that we knew of, which is under a mountain. The ambassador who conveyed these offerings is named Abba Azerata, and now he is chief guardian of the Prester's sisters, and they say that he took with him fifteen men, among whom were gentlemen of *nagaridas*, or as we should say in our language, of kettledrums,[1] and the number of their kettledrums was sixty. And I heard tell by those who went with him that they sounded them all along the road, and in the city of Cairo, as far as Jerusalem; and on their return they came in flight, because the Turk was coming against the Sultan,[2] and against his great city, through which they had to pass.

CAP. CXXVIII.—*How three hundred and odd friars departed from Barua in pilgrimage to Jerusalem, and how they killed them.*

In this country many friars are accustomed to go every year in pilgrimage to Jerusalem, and also some priests. While we, Portuguese and the Franks who were in the country, were at Barua, the country and chief town of the Barnagais, a caravan of friars was prepared to make the said journey and pilgrimage as they are accustomed. There went together three hundred and thirty-six friars, and in this number entered fifteen nuns, and this about Christmas, because they depart after the day of the kings, and reach

---

[1] *Atabales.*   [2] Of Egypt.

there in holy week, because they go very slowly; and they make this journey at this time because they say that the winter ends in Nubia, which is the beginning of Egypt, and that in the most part of Egypt and in Cairo it does not rain, and so at this end of the winter water is still to be found. The manner in which these friars set out was this: they came together from all parts to the said town, and when the day of kings had passed, they were entrusted by the Barnagais Dori (who then reigned) to some Moors to convey them safely. These Moors were from Suaquem and Rifa. Suaquem is at the end of the countries of the Prester, and at the entrance of Egypt, and on that account they were entrusted, and Rifa is in the middle of Egypt, and the river Nile passes through the middle of that city. These Moors were obliged to place these pilgrims in safety in the city of Cairo, and they were well known Moors, traders in the Prester's countries, and therefore they were entrusted to them. They commenced their journey to another town, which is one march from this place (Barua), which is named Einacem; they say that it is a town and district abounding in provisions, and many monasteries; and here they finish making up the caravan. This town belongs to the lordship of Dafila, subject to the Barnagais. At the time they set out these friars travelled very slowly, for at hours of vespers they encamped in their halts,[1] and then they pitched their churches which they carried with them, and there were three churches, and they said their hours and masses, and then all received the communion. Next day at the hour of tierce they arose and began to travel; and they all went laden with their provisions, and gourds and waterskins, and their churches by turns,[2] that is to say, the tabutos or altar stones, for let me say that the tents of the churches went on camels. So each day they did not make a journey exceeding two leagues; and to see their customs I travelled for two days

---

[1] Meijoadas.　　　　　[2] Or, alternately, revezadas.

with these friars, and saw what I relate. In those two days
we may have travelled, according to good judgment, three
leagues and little more. From the town of Einacem as far
as Suaquem two lords rule, namely, Dafella and Canfella,
and both are subject to the Barnagais ; and they say that
from this town to Suaquem there are fifteen days' march of
a caravan of merchants, who travel a little more than three
leagues in a day's march. From Suaquem to Rifa there are
fourteen days of the same pace of a caravan. On this road,
on leaving Suaquem Egypt begins, and they say that all
the country is inhabited, except for two days where there
are no dwellings or water ; and they say that along this road
there are many churches and many Christians, who give
much alms to these pilgrims, and they are subject to the
Moors. They say that on this road is the monastery in
which St. Antony abode, and of this order are all the friars
of the Prester's countries. And from Rifa to Cairo they say
the country is very cool, always going down the river Nile
(as they say) there are eight days' journey. This caravan of
friars departed before we did, and as soon as it passed Suaquem other Moors attacked them, and it seems that they
were more powerful than the Moors who conducted them, and
they took all the pilgrims, and killed the old men, and made
captives of the young ones, and sold them ; and of 348
friars there did not escape more than fifteen. These did the
pilgrimage, and later I heard three of these fifteen, who
related to me all their fatigues, and told me that what had
happened to them was because they were great friends of
the Portuguese ; and in truth it is so, because they receive
bad treatment from their neighbours for our sake. From
Rifa to Cairo is a pleasant country for travelling, with white
people, Moors, Jews, and Christians. And in Cairo they
say they make their stations at Cosmo, Damiano, and St.
Barbara, and at the fountain which is in the garden of the
balsam. They also say that from Cairo to Jerusalem there

are eight days' journey. Since this destruction of friars till now no more friars or priests have gone to Jerusalem in a caravan, and if any go, they go like concealed passengers; and those who go there and return are held to be holy men. And because the people of Jerusalem are white people, when we arrived in this country, they called us Christians of Jerusalem. There is another road from here by sea which takes less time; embarking at Masua for Mount Sinai, they go in fifteen days or less (according to the weather), and from Mount Sinai to Jerusalem they go in eight days. The Abyssinians are not much able to travel by this way, because they have not got any navigation, and they hope that our Portuguese will make this way secure, if a fortress were made in Masua by the King our Sovereign.

CAP. CXXIX.—*Of the countries and kingdoms which are on the frontiers of Prester John.*

The countries, kingdoms and lordships which confine with the kingdoms of the Prester, as far as I could learn, are these. First, they commence at Masua, opposite the Red Sea, which is opposite to the south, then they are at the outskirts[1] of the Moorish Arabs who keep the herds of the great lords of the countries of the Barnagais, and they go about in encampments[2] of thirty or forty, with their wives and children. All these Moors have a Christian captain, and all are thieves, and they rob the poor on the roads by their power and the favour of the lords whose herds they keep. Next further on comes the kingdom of Dangalli,[3] which is a Moorish kingdom. This kingdom has a seaport which is named Belic, this is behind the gates of the Red Sea, inside to the parts of Abyssinia; and this kingdom runs on till it

[1] *Na falha.*   [2] *Aduares.*   [3] *Dankali.*

meets the kingdom of Adel, which is the sovereignty of
Zeila and Barbora; where these two kingdoms join in the
interior, which is towards the country of the Prester, there
are twenty-four large lordships or captaincies, which they
call Dobaas; and 1 have already spoken of these Dobaas
above in the Chapter xlviii.

CAP. CXXX.—*Of the kingdom of Adel, and how the king is
esteemed as a saint amongst the Moors.*

The kingdom of Adel (as they say) is a large kingdom,
and it extends over the Cape of Guardafuy, and there in
that part another rules subject to Adel.   Among the Moors
they hold this King of Adel for a saint, because he always
makes war upon the Christians; and he sends of the spoils
of his battles (as they say) offerings to the house of
Mekkah, and to Cairo, and presents to other kings, and
they send him from their parts arms and horses, and other
things to assist him in his wars; and I have before related,
in Chapter cxxxiii, how this king was routed and his captain
Mafudy killed.   This kingdom of Adel borders upon the
kingdom of Fatigar and Xoa, which are kingdoms of the
Prester John.

CAP. CXXXI.—*Of the kingdom of Adea, where it begins and
where it ends.*

In the middle of the kingdom of Adel, more in the
interior, commences the kingdom of Adea, which is of
Moors, and they are peaceful and subject to the Prester:
they say that this kingdom reaches to Magadaxo.   In
Chapter cxxix I have related how Prester John went there
in person, to make peace, and made in it churches and

monasteries, and left there priests and friars. This kingdom of Adea borders upon the kingdom of Oyja, which
belongs to Prester John, and all these above-mentioned are
towards the sea and the east.

CAP. CXXXII.—*Of the lordships of Ganze and Gamu, and of
the kingdom of Gorage.*

To the middle of this kingdom of Adea, towards the
west, begin some lordships of pagans which are not kingdoms, and are at the extremities of the kingdoms and lordships of the Prester. Of these lordships or captaincies the
first is called Ganze, and it is a mixture of pagans and of
Christians who are gradually entering it. Next after this
comes another large lordship, and (as they say) in size
almost a kingdom ; they are pagans, little valued as slaves;
they have no king, only chiefs who rule separately. This
is called Gamu, it runs more towards the west. Also to
the south is the kingdom called Gorage, and its inhabitants
Gorages ; they say they have a king ; in Chapter cxi, I
spoke of it. This kingdom and the lordships of Ganze and
Gamu border upon the kingdoms of Oyja and Xoa, which
belong to Prester John.

CAP. CXXXIII.—*Of the kingdom of Damute, and of the much
gold there is in it, and how it is collected, and to the
south of this are the Amazons, if they are there.*

Going more to the west by the same extremities of the
Prester's kingdoms, and principally to the west of the
kingdom of Xoa, there is a very great country and king-

dom which is called Damute. The slaves of this kingdom
are much esteemed by the Moors, and they do not leave
them for any price; all the countries of Arabia, Persia,
India, Egypt, and Greece, are full of slaves from this
country, and they say they make very good Moors and
great warriors. These are pagans, and among them in this
kingdom there are many Christians. And I say there are
some there because I saw them at the Court; there came
many priests and friars and nuns, and they say that there
are many monasteries and churches there, and the king's
title is King of the Pagans. From this kingdom comes
most of the gold that is in the country of the Prester
which can be made use of, and it is very fine. In this
kingdom there are (as they say) plenty of fresh provisions
of various sorts, and when we kept Lent in Gorage there
came from this country much green ginger, grapes, and
peaches, which in this country are found at that time, and
later, in flesh days, many large sheep, and cows of great size.
They say that at the extremity of these kingdoms of Damute and Gorage, towards the south, is the kingdom of the
Amazons; but not as it seems to me, or as it has been told
to me, or as the book of *Infante Don Pedro* related or
relates to us, because these Amazons (if these are so) all
have husbands generally throughout the year, and always
at all times with them, and pass their life with their husbands. They have not got a king, but have a queen, she
is not married, nor has she any special husband, but withal
she does not omit having sons and daughters, and her
daughter is the heir to her kingdom. They say that they
are women of a very warlike disposition, and they fight
riding on cows, and are great archers, and when they are
little they dry up the left breast, in order not to impede
drawing the arrow. They also say that there is very much
gold in this kingdom of the Amazons, and that it comes
from this country to the kingdom of Damute, and so it

goes to many parts. They say that the husbands of these
women are not warriors, and that their wives dispense them
from it. They say that a great river has its source in the
kingdom of Damute, and opposite to the Nile, because each
one goes in its own direction, the Nile to Egypt, of this
other no one of the country knows where it goes to, only
it is presumed that it goes to Manicongo. They also say
that they find much gold in this kingdom of Damute, I tell
it as I heard it. They say that when winter comes they
expect rains and storms, and without necessity they dig
and till the earth that it may be soft : and the waters wash
the earth and leave on the top of it the clean gold : and
that they find most of this gold by night by the light, because they see it glitter. And in the town of Aquaxumo,
which is in the kingdom of Tigray, I often saw it searched
for in the above-mentioned manner, and they said that they
found it, but not at night. This Damute borders upon Xoa,
which belongs to Prester John.

CAP. CXXXIV.—*Of the lordships of the Cafates, who they say
had been Jews, and how they are warriors.*

Making more for the west, and almost west through this
Damute, are other lordships which they call the Cafates,
people who are not very dark, and large of stature. They
say that they had been of the race of the Jews, but
they have no books or synagogues, they are more subtle
people than any that are in this country; they are pagans
and great warriors, and always carry on war with the
Prester. They border upon part of Xoa and Gojame, which
are kingdoms of the Prester. I say this for I never reached
there, and some of our people went there with the great
Betudete, and afterwards the Prester in person. They said

that these Cafates gave them much to do, chiefly at night, when they came to kill and plunder, and by day they took refuge in the mountains and thickets, and the mountains (as they say) consist more in ravines than in heights.

CAP. CXXXV.—*Of the kingdom of Gojame which belonged to Queen Helena, where the river Nile rises, and of the much gold there is there.*

Now leaving the south and turning west, there is another kingdom of the Prester, named Gojame, of which a great part belonged to Queen Helena. They say that in this kingdom rises or issues the river Nile, which in this country they call Gion; and they say that there are in it great lakes like seas, and that there are in them marine men and women, and some report this from eyesight. I heard Pero de Covilham say that he had gone by order of Queen Helena to show how an altar should be made in a church which she had ordered to be built in this kingdom, where they buried her, and they made this altar of wood, and covered it all over with gold, and also the altar stone was of solid gold. I state what he told me, and I think he spoke the truth; and as to the altar stone, the Abima who had consecrated it, told me that it was large and of great weight and price. I always heard say while we were in the neighbourhood of this kingdom that there were numerous guards at that church, who guarded it on account of the much gold that was in it. They say that there is much gold in this kingdom also, and that it is inferior gold. I could not learn what this kingdom borders upon on the other side, only they said that there were deserts and mountains, and beyond them Jews. I do not credit it or affirm it; I speak as I heard general report, and not from persons whom I can quote.

CAP. CXXXVI.—*Of the kingdom of Bagamidri, which is said to be very large, and how silver is found in its mountains.*

At the end of this kingdom of Gojam begins another kingdom, which they say is the largest kingdom in the Prester's country, and it is called Bagamidri. This they say extends along the Nile. And it cannot fail to be large as they say, because it begins at the kingdom of Gojame, and runs along the edge of the kingdoms of Amara and Angoir and Tigray of the Tigrimahom, and of the kingdom of the Barnagais : so it extends far more than two hundred leagues. Between the kingdoms of Angoir and Tigray, at the end of them are other lordships which are named Aganos, in them Christians and Pagans are intermingled. I do not know what these border upon on the other side, they must border upon this kingdom of Bagamidri. I have heard many people say that there was a mountain in this kingdom of Bagamidri which contains much silver, and that they do not know how to extract it; and that when they got any, it was in this manner, namely, where they saw any hollow or cave they filled it with wood, and set it on fire, as in a limekiln, and that this fire melted the silver and it ran in spouts, a thing not to be believed. I asked Pero de Covilham about this; he said he did not doubt that it was quite true. I tell it as I heard it, and I know that the silver is much sought after.

CAP. CXXXVII.—*Of some lordships which are called of the Nubians, who had been Christians, and of the number of churches which are in the country which they border upon.*

At the end of the kingdom of Bagamidri there are Moors who are called Bellonos, and are tributaries of

Prester John for a great number of horses. Towards the north, these Bellonos border upon a people who are called Nubiis ; and they say that these had been Christians and ruled from Rome. I heard from a man, a Syrian, a native of Tripoli of Syria, and his name is John of Syria (he went about with us three years in the Prester's country, and came with us to Portugal), that he had been to this country, and that there are in it a hundred and fifty churches, which still contain crucifixes and effigies of Our Lady, and other effigies painted on the walls, and all old : and the people of this country are neither Christians, Moors, nor Jews ; and that they live in the desire to become Christians. These churches are all in old ancient castles which are throughout the country ; and as many castles there are, so many churches. While we were in the country of the Prester John there came six men from that country as ambassadors to the Prester himself, begging of him to send them priests and friars to teach them. He did not choose to send them ; and it was said that he said to them that he had his Abima from the country of the Moors, that is to say from the Patriarch of Alexandria, who is under the rule of the Moors ; how then could he give priests and friars since another gave them. And so they returned. They say that in ancient times these people had everything from Rome, and that it is a very long time ago that a bishop died, whom they had got from Rome, and on account of the wars of the Moors they could not get another, and so they lost all their clergy and their Christianity. These border upon Egypt, and they say they have much fine gold in their country. This country lies in front of Suaquem, which is close to the Red Sea. These lordships of Nobiis are on both sides of the Nile, and they say that as many castles as there are, so many captains : they have no king, but only captains. This Suaquem is the town which is at the extremity of the Prester's country, in the beginning of

Egypt, in front of these lordships, with the Moorish Bellonos in the middle. And they say that from this Suaquem along the coast of the sea towards Masua it is all wooded land. These are the frontier countries of Prester John's kingdoms and lordships which I was able to learn, and of them I learned by hearsay, and of a few of them by sight.

CAP. CXXXVIII.—*Of the officials that Solomon ordained for his son that he had of the Queen Sabba when he sent him to Ethiopia; and how they still draw honour from these offices.*

I said that I would relate what I heard of the officials that Solomon gave to his son when he sent him from Jerusalem to Ethiopia to his mother the Queen Sabba. I heard say that to this day these officials or officers are alive in the families of those that came, because they go in succession from father to son. They say first that when Solomon sent his son to the Queen Sabba, his mother, he gave him officials for his house ; and he gave an office from each of the twelve tribes, such as chamberlains, porters, overseers, grooms, trumpeters, chief guards, cooks, and other officials necessary for the house of a great king or lord, and that these offices are still in those families descending from them. Thus these officials honour themselves much as Israelites, and gentlemen, and our relations. All of them are in great number, because the sons of the chamberlain and their descendants, all of them are of that office ; and so also the other officials all descend in the offices of their fathers and ancestors, except the pages, who usually are the sons of the great gentlemen and lords, and now they are not so. And as has been said, when the Prester sends to summon the grandees, he does not send to tell them why : and when the sons of the grandees served as pages, they used to disclose his secrets, and for this he turned them out, and the captains who are sons of Moorish or Pagan Kings whom they take in their expeditions, serve as confidential pages, and if they see them well disposed they send them to be taught without their entering inside,[1] and if they turn out discreet and good they put them inside, and they serve as pages. And the sons of the great lords serve as outside pages, and also as pages of the halter when they travel, and pages of the kitchen, and they do not enter inside, (as they say) and we saw this. All the canons that they call *debeteras* also say that they come from the families that came from Jerusalem with the son of Solomon, and on this account they are more honoured than all the rest of the clergy.

CAP. CXXXIX.—*How the ambassador of Prester John took possession of his lordship, and the Prester gave him a title of all of it, and we departed to the sea.*

On the day that Prester John set out for the kingdom of Adea, the friar, his ambassador, and I, we set out on the road to that lordship which the Prester had then given him, and it was the road to whereour people had remained; and we arrived on the beginning of Lent,[2] that is to say of their Lent, which is ten days earlier than ours, at the land they had given him. When he had taken possession both of that which they had newly given him, and of that which they had taken from him, we made ready to depart. These lordships, that is, the one they were taking from him, is of eighty houses,[3] and it contains two churches, and it had been given him in exchange[4] for a small monastery which he before possessed near them. The lordship which they have

---

[1] The palace. [2] *Entrudo*, Shrove Tuesday.
[3] Or, inhabitants.
[4] *Era lhe dado por conto ou camara para hum pequeno mosteiro ;* or, " in payment for", as Selves translates.

now given him is to be arraz of the chavas, that is head or captain of the men-at-arms, who are in the lordship of Abrigima, and these chavas are eight hundred and upwards. About mid Lent we arrived at where our people were, with a great longing that the Portuguese might come for us this Easter. When Easter passed, which was the monsoon, and nobody came, we remained sad as before : and when it was the month of July and Prester John knew that the Portuguese had not come, he sent word to his ambassador to go to Abrigima, under the rule of which are the two above-mentioned lordships, and another lord of this lordship of Abrigima is named Abive arraz, and he is a great lord with more than ten thousand vassals, and he is like all the others in all that the Prester pleases. When this message came, there came another to us that we were to go with him, and that as the fruits of the earth which they gave him were already gathered in and they could not give us what was necessary, that he had ordered us to be given at that place five hundred loads of wheat, and a hundred cows, and a hundred sheep, and that his ambassador was to give us honey for wine. We were in great doubt as to whether we should make this journey or not, because it removed us a long way from the sea, and by very much travelling we should not be able to reach the sea from that district in less than one month, and this with long marches ; withal we went with the intention of not remaining there longer than until we had received all, and then returning. So we did, for in the middle of January following we departed from that land by the road to where we used to be near the sea, and without leave, neither did we wait for the ambassador, nor inform him, so that he should not embarrass us, but we went on our own footing. And the said ambassador, as soon as he knew of our departure, sent two men after us entreating us to take them with us, and to send one back with any news there

23

might be of the Portuguese, and that when there was certain news the other should come.

CAP. CXL.—*How the Portuguese came for us, and who was the captain.*

Whilst we Portuguese and the Franks were in the town of Barua waiting for them to come to us, and having sent two men to the sea in order that they should bring us the good news that our Portuguese were coming for us, on Saturday, vigil of Easter day, the 1st of April of 1526, the said two men whom we had sent to the sea reached us, and they came half dead and despairing, and they began to say, there are no Portuguese there, who were coming for us, nor are there in India, for all are routed and India lost; and they said that they knew this news by the Moors of three ships which had arrived at the Island of Masua with much sounding of music and festivity, and very rich merchandize, and that with much festivity they had disembarked at the said island. These Moors gave this news because such was their wish, and they founded themselves in asserting it on the capture of a Portuguese galley close to Diu, a port of the King of Cambay. These Portuguese who brought this news came half dead and fainting, and we remained in like manner with this news so bad for us. The ambassador, Don Rodrigo, said to me: "Padre, let us say mass to-morrow very early, and commend ourselves to God." I answered him that my heart was not quiet, nor in such rest as to be able to say mass, but that we would go very early to the chief church and hear mass with the Barnagais. And so we did, and when the morning became light, and the mass of the resurrection was finished, the Barnagais invited us to come and dine with him, and we excused ourselves on account of the feast day, and that each of us

wished to honour his own quarters : and we did this by
reason of the small pleasure we felt.   I went with eight
Portuguese and Genoese that I had invited to dinner, and
when we had done eating I left them in the house with my
nephew who always accompanied me, and I went alone up
a stream as far as a great rock which made shade on the
sand of the river, and I wept by the way, and with tears
and sighs I laid myself down in that shade for more than
an hour ; and, desisting from weeping, I recovered myself,
and talking to myself I said : "Now this comes from God,
and He is served by me in this land : the Lord be praised
for ever since it is so.   I know this country better than
any native of it does, because I go in pursuit of game, and
know its mountains, and waters, and the land which is
good for cultivation, and which will give all that is planted
or sown in it.   I have got some good slaves and fourteen
cows, and I have got rams which I will exchange for ewes.
I will go near to some water, and will have a strong bush
fence made to keep off the wild beasts, and I will pitch my
tent in which to take refuge with my servants, and I will
arrange a hermitage within, and each day I will say mass,
and commend myself to God, since the Lord is pleased that
I should be here.   I will order the bushes to be cut to
make gardens, and I will sow grain of all sorts : and with
my harvests and hunting I will maintain myself and servants
and slaves."   With this I remained consoled, as though
good news had come to me ; and I arose and returned
down stream to my house, where I found the ambassador
Don Rodrigo and the Portuguese and Genoese, and all our
company, playing and enjoying themselves.   As soon as I
approached them, Don Rodrigo said to me : "Padre, what
shall we do ? my opinion is that we write to the Court to
our friends to say to Prester John that he should bid us
return to the Court."   I answered him : "Do not do it,
and I shall never come from it if I go there."   And when

23 ²

he said to me, "What shall we do if the Prester orders us to go?" I answered, "If His Highness sends to say that the Portuguese should come, and does not say let Padre Francisco come, as he always says, I shall not go : and if he names me I will go, even though I should regret it." And when he asked what I would do if I did not go, I gave him an account how I had gone after dinner up stream as far as the said shade and had lain down; and of the thoughts I had had, and the determination I had taken, and that I had come away consoled. All that were there arose and embraced me except the ambassador, who did not agree to this; and all of them said, and each one separately: " This is a thing which comes from God, and we will all go with you, and we will bring our wives and sons and slaves; we have got very good mules, and we very well know the sea and the land markets, and some of us will remain with you, and others will go and trade, and we will enrich ourselves, and we will make a place of our own in which we will breed cattle, and we will make large tilled fields." When the ambassador heard this he answered nothing, and said : " You, Padre, have got much game and good things to eat, let us all sup here if you bid us, and to-morrow we will also dine here with you, and after dinner we will go with your snares after game, and we will go and sup at my house." This pleased me very much, and we all supped this Easter and dined on Monday. After that, we rode out to hunt, and killed many hares and three or four ......,[1] and went to sup at the house of the ambassador. All the Portuguese and white men of other nations being very firm in the agreement before come to through me, when it was already night, after supper, and all of us going home to our quarters, and all with me to conduct me to mine, there came up to us on the road a servant of mine named Abetay, a

---

[1] *Sysones*, omitted by Selves.

married man of the country. And he came running so fast that he could not speak from fatigue : and he began to say : " Sir, Sir, the Portuguese on the sea." I asked him : " Abetay, who told you this ?" he replied, " A man said it who has now arrived from the sea and is with the Bar-nagais." I said to him : "Abetay, if this is true, of nine mules that I have got, five mine and four of my nephew's, excepting the one the Prester gave me, on which you cannot ride, I will give you the best, and I will not sleep until I see this man." Then I took leave of my companions and went to the gates of the Barnagais' palace, and they would not open them to me ; and I waited at the gate with the said man until the cocks crew, and the man came out, to whom I at once said : " Are you the man who saw the Portuguese on the sea ?" He replied : " I did not see them with my eyes, but I heard with my ears, in the morning of Easter, firing of cannon at Dalaqua, and I bring this message from the Sultan[1] of Arquiquo to the Barna-gais." I made my calculations, as it was not new moon, for at sight of it the Moors make great rejoicing, who could these be who were firing, whether they could be Rumys, Moors, or Christians. I gave this news to all our company who came to me for it on the Tuesday morning to ask, as they knew that I had gone to seek the man who had come from the sea. As I said before, that the Prester's ambassador had sent after us two of his men for them to bring him in great haste any news of the Portuguese that we might hear, in that hour we despatched one to him, and he was one of his men, and another of this country to go night and day and take this message to the ambassador, so that he might make ready, we having some hope of good, for we had no other contrariety, except that two men of ours had brought the news from the sea that

---

[1] This man appears to be one of the Prester's officials. See before, p. 316.

India was lost, and they could not believe in the coming of
the Portuguese; on the contrary, they said this firing of
bombards was rejoicing of the Moors, on being certified of
the injury to India. This Tuesday, in the night, while we
were thus neither believing nor disbelieving either the
good or the bad news, there reached us a letter from Hector
da Silveira, captain-major of the Indian sea, who had come
for us, and remained in Masua. Here I do not know what
to say of how great was the pleasure of all of us, except
that we went out of our senses, so great was the joy. Don
Rodrigo, the ambassador, returning to us said that we
should start, and at once, next morning; some said that
that was good. I said that it did not seem to me good;
because, up to this time we had been held to be Christians,
and if we travelled on such great feast days, they would
say that we were not so, and that we should keep the
octaves until Monday. Then that night we despatched a
Portuguese, and a man of the sea coast, with our letter to
Hector da Silveira; and to the Prester's ambassador we
sent his man who was still with us, with another man of
the country, and they were to travel day and night and
take him this certain news, and the ambassador was to do
the same, and travel day and night by some other shorter
road along the sea on the way to Arquiquo.

CAP. CXLI.—*How the Barnagais made ready, and we travelled
with him on the road to the sea.*

On Monday after the octaves of Easter, the 9th of April,
we set out from Barua, the Barnagais and we Portuguese,
and the other three white men who were with us, on the
road to Arquiquo. The Barnagais and his gentlemen and
two that he sent for may have taken with them a thousand

men on mules, and a large number on foot. This day we went to sleep at a distance of two leagues from Barua, at a place called Dinguil, encamped in a plain in which every Monday at night, and Tuesday in the morning, people assemble who are going to the fair of Arquiquo, and they go together in a caravan, because this road is not travelled over except by a great assemblage, from fear of the Arabs and wild beasts. Here there joined us fully two thousand persons who were going to the said fair, and they said that there were few people, and that they had failed to come from fear of want of water. With the people who came with the Barnagais and those who came from this place, Dinguil, we set out and went to sleep at the place of scanty water. And in the distance that there may be from Barua, whence we started with the Barnagais, to Arquiquo, of fourteen leagues or fifteen at most, we passed all the week till Saturday morning, and we took up our quarters close to the town of Arquiquo, not approaching our ships because the Barnagais had to present us, and his people were not yet assembled, because besides the people who came with him from Barua, he was expecting men and captains who were to go against Suaquem, which is towards Egypt. These men did not arrive till the Monday following. At night, and we at liberty, we went to see our people, and they us. On account of the heats, which were great and insupportable, the Barnagais and captains ordered dwellings to be made of wood and tall bushes, and they also ordered dwellings to be made for us Portuguese to sleep in, covered with sails above, as there was no man could endure the heat of the country from the great multitude of people and the suffocation of tents and huts. The Portuguese who came for us had made their dwellings over the sea where there was always a breeze ; others lodged in good terraced houses, which were in the island. On Tuesday, in the morning, the Barnagais and his captains and me with him, he conducted us to where

Hector da Silveira was, and delivered us up to him with
much pleasure and joy. He ordered fifty cows and many
sheep, fowls, and fish to be given him for the ships. On
the Thursday following, Prester John's ambassador reached
us, he had travelled day and night, and as soon as the first
message which we sent was given him he ordered mules to
be put in readiness, in order that if a positive message
came, he might travel day and night, which he did as soon
as the message was given him. We Portuguese went to
wait for him at the town of Arquiquo, to come with him, and
the Barnagais also came to deliver him up. While we were
thus waiting for the monsoon, that is, wind for departure,
which always comes from the 26th and 27th of April till the
3rd or 4th of May, and if one does not go out with this
monsoon there is no other till the end of August; on the
21st of April there reached us four *calacens*, that is, four
messengers from Prester John to say that he had news by
Zeila of the Portuguese fleet having entered the Red Sea,
and that they thought they came for us; and since it was a
long time that we had left his Court, and we might be sad,
that we should at once return to him, and he would give us
much gold and clothes, and would send us joyful and contented to the King of Portugal his brother. These calacens
said that they had been sent in such haste that in each town
they had taken fresh mules from the captains, and had travelled night and day, and they requested us very earnestly
not to do anything else there except turn back : and they
required the same of Alicacanate, the Prester's ambassador,
to return with us, and we with him : they moreover requested Hector da Silveira to send us because Prester John
would feel displeasure at our going away vexed. Hector da
Silveira answered, and we with him, to the said calacens,
that by no means could we turn back, nor could he wait, nor
did the monsoon allow of it, and that if we did not go away
now at once, other ships would never come for us, and that

his ambassador might return if he liked. This was told to the ambassador of Prester John, and he replied that by no means would he return without us, because he would order him to be thrown to the lions. So we all remained with great pleasure ; and the calacems discontented because their labour had been in vain.

LAUS DEO.

IN THIS PART IS RELATED THE JOURNEY WHICH WAS MADE FROM THE COUNTRY OF THE PRESTER JOHN TO PORTUGAL.

CAP. I.—*Of how we departed from the port and island of Masua until arriving at Ormuz.*

On the 28th day of April, of 1526, we set sail, the whole fleet together; it consisted of five sail, namely three royal galloons and two carvels. We reached the island of Camaran the 1st day of May, and there the wind wearied us. We were there three days, and whilst waiting I remembered how we had there buried Duarte Galvam, the ambassador to Prester John, who was sent by the king our sovereign. I was present at his decease, and I went to his burial, and with the licentiate Pero Gomez Teixeira, who was then judge, we marked the grave, so that if at any time any of his relations or friends came, they might know it, to remove his remains to a country of Christians if they chose. And I went with a slave of mine to where we had left him buried, and I ordered him to be dug up, and to dispose all his bones in order; but we did not find more than three teeth, and I put them in a small box, and we brought his remains to the galloon St. Leon, in which I went, without anyone knowing of it except one Gaspar de Saa, factor of the said fleet, and who was of his household. As soon as we had got the said remains on board the galloon, the wind changed to a stern wind, and that hour we set sail, and this factor said to me : "Certainly, as Duarte Galvam was a good man and ended his days in the service of God, so God gives us a good wind for him." And we had the same wind till the 10th of May, when we were opposite Aden, and already in the open sea,[1] and the winter weather from India was facing us, and we facing it. The storm was so great that the second night we passed in it, what with the great darkness and high wind, we lost one another and were separated without seeing each other again, or knowing what course each ship was making. This galloon St. Leon, in which I went, had a large boat made fast astern with three ropes, and in it was a ship boy, a Frenchman by nation, who steered it. In the fourth night that we passed in this storm, the sea was so wild and high that we all thought we should be lost; and at midnight a little more or less, all three ropes of the boat broke, and the galloon gave so many and so great lurches, that we thought we should go to the bottom of the sea. The master of the galloon sounded his whistle and gave out a *Pater-noster* through the ship to all hands[2] for the soul of the ship boy who was in the boat. On the following day an auction was held, that is, a valuation and sale of the pieces and things which the ship boy had with him, and with them and a slave of his a hundred and twenty pardaos[3] were made. We sailed with this storm[4] until we got to the strait of Ormuz, and on the 28th of May we reached the port of Mazquate, which belongs to the Kingdom of Ormuz, and pays tribute to the King of Portugal our sovereign. There we found one of the carvels of our convoy and fleet, which gave an account of the storm which it had passed, and three days after that the other carvel, companion of the first, arrived; and the same day a galloon arrived, and each related the storms. Ten days after our arrival at this port of Mazquate, they saw tacking about on the sea the galloon Sam Donis, the flagship of the fleet, and she could not fetch

---

[1] *Golfam.*   [2] *De mao em mao.*
[3] *Pardao,* Indian coin worth 3 *testoons* and 3 *vintens.*
[4] *Fortuna.*

the port: two Portuguese fustas, which guarded the strait
of the port of Mazquate, went out to her, and as soon as
they reached the galloon they turned back, and with great
haste they took provisions and water to succour the galloon
and her crew, who were lost with hunger and thirst, more
with thirst than hunger. The fustas passed the night there;
and next day, in the early morning, all our boats and the
town boats set out from the town to fetch the galloon, and
they did bring her and arrived with her in the port in the
afternoon. Here they related the great straits and danger
in which they found themselves, saying that they had run
before the storm which caught them at the entrance of the
strait,[1] and they went as far as the bay of Cambay, from
which they could not come out: and the Lord was pleased
that the storm should not cease, by which the sea was secure
from enemies. They also said that for three days they had
not eaten, from being short of water. They spoke of the
great virtue and compassion of Hector da Silveira, captain-
major of this fleet, and they said that he was the first to
leave off drinking, and that with tears in his eyes and a little
water in his hand he went about distributing it among the
sick: and after the time that they found themselves in these
straits, he did not any more sleep in nor enter his cabin,
that it might not be supposed that he went to fill himself
with water and left the crews to suffer. So they said it was
true that on the day when they sighted land and we succoured them, there was not a single drop of water in the
galloon, nor had either the sound or the sick tasted it : and
that they had sight that day miraculously of the land and
port, and we of them; because they already despaired of their
lives. I heard this from the ambassadors, Don Rodrigo de
Lima who went to the Prester John, and Alicacanate, the
ambassador of the Prester, who is going to Portugal; and
generally all said it who were in the galloon. All the

1 Gulf of Ormuz.

people landed to refresh themselves and recover from the
fatigue of the sea. We were few days in this port of Mazquate, and from there our fleet sailed together, God be
praised, and with us certain fustas of those which guard
this port and strait. We went to the city of Ormuz, a fortress of the king our sovereign, and found there Lopo Vaz
de Sampayo, captain-major and governor of the Indies for
his Highness. When we reached the port, all the gentlemen
and captains of the ships, carvels, galleys, and fustas, and all
the other people, both of the fortress and of the fleet and
company of the captain-major, came out to receive us on the
beach; and the captain-major was on the beach in front of
the fortress, and there they gave us our welcome. Then
we went together to the church which is inside the fort, and
the captain-major came down there to embrace the ambassadors, and me with them, and some others of our embassy.
Then we went each to his quarters. The following day we
all came to hear mass and to speak to the captain-major,
and to give him a letter from Prester John, which we had
brought for Diogo Lopez de Sequeira, who had been captain-major and governor of the Indies, and who took us to
the country of the Prester : and we gave the letter to Lopo
Vaz de Sampayo, as he had succeeded to the said charge.
Besides, we gave him a silk robe with five gold plates before
and other five behind, and one on each shoulder, which in
all made twelve. Each one was the size of the palm of the
hand, and Prester John sent it to Diogo Lopez. The
governor, Lopo Vaz de Sampayo, gave the favour of two
hundred pardaos to Don Rodrigo de Lima, the ambassador who had gone to the Prester, and another
two hundred to the Prester's ambassador, and to me he gave
the favour of a hundred pardaos. Hector da Silveira remained few days at Ormuz, and soon returned with his fleet
to wait for the ships which come from Jiddah to Dio, and
come out with the monsoon with which we came, and they

pass the winter at Aden, and with the first wind make their voyage; and we remained until being certain that the winter had passed.

CAP. II.—*Of the translation of the letter which Prester John sent to Diogo Lopez, and which was given to Lopo Vaz de Sampayo.*

"In the name of God the Father, Who always was, to Whom no beginning is found. In the name of the Son, one only, who is like Him without being seen, light of the stars from the beginning, before the foundations of the ocean were founded. In another time He was conceived in the womb of the Virgin without seed of man, or marriage. So was the knowledge of His office, in the name of the Paraclete, spirit of holiness, who knows all secrets, where He was first in the heights of heaven, which is sustained without props or supports, and extended the earth, without its being from the beginning, nor was it known nor created from the east to the west, and from north to south; neither is He the first nor the second, but the Trinity joined together in one Creator of all things for ever, with one sole counsel and one sole word for ever and ever. Amen.

"The king of the great and very high city of Ethiopia sends this writing and embassage: the king incense of the Virgin, whose name is his by baptism: now that he has become king he is named David, the head of his kingdoms, loved of God, prop of the faith, a relation of the lineage of Judah, son of David, son of Solomon, son of the column of Sion, son of the seed of Jacob, son of the hand of Mary, son of Nahum in the flesh.

"This goes to Diogo Lopez de Sequeira, captain-major of the Indies.

"I have heard of you that you are under the king, and that you are a conqueror in all the things which are committed to you, and have no fear of the forces of the numerous Moors, and mounted on a horse you do not fear storms, and you go armed with faith; neither are you one who is conquered by concealed things, and you go armed with the truth of the Gospel, and so you sustain yourself on the edge of the banner of the cross: and for ever thanks be to God for the said faith which procured us our joy, for the love of our Lord Jesus Christ. Of the coming to us which you have come, and have announced your good embassy of your sovereign king Don Manuel; and with your present and peace, which you accomplished with so much fatigue in the ships, and upon the sea, with great winds and storms both by sea and land, coming to kill the Moors and Pagans by such distant journeys; and your ships are steered and directed wherever you wish, which is a miraculous thing: and we are amazed at your having gone for two years, at sea and in war, and with so much fatigue, without resting either day or night. That which it is usual to do, is done by day, and by day merchandise is bought and sold, and travelling is done; the night is for men to sleep and rest themselves, as the Scripture says. The day is for men to do their business from the morning till night. And the lion's cub only scratches the earth and seeks[1] and prays to God that it may find food; and when the sun rises it returns to its den. And the customs of men are like those of animals: the animals exist from the beginning of the world, and you were not conquered by not sleeping at night, nor by day with the sun, from love of the true faith, as St. Paul says. Who will it be that will contradict these words. Sickness or suffering, hunger or cruelty, knife or sword, fatigue or anything else, cannot part us from the faith of Christ, in which we truly believe

[1] Selves translates: *no hace de noche sino arañar la tierra y buscar*.

in death and in life. The great lords and rich men, when
they are sent with an embassage of that which was good
by day, it is a very deep thing; there is not one who can
separate us from Jesus Christ. The apostle moreover says:
Blessed is the man who is humble and endures good and
evil, and in conclusion deserves to take the crown of life,
and God promised him that which was his desire. There
are some men who desire to attempt and care for one thing,
God chooses another. God does not select a man for bad
things. Now may God fulfil your desire, and give you
safety, and bring you to the King Don Manuel your sovereign; and those whom you have conquered, carry them
before you, with their spoils, that is of the Pagans who
are not in the faith of Jesus Christ. May this be for good;
and your men-at-arms may they be blessed, like you; because they are martyrs for Jesus Christ, who die for his holy
name of cold and heat, with labours and fatigues; and you
and they, may God conduct you with health and peace to
see the face of your sovereign King Don Manuel. I heard,
Sir, and I had heard what you had told us, how you arrived
at our country, and there was great joy as when one takes
a large booty; and when they told me that you had gone
away, there was great sadness. After that, when they told
me that your ambassador was coming, and of your good
will up to this day, I am in great pleasure, and blessed be
the name of God the Father, one only God, and of our
Lord Jesus Christ the Saviour of the world. And they
came to me, and I heard your reputation from afar; and
now may God maintain you that you have made friendship
with me. May your goodness now be fulfilled in that which
I desire, and do you send me masters of working gold and
silver, of making swords, and weapons of iron and helmets,
and masons to make houses, and masters to make vineyards
and gardens, and all other masters that are necessary, and
of the best arts that are named, and to make lead to cover

churches, and to make earthen tiles in our country, so that we may not cover our houses with thatch : of this we have great necessity, and we are very sad at not possessing them. I have built a very large church which is named Trinity, in which I have buried my father, whose soul may it be in God's keeping; and your ambassadors will tell you how good its walls are, and I wished to cover it in great haste, because it is covered with thatch. I tell you this for the love of God to send me the total of these masters, which is ten of each art. On account of this your masters will neither be diminished nor increased. As long as they like to remain they may remain, and if they should wish to return I will pay them their work, and I will let them go in peace. And now hear another word : I send you there those Franks who were here, and who were going about as Moors in the country of Cairo ; I made Christians of them, and they will show the road to Zeila and Aden, and Mekkah, and Masua, as they know it well. On this account let your heart be glad, and I rejoice at that which is in your desire, and I write to you for the sake of the embassage which you sent, which says that you wish to build a church and a fort in the island of Masua, and you ask me for leave to do it : I give you permission to make a church and a castle in Masua and in Dalaqua, and to put priests in the churches, and strong men to guard the castles, from fear of the Moors, dirty sons of Mahomed. Do this quickly before you go to India, and do not give yourselves leisure in this, nor go to India until you have made a church and a castle. For all this we will praise you, I and the King Don Manuel your sovereign, because God has been pleased that we should love one another. And make a market where they buy and sell merchandise, and do not allow Moors to buy and sell, but Christians. And if you wish that Moors should buy and sell there, let it be as you please and with your license. And after you have done this in Masua, come

24

to Zeila and make there a church and castle, as I said before. This town of Zeila is a port of much provisions for Aden and all parts of Arabia, and many other countries and kingdoms; and those kingdoms and lands have no other favour except what comes to them from Zeila. When this is done which I send you word to do, you will have the kingdom of Aden in your hand, and all Arabia, and many other countries and kingdoms, without war nor death of people, because you will take all their provisions and they will be starved. When you wish to make war upon the Moors, send and tell me, and what you want or have need of; and I will send you horsemen and archers, and I will be with you, and we will defeat the Moors and Pagans justly for the faith, I and you. When you wish to go to India, leave Don Rodrigo de Lima as captain of Masua, and let not your ambassadors omit to go and come whenever there is anything suspicious there. These who now are going are the first who came here; the ambassadors of your embassage are great and good, and they love one another well in spite of their faults; and do to them much good for the sake of their goodness, especially to Don Rodrigo de Lima, who is very good, excepting his faults, and that he does not speak much with his lips, and he is remarkable for making himself good, better than all, and he is a servant to be trusted; do good to him, and he is a servant of the blessing. To Padre Francisco give twice as many thanks, because he is a holy man, honest, and of good conscience for the love of God: I know his disposition, and I gave him a cross and a staff of his lordship into his hand: this is a sign of his lordship, and he is an abbot in our country: and do you increase him and make him lord of Masua and Zeila and all the isles of the Red Sea, and of the extremities of our countries, because he is sufficient for, and deserving of such an office. Also, with regard to Joam Escolar the clerk, I have complied with his desire and

wishes, because he is always at the king's service, do to
him as may be best for him, because he is a man of very
good condition, and he laboured much in the writing of
this, and in things which had to be done. To the rest of
the embassy do them good, from the small to the great,
according to what each is, and give them their reward.
Our Lord give you his peace for the service of virtue, and
do good to you and to all that are with you. Do good to
them, and may the Lord illuminate you and them with his
grace. May God assist our brothers, those who love one
another well, and all those who persist in it; God is with
them, and may He be with you and succour you in all
cases; and may your feet be together on the road, and
keep you from the evil eye, and keep you from the waves of
the sea, and your ships from the storms, and you in life in
all times without any sickness, and keep you in all hours of
the day and night, in winter and summer, *in secula seculorum, amen.* I send you my blessing, but not by this
letter only, as I am accustomed so to send it; and I excuse
myself in this, and remember you, and that in all the
houses of Christians and churches which were built by our
ancestors, the prayer which we make says thus: "We will
pray for that which we want of the Lord God and Jesus
Christ his Son for those who come in pilgrimage, our
brothers, and those also who have come this pilgrimage by
sea or rivers or lakes or difficult roads, wherever it may be.
To Thee they belong; God bring them and conduct them
in safety with a smooth sea: the Lord sustain them all."
So the deacons say, praying for the priests, and in another
part the priests say: "God be with you, because He is with
all, and we ask for that which He has for good, and we ask
for those who are brothers in dangers, and they are so now,
and they come in pilgrimage a straight road with those of
the road which they desire, and that we may soon find
what we desire, may the Lord give it us." The deacon says,

2 t ²

and all the people say : " Lord God have mercy upon us."
So says the third priest : " May God bring them in safety on
a smooth sea, and bring them to their relations with pleasure and peace which they desire, and may they see pleasure by His Son Jesus Christ. May He be with you, and
you with Him, and with the Holy Spirit, which is eternal
glory, now and for ever *in secula seculorum, amen.*"

" So, as I say, prayer is made in all the churches and hours
of the offices, with incense, not for you alone, but for all of
us, that He may be with us in pilgrimage, and that this pilgrimage should not come to us, but over the sea inside our
country as in yours; for the sake of this do you make prayer
in this office so that you may be saved, and that you may
be against bad men, and that bad imaginations may not
enter you. And while you live, in order to defeat the
Moors and Pagans, those who do not believe in the faith of
our Lord Jesus Christ, I will send assistance to make war,
and many men and provisions and gold : not only to Masua,
but to Zeila and Adel, and all the countries of the infidels,
defeating the sons of Mahomed, the heretics. With the
assistance of the Queen St. Mary our Lady I have defeated
them, and we will defeat them. You will come by sea, and
we will go by land together with consultation, with the
strength of the most Holy Trinity."

Cap. III.—*Of the voyage we made from Ormuz to India, as
far as Cochim.*

We left Ormuz with the captain-major, Governor Lopo
Vaz de Sampayo, in his fleet, because Hector da Silveira had
already sailed with his galloons and fleet to wait for the
Mekkah ships which had wintered at Aden, as has been
said; and coming out of the strait of Ormuz, we already met
the wild winter weather of India, which could be navigated

without a storm, and we went to the fortress of Chaul, ·
which belongs to the king our sovereign, a country which is
very strong and flourishing, of much wheat, which comes
from Cambay, and much meat of the country, namely, cows,
rams, fowls, fish, an infinite quantity of shad fish, and very
good, and the rest remain in the canals, (where the ship
sunk with Don Lorenzo d'Almeida, a great knight, son of
the Viceroy Don Francisco d'Almeida), many Indian figs,
large vegetable gardens and delicacies, all made by the
Portuguese. Many days did not pass but what Hector da
Silveira, who was waiting with his fleet for the Mekkah
ships, came and brought three ships as prizes, very large
and rich, with much gold, because as yet they did not
bring merchandize, and they came for it to India. All the
Moors that they captured in them (and the fortress was full
of them), those that were young and able for the galleys, all
were taken for the king our sovereign for his galleys, and
they were taken at a price of ten cruzados each, for such is
his regulation. And the other old men or who were not
able, they gave them also for ten cruzados to whoever
wanted them for ransom, or to make use of them. Among
these that were taken in the prizes came many Jews, among
whom was an old Jew who had done honour and given hospitality in his house to some Portuguese who had been lost
in the kingdom of Fartaque,[1] they went about the country
like desperate men, asking the way to Ormuz, and God
brought them to the house of this Jew. The Jew took
them in and gave them food and drink and stuffs to cover
themselves with, and some money for the road. The Lord
was pleased that this benefaction of his should not pass
without a reward. One of the men to whom the Jew did
this good happened to be here, and to know him in a prison
where he was lying with others ; and he was a man who was

---

[1] The kingdom of Fartaque was on the Arabian coast, east of Aden.
It contained the town of Dhafar.

poor enough, a native of Viseu : compassion and virtue
worked in him, and remembering what he had received from
the Jew, he went to the captain-major and told him that the
Jew had done much good to him and to other Portuguese,
in the kingdom of Fartaque, and had given them their lives,
and that he was now a captive with the Moors that Hector
da Silveira had taken in the prizes, and that he was very old
and not fit for the galleys, and that he himself had no money
with which to buy him, and that he entreated his lordship to
give this Jew to him on account of his pay for ten cruzados,
as they gave for the others. The captain-major sent for the
Jew and told him to look and see if he knew any men of
those who stood there. Looking at all of them, he pointed
out the one who had been in his house, and to whom and to
others he had done good. Then the captain-major granted
this Jew to that poor man for the good which he had done
to him and to the Moors who went with him in that voyage
and storm, in which they had come to his house. This man
took the Jew by the hand, and went with him among the
Portuguese relating the benefit which he had received from
him, as also other Portuguese who were not present, and he
collected fifty pardaos of alms for him. All Christians,
Moors, and Jews said publicly that no other good act received thanks, and that there was no other recompense except for what was done to the Portuguese; and so they
would do good to them when they fell in with them in their
own countries. We sailed from here and arrived at the city
of Goa on Saturday, the 25th of November, the vigil of St.
Catherine ; and because this city was taken from the Moors
and Gentiles on St. Catherine's day, on the Sunday,[1] which
was St. Catherine's day, they made a very great and solemn
procession, with all the plays and festivities which are customary in Portugal on the day of Corpus Christi. Prester

[1] The 25th of November is St. Catharine's day, so that there must be
an error as to Saturday or Sunday. Selves avoids this difficulty.

John's ambassador and certain friars who came with him from his country said that here they completed their belief and knowledge that we were Christians since we made so solemn a procession. We did not remain in this city more than three days. Prester John's ambassador left in this city of Goa four slaves, namely, two to be taught to be painters, and two others to be trumpeters, and the captain-major ordered maintenance to be given them and that they should be taught. We sailed for Cananor and remained there six days; the ambassador and the friars there also rejoiced at seeing the chapel of Jacob, which Matheus had ordered to be built, and the honoured bell which lies over his tomb. From the fortress and town of Cananor we sailed by this sea on the way to Cochim : on reaching it we found Antonio Galvam, son of Duarte Galvam, the ambassador who was going to Prester John and who died in Camaran, whose remains I was bringing with me. I sent word to his son how I was bringing them : he rejoiced much and begged me not to bring them on shore, because he wished to come for them with a procession; which he did with all the clergy and friars of the city, and the confraternities with all their tapers. He ordered an honourable memorial service to be performed in the monastery of St. Anthony, with offerings of sacks of wheat and barrels of wine. And because the seamen would hesitate about carrying dead bodies in the ship,[1] they made a small recess on the Gospel side, close to the high altar, so that it should seem that the box in which the remains were was put in there, and when the people had gone they closed the recess and the box remained outside. As Antonio Galvam was captain of a ship which was going to Portugal, he had the box with his father's remains taken to his ship. All the time that we remained at Cochim was spent in loading three ships and getting ready the people who were to go. Each ship, when it had got its cargo

---

[1] This superstition still exists among sailors.

of pepper and cloves, sailed for Cananor, which is thirty
leagues from Cochim, to take in ginger and provisions of
biscuit and fish, and also palm wine and gunpowder. All
the three ships assembled at Cananor in the beginning of
January, and one of the three ships sailed at once.

CAP. IV.—*Of the voyage we made from Cananor to Lisbon, and
of what happened to us by the way.*

The ship which first reached Cananor of those which
loaded in Cochim, the captain of which was Tristan Vaz da
Veiga, in which went the ambassadors Don Rodrigo de
Lima and Licacanate, ambassador of the Prester, first took
what was necessary in that fortress, namely, ginger, biscuit,
arrak, fish, and she sailed on the 4th of January of 1527
for Portugal. The ship of which Antonio Galvam was
captain, and in which I went on account of his friendship,
arrived at port after the first which had already sailed, so
they at once equipped us, and we sailed on the 18th of
January for Portugal; and according to what they told us,
the ship which had remained in the port of Cananor, taking
in what it had to take sailed fifteen days after us, which
was twenty-nine days after the departure of the first ship,
which went out of port before us. Each ship made its
course full speed as God might assist them, without first
talking of waiting for one another. On the morning of
the 2nd of April the look-out man of our ship, who slept
in the top, began to say, "There is a ship a-head of us a
distance of two leagues". All those who still slept arose,
and with those who were already up we placed ourselves in
the castles to look with much amazement what ship it
might be, because we were very far out in the middle of
the sea. When it was clear day they knew that she was
Portuguese, and one from India. Upon this the look-out

man said he saw a ship astern of us. The ship which went in front having knowledge of us, as we had of her, began to wait until we approached and saluted her, and she us. Then the ship which came astern was well in sight, and the two ships agreed to wait for her, and towards night she reached us. There was much pleasure among the crews of the three ships, asking one another how they had fared, and asking the foremost ships if anything had happened to them, or how they had not sailed faster. They said, or we said, that we had sailed as much as we had been able, without anything happening to us by the way; and all in good health, God be praised. Here we went in convoy, and sailed together for three days. And because the ship named *Sta. Maria do Espinheiro*, Captain Antonio Galvam, in which I went, heeled over a great deal, and did not sail as fast as the others, one day early in the morning one of the ships was a long way off, and the other waited for us to speak us. When we reached her and saluted her, she said that the other ship which had gone a-head, and she, asked our pardon, but they could not wait for us, because they saw our ship heel so much that it seemed to them that we could not go to Portugal. We remained very disconsolate, and they went on their course. We made our course for the island of St. Helena to take in water there. The two ships which had left us fetched the said island, and we on Easter Sunday, which was the 21st of April 1527 ran by the island in the night which ended on Monday. And as at midnight, a little more or less, there came a heavy shower, some said that then we ran by the island, because the shower came from the land; others said that it was still a-head of us. We remained some days in this doubt, until we saw signs that we were beyond the island, and we ran very short of water; already we did not boil anything from want of water. Here the Lord succoured us with his mercy, giving us three days and three nights heavy rain, during which much good water was taken. They took thirty pipes of water for the ship, and for me they took three, and so also each one took what he wanted in whatever he had got, and we remained with abundance of water. From this time forward we made our usual meals. When we were near the island of Terceira we sighted a ship, and we feared much, thinking that she might be French. This ship fell off from the island to seaward, and we got as close in shore as we could; and then they sighted from our top a canoe[1] in which were men castaway, and they launched another canoe from our ship, which they had brought from India, and some seamen and shipboys went to it and took the canoe and nine persons that were in it, namely, five white men and four slaves, who were half dead; for the canoe had capsized with them because it is long and narrow and all of one piece of timber. They placed all these men thrown one upon another as they could not move, and had all been overflowed with water. On reaching the ship they seemed more dead than alive. They at once stripped them and put on them dry clothes, and some of them in beds, others by the fire, and some spoke three hours after that, others four hours, and others next day. Next day at dawn we made the port of the island Terceira, where we found caravels which were waiting for ships, and also alarmed at the ships which appeared at sea, thinking they were French, as they ran by the island, and were thinking of going to them. Upon this, the men whom we had picked up, and who were now somewhat in their senses and wits, said that those were the Portuguese ships which came from India and had separated from our company, and that they had sent them in the canoe to buy some fowls at an island where they were cheap, and the canoe had capsized with them, and they did not know what had become of the ships. After we had been five days at anchor in the port,

[1] Almadia.

the said two ships reached the port, and they told how they
had run by so much that they could not make the island,
and if it had not been on account of the king our sovereign,
and fear of the French, they would have made their course
for Portugal. They gave great thanks to God for saving
their men and slaves, and also for our coming, swearing
that they had left us for lost on account of our ship heeling
so much, and they entreated us for the love of God to
pardon them. They also told us that on Saturday, vigil of
Easter, they made the island of St. Helena, and we told
them that on the night of Easter Sunday, dawning on
Monday, we had run by it with a shower. They also said
that it rained there that night. We remained at Terceira
eighteen days waiting for a carvel which was at the mine,
and ships from the islands of St. Thomas and Cape Verde
and from Brazil, for such was the regulation. The carvels
that we waited for had to go together with the fleet that it
might be secure from the French, and though this island is
the mother of wheat it was very dear: and this was caused
by its raining every day and not allowing of reaping, and
still less carrying what was reaped. As soon as we reached
this island they at once sent a carvel with a message and
news of our arrival to the king our sovereign. When the
ships that we were waiting for had assembled, we made our
course for Lisbon, and one morning that we sighted Portugal and were not very far from land, we were still three
days without being able to fetch the port, and with fear of
running by it, and going to Gallicia. The Lord was pleased
that on the 24th of July, which was the vigil of St. James,
we entered the bar of Lisbon, and before we reached it, at
Cascaes a carvel came out with a message from the king,
saying, that His Highness ordered that those who came
with the embassy of the Prester John were not to land in
Lisbon, because it was prevented by the pestilence. In
this carvel there came a servant of the king, who was to

provide us with boats at Santarem, and pay expenses as far
as Coimbra where His Highness was. This day we entered
and anchored in front of the city of Lisbon, which gave us
much pleasure.

CAP. V.—*Of the journey we made from Lisbon to Coimbra,*
and how we remained at Çarnache.

As soon as we anchored in the Lisbon river, in front of
the bulwark of the palace of the King our Sovereign, that
day, the vigil of St. James, the king's servant caused boats
to come alongside to take us, all those belonging to the
embassy, and convey us to Santarem, and also boats to
take our goods with care to the India House. And because
I and my nephew we had there a brother of his, also my
nephew, who was representative of the monastery of Santos
o Novo, which was outside in the parish of Sta. Maria dos
Olivaes, he, learning our arrival, came on board, and we entrusted to him to keep for us some baggage which had not
got to go to the India House, namely, bed clothes, both
that on which we slept at sea, and also new and clean bedding, and dresses of silk, many new shirts, table napkins,
head dresses, and all other small articles; and he collected
it all within the enclosure of the monastery of Santos, of
which he was the representative, in order to come next
day with carts and take it all to his house. And we went
on our road in the boats which had been assigned to us.
On the following night that the said goods remained there,
they took away all that was good and select, and left the
old and worn, and even with that I and my nephew received
a loss of more than fifty cruzados. We did not learn this
till many days later, when they told me at Coimbra that a
letter of excommunication had been published for my goods.
We went this time in the boats to Santarem, and there

the king's servant provided us very good lodgings; he lodged me and the Prester's ambassador in Alfauge, and Don Rodrigo lodged in Marvila, in houses which had belonged to his father. We remained six days in this town, during which we dressed ourselves after the fashion of Portugal, and we bought mules and what we required because we came battered by the sea. One day we departed from Santarem at ten o'clock, in the greatest heat I ever saw, and in order to lodge separately, so we started in a straggling way, the king's servant and I went together, and the Prester's ambassador and the clerk of the embassy and his friars and servants in a party by themselves, and Don Rodrigo de Lima with his servants and slaves in another party. Don Rodrigo brought with him two Moorish pilots, who had been captured in the ships which Hector da Silveira took, as was said before in chapter III, who were sent to the King our Sovereign. And he dressed them in skin jackets, shirts, trousers, shoes, and caps, to present them to the king. The Prester's ambassador, with his company, went in the narrow path half dead with heat. The king's servant took me out of the town, and we went to stop at Ponte d'Almonda, where I expected my death from the heat. The Lord was pleased that I should find a lodging with much cold water, and a very good host, who when he saw me thus, began to encourage me and to give me cucumbers and cool wine, with which he cooled me and drew out the heat. Upon this, Don Rodrigo arrived galloping on a horse, shouting and saying, "For the sake of God let them run to me with beasts, for the Moorish pilots of the king and my slaves have remained half dead of heat." There were there some muleteers, who at once went in haste with four beasts and Don Rodrigo with them, and they brought the said Moors and slaves, and they came in such a state that one of these Moors never returned to his senses. It did not profit him to anoint him with verjuice,[1]

¹ .Agraço.

and many other remedies which they applied to him, he died at midnight; and the fever never left the other Moor until he died. We said with regard to this that they were suffocated with the clothes which they were not used to. We who were used to them passed a sufficiently bad time of it. After this the consequence was the suspicion that arose here whether we had entered Lisbon, and we all went to take oath, going before the king's servant who conducted us, or ordered us to be brought. We gave our testimony that we were in good health and very sound, and from a very wholesome country: and that we had not entered Lisbon nor any other infected[1] country, but that we thought that these Moors, although they belonged to hot countries with great heats, had not the custom of going clothed, but wore only a cloth round them from the waist downwards, and above that their skins to the sun, and so it seemed to us they had been suffocated in their clothes. Several days later we learned that that day had been pestiferous, and that many people had died on it of heat; as for instance, a woman, an inhabitant of the monastery das Celas, in the olive gardens of Coimbra; coming from the Campo do Bollan, with other women, from washing her linen, she died of the heat at the entrance of the oliveyards, at a place named Fontoura. And a friar of Conception da Veiro, who was a native of Coimbra, going with another friar as was his custom from Botan, which is two leagues from Coimbra, to Pennacova, which is four leagues from the same city, died close to a village which is named Gavinhos, of the heat, though he was a young man not more than twenty-four years old. The night that the first Moor died we went on to Golegan, which was a league from there, and thence further on from fear of the heat, and on account of the other Moor that we carried, who was sick, we travelled very little. From Golegan we went to sleep at

_____
[1] _Impidosa._

Tomar, and from there to Almayazaro, and from there to Ansiam. Here the king's servant separated from us and went to Coimbra; and we made our journey, and on arriving at Çarnacho we found a message from the king, bidding us take up our quarters there, and remain there till His Highness sent for us. In our opinion, this was on account of what his servant told him of the Moor who had died with us: and in order to allay the suspicion and doubt about his death. We remained there twenty-eight days. When these were ended the King our Sovereign sent to call Don Rodrigo and me, and we went to kiss his hand, and give an account of those things as to which he questioned us; and he ordered, that two days after that day we should get ready to go all of us to the city.

CAP. VI.—*How we departed from Çarnacho on the way to Coimbra, and the reception that was made, and how the embassage was given, and of the welcome which the King our Sovereign gave us.*

When we had now been thirty days in Çarnacho, well provided with what we required by order of the king, through his servant who accompanied us, one day very early in the morning there came to us Diogo Lopez de Sequeira, chief officer of the household[1] of His Highness, and who when he was captain-major had taken us to the country of Prester John, and looked upon this embassy as a thing of his own, and done by his hand : he came to embrace the ambassador, and the Prester's ambassador, and all of us separately, saying that the king had bid him come here, and that we were to eat heartily, and set out and go with him by the field road, because all the Court was coming to receive us. Diogo Lopez de Sequeira had or-

[1] *Almotacem-mor.*

dered dinner to be prepared here, without our knowing of
it. We all dined with him, and very early, except the
Prester's ambassador, who said he was not very well.
Dinner over we got ready and set out. On reaching a
place called d'Antanhol (which is a league from the city), we
found there many people of the Court, who came there to
meet us or receive us. From this place to San Martinho,
which is half a league from the city, we found the roads
full of all the Bishops and Counts and gentlemen that were
at the Court. They conducted us by the quarter of Ra-
poula, and we entered by a street which is called Figueira
velha, and thence by the gate of the monastery of Santa
Cruz; and by another street named rua de Coruche, and
by the road passing the gate of Almidina,[1] by the street
das Fangas, the street of Sam Christovam, and by the
Cathedral See, house of Our Lady, until we arrived at the
palace of His Highness. The Marquis of Vilareal led the
ambassador of Prester John by the hand until he kissed
the hands of the King and Queen our Sovereigns, and of
the Cardinal and the Princes, and all of us likewise kissed
them. The king asked the ambassador how he had left
Prester John his Sovereign, if he was in health, and likewise the Queen his wife, and his children. The ambassador
answered, that all had remained in good health, and very
desirous to learn and hear good news of His Highness, and
of the Queen, and his brothers. The King our Sovereign
said, that he received very great pleasure by this visitation
and embassage, and he hoped that by it great service would
be rendered to the Lord God, and to them as brothers much
honour. His Highness, moreover, asked the ambassador
how he had been by sea and land, and if he had been well
provided for and welcomed since he had been in his dominions, fortresses, and ships, and also since he had come to

---

[1] This would be the gate of the oldest part of the town. Selves omits
all reference to the topography of Coimbra.

his kingdoms. The ambassador replied, that the blessing of His Highness was so great, that whoever was comprised in it was in the grace of God. The king said to him that he had arrived tired, and that he should go in peace to his lodging, and all of us in company with him, and that we should rest ourselves; and His Highness would send to call us in order that we might give complete news of Prester John. Then we went away and mounted, and even many bishops and lords and gentlemen returned to accompany us, that is the Prester's ambassador and all of us, as we had come, as far as the monastery of St. Dominic, where they gave him his quarters. Two days after that the Bishops and Dean of the Chapel and some chaplains came to seek the Prester's ambassador and us who came with him, and we all went to the palace. The Prester's ambassador presented to the King our Sovereign a crown of gold and silver, with the sides two palms high, and not very rich, which the Prester sent him; and two letters folded like books on parchment, each written in three languages, namely, Abyssinian, Arabic, and Portuguese, and two of each language, because they came thus in two little bags— they were made for Don Manuel, may he be in holy glory— and another little bag for the King our Sovereign. Lica- canate, the ambassador of Prester John, then said to the king: "The King David, my Sovereign, sent this crown with these letters to the king your father, may he be in holy glory; and he sent to tell him that a crown never went from son to father, but that it comes from father to son, and that by the sign of this crown he, King David, was known, loved, feared, and obeyed in his kingdoms and lord- ships; and being a son he sent to the king his father this crown, in order that he might be assured that his king- doms, lordships, and peoples were for whatever His High- ness might command; and when he was certain that the king his father had died, he said, the crown and letters

25

which he was sending to his father Don Manuel, are going
to my brother the King Don Joan, with other letters which
I will write to him": and thus he presented to him the said
crown and letters. And he gave all into the hands of His
Highness. His Highness gave the crown and letters to
Antonio Carneiro his secretary: and as His Highness was
very gay and showed that he rejoiced much with this embassy, the said ambassador Licacanate and I presented to
His Highness two little bags of brocade with letters inside,
and a small cross of gold, which he sent to the Holy Father
of Rome, telling His Highness how the Prester had ordered that these letters and cross should be delivered to
His Highness, and should be given by the hand of His
Highness to me, Francisco Alvarez, to take them to His
Holiness. These His Highness took in his hands, letters
and cross, and kissed them and gave them to his secretary
Antonio Carneiro, saying, that he gave great thanks to the
Lord that for the intercession of the King his sovereign
and father such service was done to the Lord God; and that
he trusted in the Lord to complete it very soon. He sent us
away to our quarters very happy. And as up to this time
we all ate as we travelled, the king ordered a regular maintenance and animals for riding to be given to the ambassador, namely, three mules, one for him, and two for two
friars who came with him; and two cruzados each day for
his table, that is, sixty cruzados a month, and one testoon
every day for fodder for the mules; and a rich bed and
bedding for him to sleep on, silver vessels for his table,
napkins, and all that was necessary for him, and a steward,
by name Francisco Piriz, to take charge of the silver, bed
and tapestry, for he ordered everything to be given him.
He also gave him one Francisco de Lemos, a gentleman of
His Highness's guard, as Arabic interpreter to speak for
him, and to receive his maintenance, and do what might be
necessary for him.

CAP. VII.—*Of the translation of the letter which the Prester sent to Don Manuel.*

"In the name of God the Father, as always was, in Whom we find no beginning. In the name of God the Son, one only, who is like Him without being seen: light of the stars, from the first before the foundations of the ocean sea were founded: who in former time was conceived in the womb of the Virgin without seed of man, or making of marriage: so was the knowledge of His office. In the name of the Paraclete, spirit of holiness, who knows all secrets, where He was first in the heights of heaven, which is sustained without props or supports, and extended the earth, without its being from the beginning, nor was it known nor created from the east to the west, and from the north to the south; neither is the first nor the second, but the Trinity joined together in one Creator of all things, for ever by one sole counsel and one word for ever and ever. Amen.

"This writing and embassage is sent by the Incense of the Virgin, for that is his name by baptism, and when he became king he was named King David, the head of his kingdoms, beloved of God, prop of the faith, a relation of the lineage of Judah, son of David, son of Solomon, son of the column of Sion, son of the seed of Jacob, son of the hand of Mary, son of Nahum in the flesh; emperor of the high Ethiopia, and of great kingdoms, lordships, and lands, King of Xoa, of Cafate, of Fatiguar, of Angote, of Barua, of Baliganje, of Adea, and of Vangue, King of Gojame, of Amara, of Bagamidri, of Dambea, and of Vague, and of Tigrimahom, and of Sabaim, where was the Queen Saba, and of Barnagais, lord as far as Egypt. This letter goes to the very powerful and most excellent King Don Manuel, who always conquers, and who lives in

25 2

the love of God, and firm in the Catholic faith, son of
Peter and Paul, King of Portugal and the Algarves, a
friend of the Christians, an enemy of the Moors and Gentiles; Lord of Africa and Guinea, and of the mountains
and island of the moon, and of the Red Sea, and of Arabia,
Persia, and Ormuz, and of the great Indies, and of all its
towns and islands; Judge and conqueror of the Moors,
and strong Pagans, lord of the Moors and very high lands.
Peace be with you King Manuel, strong in the faith, assisted by our Lord Jesus Christ to kill the Moors, and
without lance or buckler you drive and cast them out like
dogs. Peace be with your wife, the friend of Jesus Christ,
the servant of our Lady the Virgin, mother of the Saviour
of the world. Peace be with your sons at this hour, as to
the flowers and fresh lily at your table. Peace to your
daughters, who are provided with clothes like good palaces.
Peace be with your relations, seed of the saints, as the
Scriptures say, the sons of the Saints are blessed and great
in graces in their house. Peace to those of your council
and offices, and to the lords of your jurisdiction. Peace to
your great captains of the camps and frontiers of strong
places. Peace to all your people and populations who are
in Christ. Peace to your great cities, and to all those
that are within them who are not Jews or Moors, only to
those who are Christians. Peace to all the parishes which
are in Christ, and to your faithful grandees. Amen.

"I heard say, king and my father, that when it reached
your knowledge, you ordered archbishops and bishops to
be summoned in the name of Matheus, for the sake of this
I am very joyful and satisfied, and give many thanks to
God: and not I alone, but all my people are very joyful.
When I enquired, they told me how Matheus had died as
soon as he entered my countries, at the monastery of Bisan.
I did not send him, but Queen Helena sent him who governed me as my mother, because at that time I was eleven

years of age : for I remained of that age at the death of my father, when I succeeded to the crown of my kingdoms, and the Queen Helena governed for me. Matheus was a merchant, and changed his name because he was named Abraham, and he called himself Matheus : and going through the country of the infidels with his merchandise to pass as a merchant, he reached Dabul,[1] and the Moors learned that he was a Christian, and they took him and put him in a prison. He, seeing himself a prisoner, sent a message to your captain-major, complaining and saying that he was arrested without justice, and he sent to say that he was my ambassador, and that the King of Ethiopia sent him to the King of Portugal, and that he should come and deliver him from that place. When your captain-major heard this word, and heard that he was a Christian ; and that the King of Ethiopia sent him, and that he was confined in prison, and robbed of what he had, for all this he had sent to tell him ; your captain hearing these words, and his heart being very strong in the love of the faith, he had great anger, and sent ships and people in great strength to kill those who kept him a prisoner, and they asked of all how the case was, and for what reason, and they told him. And he said to Matheus : ' Tell me the embassage of the King of Ethiopia which you carry to the King of Portugal', and when he said these words, they let him go. And he reached you, king, and said : ' I bring here a cross of Jesus Christ', and he gave you the cross. Also he said many other words of himself, and others as to what you, king, inquired of him, and he replied. And for what he told you, you honoured him and made him great in many things ; as was said by the letters which he brought. And before he arrived here, he died in the monastery of Bisam ; and others who came with him, men of Portugal, came here and gave the letters

_____
[1] On the coast of India, to the north of Goa.

of this embassy. When I saw the letter I gave thanks to God, and thanked Him for their coming and embassy. I am very joyful on account of you and your peoples, and I was very joyful when I saw the crosses on their heads and breasts, and also in their hands. When I asked about the faith, I found it proved that you were Christians, and I saw people who had never come to me, and who told me how they had found the way and country of Ethiopia, because as yet it had not been found, and I felt vexation. And when they were as though despairing of finding it, and wished to return to the seas of India, fearing the storms and fatigues, at night they miraculously saw a red cross in the sky over the lands of Ethiopia, and it was adored by all, both by the lords and by the mariners. By this they knew that their navigation was directed by God, and I was extremely amazed at this. Certainly this signal and word came by the will of God, and it was not from the devil; but it was for you to send here an embassy to me, of your embassage to me. This was first prophesied by the prophet in the life and passion of St. Victor in the book of the Holy Fathers, that a Frank King should meet with a King of Ethiopia, and that they should give each other peace, and I did not know if this would be in my days and time or in another. God knew it for certain, praised be His name, who brought me your embassy, in order that I might send to you as to my father and friend, and we are united in one faith. Before this I had not seen any embassy from a Christian king, and now you are near to me, before all were Pagans and Moors, dirty sons of Mahomed, and others are slaves who do not know God; and others pay reverence to sticks and to fire, and others to the sun, and others to serpents : and there are great differences. I was never at peace nor did I rest, because they would not believe the truth, and I always preached the faith, and now in my time I am at rest: God gives me rest from these our enemies;

and in all my borders when I go to meet the Moors, they
cannot set their faces straight, nor turn their face to us.
When I send the camps to war, my captains obtain the
victory over the enemies, and so I have victory; and God
does not weary me with His favour, as the Psalter says.
God rejoices at your power, the King and many rejoice
at your safety, and that which the will desires, that He
grants if just petition is made to Him, each one saying this
for himself. We owe not only praise but thanks to God.
To you, father, God has given the world, and has given you
the country of the Gentiles for ever; and the countries of
other people, which are your countries, as far as the beginning of Ethiopia: and God has placed in my hands many
worlds, and for the sake of this I give many thanks to God.
And I speak of your great power, hoping that your sons
who are to come will be in the knowledge of the truth;
and I and you will be very joyful on account of His goodness, because He has given us everything. And now do
you not cease to make your prayer until God gives into
your hands the holy house of Jerusalem, which is in the
hands of rebels against Christ, and they are Moors, and
pagans, and heretics. When this shall be attained, who
will be greater than you, for there will be no other name,
but only yours alone : and in this I have thought and kept
it, as a good messenger, and the guards that are given him
are the messengers of Jesus Christ. When you do this
you will have your fill of the praise of men. I heard how
you sent your ambassadors with Abraham who changed
his name for Matheus, and who brought me your words.
These ambassadors who came with Abraham, three died
and did not come to me, and the great captain head of the
captains came as far as Masua, and saw the Barnagais (who
is a king subject to me), and he sent ambassadors, and I
rejoiced greatly at hearing your good news; and of all the
treasures in the world, your name is better than all rich

and precious stones. I heard you with great satisfaction.
Let us leave this and go and seek something else to take
up. I would give two hundred millions[1] of gold and we
will meet with friendship, and if you will choose to do this
according to my desire, why is it not in me to send an
ambassador of peace with a similar embassage; and you
first sent one to me to seek me with truth, to fulfil the
words of Jesus Christ as he said it. And by this you will
see how I am disposed for this, as did the Apostles of
Jesus Christ, who all were of one heart and one will; so
you have made me very joyful. The one only God keep
and sustain you my father, King Manuel, the one only God
of the heavens, whose substance is ever, without being
younger or older. The embassy which your great captain
sent by your order, they were good those who brought it.
When they came to me, I received them with honour, and
Don Rodrigo de Lima came as the head of it, and I did
good to him as he was the head. And Padre Francisco
Alvarez, who came with your embassy, and came to my
person, and I showed him much favour and affection, because I found him a just man and very truthful in speech,
and in all matters which concern the faith : do you increase
him, and make him master and converter of Masua, and
Dalaqua and Zeila, and all the islands of the Red Sea, because they are on the borders of our countries; and we
granted to him and gave into his hand a cross and crozier
in sign of his lordship, and do you order to be given to him
so that he may be bishop of the said countries and islands,
and this because he is deserving and sufficient and capable
for this. And you, may God do you much good, that you
may be very strong and not grow weak before your
enemies, and cause them to fall down at your feet. May
God prolong your life, and give you a part in the kingdom
of heaven, and a good abode, such as I wish for for myself.

---

[1] *Milhões.*

And I have heard good things with my ears, and did not see them with my eyes, and now my eyes have seen that which they never thought to see. May God do you good, as for the best of those He loves : may your part be on the tree of life, and your dwellings like the dwellings of the saints. Amen. Also I send you my embassage through Licacanate, who will tell you what I want : and I send Padre Francisco Alvarez to the Pope with my obedience, which is a direct matter for me. Also do you command, as a father commands his little son, and I will do it when you send me ambassadors. Do you always write to me that we may assist one another. On the arrival of those that you sent to Masua, and also of those who may come in future, both to Masua and Dalaqua and the other ports, I will do what you have commanded, because thus I desire that we should both assist one another : and as your people will be there, I shall be there, because there are my lands : there are no Christians and churches there, and all are Moors and Pagans. I am pleased that your people should settle there at the extremities of my countries; for the sake of this do you accomplish what you have at first begun. Send me masters who can make figures of gold and silver, copper, iron, tin, and lead, and send me lead for the churches : and masters of form to make books of our characters; and masters of gilding with gold leaf, and of making gold leaf; and this soon, and let them come to remain with me here and in my favour. And when they may wish to return at their desire, I will not detain them, and this I swear by Jesus Christ, Son of the living God. And do you send me this without holding yourself as under obligation. I send this to you knowing your virtue and goodness, because I know how well you love me, and also you did good to Abraham. For the sake of this I take courage to make requests to you, and do not hold this to be shameful, for I will repay it. Because when a son asks of his father, he

cannot say him nay, and you are my father, and I your son:
and we are close together as the stones in a wall, and also
we are both joined in heart in the love of Jesus Christ,
who is the Head of the world. He, Jesus Christ, and also
all those who are with Him are joined together like stones
well bound together in a wall."

CAP. VIII.—*Translation of the letter of Prester John to the
King Don Joam our Sovereign.*

"In the name of God the Father, Almighty, Creator of
heaven and earth, and also of all things made by Him,
visible and invisible. In the name of God the Son, will and
counsel and prophet of the Father. In the name of God
the Holy Ghost, Paraclete, living God equal to the Father
and to the Son, who spoke by the mouth of the prophet,
inspiring the apostles so that they should give praise to the
Trinity in heaven, in earth, in the sea, and in the depth
for ever. Amen.

"I, Incense of the Virgin, King of Ethiopia, send you this
letter and embassy, the son of Nahum, son of the King of the
hand of Maria, son of the King of the seed of Jacob, these
are those who were born of the house of David and Solomon, who were Kings in Jerusalem. May this reach the
King Don Joam, King of Portugal, son of the King Don
Manuel. Peace be with you, and the grace of our Lord
Jesus Christ be with you for ever. When they gave us
news of the power of the King your father, how he broke
the power of the Moors, sons of Mahomed, I gave thanks
and praise to the Lord God for the raising up and greatness and crown of salvation in the house of Christendom.
I also greatly rejoiced when the speech of your embassy
reached me, which came to make affection and friendship
and acquaintance between the King and me; in order to

tear out and cast forth the bad Moors, Jews, and Pagans
from his and my kingdoms. And being in this pleasure, I
heard news that the King your father had died before we
had despatched his ambassadors from my kingdoms, on
which account my pleasure was turned into grief, and re-
grets were increased in my heart when I remembered the
passing away of his life ; and all the great men of my court
grew sad, and wept along with me ; also all the clergy
carried their weeping and lamentation to the monasteries ;
and as much pleasure as they had felt at the first news, so
much grief had they with the second. Sir brother, from
the beginning of my kingdoms until now no ambassador
had come from the Christian kings and kingdoms of Portugal ; only we heard of the dangers of those who go of
their own desire to those parts in pilgrimage to Jerusalem
and Rome, and they are scattered about those kingdoms
and countries and provinces, and I never had any certain
information, only in the lifetime of the King your father,
who sent his captains and gentlemen with many people and
priests and deacons, who brought all things necessary for
saying mass, and on that account I was very joyful, and
ordered them to be received, and received them with great
honour. Then I despatched them, pleased and contented,
with much honour and peace. And after that they reached
the seaport which is at the extremity of my kingdoms in
the Red Sea, they did not find there the great captain
whom your father had sent there, nor did he wait, as he
had sent to tell me. And as it is your custom to make a
captain-major every three years, he could not wait or come,
as another captain-major came in that time, and for this
reason the ambassadors of the King your father, who had
come to me, were detained. I have sent them to you,
those that I sent to your and my father, to give you my
embassage ; and that which I send to the Pope, Sir king
and brother, fulfil the friendship and affection which the

King your father opened between us, and always send me
your embassies, which I much desire as from a brother, and
such is reason, since we are Christians, for the Moors, who
are vile and bad, concert together in their sect; and now I
do not wish for ambassadors from the kings of Egypt, nor
from other kings who used to send them, but only from
your highness, which I much desire, because the Moorish
kings do not hold me as a friend on account of the faith,
but only on account of their trade and merchandise, from
which much profit accrues to them, and they take away
from my kingdoms much gold, of which they are great
friends, and of me little; and their pleasures do not rejoice
me, only I trade with them because it was the custom of
my predecessors. And if I omit to make war upon them,
and to destroy them, it is in order not to destroy the holy
house of Jerusalem, in which is the tomb of Jesus Christ,
which God has left in the possession of the vile Moors; and
so they destroyed all the churches which are in the land of
Egypt and Syria; and for this reason I omit destroying
them. For which I feel my heart sufficiently angry and
sad; and from not having near me any Christian king to
assist me and rejoice my heart. And I, Sir brother, am not
pleased with the kings of Frankland, who, being Christian,
are not of one heart, and are always fighting with one another. If I had a Christian king for a neighbour, I would
never separate from him for an hour. As to this, I do not
know what to say nor what to do, since these are things
which God ordains. Sir king and brother, always send me
your embassy and write to me, because, seeing your letters
it seems to me that I see your face, for much more love
exists between those who are distant than between those
that are near, on account of the desires they feel, as in my
case, who do not see your treasures and love you well always
in my heart. As our Lord Jesus Christ says in the gospel:
'Where the treasure is, there is thy heart.' Thus my heart

is for you, and you are my treasure; and do you make me your treasure, and join your heart to mine. Sir brother, keep this word, for you know a great deal, and also I dare to say that you know more than your father, and for this which I thus know, I give thanks to God, and leave sadness and take pleasure and say, 'Blessed be the learned son of great understanding of the King Don Manuel, who has sat on the seat of his kingdoms.' Look, Sir, and do not weary against the Moors and Pagans, for, with the help of the Lord God, you will destroy them; do not say that you have less forces than your father, because they are many, and God will assist you. I have got men, gold and provisions like the sands of the sea and the stars of heaven. Both of us together we will destroy all the Moorish State. Neither do I want anything from you except people to set in order and arm our people, and you are an entire man. The King Solomon reigned at twelve years, and had great strength and had more knowledge than his father. I also, when my father Nahum died, was left very little, and succeeded to his seat, and God gave me greater forces than to my father, and I have got all the people of my kingdoms and districts under my hand, and I am at rest. For this let us together give thanks to God for such great favour. Sir brother, hear another word now, I want you to send me men, artificers to make images, and printed books, and to make swords and arms of all sorts for fighting; and also masons and carpenters, and men who make medicines, and physicians, and surgeons to cure illnesses; also artificers to beat gold and place it, and goldsmiths and silversmiths, and men who know how to extract gold and silver and also copper from the veins, and men who can make sheet lead and earthenware; and masters of any trades which are necessary in these kingdoms, also gunsmiths. Assist me in this which I beg of you, as a brother does to a brother, and God will assist you, and save you from evil things. Our Lord receive

your prayers and petitions, as He received the holy sacrifices
in their time.   First, the sacrifice of Abel, and of Noah
when he was in the ark, and of Abraham when he was in the
land of Midian, and of Isaac when he went away from the
Cave of the Oath, and of Jacob in the house of Bethlehem,
and of Moses in Egypt, and of Aaron on the mountain, and
of Jasom, son of Hu, and of Galgala, and of Gideon on the
shore, and of Manoe and his wife, and of Samson when he
was thirsty in the dry land, and of Jepthah in the battle,
and of Baron and Debora when she went against Sisera the
captain on Mount Thabor, and of Samuel and Rama the prophet, and of David on the threshing floor, and of Arbana,
and of Solomon in the city of Gabon, and of Elias on Mount
Carmel, when he raised up the dead son of the widow, and
of Rica at the well, and of Josaphat in the battle, and of
Manasse after he sinned and returned to God, and of Josias
bepaca after he turned, and of Daniel in the lions' den, and
of Jonas in the belly of the fish, and of the three companions,
Sidrach, Misaac, and Abdenago in the fiery furnace, and of
Anna, within the tent of the altar, and of Nehemiah who
made the walls with Zorobabel, and of Matatias with his
sons upon a quarter of the world, and of Esau upon the
blessing.   So, Sir, God will receive your sacrifices and
prayers, and will assist you to go forward against evil adversaries in all times and all days.   Peace be with you, and
I embrace you with the embrace of holiness, and so I embrace those of your holy council of the kingdom of Portugal,
and the archbishops, bishops, priests, and deacons, men and
women.   The grace of God, and the blessing of Our Lady,
Mother of God, be with you and with all.   Amen."

CAP. IX.—*Of certain questions which the Archbishop of Braga put to Francisco Alvarez, and the answers which he gave.*

While we were at the Court in the city of Coimbra, no long time elapsed before the King, our sovereign, departed with his Court to Almeirim, where on some occasions I reminded his Highness about sending me to carry out the journey which I had promised and sworn to Prester John to make, namely, to carry his letters and a cross of gold and his obedience to the Holy Father in Rome. His Highness told me that he was fully mindful of this, but that the roads did not give an opportunity for this, on account of the wars with France. From Almeirim His Highness departed with his Court for the city of Lisbon, where, in the manner above mentioned, I reminded His Highness of my despatch to Rome. He gave me the same answer as before. Upon this, Bras Neto was named ambassador; it was not said to what place. He, Bras Neto, begged me to ask the King to send me with him. I begged of the King the favour to send me with Bras Neto, since he was going to Rome. His Highness told me that Bras Neto was going to the emperor and not to Rome, and that he well remembered about sending me, but that I could not go except when Don Martinho went, and that he would soon despatch him. At this time a benefice becoming vacant in the archbishopric of Braga, His Highness did me the favour to bestow it on me, and, with his presentation, sent me to the archbishop, for him to confirm me in it. Whilst I was with his lordship, he never ceased asking me about the affairs of Prester John. I answered him truly, as I knew them very well, and his lordship ordered everything to be written down, and the questions and answers are the following :

Questions which Senhor Don Diogo de Sousa, archbishop

of Braga, put to Francisco Alvarez, chaplain of the king our
sovereign, respecting some particulars of the country of
Prester John, beyond those which the said Francisco
Alvarez has written in his book; the said Francisco Alvarez
having gone to the said Prester in the company of Don
Rodrigo de Lima, who went as ambassador to the said Prester, on account of the death of Duarte Galvam, who was
sent there by the King Don Manuel, may he be in holy
glory; which persons reached the port of Masua, an island
in the Red Sea, close to the town of Arquico, country of the
Prester, on the 27th day of April 1520, and they passed six[1]
years in the said country and lordships of the Prester, and
they returned to embark at the said port of Masua, close to
Arquico, in the year 1526 on the 28th day of April; and the
said Francisco Alvarez came to this city of Braga to be confirmed in the benefice which the King our sovereign gave
him. He remained in it some days, and the said Francisco
Alvarez reached this city of Braga on the 30th July, of the
year 1529.

He said that usually the people do not eat only once a
day, and this at night, and that the monks and clergy fast
strictly during Lent, so that many only eat three times in the
week, namely, Tuesdays, Thursdays, and Saturdays, that
they do not drink wine of grapes nor of honey, and that
they drink other beverages which are made of other vegetables.

In Lent they eat neither meat not milk, nor eggs nor
butter, even though they are near dying, they eat vegetables and some few fruits which are in the country. All
the men and women, great and small, fast all the Wednesdays and Fridays in the year; this is not to be understood
from Christmas to the Purification of Our Lady, nor from
Easter to Trinity, when there is no fast. Friars, priests,
gentlemen and noblemen, fast all the week excepting Saturday and Sunday.

[1] Should be seven years.

He said that no men died at the hands of justice, that they flogged many, and put out the eyes of some, and of others they cut off a foot or a hand, according to the quality the crime; but that he had seen a man burned because he was found to have committed two robberies in a church.

That the Pope or Patriarch of the country of Prester John is called Abima, which means father, and that there is nobody else in all the kingdoms and lordships of the Prester who confers orders except him.

The Prester John is called Acegue,[1] which means emperor, and he is called Neguz, which means king.

There is no manner of physic, only they apply fire; in some sickness they use cupping without fire, and for headaches, they bleed on the head with a knife placed on the vein, and they strike it with a stick so that it should draw blood, and also they take some herbs as a beverage to cure themselves.

In all the country there is no town which exceeds one thousand six hundred inhabitants, and of these there are few, and there are no walled towns or castles, but villages without number. The houses generally, or most of them, are round, and all of one story, covered with terraces or thatch, and court-yards round them. People generally sleep on ox-hides, others on beds made of straps of the same hides; no kind of table. They eat in flat trenchers, like trays of great width, without napkins or tablecloths. They have basins of very black earthenware like jet, and pipkins of the same clay for drinking water and wine. Many eat raw meat, and others eat it roasted on the ashes, others roasted over woodfire, and others over cowdung where there is no wood. There is much wax there, and tapers and candles; they do not make candles of tallow. There is no oil there except a kind which they call hena, and which is made from some herbs like Mayweed;[2] it has no taste, and is beautiful as gold. There

---

[1] _Akegue_, an Emperor.   [2] _Pampilhos_, also called _olho de boy_.

is no fish there except very little from the rivers; from the sea none.

There are no monasteries except of St. Anthony, and not of any other order, as some friars say who come from there.

The gentlemen, monks, canons, and priests are clothed; most of the other people are bare from the waist upwards, and a sheepskin on the shoulders, with the front and hind feet tied together.

Most of the monasteries are situated on high mountains, or in great ravines; they have large revenues and jurisdiction. In many monasteries they do not eat meat all the year, and fish very few times, as they have not go it in the country. The services of these monasteries are psalms and prose, and so it is done in the churches of the canons.

Every church has two curtains, one on this side of the altar with little bells, and no one but priests enter inside this curtain; and another curtain in the middle of the church. And no one but persons in orders enter the church, and many gentlemen and honourable persons are ordained in order to enter the church. They go to the door of all the churches and monasteries to read the epistles and gospels, and they say them rapidly, and there they give the communion to the people.

The priests consecrate at the altar, and do not show the sacrament. When the priest who says mass comes to take the communion, he takes a particle from the top, and the other two large parts he leaves for the communion of the people. All the people who come to the church have to receive the communion every day, or else not come to church. When the communion is ended, they give them a little blessed water with which they wash their mouths.

Nobody sits down in the church, nor do they enter it shod; they do not hem or spit, nor do they let any dog or other animal come into the church. They confess standing, and so receive absolution. They pray in the churches of the canons as in those of the friars. Friars do not marry, canons and priests do so. When the canons live together in the circuit they eat in their houses, and the friars eat in community. The chiefs of these churches are called Lica-canate. The wives of the canons have houses outside of the circuit, where they go to live with them : the son of a canon remains a canon, and the son of a priest not, except he chooses later to become one. No tithes are paid to any church, they live on the large properties which the churches and monasteries possess. Complaints against the clergy are dealt with before the secular justice.

The vestment is made like a shirt, and the stole with a hole in the middle, and put over the head ; they have no maniple, nor amice, nor girdle ; priests and friars all have their heads shaved, and the beards not. The friars say mass with their hats on their heads, and the priests with their heads bare.

In no church is more than one mass said, and no mass is said for alms, not even for the dead. When any person dies, the priests come with cross and holy water and incense, and recite certain prayers for him, and carry him off to burial very hurriedly : next day they bring offerings : the churchyards are all closed, so that nothing can enter them.

Prester John has no determined place of abode, he always goes about the country in tents, and he will always have in his camp five or six tents among good and common ones : and there will always be at Court of people for the horses and mules from fifty thousand upwards.

The kitchen of Prester John is a good crossbow shot behind his quarters, and they bring his food in this manner: all that he has to eat comes in porringers and dishes of very black earthenware on wooden trays, and pages bring them, and above the pages come a pallium of silk, which covers them so that these viands come with reverence.

There are many royal farms belonging to the Prester, in which a great quantity of bread is gathered, which is given to honourable persons, and the poor, and to poor monasteries and churches, without Prester John making any profit of the produce and revenue of these farms, but only alms.

In all the country there is much bread, wheat and barley; in other lands there is more millet than wheat or barley, in these, and where wheat and barley, there is much taff and dagusha (seeds not known to us), pulse, beans, pease, and all vegetables; and in other lands all sorts of grain and vegetables in great quantity and abundance. There are many water springs, but no fountains made of stone. In the town of Aquaxumo, where the Queens Saba and Candacia were, there are many wells and tanks made with good masonry.

In the town of Aquaxumo there are images very well made, and figures of lions and dogs, and oxen, and other antiquities made of stone. In this town Queen Candacia became a Christian by the advice of her eunuch, whom St. Philip baptized by inspiration of the Holy Spirit.

In all this country there is no bridge of stone or of wood; in no part of the kingdoms or lordships of Prester John are there Jews. There are infinite quantities of sugar canes, and they do not know how to make it; grapes and peaches are ripe in the month of February and end in April: there are many oranges, lemons and citrons, and few pot herbs, because they do not plant them.

Animals, namely lions, ounces, tigers, wolves, deer, antas,[1] wild cows, foxes, lynxes,[2] wild boars, porcupines, civet cats, roedeer, gazelles, elephants, and other animals not known to us, of which the country is full, except two which I never saw there, namely bears and rabbits.

Birds, partridges of three kinds, like ours, other fowls

---

[1] *Anta* is a South American animal.   [2] Probably hyænas.

which we call of Guinea, there they are called zegra, quails, pigeons, turtles, hawks, falcons, kites, eagles, thrushes, sparrows, swallows, nightingales, larks, wild ducks, of different kinds,[1] and other waterfowl, herons, cranes, *hemas*, and all other birds that may be in the world, and not known to us; and there are all in this country except magpies and cuckoos, which I never saw, nor heard of their being there.

There are so many apes, that in the kingdom of the Barnagais, in a town which is named Ceroel, at the time the harvest is ripe, they pursue them till they make them pass a mountain; and they keep guard over them in a pass by day, because at night they do not move about, and they give a certain provision to two men who keep guard over them until the corn is gathered in, when they let them loose, or leave off keeping watch over them.

There is much basil in the thickets, and there are none of our trees except cypresses, plumtrees, and willows by the rivers; there are no melons, cucumbers, nor horseradish.

In the country there is no gold or silver money, and purchases are made by exchange of one thing for another, principally salt, which is current throughout the country as money.

There is linen there, but it gives no fibre, and no stuff is made with it; there is much cotton, and stuff made of it; there is much coloured cloth, and there is a very cold country where they wear serge.

The churches there are well built, but the walls are not well wrought, and they do not place anything upon them; they pitch [the roof] upon props, which reach from the ground upwards.

In the country there is gold, silver, copper and tin, but they do not know how to get it out of the mines.

---

[1] *Adens, marreças.*

There are many lepers in this country, and they do not live separated from the people, they live all together; there are many people who, out of their devotion, wash them, and tend their sores with their hands.

There is a great quantity of honey in all the country, and the bees are not in hives, but inside the houses, where the cultivators live, clinging to the walls on the inside, where they have a mode of egress outside, and also inside they surround the house: but they do not on this account desist from dwelling in the house, because the bees go outside. There are a great number of these swarms of bees, chiefly in the monasteries, there are also many in the woods and mountains, and the men put hives near the trees and fill them with bees, and bring them in them to the houses.

Since no one sits in the churches, at their doors outside of them, and within the circuit, there are always a great quantity of staves with cross pieces like a ......[1] or cripple's crutch, and each one takes his staff and leans upon it as long as he is at the offices of the church. In the churches there are many effigies painted on the walls. Effigies of our Lord and our Lady, and of the apostles and patriarchs, and prophets and angels, and in all the churches St. George. They have not got solid images. There are many books in the churches all written on parchment, because there is no paper there, and the writing and language is Tigray,[2] which is that of the first country in which Christianity began.

In this country they are not accustomed to write to one another, neither do the officers of justice write anything. All the justice that is done, and what is ordered, is by messengers and speech. I say only that I saw the property of Prester John written down on being delivered up and received.

There would be much fruit and much more tillage in the country, if the great men did not ill treat the people, for

---

[1] *Tahu.*   [2] *Tigia.*

they take what they have, and they do not choose to provide more than what they require and is necessary for them.

In no part that he went about in were there butchers'
shops, except at the Court, and no person of the common
people may kill a cow (even though it is his own) without
leave from the lord of the country.

The people speak the truth little, even when they make
oath, unless they swear by the head of the King. They
much fear excommunication, and if they are ordered to do
something, and that it be to their prejudice, they do it
from fear of excommunication.

The oath is administered in this manner. They go to the
door of the church with two priests, and they have there
incense and embers, and he who has to swear puts his hands
upon the church door, and one the priests tells him of the
oath to speak the truth, and that if he speaks falsely, that as
the lion swallows his prey in the woods, so may his soul be
swallowed by the devil; and as the wheat is broken between the stones, so may his bones be ground by the devils;
and he who swears, at each thing answers Amen; and as
the fire burns wood, so may your soul be burned in the fire
of hell and made dust. He says Amen. And this if you do
not speak truth; he says Amen. And if you speak truth,
may your life be prolonged with honour, and your soul
in paradise with the blest. He says Amen. And this
ended, he gives his testimony.

He says that the movable feasts, Easter, Ascension, Pen-
tecost, are celebrated on the same days and seasons that we
celebrate them. The birth of Christ, Circumcision, Epiphany,
and other feasts of saints also agree with us, and others not.
The year and months begin on the 29th day of August, on
which was the beheading of St. John, and the year is of
twelve months, and the month of thirty days. When the
year is ended, there are five days over, which they call pago-
men, which means fulfilment of the year, and in the bissex-
tile year there are six days over; so they keep with us.

He says that during all Passion week they are dressed in black or blue, and do not speak to one another for grief, saying that Judas by a kiss of peace betrayed his Lord.

Although there are in the churches effigies painted on all the walls, and also crosses, nevertheless on no cross is a crucifix painted, neither have they any of solid carving; because they say they are not deserving to see Christ crucified. All the priests, friars, and gentlemen carry crosses in their hands, both on foot and on horseback; and the laymen of the people and lower people carry crosses round their necks. Every priest and friar carries a little horn of copper with holy water, and the hosts where they arrive beg of them water and a blessing, and they give it. Before they eat they · throw drops of water on the food, and also in the drinking vases.

Their arms are assagays, few swords, a few shirts of mail, long and narrow; our Portuguese say that they are not of good mail.

There are many bows and arrows, they have no feathers like ours; there are very few helmets and casques. Those that there are have come since they have had intercourse with the Portuguese. There are plenty of strong bucklers; there are no cannon, except two swivel guns which we brought them. At our departure there were fourteen muskets at Court, which they bought from the Turks who come there to trade. The Prester ordered whatever they asked to be given for them, and ordered men to be taught to shoot.

There are trumpets, but not good ones; there are many drums of copper which come from Cairo, and others of wood which have leather on both sides; there are tambourines like ours, and large cymbals which they sound. There are flutes and some instruments with chords, square like harps, which they call David moçanquo, which means the harp of David. They play these to the Prester, and not well.

In this country there are in some parts very flat lands, and in others mountainous; and altogether they are fruitful lands. There are no snowy ranges, but withal severe frosts, especially in the flat lands. In all the lands there is great breeding of cattle.

He says that he did not see the river Nile, and he reached to two days' journey from it, and the days' journey which they went were small ones, namely, four or five leagues, a little more or less. But some of those in his company reached its source, and they say that it rises in the Kingdom of Gojame, and its source is in great lakes, and where it rises there are islands, and thence it commences its course and goes to Egypt.

The time when the Nile rises in Egypt is (as they say) from the 15th day of September and later, and in all October; and the reason of this is, because the winter of Ethiopia begins from the middle of June to the middle of September, and on account of the great rains which take place in it without this winter ever changing, the Nile overflows in Egypt at that time.

It is the general custom of Prester John and all the people for no man on horseback to pass a church, but before they reach it they dismount, and so pass it, and lead their beasts by the bridles, and after passing they mount.

When Prester John and all his people travel, the altar and the altar stone on which mass is said, all goes on the shoulders of the priests as on a litter, and there go eight priests with each altar by turns, that is, four and four : and a priest goes in front of them with a thurible, and further in front a zagonay ringing a bell, and all the people go away from the road, and those that are on horses dismount, and show reverence to the altar stone or altar.

There is no grape wine there, more than in two houses, where it is made publicly, namely, in the house of Prester John and the house of the Patriarch Abima Marcos ; and if

27

any other is made, it is secretly. The wine with which mass is said in all the churches and monasteries is made in this manner. They take raisins which they have stored in the sacristies and they put them to soak in water for ten days, and they swell, and they let them dry, and they crush them and press them in a cloth, and with that wine which comes out they say mass.[1]

The horses, natives of the country of Prester John, are many and not good, for they are like Gallician beasts; those which come from Arabia are very good, like Moorish horses; those from Egypt are much better, very tall and big and handsome. Many lords breed horses from the mares they get from Egypt in their stables. In this manner, namely, when they are born, they do not suck the mother more than three days, and they at once put the mares to the horses[2]; and they tie up the little colts somewhat apart from the mothers, and they keep for them many milch cows, and give them their milk to drink.

DEO GRATIAS.

---

[1] The Malabar Christians had the same custom. See Duarte Barbosa.

[2] *As mais acavalanas logo.*

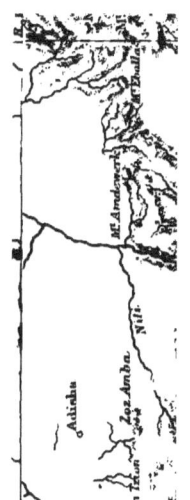

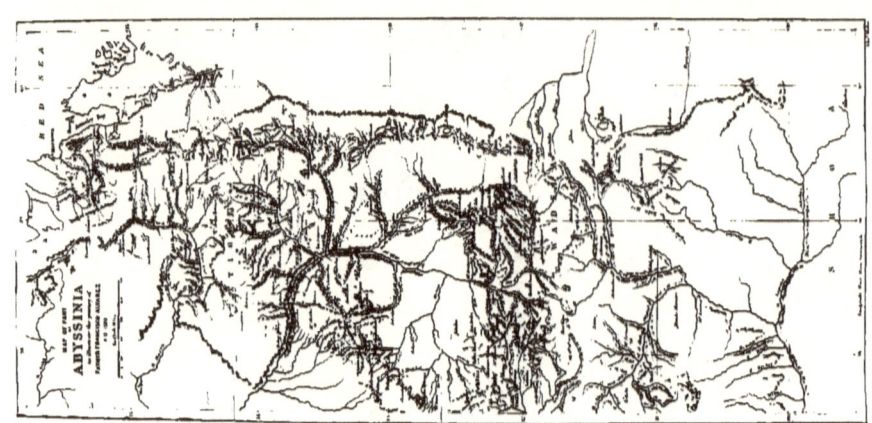

INDEX.

GENERAL INDEX.

INDEX.

GENERAL INDEX.

NAMES OF PERSONS.

NAMES OF PLACES.

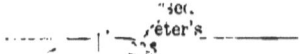

ANTIQUATED PORTUGUESE WORDS AND TERMS.

T. RICHARDS, PRINTER, 37, GREAT QUEEN STREET.

www.ingramcontent.com/pod-product-compliance
Lightning Source LLC
Chambersburg PA
CBHW020858130726
47900CB00014B/1020